This box was her secret.

Dorothy got stiffly to her feet and carried the box to the bed, setting it on the tumbled blanket. Slowly, slowly, she lifted the lid and gently folded back the layers of tissue.

She had not looked at them in a very long time. They lay innocently in their bed of tissue, gleaming with a color that no longer existed in Kansas. Red was not an adequate word for this color. It was crimson, cardinal-red. It was the color of rubies, glowing from within, deeply, vibrantly, the very color of imagination.

Of magic.

She touched the shoes with one finger and felt their power surge through her skin, tingle up her arm, shiver in her chest.

Dorothy pulled her hand back. She glanced up at the mirror that lined the closet door, seeing a plain woman with one pudgy hand at her throat. A dull woman, whose life had lost every shred of its magic. She looked back at the ruby shoes, yearning toward them.

No, no, she told herself. She couldn't. She shouldn't.

—from "Technicolor" by Louise Marley

Also Available from DAW Books:

Hags, Harpies, and Other Bad Girls of Fantasy, **edited by Denise Little**
From hags and harpies to sorceresses and sirens, this volume features twenty all-new tales that prove women are far from the weaker sex—in all their alluring, magical, and monstrous roles. With stories by C.S. Friedman, Rosemary Edghill, Lisa Silverthorne, Jean Rabe, and Laura Resnick.

If I Were an Evil Overlord, **edited by Martin H. Greenberg and Russell Davis.**
Isn't it always more fun to be the "bad guy?" Some of fantasy's finest, such as Esther Friesner, Tanya Huff, Donald J. Bingle, David Bischoff, Fiona Patton and Dean Wesley Smith, have risen to the editors' evil challenge with stories ranging from a man given ultimate power by fortune cookie fortunes, to a tyrant's daughter bent on avenging her father's untimely demise—and by the way, rising to power herself—to a fellow who takes his cutthroat business savvy and turns his expertise to the creation of a new career as an Evil Overlord, to a youth forced to play through game level after game level to fulfill someone else's schemes for conquest. . . .

Under Cover of Darkness, **edited by Julie E. Czerneda and Jana Paniccia**
In our modern-day world, where rumors of conspiracies and covert organizations can spread with the speed of the internet, it's often hard to separate truth from fiction. Down through the centuries there have been groups sworn to protect important artifacts and secrets, perhaps even exercising their power, both wordly and mystical, to guide the world's future. In this daring volume, authors such as Larry Niven, Janny Wurtz, Esther Friesner, Tanya Huff, and Russell Davis offer up fourteen stories of those unseen powers operating for their own purposes. From an unexpected ally who aids Lawrence of Arabia, to an assassin hired to target the one person he'd never want to kill, to a young woman who stumbles into an elfin war in the heart of London, to a man who steals time itself . . .

PANDORA'S CLOSET

EDITED BY
Jean Rabe
and Martin H. Greenberg

DAW BOOKS, INC.
DONALD A. WOLLHEIM, FOUNDER
375 Hudson Street, New York, NY 10014

ELIZABETH R. WOLLHEIM
SHEILA E. GILBERT
PUBLISHERS
http://www.dawbooks.com

First Printing, August 2007
1   2   3   4   5   6   7   8   9

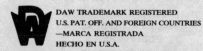

DAW TRADEMARK REGISTERED
U.S. PAT. OFF. AND FOREIGN COUNTRIES
—MARCA REGISTRADA
HECHO EN U.S.A.

PRINTED IN THE U.S.A.

ACKNOWLEDGMENTS

Introduction copyright © 2007 by Jean Rabe

"The Ring," copyright © 2007 by Timothy Zahn

"What Quig Found," copyright © 2007 by Christopher T. Pierson

"Technicolor," copyright © 2007 by Louise Marley

"Loincloth," copyright © 2007 by Wordfire, Inc.

"Seamless," copyright © 2007 by Michael A. Stackpole

"Ancestral Armor," copyright © 2007 by John Helfers

"The Opposite of Solid," copyright © 2007 by Linda P. Baker

"The Travails of Princess Stephen," copyright © 2007 by Obsidian Tiger, Inc.

"The Lady in Red," copyright © 2007 by A. M. Strout

"Another Exciting Adventure of Lightning Merriemouse-Jones: A Touching Ghost Story," copyright © 2007 by Belle Holder and Nancy Holder

"Revolution: Number 9," copyright © 2007 by Judi Rohrig

"Cursory Review," copyright © 2007 by Donald J. Bingle

"Jack's Mantle," copyright © 2007 by Joe Masdon

"Irresistible," copyright © 2007 by Yvonne Coats

"Seebohm's Cap," copyright © 2007 by Peter Schweighofer

"Cake and Candy," copyright © 2007 by Kelly Swails

"A Clean Getaway," copyright © 2007 by Keith R.A. DeCandido

"Off the Rack," copyright © 2007 by Elizabeth A. Vaughan

"The Red Shoes," copyright © 2007 by Sarah Zettel

CONTENTS

INTRODUCTION

**If the shoe fits . . .
there's a story in this anthology about it.**

Garments and accoutrements have played key roles
in fact and fiction throughout the ages—
Cinderella's glass slipper, Superman's cape, Abe Lincoln's top hat, Sherlock Holmes' coat and pipe—none
of which you'll find here, but I use these as examples.
I've no intention of spilling any proverbial beans and
ruining the authors' surprises in this simple introduction.

What you will find tucked inside the following pages
is an incredible collection of stories featuring clothes,
shoes, jewelry, and more . . . things that you might discover in some fantastical closet hidden away in the
minds of our tale-spinners. Some stories are linked to
history, some to beloved fables, and some spring from
the authors' own worlds. All of them should either
bring a smile or send a shiver.

Hmmmmm . . . just what did Quig find?

And what is the opposite of solid?

The collection of talent is amazing—from Hugo-
winning veterans to promising newcomers who reached
into Pandora's closet and pulled out something that
turned into their first professional sales.

The stories are worth rereading. All nineteen of
them.

That's quite a few tales for one anthology, and it's

due in part to the calculator I pulled out of the closet in my office.

I dutifully jotted down the word count of each story as it came in and double-checked it with Microsoft Word's wonderful word tallier. Next, I added all of the individual stories' word counts with . . . that calculator from my closet. Horrors! I was short on content. So rather than use Word's wonderful word tallier, as I hadn't yet started stringing the stories together, I contacted more authors to see if they had something interesting in their closets that they might write about.

And I used . . . that calculator . . . again.

Still short.

One more author.

One more . . .

Before I started putting them all together for the publisher and returning to Word's word tallier.

Uh-oh, I guess I wasn't as short as I first thought.

Now, I'm not saying the calculator out of my closet didn't work properly. I well and truly could have hit the wrong buttons every time I used it. I have been known to unbalance a checkbook. But I tried it again a moment ago and got the same result. So that malfunctioning calculator (or my defective finger) is responsible for you holding a slightly thicker book in your hands and getting to read so many great stories.

I'd prefer to think that Pandora had a hand in putting this collection together.

Enjoy,
Jean

THE RING

Timothy Zahn

It had been the fifth free-fall day in a row on Wall
Street, the kind of day that grinds all the anger and
frustration out of an investor and leaves him feeling
nothing at all, unless it's a weary desire for rest or
death, and either would be fine with him.

Which was why Nick Powell, department store floor
manager and formerly hopeful stock market investor,
walked completely past the small curio shop on his
way home from work before the exotic gold ring sitting on its black velvet pad in the window finally
registered.

Even then, he almost didn't stop. His modest and
carefully nurtured portfolio had been nearly wiped out
in the bloodletting, and there was no place for impulse
purchases in a budget that included food and clothing
and a Manhattan rent.

But his girlfriend Lydia loved odd jewelry, and a
week's worth of preoccupation with the markets had
turned their permanent simmering disagreement about
money first into a shouting argument and then into a
cold and deadly silence. A suitable peace offering
might help patch things up.

And who knew? In a little shop like this the ring
might even be reasonably priced. Retracing his steps,
Nick went inside.

"Afternoon," the shopkeeper greeted him. He was an old man, tall and thin, with wrinkled skin and a few gray hairs still holding tenaciously to his pale skull. But his blue eyes were sharp enough, and there was a sardonic twist to the corners of his mouth. "What can I do for you?"

"That ring in the window," Nick said. "I wonder if I might look at it."

The old man's eyes seemed to flash. "Very discerning," he said as he left the counter and crossed to the window. Nick winced as he passed, something about the air that brushed across his face sending a tingle up his back. "Antique German," the shopkeeper went on as he turned around again, the ring nestled in the palm of his hand. "Here—don't be afraid. Come and see."

Don't be afraid? Frowning at the odd comment, Nick leaned over to look.

Sitting behind a dusty window in the fading sunlight, the ring had been impressive. Pressed against human flesh in a bright, clean light, it was dazzling.

It was gold, of course, but somehow it seemed like a brighter, clearer, more vibrant gold than anything Nick had ever seen before. The design itself was equally striking: a meshed filigree of long, thin leaves intertwined with six slender human arms, each complete with a tiny but delicately shaped hand. "It's beautiful," he managed, the words catching oddly in his throat. "German, you say?"

"Very old German," the shopkeeper said. "Tell me, are you rich?"

Nick grimaced. So much for any peace offering to Lydia. It probably would just have earned him a lecture on extravagance anyway. "Hardly," he said, taking a step toward the door. "Thanks for—"

"Would you *like* to be rich?"

Nick frowned. There was an unpleasant gleam in the old man's eyes. "Of course," Nick said. "Who wouldn't?"

"How badly?"

The standing disagreement with Lydia flashed through his mind. "Badly enough, I'm told," he muttered.

"Good." The old man thrust his hand toward Nick. "Here. Take it. Put it on."

Slowly, Nick reached over and took the ring. The old man's skin felt cold and scaly. "What?"

"Put it on," the old man repeated.

"No, it's not for me—it's for a lady friend," Nick said.

"It doesn't want her," the old man said flatly, an edge to his voice. "Put it on."

Nick shook his head. "There's no way it'll fit," he warned, slipping the filigreed gold onto his right ring finger. Sure enough, it stopped at the second knuckle. "See? It—"

And broke off as the ring somehow suddenly slid the rest of the way to the base of the finger.

"It likes you," the old man said approvingly. "It knows you can do it."

"It knows I can do what?" Nick demanded, pulling on the ring. But whatever trick of flexible sizing had allowed it to get over the knuckle, the trick was apparently gone. "What the hell *is* this?"

"It's the Ring of the Nibelungs," the old man said solemnly.

"The *what*?"

"The Ring of the Nibelungs," the old man repeated, the somber tone replaced by irritation. "Crafted hundreds of years ago by the dwarf Alberich from the magic gold of the Rhinemaidens. It carries the power to create wealth for whoever possesses it." His lip twisted. "Don't you ever listen to Wagner's operas?"

"I don't get to the Met very often," Nick growled, twisting some more at the Ring. "Come on, get this thing off me."

"It won't come off," the old man said. "As I said, it likes you."

"Well, I don't like it," Nick shot back. "Come on, give me a hand."

"Just take it," the old man said. "There's no charge."

Nick paused, frowning. "No charge?"

"Not until later," the other said. "Shall we say ten percent of your earnings?"

Nick snorted. The way things were going, a deal like that would soon have the old man owing *him* money. "Deal," he said sarcastically. "I'll just back up the armored car to your door, okay?"

The other smiled, his eyes glittering all the more. "Good-bye, Mr. Powell," he said softly. "I'll be seeing you."

Nick was two blocks away, still trying to get the Ring off, when it suddenly occurred to him that he'd never told the old man his name.

There weren't any messages from Lydia waiting on his machine. He thought about calling her, decided that it wouldn't accomplish anything, and ate his dinner alone. Afterward, for the same reason people tune into the eleven o'clock news to see a repeat of the same multicar crash they've already seen on the six o'clock news, he turned on his computer and pulled up the data on the international stock markets.

Only to find that, to his astonishment, the six o'clock crash wasn't being repeated.

He stared at the screen, punching in his trader passcode again and again. The overall Nikkei average was down by nearly the same percentage as the Dow. But somehow, impossibly, Nick's stocks had not only survived the drop but had actually increased in value.

All of his stocks had.

He was up until after four in the morning, checking first the Nikkei, then the Hang Seng, then the Sensex 30, then the DJ Stoxx 600. It was the same pattern in all of them: The overall numbers bounced up and down like fishing boats in a rough sea, but Nick's own stocks stubbornly defied the trends, rising like small hot-air balloons over the violent waters.

He fell asleep at his desk about the time the London exchanges were opening . . . and when he awoke, stiff and groggy, the NYSE had been open for nearly an hour, he was two hours late for work, and already he'd made up nearly everything he'd lost in the previous two days. By the time the market closed that afternoon, his portfolio's value had made it back to where it had been before the free fall started.

By the end of the next week, he was a millionaire.

He broke the news to Lydia over their salads that Saturday at Sardis's. To his annoyed surprise, she wasn't happy for him.

In fact, just the opposite. "I don't like it, Nick," she said, her face somber and serious in the candlelight. "It isn't right."

"What's not right about it?" Nick countered, trying to keep his voice low. "Why shouldn't one of the little people get some of Wall Street's money for a change?"

"Because this was way too fast," Lydia said. "It's not good to get rich so quickly."

Nick shook his head in exasperation. "This is one of those things I can't win, isn't it?" he growled. "I head into the Dumpster and you don't like it. I turn around and bounce into the ionosphere, and you *still* don't like it. Can you give me a hint of what income level you *would* like me to have?"

"You still don't get it, do you?" Lydia said, her eyes flashing with some exasperation of her own. "It's not about the money. It's about your obsession with it."

"Could you keep your voice down?" Nick ground out, glancing furtively around the dining room.

"Because you're just as focused on money now as you were a week ago," Lydia said, ignoring his request. "Maybe even more so."

"Only because I've got more to be focused on," Nick muttered. Heads were starting to turn, he noted with embarrassment, as nearby diners began to tune in on the conversation.

"Exactly," Lydia said. "And I'm sorry, but I can't believe someone can make a million dollars in two weeks without some serious obsessing going on."

Heads were definitely turning now. "Half the people in this room do it all the time," Nick said, wishing that he'd waited until dessert to bring this up. Now they were going to have to endure the sideways glances through the whole meal.

Still, part of him rather liked the fact he was being noticed by people like this. After all, he was on his way to being one of them.

"I'm just worried about money getting its claws into you, that's all," Lydia persisted.

Out of sight beneath the table, Nick brushed his fingers across the filigreed surface of the Ring that, despite every effort, still wouldn't come off. "It won't," he promised.

"Then prove it," Lydia challenged. "If money's not your master, give some of it away."

The old shopkeeper's face superimposed itself across Lydia's. *Ten percent of your profits, Mr. Powell.* "I can do that," Nick said, suppressing a shiver. "No problem."

"And I don't mean give it to the IRS," Lydia said archly. "I mean give some of it to charity or the community."

"No problem," Nick repeated.

Lydia still didn't look convinced. But just then a pair of waiters appeared at their table, one sweeping their salad plates deftly out of their way as the other uncovered freshly steaming plates, and for the moment at least that conversation was over.

Despite the rocky start, the meal turned out to be a very pleasant time. Lydia might like to claim the high ground in her opinions about money, a small cynical part of Nick noted, but she had no problem enjoying the benefits that money could bring.

They were halfway through crème brulee for two when a silver-haired man in an expensive suit left his table and his dark-haired female companion and came over. "Good evening," he said, laying a gold-embossed business card beside Nick's wine glass. "I couldn't help overhearing some of your conversation earlier. My congratulations on your recent achievement."

"Thank you," Nick said, his heartbeat picking up as the name on the card jumped out at him. This was none other than David Sonnerfeld, CEO of one of the biggest investment firms in the city. "I was just lucky."

"That kind of luck is a much sought-after commodity on Wall Street," Sonnerfeld said, smiling at Lydia. "Would you by any chance be interested in exploring a position with Sonnerfeld Thompkins?"

"He already has a job," Lydia put in.

"Actually, I don't," Nick corrected her. "I quit this afternoon."

Lydia's eyes widened. "You *quit*?"

"Why not?" Nick demanded, feeling the heat rising to his cheeks. Was she *never* going to let up? "It's not like I need it anymore."

"Quite right," Sonnerfeld put in smoothly. "A man with the talent for making money hardly needs a normal job. On the other hand, the right position with the right people can certainly enhance both your career and your life." He gestured down at the card. "Why don't you come by the office Monday morning. Say, around eleven?"

"That would be—yes, thank you," Nick managed.

"Excellent," Sonnerfeld said, reaching out his hand. "Mr.—?"

"Powell," Nick said, reaching out and taking the proffered hand. "Nick Powell."

"Mr. Powell," Sonnerfeld said, giving his hand a quick, firm shake. "That's an interesting ring. Oh, and

do bring your portfolio and trading record with you."
With a polite smile at Lydia, he returned to his waiting
companion and they headed toward the exit.

"I take it he's someone important?" Lydia murmured.

"One of the biggest brokerage men in the city,"
Nick told her, his hands starting to shake with reaction. "And he's interested in *me*."

"Or he's just interested in your money." Lydia
dropped her gaze to his hand. "So you're still wearing
that thing?"

"I happen to like it," Nick said, hearing the defensiveness in his voice. He'd been too embarrassed at
first to tell her he couldn't get it off, and now he was
stuck with the lie that he actually liked the damn
thing.

"It's grotesque," she insisted, peering at the Ring
like it was a diseased animal. "Those leaves look half
drowned. And the hands all look like they're grabbing
desperately for something."

Nick held the Ring up for a closer look. Now that
she mentioned it, there *did* seem to be a sense of
hopelessness in the arms and hands. "It's old German," he said. "Styles change over the centuries,
you know."

"I don't like it," Lydia said, a quick shiver running
through her.

"I'm not asking *you* to wear it," Nick growled,
scooping up a bite of the crème brulee.

But the flavor had gone out of the delicate dessert.
"Come on, let's get out of here," he said, laying down
his spoon. "You coming back to my place?"

"That depends," she said, gazing evenly at him.
"Will you promise not to check on your money every
ten minutes?"

"What, you mean go into the vault and count it?"
he scoffed.

"I mean will you leave the computer off?"

He sighed theatrically. "Fine," he said. "I promise."

But later, an hour after she'd fallen asleep, he stole out of the bedroom and went online to check the foreign market predictions. What she didn't know wouldn't hurt her; and besides, his finger underneath the Ring was suddenly hurting too much for him to sleep.

An hour later, his curiosity satisfied and the pain gone as inexplicably as it had appeared, he crept back into bed.

And in his dreams he was the master of the world.

The Monday meeting at Sonnerfeld Thompkins was every bit as impressive as Nick had expected it to be. Sonnerfeld pulled out all the stops, introducing him to the rest of the firm's top people and studying Nick's portfolio with amazement and praise.

Midway through lunch, under Sonnerfeld's polite but steady pressure, Nick agreed to join Sonnerfeld Thompkins on a trial basis.

The first month was like a chapter from a financial success book. Nick's Midas touch continued, with every stock or bond or commodity he picked turning to gold with a perfect sense of timing. There were a few false starts, but every time he tried to buy a property that he would later find was irretrievably on its way down, his finger started hurting so badly he could hardly type. Eventually, he learned how to read the telltale twinges that came before the actual pain started.

Pain or not, though, his purchases made money for himself and the firm and its clients, and that was the important thing. By the end of the month Sonnerfeld was talking—just theoretically, of course—of putting Nick on the fast track to full partner and wondering aloud about the flow of the name Sonnerfeld Thompkins Powell. Everything was going perfectly.

Everything, that is, except Lydia. In the midst of all the success she continued her self-appointed role as rainmaker to Nick's private parade. Before the Ring had come to him, Nick had been ready to ask her to marry him, his lack of strong finances the only thing holding him back. But now, just when he was gaining the sort of wealth and power that would attract most women, Lydia was instead growing more distant. While she still permitted him to spend money on her for dinners and modest gifts, her disapproval of what she called his obsession was never far below the surface. He couldn't pause in the middle of an evening to check the international funds without getting a lecture, and she went nearly ballistic when he tried to give her a simple little thirty-thousand-dollar necklace.

Nothing he did seemed to make any difference. He set up a charity distribution trust fund with direct access from one of his accounts to fulfill his promise to share the wealth; she applauded it as a good first step but thought the five percent he routinely sent to it was far too small for a man of his means. He bought a new cell phone with internet trading capabilities programmed in so that he could make any last-minute trades on the way home from work. He put Sonnerfeld and the rest of his staff on a special vibration mode on his cell phone and a special flashing-light code on his home phone so that he could let any late-night calls go to voice mail if Lydia was around to disapprove.

None of it helped. Lydia seemed bound and determined to make him feel guilty about his success.

And finally, midway through the last weekend of that otherwise glorious first month, Nick decided he'd had enough of her complaining.

He was still brooding over it Monday morning when the runaway bus slammed into a line of pedestrians twenty feet in front of him.

"I'm surprised you even came in," Sonnerfeld said, sitting on the corner of his desk as he handed Nick a cup of coffee. Or rather, tried to hand it to him. Nick's hands were shaking so much that he couldn't even hold it. Eventually Sonnerfeld gave up and instead set it down on the desk. "Why don't you just go home?"

"I'm okay," Nick said, gazing out Sonnerfeld's floor-to-ceiling windows at the brooding clouds hanging over the New York cityscape. "It was just a freak accident."

"Still had to be pretty unnerving," Sonnerfeld said. "But if you think you're okay . . . ?"

"I'm fine," Nick said, getting up and heading for the door. "Time and tide, and all that."

Sonnerfeld gave him a thumb's up. "Good man."

It was midafternoon, and Nick had finally managed to put the bus crash mostly out of his mind when he heard that one of the firm's up-and-coming young brokers had been mugged and beaten while returning from lunch. Returning, in fact, from the very restaurant Nick had been planning to go to until he'd been pulled into a last-minute emergency meeting.

Ten minutes later Nick was in a cab, heading for the bank. Ten minutes after that, he was on his way to the shop where he'd gotten the Ring.

The old shopkeeper was waiting. "I've been expecting you," he said gravely. "How are you enjoying your new success?"

"I've got your money," Nick said, pulling out a certified check. "You said ten percent—I've made it twenty."

"Very generous of you," the old man said approvingly, his hand darting out like a striking rattlesnake to pluck the check from Nick's fingers.

"So we're square, right?" Nick said, wincing again at the unpleasant touch of the other's skin. "So call them off."

"Call who off?"

"Whoever it was tried to run me down with a bus this morning and then mugged Caprizano at lunch," Nick said. "I got the message, and you've got your money. Okay?"

The other shook his head. "I had nothing to do with

any of that, Mr. Powell," he said. "It's the curse working."

"No, but look, I got you the—" Nick broke off. "The *what*?"

"The curse," the old man said softly. "You didn't think all that money was just going to fall into your lap without any consequences, did you?"

Nick's skin began tingling. The whole idea of a curse was absurd . . . but then, so was a ring that could make you rich. "What kind of curse are we talking about?" he asked carefully.

"Death and destruction, of course," the old man said, his eyes taking on a faraway look. "The Rhine-maidens laid it on the gold when Alberich stole it from them." His eyes came back and he smiled tightly. "That's the one part Wagner got wrong. He said it was *Alberich* who cursed it."

"Never mind who cursed it," Nick snapped. "Are you saying it's coming after *me*?"

"Of course," the old man said, sounding surprised that Nick would even have to ask. "You have the Ring."

"So that's why you let me have the damn thing instead of using it yourself," Nick bit out, twisting at the Ring.

The old man shook his head. "It won't come off, Mr. Powell," he said. "It likes you. More than that, it likes the money you're making." He cocked his head to the side. "I don't suppose you'd consider turning your assets into gold? It especially likes gold."

"In a minute I'm going to get on the phone and convert it to Rwanda francs," Nick growled. "Now tell me how I get it off."

"You don't," the old man said softly. "Not while you're alive."

Nick stared at him. "How do you know so much about this?"

"Because I was there from the beginning." The old

man lifted his hand to the side of his head and tugged at something.

And abruptly shrank into a short, wide, bearded man holding a sort of metal cap in his hand. "I *am* Alberich," he said.

Nick looked at the metal cap. "The Tarnhelm," Alberich answered his unspoken question, wiggling the cap between his fingers. "It gives its owner the power to change shape at will." He smiled. "Wagner *did* get that one right."

And with that, the reality of magic Rings and their curses suddenly came sharply into focus. "This curse," Nick said between dry lips. "If it's coming after me, why did Caprizano and those people just walking down the street get hurt?"

"The Ring's trying to protect you," Alberich said. "It will succeed, too, for awhile. And I can also help."

"For a price, I suppose?"

"Of course," Alberich said.

"Why am I not surprised?" Nick growled. "And if I refuse, or you miss one? The curse nails me, I die, and the Ring moves on to someone else?"

"Basically," Alberich said casually. "But at least your heirs will still have your money." He shrugged. "If any of them are still alive."

And right on cue, Nick's cell phone vibrated.

He snatched it from his pocket, his heart suddenly pounding. "Powell."

"Nick, its Amy," the choked voice of Sonnerfeld's assistant said. "There's been a terrible accident. Mr. Sonnerfeld's fallen down an elevator shaft."

Nick looked at Alberich. How many times, he wondered, had the dwarf watched this same scenario play itself out, losing victim after victim to the Ring's curse while he grew rich on his ten percent?

Amy was still talking. "I'm sorry—what was that?" Nick asked.

"I said you need to get back here right away," she

said. "The whole board's coming in for emergency session—oh, *God*—"

"I understand," Nick cut in. "I'll be right there."

"Your boss?" Alberich asked as he closed the phone. "Yes, that's the usual pattern. From the edges of your life inward—strangers, co-workers, boss. Fortunately, you don't have a wife or children, or they'd be next."

Nick's stomach twisted into a hard knot. *Lydia.* . . . "I've got to go," he said, his voice sounding hollow in his ears as he headed for the door.

"Remember what I said," Alberich called after him. "For an extra forty percent I can help protect you from the curse."

"I'll think about it," Nick called over his shoulder.

To his relief, Lydia was sitting safe and sound at her desk when he barged into her office. "Come on," he said, without preamble, grabbing her wrist and all but hauling her out of her chair. "We're going on a trip."

"Nick, what in the world do you think you're doing?" she demanded as she tried to pull from his grip.

"I've got a cab waiting," he said, ignoring her struggles as he pulled her across the room under the astonished stares of her colleagues. "You've got ten minutes to pack, and you'll need your passport. We've got just three hours until the next flight to Frankfurt."

"To Frankfurt?" she echoed as he got her out the door. "You mean . . . *Germany?*"

"I don't mean Kentucky," Nick said. "Come on."

A moment later they were in the cab, weaving their way through the city's streets. Nick could feel Lydia's puzzled and hostile glare on him, but he ignored it. As long as he kept her close, maybe the Ring's protection would extend to her, too.

Meanwhile, he had to find a permanent solution to the problem. It was these damn Rhinemaidens who had put the damn curse on the damn Ring. Maybe they could take it off.

The sky had been clouding over as they landed at Frankfurt International Airport. The commuter flight to Stuttgart had run into some more serious weather, and as Nick got them on the road in their rental car, the rain was starting in earnest.

By the time he pulled off the road beside the slope leading down to the Rhine River the full fury of the storm had broken.

"This is the place?" Lydia shouted over the wind as they picked their way carefully through the trees and rocks toward the surging water below.

"Assuming Wagner knew what he was talking about," Nick called back. "This is definitely the place he described for the scenery in the first Bayreuth production of *Gotterdammerung*. We'll just have to see if he got it right."

They fell silent, concentrating on the climb, and Nick found himself marveling once again at the remarkable woman beside him. He'd told her the whole story on the way to the airport from her apartment, fully expecting her to order the cabby to forget Kennedy and take them straight to Bellevue. But to his surprise, she'd not only taken it calmly but had actually believed the story.

Or at least she'd pretended to believe it. Still, that was more than he would have gotten from anyone else he knew.

The rain had moderated a little by the time they reached the bottom of the slope, but the winds had become more turbulent. Carefully, Nick moved to the edge of the river, wiping at the sheet of water streaming down his face as he peered across the roiling whitecaps spilling over the treacherous rocks. "Rhinemaidens!" he shouted. "I've brought you your Ring. Come and get it."

There was no answer but the whistling of the wind. "What if they're not here?" Lydia asked.

Nick shook his head wordlessly, looking back and forth down the shoreline.

And frowned.

There, about fifty yards downriver, he could see a squat figure standing with the stillness of a rock, facing their direction.

It was Alberich.

"I knew you'd come," the dwarf said as Nick and Lydia slogged through the wet grass to him. "They all do, sooner or later. Hoping to bribe or beg or threaten their way out of the curse."

"News flash—I'm not here to beg," Nick told him. "I'm here to give them back their Ring."

Alberich snorted in disgust. "Fool. You really think you're the first one to think of *that*?"

"They won't take it back?" Lydia asked.

Alberich looked her up and down. "You must be the one he was going to buy the Ring for." He snorted. "Waste of effort. You're not nearly ambitious enough."

"You mean I'm not greedy enough," Lydia shot back. "Why won't they take it back?"

"Of course they'll take it back," the dwarf said maliciously. "The problem is, the Ring won't leave him. That means the Rhinemaidens will have to take a bit more than just the gold."

Lydia inhaled sharply. "You mean . . . his *finger*?"

"Or his hand," Alberich said. "Possibly his whole arm."

Lydia looked at Nick in horror. "No! They *can't*."

"They will." Alberich pointed to a jagged rock in the middle of the river, barely visible above the surging water. "That's their rock, and they're already on their way. But there *is* an alternative."

"What is it?" Lydia asked.

"Forget it," Nick snarled. "He's just playing another angle."

"I'm as strong as they are," Alberich told her. "For another twenty percent I can keep them away from him."

"I said forget it," Nick said again. He could see something in the water now, moving toward him just below the surface. "Even if it costs my whole arm, it'll be worth it."

"Nick, that's insane," Lydia said urgently. "We're in the middle of nowhere, with our car fifty feet up a hill. You'll bleed to death before we can get you to a hospital."

And then, abruptly, three slender bodies surged out of the water onto the shore, and six hands grabbed at his clothing.

"Back!" Alberich snapped, leaping to Nick's side and pulling his right arm away from the grasping hands.

"The Ring!" the Rhinemaidens called in unison, their voices thin and ancient and terrifying. One of them shoved her way beneath Alberich's grip, and suddenly there was a tug-of-war going on for Nick's right arm.

"Give us the Ring," one of the Maidens said, her hand wrapping like a vise around Nick's ankle and tugging him toward the river. "You retain it at your peril."

"I know," Nick said. "I want to give it to you—really I do."

"Only the waters of the Rhine can wash away the curse," the third Maiden said, her hands on Nick's jacket, her face up close to his. Over the smell of fish he caught a glimpse of sharp barracuda teeth.

"It won't let go," Nick pleaded.

"It likes him," Alberich said, pushing the first Maiden's hands off Nick's arm. "Don't be a fool, Nick. I can still save you."

Nick blinked. *It likes you.* Alberich had said the same thing the first time Nick had set eyes on the Ring.

Only the Ring didn't like Nick. All it liked was his money.

His money. "Lydia!" he shouted, shaking his left arm free long enough to dig his phone from his pocket. "Here," he said, tossing it awkwardly toward her.

For a second she fumbled, then caught it in a solid grip. "Who do I call?" she shouted back, flipping it open.

"Phone list one—second entry," Nick said, stumbling as the third Maiden got a fresh grip on his left arm and pulled him another step closer to the river. The one who'd been tugging on his ankle abandoned that approach and moved instead to Nick's right arm, and now Alberich had two sets of hands and teeth to fight off. "Input trader passcode 352627."

Lydia nodded and leaned over the phone. The Maiden on Nick's left arm shifted one hand to his belt. He kicked at her legs; it was like kicking a pair of oak saplings. "I'm in," Lydia called.

"There are five funds listed." On Nick's right arm, one of the two Maidens opened her mouth and lowered the pointed teeth toward the Ring. Nick cringed, but Alberich slapped the creature's cheek and shoved her back again. "Transfer everything in the first four into the fifth."

"What are you doing?" Alberich demanded, frowning at Nick in sudden suspicion.

"The Ring doesn't like *me*," Nick said. "It just likes my money."

"What?" The dwarf spun toward Lydia. "No!" Abandoning Nick's arm, he charged toward Lydia.

And suddenly Nick was fighting all three Maidens by himself. "Alberich!" he shouted as they dragged him toward the river. "Help me!"

"For what?" the dwarf spat, lunging for the phone. But Lydia was faster, twisting and turning and keeping it out of his reach even as she continued punching in numbers. "Seventy percent of nothing? She's throwing it all away, isn't she?"

"She's transferring it into my charity distribution account," Nick said. His feet were in the icy water now, the Maiden on his left arm already in up to her knees. "All the Ring cares about is money. And as of right now—"

"You're broke!" Lydia shouted in triumph. "You hear me, Ring? He's broke."

Spinning away from Lydia, Alberich threw himself back at the Ring. "Get away from the Ring!" he shouted.

"The Ring is ours," the Maidens chorused in their eerie unison.

"It's mine!" Alberich snarled, grabbing Nick's wrist.

Something cold ran up Nick's back, something having nothing to do with the water swirling around his feet. Lydia was right—with all his money now in the irrevocable trust fund, he had nothing left in the world.

But the Ring still wasn't letting go.

"Is this how you want to die?" Alberich demanded, pulling at Nick's arm with one hand as he shoved at the Maidens with the other. "Drowned in the Rhine by ancient creatures who have nothing left but hate and greed? There's still time for us to make a deal."

"I don't want a deal," Nick said. He was knee deep in the river now, the numbingly cold water threatening to cramp his calf muscles. Out of the corner of his eye, he could see Lydia doing something with the phone. "I don't want money. All I want—"

And without any warning at all, the Ring came loose.

Nick's arms were still pinioned, but for the moment no one was gripping his hand. With a desperate flick of his wrist, he sent the Ring arcing into the air toward the center of the river and the Rhinemaidens' rock. "No!" Alberich screeched, diving toward it.

But the Maidens were ready. Two of them twisted their arms around the dwarf's neck and dragged him into the river, swimming backwards toward their rock. The third Maiden dove into and then out of the water like a dolphin, reaching up and catching the Ring in midair as it fell. For a moment she held it triumphantly aloft, then turned and disappeared with her sisters beneath the waves.

And then Lydia was at Nick's side, pulling at his now aching arms, helping him back to the shore. "What did you do?" Nick asked, shivering violently. The storm, he noticed, was starting to abate. "How did you get it to let go?"

"You had no money," she told him, wrapping her arm around his waist and leading him toward the cliff where their car waited. "But you still had the potential to earn it all back."

He nodded in understanding. "So you fired me."

"I text-messaged your resignation to Sonnerfeld Thompkins," she confirmed. "I guess it'll never be Sonnerfeld Thompkins Powell now. I'm sorry."

Nick blinked a few lingering drops of water from his eyes. "I'm not. Thank you."

"I'm glad it worked." She paused. "Nick . . . your phone list. Number two was your online investment number, three and four and five were Sonnerfeld and your office. Number one . . ."

"Is you," Nick confirmed with a tired sigh. "You've always been number one. I just forgot that for awhile."

She squeezed his hand. His aching, ringless, *free* hand. "Come on," she said softly. "Let's go home."

WHAT QUIG FOUND

Chris Pierson

This all happened at a restaurant in Rhode Island, the name of which I don't care to recall.

Well, actually I *do* recall it. I just can't tell you what it is.

I'll explain.

What happened there caused a bit of what my mother would call a *foofaraw,* which means publicity, and not the kind a major restaurant chain enjoys. So the first time I tried to get this story published, I mentioned the name, and next thing there were cease-and-desist orders flying, and . . . well, they're a multinational corporation worth billions. I'm a database programmer with student loans and a car to pay off. You tell me who'd win in court. So turns out I can't tell you where the story takes place.

Ah, narrative in the modern era.

But I *can* tell you the type of restaurant I'm talking about. It's the sort of joint that always springs up in that special kind of strip-mall hell you find in the suburbs. The kind you find next door to the mini-golf course, where they play bad classic rock and serve fajitas and triple cheeseburgers and other things sure to kill you before you start collecting Social Security.

They're also the kind where there isn't a square inch of wall that isn't covered in some old piece of random junk. Pair of snowshoes, washing board, stuffed wolverine, Alaskan license plate. You know the sort. They always have a cute name, like *J.P. Fernstubble's Goode Tyme Emporium,* or *Holy Crap, It's Still Thursday's.* You've probably eaten there, then spent the evening scrounging for antacid.

Anyway, I used to work about half a mile from a place like that. Little startup company, sold baby products online. I'll spare you the glamorous details. This was back in '99, before the tech bubble popped, and half of America was made up of little places like that, with way more venture capital than clue. Since *Footwell McBucketfish's Olde-Style Roadhouse* was just down the street, my team went there for drinks after work. A lot.

So there we were, five of us. There was me—I'm Jered, by the way—and the rest of my crew. Rick was one of the company founders, a burnout who didn't get any work done. Gabby was the best user interface programmer I've ever met, but she hated her job and spent half her time using the office copier to make dupes of her résumé. Ravi did server work; he moved to Canada last year after some drunk morons who thought he was Iraqi set fire to his lawn.

And then there was Alex Quigley. We called him Quig. He was our project lead, and he was older than us—fiftyish, a bit fat and nerdy (in a tech company, you say? Egad!), on his second career. Good guy to work for. He used to be an actor, when he was my age; he even did a little off-Broadway before he got tired of being poor.

We were regulars at the *Muggawugga Gulch Saloon,* which meant we had a regular booth, with a waitress named Donna. She brought us oversized margaritas and their special chili-cheese-'n'-bacon fries ("They're Defibrillicious!") and kept the families with shrieking babies at least three tables away. We never tipped her less than twenty percent.

"Rough day?" she asked that rainy night, setting

down our second round of drinks. "You all look like you just found out Jar Jar Binks was going to be back in the next *Star Wars*."

Nerd humor. Usually it got a laugh, but all we could manage were pained grimaces.

"God," said Ravi. "Don't depress us even more."

"Quig got yelled at," Gabby said, and shrugged. "But what else is new?"

Rick took a long pull off his beer. "Nah. It's bad this time."

We all looked at Quig. He and the CEO had had a blowup that afternoon. See, the CEO thought we should all be working sixteen-hour days until we shipped our product. Quig thought that was just going to make us tired and sloppy, which meant delays. It got to shouting, and Quig lost. Now he looked as though someone had stolen his car in order to run over his dog.

"You gonna get fired?" Donna asked.

Quig shook his head and sighed, watching his margarita melt. "That'd be too merciful."

"They're setting him up to fail," I said. "They want someone to blame."

"I told them from the start: Fast, Cheap, Good— you only get to pick two," Quig said, and shook his head. "But these guys have MBAs, so they knew better."

"So now we're gonna work our asses off on something we *know* is gonna fail, and Quig'll take the fall," Rick said. He raised his drink. "To the New Economy."

That got a few morbid laughs. We toasted with Rick—everyone but Quig. He just sat still, moping.

"Jeez." Donna touched his shoulder. "You should just quit. Life's too short for that crap. I'll get you some Alamo Massacre Wings. You eat 'em, the pain'll take your mind off things."

Quig looked up at her and managed a smile. "Thanks, D. You're a peach."

Off she went, dodging a table of half-drunk biker-looking dudes a short way away. There was a lot of shouting, and one of the bikers tried to grab Donna's ass, but she escaped and vanished toward the kitchen.

"Jackasses," Gabby muttered, giving the drunks a dirty look.

"Donna's right," Ravi told Quig. "You *should* walk."

"I can't do that to you guys," Quig replied. "They'll ride you into the ground without me there."

Rick finished his beer. "It's happening anyway. It's not like you're protecting us from anything."

"Jesus, Rick," Gabby said.

"What?" he shot back. "It's true. Or are we *not* staying for 'Productivity Nights' starting next Monday?"

"All right, enough," I said. "We talk about work any more, I'm going to jam this fork in my eye. Who's up for a game of Spot the Tchotchke?"

I'd come up with Spot the Tchotchke one day after realizing the stuff on the walls of *Q.T. von Thunderpants's Publick Haus* wasn't always the same from one week to the next. Believe it or not, they add and remove things on a regular basis—I don't know if they rotate it between restaurants, or buy new junk, or what. I suspect magic gnomes are involved, but that's just a guess.

Anyway, in Spot the Tchotchke, you take turns trying to find stuff that wasn't there last time you visited. Whoever finds the weirdest thing gets their meal paid for by the rest of the table.

"I'm in," said Ravi, and pointed across the room. "New traffic sign over there. Armadillo Crossing, I think."

"That's an aardvark," Gabby said, squinting.

"Even better. Beat it."

"Easy," she said. "There, behind that flock of teenagers. That's an old medieval instrument called a serpent."

I looked. The teens were busy throwing food at each

other and generally acting like idiots. Hanging nearby, smeared with ketchup, was a wavy thing that looked like a clarinet that had been in an accident.

"Advantage: Gabby," I said. "Obscure musical instrument beats road sign."

"Does not!" Ravi protested.

"It's in the rulebook." There was no book, of course, but as the game's creator, I made the call. "Anyone else?"

"Got you all beat," said Rick. "Look up."

I did, and flinched. Poised above me, like I was Damocles or something, was a huge pair of old, rusty blades. I mean, the suckers were *big*. "What the hell?" I asked.

"Gelding shears," Rick said. "They used to use 'em on horses."

There was a moment's silence. I shuddered.

". . . *annnnnd* I'm vegetarian tonight," said Ravi.

Everyone accepted that Rick had taken the lead. "I'm not even going to try to top that," I said. We turned to Quig, who was still poking at his half-thawed margarita. "How about you, boss? Can you beat the Amazing De-stallionizers?"

"Hmmm?" he asked.

"Come on, Quig," said Gabby, shaking his arm. "We're trying to cheer you up. Can you see anything stranger than those godawful things?"

Quig sighed, glanced at the shears, then started scanning the room. He usually won the game. He had a good eye for weirdness. I watched him go from wall, to wall, to. . . .

"Mother of God," he said.

"What?" we asked.

Saying nothing, he got up and went over toward the bar. There was a ghastly old puppet that must have provided nightmare fuel for kids fifty years ago, and I thought he was going for that, but instead he reached to the right and picked up something else. He brought it back to the table.

It was round and wide, a tarnished disc of brass with a deep bowl in the middle and what looked like a bite out of the rim. He held it up.

"I give you the Golden Helmet of Mambrino," he said.

"The who of the what now?" I asked.

"You never read Cervantes?"

I gave him a look. "Sorry. I'm still working my way through the collected works of Proust. Come on, Quig. That thing's just an old bowl."

"Close," he said, his eyes shining. "Shaving basin. You put your throat in the niche, here, fill it with water, and a barber shaves you."

"I thought it was a helmet," Gabby said.

"It is. *Don Quixote*. He met a barber on the road, and he thought the man's basin was a famous helmet. He wore it on his head after that. Like so."

He raised it, ready to put on the bowl. Other tables were staring at him now. So was the restaurant manager, a beefy, humorless guy named Stan who rumbled toward us from across the room. "Hey!" he yelled. "What have I told you guys about taking stuff off the walls?"

People at the other tables chuckled. Quig turned a little red, then lowered the bowl—basin—whatever—and handed it to Stan. "My apologies, good sir," he said. "It was not my intent to weigh upon the hospitality of your inn."

Ravi nearly folded up, he was laughing so hard. The others at least tried to contain it. I wiped tears from my eyes as Stan took back the basin and rumbled away.

"I say my thing still beats that," Rick said.

"Nah," I replied. "The demonstration put it over the top. You win, Quig."

Rick gave me a dark look. "I could arrange a demonstration . . ."

"Easy, now," Gabby said. "Where'd you find out about the helmet, Quig?"

Quig watched Stan hang the basin back on the wall.
"Oh, I played the Don once, in a production of *Man
of La Mancha*. Dinner theater in Connecticut, back in
the eighties."

"Ah," Ravi said, still laughing. "Glamour."

"Shut up," Gabby told him.

Quig wasn't listening. He'd gone back in time. "I
got to wear the helmet every night, and sing 'The
Impossible Dream.' " He hesitated, then sighed as he
sat down again. "And I gave that up for e-Baby."

"At least you've got me, hon," said Donna, coming
back over. She was older than most waitresses at
Chuckles Feeblebuzzard's Cholesterol Hut, maybe
forty, and still good-looking. She flirted with Quig
constantly—and not, I got the feeling, just because he
tipped well. She set down a plate of wings that gave
off eyeball-melting fumes and another round of drinks.
"You guys know what you want?"

We told Donna our orders. She gave Quig another
wink and went back toward the kitchen. We laid into
the wings—all but Ravi, who kept looking up at the
shears.

As we were eating, I noticed Quig glancing back at
the basin. "You could go back to it, you know," I said
after a while. "Acting, I mean. Give up this crap, sell
your condo, try again. God, you could probably put
together your own little troupe of disenchanted pro-
grammers, tour the country."

"I'd join," said Gabby. Rick, sucking meat off a
bone, nodded too.

Quig shook his head. "It's a hard life, J. I can't
go back to cinder-block furniture and insta-noodles
for dinner."

But then he looked at the basin again.

By that point, Donna was on her way with our food.
With the drinks and all, the tray must have weighed
twenty pounds, but she carried it one-handed, weaving
through the place like it was nothing. And the damn
thing is, I saw what was about to happen, saw the

biker-types snickering, but I froze up and couldn't say anything until it was too late.

It all went in slow motion, like so:

The biker who nearly grabbed her ass before, a fat guy with a bushy beard that looked like his neck had thrown up, gives it another shot. And this time Donna can't get away. He gets a handful. She stumbles. The tray rocks, she twists, her ankle rolls, and down she goes—along with about a hundred dollars' worth of greasy food and frozen drinks. She doesn't make a sound, but glasses smash and cutlery clatters and plates go *crrrang,* and there's about a fifteen-foot spray of fries and ice and Krazy Tequila Lime Dippin' Sauce splatted across the floor. Somehow, she manages to miss all the customers. The noise is ridiculous—and all the talking and laughing stops, just a lousy Foreigner song playing in the background. Count to three, and no one moves.

Then someone says something. It's one of the food-throwing teens. "Two points!" he shouts.

The idiot teens laugh and go back to flinging onion rings. But everyone else is paralyzed—even the bikers, who stare at Donna, sprawled on the tiles. Mortified.

I stare, too. Your brain just kinda locks.

But then a chair squeaks, and next thing I know, Quig's on his feet. And the look on his face—well, there's anger and then there's blank, white-lipped rage. He walks to Donna, through broken glass and mango salsa, and offers his hand.

Oh, yeah . . . I have no idea how he got it down from the wall again, but that brass bowl-thing? It's on his head.

"Milady," he says.

"His *what*?" murmurs Rick. Gabby kicks him under the table.

Donna looks up at Quig. There's a smear of cole-slaw on her cheek. She's got rice in her hair and tears in her eyes. She takes his hand, and he helps her up. The whole restaurant applauds. I've never been so proud of anyone. He should've looked like a fool with that thing on his head, but he didn't. He looked . . . well, noble.

But the slow motion doesn't stop there. Quig offers Donna a napkin to clean herself up, then turns to the bikers. If looks could blow things up, there would have been a smoking crater there in the middle of the restaurant. But looks can only . . . well, *look*. So he reaches out, grabs a beer mug off the table, and dumps it over Neck-beard's head.

That's when things started moving normal speed again. Maybe even a little faster.

The bikers all got up at once, yelling stuff that sent moms diving to cover their kids' ears. Neck-beard was dripping—with the beer on him, he smelled like a college dorm stairwell—and he took a swing. Quig ducked, and Neck-beard slipped in the goo on the floor and went down. Our table got up next, and we grabbed hold of Quig before he could hit back. I saw his eyes—he was going to. Donna helped us drag him away, while two truckers, three college kids, and a guy who looked like a retired accountant surrounded the bikers, trying to break up the fight.

The bikers looked ready to grab chairs, flip tables, just trash the place—but Stan the manager came barreling out of the back, his face a really spectacular shade of purple. I remember there was this vein throbbing on his right temple. I thought it was going to pop, and boom, down he'd go with an aneurysm, but it didn't.

"What in the flying hell is going on here?" he roared. "Anyone touches a stick of furniture, and I'll have the cops here. Any of you have any outstanding warrants?"

The bikers quieted down.

"Asshole dumped beer on my head!" yelled Neck-beard, getting up off the floor. He pointed at Quig.

"And you tripped me!" said Donna.

Stan looked at her, at the mustard-and-ketchup

Jackson Pollock all over the floor. His lips moved, and I could see he was counting to ten. When he was on seven, Quig stepped forward.

"Sir," he said, "it's true, I did what that man said. But I was avenging the honor of the lady—"

Stan glared at him, his eyes flicking up to the basin as if wondering how it got on Quig's head. "Shut it," he snapped, and turned back to the bikers. "All right, you lot—out. If I ever see you back, spilled beer's the least of your worries."

The bikers muttered, suddenly sheepish. Stan had this effect on people—they could have crushed him into the ground, but the guy was built like a fire hydrant. He intimidated people.

"Now," he said, and they skulked out.

There was some scattered applause, but Stan gave the room the stink-eye and it stopped. Next he turned to Quig. "You, too."

"Him?" Ravi asked.

Gabby pointed at Donna. "He was defending *her!*"

Rick and I joined in, and so did a bunch of other people, with variations on "yeah!" and "that's right!"

"Stan," Donna said. "Those jerks are waiting for him in the parking lot. You know that."

But he just shook his head. Stan could be a bit of a dick, sometimes. "Company policy. Anyone fights or disturbs the other diners, I have to throw them out."

And there's the part that the legal department of *P.F. Whistlefart's Grease-a-torium* didn't like me telling: how their corporate policy was to send a fifty-year-old software engineer out to get the snot knocked out of him by six guys who could crush beer kegs against their foreheads. It's the sort of bad press that could make America want to buy its two-thousand-calorie meals elsewhere.

Gabby began to explain, in precise anatomical detail, what Stan could do with company policy. She was just getting into the part about twisting it sideways when Quig held up a hand. "It's all right," he said. "I don't fear those riffraff. If it's a fight they want, then a fight they shall have. Stand aside."

And he made for the door.

I watched him go. We all did, a bit too stunned to react. Quig looked different—maybe it was because he was balancing that bowl on his head, but he was standing straight, his programmer's hunch gone. And he was *thin,* which was weird. He'd always had a bit of a gut.

Donna broke the silence. She stepped forward, ripped the nametag off her uniform, and threw at Stan. The pin stuck in his tie and it hung there, upside-down, proclaiming him to be ∀NNOᗡ.

"Prick," she said, and went after Quig.

We followed him, too. Looking back, I was asking for what happened to me out in the parking lot, but I'd do it again. Quig was my boss, but he was also my friend. I wasn't going to let him go out there alone.

Anyway, we all gathered around Quig near the coat rack. He was rummaging through the umbrella stand and came up with his—a sturdy old thing, not one of those collapsibles that blow inside-out if you breathe on them wrong.

"Trouble yourselves not for me," he said, holding up the umbrella. "I can fend for myself, even against such a horde."

"Uh, Quig?" I asked. "What are you going to do?"

"And why are you talking like that?" Rick added.

I heard a sound, and there was Stan again, coming up behind us. "Not so fast," he said. "Give that back."

He reached for the basin, then yelped when Quig hit him with the umbrella. It was a quick blow, and precise. Quig hadn't forgotten his stage-fight training, I guess. Stan pulled back, clutching his wrist.

"Uncouth rogue!" Quig said. No, not said— *proclaimed.* "Do not despoil the Helm of Mambrino with your innkeeper's hands. Now begone!"

Stan looked at him, pop-eyed. He could have had Quig arrested for assault, even for that little smack, but he just stepped back, blinking.

"No, seriously," Rick said, "why do you sound like someone from a Monty Python movie?"

"Shhh," said Gabby. She started grabbing more umbrellas and handing them out. "We're coming with you, Quig. We're your men at arms."

"What?" asked Ravi. He stared at the umbrella in his hand.

Quig smiled. "Very well," he said, and his eyes fell on Donna. "But not you, milady. You must wait until the battle is done—but if you would give me a token to wear as I sally forth. . . ."

She looked like she was going to argue, but she didn't. There was something irresistible about Quig just then, the same thing that made me not question going out to face six thugs armed only with a bumbershoot. I didn't know the word for how he looked at the time, but I learned it later. He looked *gallant*.

"All right," Donna said. She looked at herself, frowned, and pulled a button off her uniform. Carefully, she pinned it onto Quig's shirt. It read:

ASK ME ABOUT OUR DOUBLE-FUDGTASTIC BROWNIE SPLITZ™!

Then, leaning forward, she kissed his cheek.

"All right," Rick said. "Everyone ready to get their asses kicked?"

"Wait," said someone behind me.

I turned, and there was the retired accountant. And the truckers. And the college kids. And even one of the idiot teens, a pimply, quiet kid who'd been sitting off to the side.

"How many more umbrellas you have?" the accountant asked.

We armed ourselves. No one tried to stop us. Then out we went. It was still raining in the parking lot. And there, waiting by the mini-golf course, were Neck-beard and company. They were armed, too—

three had pipes, a couple had knives, and one big bald dude had a freaking bicycle chain. They grinned when Quig stepped out, the bowl glinting under the street-lights—but they faltered when the rest of us followed him. We had them outnumbered, two to one. Behind us, Donna and half the restaurant watched through the window.

"What the hell?" blurted Neck-beard. "You put together a posse, freak? And what's that thing on your head?"

Quig looked at him. Slowly, he raised his umbrella. "Yield, varlet," he said. "Beg forgiveness and quit this field, or taste my steel!"

The bikers laughed, and can you blame them? This was insane. Except it didn't *feel* insane, not at the time. It was exciting. I felt every raindrop as it hit me. I raised my umbrella too, and stepped forward. So did Rick, and Ravi, and Gabby. And the rest.

I'm amazed none of the passing cars drove off the road at the sight of us.

The bikers must have felt a little of what I was feeling, because they quit laughing and spread out. The guy with the chain started to whirl it slowly. They looked different than they had inside—bigger, cruder, more savage. Like ogres. It could have been a trick of the light . . . but you know, I doubt it.

"As you will," Quig said. He kissed the Double-Fudgtastic button, then raised his head again. I wondered how I'd ever thought the thing he was wearing was a bowl. Couldn't everyone see it was a helmet?

The bikers charged.

We ran to meet them, our weapons held high.

So here's the problem: Quig had his army, but he'd overlooked one thing. None of us knew how to *fight*. Plus we had *umbrellas*, for the love of God. What I'm saying is, it was sort of a lopsided battle. The truckers managed to break one guy's teeth, but the rest of us didn't accomplish much except for a lot of shouting and falling down and yelling in pain. Bicycle Chain took out all three college kids by himself. The accountant got stabbed through the hand. The high school kid ended up with a cut that took thirty-three stitches, I found out later.

After that, things get a bit blurry, because I met up with Neck-beard. He had a pipe. He swung and I tried to parry, except I had no idea what I was doing, and I ended up getting hit full-force on my right elbow.

So I hear a *snap,* and suddenly the umbrella's on the ground and my arm's hanging limp at the shoulder and it feels *really* weird, like anything it touches is moving around all over the place. And there's no pain yet, not really, because I'm in shock. I fall to my knees and throw up margaritas and Alamo Massacre Wings all over the biker's boots. You wouldn't believe the colors.

Neck-beard stood over me, and he raised the pipe. I couldn't even get my arm up to protect myself. I just felt bits of bone grinding together where my humerus ought to be. I knew the next thing I was going to feel break was my skull.

Only the pipe never came down. Just then, Quig came out of nowhere, yelling . . . well, I guess it was a battle-cry. I didn't catch the words—they sounded Spanish—but it caught Neck-beard's attention. He took a swing at Quig, but Quig twisted out of the way, then snapped his umbrella around and hit Neck-beard in the face. There was another *crack,* and Neck-beard dropped his pipe and clutched his nose, which was starting to pour blood. Quig didn't miss a beat; he spun around, rammed the butt of his umbrella into the back of Neck-beard's head, and the big ox fell on his face and stayed down.

I just knelt there, grunting and grinding my teeth, while Quig stood above Neck-beard silhouetted against the lights of the mini-golf course. "You all right, J.?" he asked.

"Not . . . really," I said, and managed a weak, crazy kind of laugh. I shook my arm, which flopped in a way I still don't like thinking about. "But I'll live."

Quig smiled at me. Then, with another battle-cry, he was gone. A moment later, the pain finally hit, and I don't remember anything more.

It was a wonder nobody on either side was killed. I was one of the worst hurt—it took the surgeons five hours, a steel plate, and seven screws to put my arm back together, and the elbow still doesn't straighten all the way—but there were a few other broken bones, a whole lot of concussions, and plenty of cuts, scrapes, and bruises. By the time the cops showed up, it was over. One of the bikers ran away; they found him hiding behind the restaurant's dumpsters. The rest were unconscious. Gabby and Ravi were still standing; Rick was one of the concussed. And then there was Quig, still wearing that damn bowl on his head, and not a scratch on him.

The media loved it. Quig's picture ended up on the front of the Providence and Boston papers and even made it into the *New York Times*: "Rhode Island 'Knight' Wins Parking Lot Brawl." He got calls to appear on talk shows, but he never did. There were various charges of assault and mischief, but we got off—there were plenty of witnesses who confirmed that anything we did was self-defense. The bikers weren't as lucky—as Stan figured, most of them had warrants.

Things at work weren't the same after that. Rick never came back; he cashed in his stock options and moved out west. I hear he's working in games now. Gabby and Ravi and I stayed a while longer, but we each left the company before too long. After that night in the parking lot, any attraction to baby product websites was pretty much gone. Me, I'm still programming. But I'm writing and taking acting classes too, because hey, why not? Plus aikido. Next time I'm in a fight, I want to be ready.

And Quig . . .

Ah, Quig.

He fought for us. He went to the CEO Monday morning and told him *we* wouldn't be working late to make up for *their* mismanagement. Said if they didn't like it, they could fire him. So they fired him, of course. No, he wasn't wearing the helmet when it happened.

Two weeks later, he showed up in the street outside the office. He was riding a motorcycle—a big, beautiful hog that would have made Neck-beard insane with jealousy. Written on the side was its name: *Rocinante.* Sitting on the back, behind him, was Donna, and tucked into one of the saddle-bags was the Golden Helmet.

"Where you headed, Quig?" I asked him.

He shrugged. "Don't know yet. Just driving around the country a while. We'll probably end up out west. Maybe I can find work in Hollywood, teaching stage fighting."

He'd changed. He was happy. I never asked him if it was the helmet that did it. That seemed too obvious.

Donna slid her arms around his waist, gave him a squeeze. "Don't worry," she said. "I'll take care of him."

And like that, with a noise that rattled the windows, he was gone.

I watched the bike head down the street, then turn left and disappear.

I went home early that day.

Oh, and if you're looking for *The All-American Alimentary Adventure,* don't bother. After all the bad press, the company closed the location. The mini-golf people bought it, and they opened a restaurant of their own.

It's called *Windmills.*

TECHNICOLOR

Louise Marley

The screen door slammed, making the breakfast dishes jump. Dorothy winced, and Lin rolled her eyes in a manner only possible for a twelve-year-old. *"Mother,"* she complained. "Do you two have to fight *every* morning?"

Dorothy sighed and looked away from her daughter's pouting face. She watched Phil stamp across the sunburned grass of the backyard. His back was stiff, and he slapped at his leg with his ancient baseball cap as he stalked toward the barn. Today, it was because Dorothy had forgotten to buy tractor oil on her weekly trip to the mercantile. Yesterday, it had been something else.

Dorothy wanted to defend herself, but the words wouldn't come. In fact, it was hardly fair of Lin to accuse her of arguing, since Phil had done all the talking. Dorothy hadn't said a single word yet this morning. She couldn't remember if she had said anything yesterday morning, either. Silence was easier. And less provoking.

She looked across the jumble of cereal bowls and dirty glasses at her pigtailed daughter and forced words to her lips. All she could think of was, "Did you make your bed, Glinda?"

A mistake. "*Mother!* Don't call me that! I've *told* you!"

"Sorry."

"Breakfast was late because you two were fighting, and now I don't have time," Lin said triumphantly, pointing out past the porch to the plume of dust winding toward the farmhouse. "The bus is coming!"

Dorothy stood, crumpling her napkin. She carried the cereal bowls to the sink and stood gazing out over the pile of dirty dishes. The school bus, covered in dust, was all but indistinguishable from the dry wheat fields, the dirt lane, the browning leaves on the oaks and alders that drooped around the house. "Monochrome," she murmured to herself.

"What?" Lin asked.

Dorothy just shrugged.

Lin was shouldering her backpack. "Where's my lunch?"

"On the counter," Dorothy said absently.

Lin snatched it up, and opened the bag. "Oh, Mother! *Peanut butter?*" Another roll of the eyes, with the bonus of an exasperated snort. Twelve-year-olds, Dorothy thought. Surely, I never snorted at Aunt Emily. Not even when I was twelve.

She crossed the kitchen to help stuff the lunch sack into Lin's backpack. "Wait," she said. "Your shoes are untied." She bent to reach for the laces of Lin's hightops, but Lin pulled her feet away, saying, "Never *mind*, Mother."

Dorothy tried to brush her lips across her daughter's forehead, but Lin spun away before she quite reached her. A moment later, she was on her way out the door. "Have a good—" Dorothy began, but the screen door slammed once more, and Lin was off, dashing across the yard to meet the bus. Her hightops, laces flying loose, disappeared up the steps, and the door folded closed behind her. Dorothy raised one hand in farewell, but her daughter never looked back.

Dorothy stood by the screen door to watch the bus

rumble away in its cloud of beige dust. Did nothing, in all this landscape, have any color? Even the last of the hollyhocks had died. All of Kansas, it seemed to Dorothy, was painted in shades of brown.

She pulled the kitchen blinds against the rising heat and turned to face the piled dishes and the waiting laundry. It was as oppressive a sight as the dry fields stretching to the horizon. Dorothy knew a woman who started on a bottle of Dewar's at just this moment every day, right after the school bus left. Today Dorothy could understand. She sighed again and started up the stairs, her house slippers scuffing on the bare wood.

She passed her old high school painting, still hanging on the landing despite Phil's scoffing. She had tried, in her amateur way, to capture the colors, to remember them. Now the sun had faded them to the same brown she saw everywhere around her.

Lin's bedroom door opened on chaos, the bed unmade, the floor littered with clothes, shoes, scattered schoolbooks. The years of her daughter's childhood seemed to Dorothy at once endless and unbearably brief. She couldn't remember the last time Lin had kissed her, or hugged her. When, she wondered, as she bent to pick up a pair of black jeans, had her daughter begun to disdain anything she said and everything she did? It had happened gradually, inching up on Dorothy until, all at once, her daughter had escaped her. She hadn't seen it coming. She didn't know what she could have done about it, or should have done about it. Maybe it was because Lin's childhood was so different from her own. Or maybe Lin was following Phil's example. He had not hugged or kissed Dorothy in a long time, either.

Dorothy crossed to the hamper with the jeans, and as she reached for the lid, she caught sight of herself in the mirror above the bureau. She stopped and stared at her reflection.

The jeans hanging from her hands were impossibly

narrow. Had she ever, when she was twelve, been so slim-hipped? She straightened, holding them before her. She was twice the size of these jeans now, round-bodied, soft of breast and stomach. Even her hair had begun to gray in the front, the way Aunt Emily's had. In fact, she had begun to look like Aunt Emily. It was a look she had taken for granted when she was young, as if Emily had been born that way, looking as if the sun had baked her dry, the prairie winds weathered her like the boards of the barn. And now the sun and the wind—and her life—were doing the same to Dorothy.

Dorothy dropped the jeans in the hamper and bent across Lin's bed to untangle her sheets and blanket. She plumped the pillow, letting her hand linger a moment in the shallow depression where her daughter's head had lain. She picked up the quilt to fold it across the foot of the bed.

Aunt Emily had made the quilt, in a wedding-ring pattern, its blue and red circles faded now. Dorothy traced them with her finger, remembering her long-ago wedding shower. How different the world had seemed on that day. It had been full of promise. Full of color.

Dorothy's vision blurred with sudden tears. She dropped the quilt, turned her back on the mess, and hurried to her own bedroom. She ignored her own unmade bed—Phil had pulled the sheets loose again—and went to the closet. She slid the mirrored door aside and knelt to reach far into the back.

Her fingers scrabbled through boots and pumps and old sandals until she felt the stiff edges of the heavy, old-fashioned pasteboard box. She pulled it out and then stopped, listening to be certain she could hear the grumble of the tractor moving compost behind the barn. Phil must have found some oil after all, she thought resentfully. He could have told her, could have apologized, but he wouldn't do that. She couldn't remember him ever having apologized for anything. At least he was occupied, so he wouldn't interrupt her. This box was her secret.

She got stiffly to her feet and carried the box to the bed, setting it on the tumbled blanket. Slowly, slowly, she lifted the lid and gently folded back the layers of tissue.

She had not looked at them in a very long time. They lay innocently in their bed of tissue, gleaming with a color that no longer existed in Kansas. Red was not an adequate word for this color. It was crimson, cardinal-red. It was the color of rubies, glowing from within, deeply, vibrantly, the very color of imagination.

Of magic.

She touched the shoes with one finger and felt their power surge through her skin, tingle up her arm, shiver in her chest.

Dorothy pulled her hand back. She glanced up at the mirror that lined the closet door, seeing a plain woman with one pudgy hand at her throat. A dull woman, whose life had lost every shred of its magic. She looked back at the ruby shoes, yearning toward them.

No, no, she told herself. She couldn't. She shouldn't.

She left the open box on the bed and crossed to the window. She lifted the print curtains she had made on her old Singer machine and gazed out at the fields. The sky was a flat, lifeless bowl, as if the sun had faded it, too. The sun glared on the house and the barn, the pigsty, the milk cows huddling in the shade of the silo. None of it had seemed so bleak in her childhood. In those days, possibility shone from every leaf, every wheat stalk. When she was young, enchantment rose with the sun every new day, and she had run, with her little dog at her side, to meet it.

Dorothy rested her forehead against the glass and let the tears roll down her cheeks. How had she come to settle for this? How had she let this happen, that her husband spoke to her only to criticize, and that her only child treated her like a piece of furniture?

It was her own fault, of course. She had drifted into it, letting the independent girl she had been transform into someone else, someone she didn't recognize.

Dorothy turned back, letting the curtain fall closed behind her, and stared at the vivid shoes sparkling from their box. Lin would sneer at them, call them old-fashioned. Phil would have a fit if he even knew she had them. She had hidden them away the day he asked her to marry him.

The sudden wish that he hadn't married her, after all, made her press her hands to her eyes. That wasn't right. If she hadn't married Phil, if they hadn't taken over the farm after Emily passed away—she would never have had Lin. She could hardly wish her daughter away, could she? She could hardly . . . no matter how bad things were . . .

Dorothy dried her cheeks and dropped her hands. The shoes glimmered their scarlet invitation.

She had resisted their temptation for such a long time. Not for her the scotch bottle, or romance novels, or soap operas. For her there were only these ruby shoes.

As if in a trance, one foot before the other, she moved back to the bed. She knelt on the rug and reached for the shoes.

She turned them this way and that, letting the sun glint on their sequins. Their rounded toes and stubby heels were out of date, but Dorothy didn't care about fashion. What she cared about, what she longed for, was magic.

She cradled the shoes against her chest. She knew why she had kept them in the back of her closet, why she had hidden them all these years. They signified something that threatened her life with Phil and with Lin. They seemed to sing in her hands, to call her away. They invited her to step out into enchantment.

They were, like the Dewar's and the romance novels, an escape.

Her toes curled with the urge to put them on.

Dorothy set the shoes neatly on the floor, side by side. She kicked out of her house slippers. She fitted her feet, first the left, and then the right, into the shoes.

They felt wonderful on her feet! She had thought the heels might be uncomfortable after years of wearing flats, but they were perfect. They made her ankles looked trim, her calves seem longer. Even her cotton skirt looked crisper above the ruby glow of the shoes. Smiling, Dorothy lifted her eyes to the mirror.

Her eyes shone with a gleam of excitement. Her cheeks glowed, and the gray in her hair looked like threads of silver in the morning light. Even her waist looked smaller, perhaps because of the heels, or perhaps . . .

Perhaps the magic still existed.

Dorothy took a step closer to the mirror, pulling off her apron as she moved, dropping it to the floor. Behind her the jumble of bedclothes, the glare of sun on the wheatfields, faded to a blur. She caught her lower lip between her teeth. She shouldn't do it, of course. It was silly, and childish, but . . .

She giggled. And then—and then she closed her eyes tightly, and she did it.

Click. Click. Click.

Three times she touched her heels together. The shoes made a slight, plasticky sound. Dorothy started to giggle again.

A sudden, sharp pain lanced through her chest, and her giggle turned to a gasp. She struggled to breathe, but her lungs cramped. She couldn't open her eyes, either, and beyond the closed lids was only darkness. Something was wrong.

She couldn't tell what was happening. She heard a loud rush that seemed familiar, like a great, whirling wind, and then, in the darkness, came a stupendous silence. Dorothy went spinning into the blackness, shooting into some place where up and down had no meaning, where gravity was gone. She flew backward, and then tumbled forward. She clenched her hands together, having nothing else to hold on to. Had she had breath, she might have screamed, but there was nothing in her lungs, and her throat wouldn't work.

And then, just when she felt as if her chest would burst . . .

Thud.

Her lungs released, all at once, and a great draught of sweet, moist air rushed to fill them. The pain in her chest vanished all at once, leaving a sense of lightness. There was light beyond her closed eyelids now, golden light. The silence was filled by the burble of running water, the whisper of a gentle breeze. Cautiously, she opened her eyes.

Her cluttered bedroom, with its unmade bed, her apron on the floor, was gone. The farmhouse was gone. Kansas was gone.

Around her, on every side, were green fields and blue houses and vivid flowers. A stream sparkled between grassy banks. The sun was gentle on her head, and Dorothy felt as if she had opened her eyes inside a kaleidoscope, her eyes dazzled by pink and rose and yellow and violet and other colors she had no name for, colors that existed nowhere else.

With a soft cry, she sank to her knees on the soft grass. Her palms crept to her cheeks, and she gazed about her in wonder. It was still here! The magic had waited for her all these years. She spread her arms wide, to embrace the bright world. "Hello!" she called. "Hello!"

For long moments she was alone in the world of color, and then, as if they too had been waiting, they began to come, creeping forward through the banks of flowers, popping up from hedges, peering around the blue houses. They were as perfect as she remembered, and as funny, small and smiling, bright-eyed.

Dorothy laughed to see them and held out her hands.

The little people in their motley clothes crowded around her, twittering in their high voices. They patted her arms and then her cheeks with soft hands. They touched her hair, and the cotton of her dress. They hugged her.

They smelled of berries and cotton candy and sweet tea, scents that mixed with the perfume of flowers, the smell of new grass, the taste of rain not long past. For a long time they greeted her in this way, welcomed her back, and Dorothy remembered how good it felt to be touched, to be caressed.

After a time, they tugged at her arms, and she stood up.

She was twice as tall as they were.

Their twittering ceased, and their eyes went round with confusion. They stared up at her, dismay in their soft faces, their hands falling by their sides.

Dorothy said, "What—what's the matter?"

They stared at her shoes and then at her face. They backed away, now beginning to murmur urgently to each other. One or two turned and ran, like fat puppies tumbling over the grass.

Dorothy put one hand on her chest. "It's me," she said, a little diffidently. "Don't you remember me?"

Heads were shaken, brows furrowed.

"You have to remember me!" Dorothy cried. "I remember you so well! I remember all of you, and I remember this place, and the flowers, and the sky . . ."

"Oh, but, Dorothy," came a melodic voice behind her. "Of course you remember us! We haven't changed. But you—you have changed a great deal."

Dorothy whirled.

She was just stepping out of her iridescent bubble, her spangled skirt as white as pearl, her hair like spun gold.

"Oh!" Dorothy cried. "Oh! I can hardly believe it's you!"

Bright blue eyes twinkled up at her. "Of course it's me, dear. But I would hardly have known you if it weren't for the shoes! You're not the same girl at all."

"I know," Dorothy said mournfully.

"Why is that, Dorothy? Is that because of Kansas?"

Dorothy's shoulders sagged. "I don't know. I think it's because of growing up—and growing dull."

"Dull? But you were so strong, so bright and clever!"

"I lost myself," Dorothy whispered.

The little woman tipped her golden head to one side. "You've come back to find yourself, then. And about time. What took you so long?"

"I didn't know I *could* come back," Dorothy said. "And I didn't think I should! I just—I was having such an awful day—"

"And you ran away?"

"Oh, no," Dorothy said. "I can't run away. I'm a grown-up now. Grown-ups don't run away." She looked around her at the vivid scenery. "And grown-ups don't believe in magic."

"*You* believe in magic!" the tiny woman said stoutly.

"Well, but—grown-ups in Kansas don't."

"Then I think," the little woman said, putting her hands on her hips, "that Kansas must be a terrible place."

Dorothy sighed. "It's not, really . . . it's just . . . oh, I wish I could stay right here and never leave!"

"Why can't you?"

"I have responsibilities. I've made promises."

Her companion only laughed. "Break them!" she said in her tinkling voice.

"I just—I don't think I can do that." Dorothy looked around her. All the little faces had disappeared, except for one brave one peeping over the hedge. But the colors were just as bright, the sweet breeze just as inviting, and there was a glimmer of gold in the distance, winding through emerald fields.

Her companion put a small, cool hand under her arm. "Come, Dorothy. Look!" She turned her around to face the shining bubble. "Let me show you something."

She lifted her arm and waved at the bubble. The side of it opaqued, its iridescence fading until it turned as gray and hard as a television screen. And there, reflected or projected, Dorothy couldn't tell, was Kansas.

The vivid green grass on which the bubble sat, and the bright blue of the sky above it, made the farmhouse and the wheatfields and the dusty lane look painfully drab. As Dorothy watched, her mouth open in wonder, the view zoomed through the screen door and into the kitchen. And there, bent over the sink scrubbing potatoes, was . . .

"It's me!" Dorothy cried. "But that can't be!"

The tinkly laugh again. "Of course it can be, Dorothy dear! So little of you was there in the first place— just a shell, really, a shadow—that it cost you nothing to leave that much behind. The main part of you— the *real* part—is right here!"

Dorothy stared at her own dumpy figure moving about the kitchen. She saw the graying hair, the thickening ankles, the rounded shoulders. Past the barn, she saw the thin plume of dust raised by the tractor, and coming down the lane, a thicker stream of dust whirling behind the school bus. "Oh, no," she breathed. "Lin!"

She watched her daughter jump down from the bus, wave to her friends, and run across the yard. She could hear nothing, but still her nerves jolted as Lin slammed the screen door. She tossed her backpack into a corner and went to the refrigerator. Dorothy— the shell of Dorothy—turned from the sink with a potato in her hand, and her lips moved.

Lin didn't even look at her.

Dorothy watched in bewilderment as Lin took her sandwich from the fridge, turned her back on her

mother, and ran lightly up the stairs to her room. A
moment later, Phil came in and sat at the kitchen table
with a newspaper in front of him. He didn't speak
either.

The shell of Dorothy turned back to the sink.

The real Dorothy looked away. It was too painful
to watch.

"You see, dear," her companion said in her ear,
very softly, "there's enough of you there." She flicked
her fingers, and the scene disappeared from the side
of the bubble. In its restored shimmer, Dorothy saw
herself, looking tall, and slim, and straight.

"Is that the way I really look?" she whispered.

"Of course you do! You're a lovely woman in the
prime of your life!"

Dorothy touched her hair. It curled crisply around
her chin and forehead. She smiled, and lines of wisdom and good humor curved around her mouth,
brightened her eyes. "The prime of my life," she
whispered.

"Precisely!" The little woman laughed again. "Just
as it should be!"

Dorothy looked down at the red shoes. She wiggled
her toes to make them sparkle in the sunshine. "The
prime of my life," she repeated. "Just as it should be."

She looked into the bubble again, but Kansas was
gone.

She giggled, and then she laughed. She slipped off
the shoes, and her bare toes sank into the soft grass.
She hesitated only a moment, and then she picked up
the shoes and turned toward the river.

One by one, first the left and then the right, she
threw the shoes into the blue water.

They splashed, and floated for a moment, turning
and dipping in the current. Then, glittering like rubies
in the soft sunlight, they sank, and disappeared.

LOINCLOTH

Kevin J. Anderson and Rebecca Moesta

All alone in the props warehouse on the back lot of Duro Studios, he made his case to Shirley in his mind, rehashing the argument they had had the night before. This time, though, he was bold and articulate, and he easily convinced her.

Walter Groves opened another one of the big crates and tore out the packing straw mixed with Styrofoam peanuts. "Not exciting enough for you, huh? You don't feel fireworks? I'm too sedate—not a man's man? Think about it, Shirley. Women say they want nice guys, the shy and sensitive type, men who are sweet and remember birthdays and anniversaries. Isn't that what you told me you needed—someone just like me? You've always despised hypocrites. But what do you do? You fall for a bad boy, someone with tattoos and a heavy smoking habit, someone who can't keep a job for more than a month, someone like that last jerk you dated, who treated you rough and left you out in the cold.

"But I loved you. I treated you with respect, drove you to visit your grandmother in the hospital, and fixed your computer when the hard drive crashed. I got out of bed when you called at three in the morning and came to your apartment just to hold you because you had a nightmare and couldn't sleep. I gave you flowers, dinners by candlelight, and love notes—not to mention the best six months of my life. 'Someday, you'll regret it. Maybe not today. Maybe not tomorrow, but soon' "—he pictured himself as Bogart in *Casablanca*—"you'll realize what you threw away. But I won't be waiting. I'm a good man, and I deserve a wonderful woman who values me for who I am, who appreciates my dedication, and wants a nice, normal life. Go ahead. Have your shallow, exciting fling with Mr. James Dean in *Rebel Without a Cause*. I'll find someone sincere who wants Jimmy Stewart in *It's a Wonderful Life*."

Scattering straw and packing material, he pulled a long plastic elephant tusk out of the prop box. The faux ivory was sharp at one end and painted with "native symbols." He glanced at the label on the box: JUNGO'S REVENGE. After marking the name of the film on his clipboard, he listed the stored items beneath the title. He sighed.

If only he could have come up with just the right answers last night, maybe Shirley wouldn't have dumped him. If only he could have been tough like Mel Gibson in *Braveheart*, confident like Clark Gable in *Gone with the Wind*, or romantic like Dermot Mulroney in *The Wedding Date*. Instead, he had squirmed, speechless with shock, his lower lip trembling as if he were Stan Laurel caught in an embarrassing failure. Walter had made no heartfelt appeals or snappy comebacks; those would have been as much fiction as a script for any Duro Studios production.

Shirley had grabbed her stuff—along with some of his, though he hadn't had the presence of mind to mention it—and stormed out of the apartment.

Sharon Stone in *Basic Instinct*. That's who she reminded him of.

The large black walkie-talkie at his hip crackled, and even through the static of the poor-quality unit, he heard the lovely musical speech of Desiree Drea. Her voice never failed to make his heart skip a beat, then go back and skip it all over again. "Walter? Mr. Carmichael wants to know how you're coming with the props. He needs me to type up the inventory."

"I . . . um . . . I—" He looked down at the box, searching for words, and seized upon the letters stenciled to the crate. "I'm just now up to *Jungo's Revenge*. I've finished about half of the work."

As Desiree responded, he could hear the producer's voice bellowing in the background. "Jungo! It's all worthless crap. Trash it."

The secretary softened the message as she relayed it. "Mr. Carmichael suggests that it's of no value, so please put it in the Dumpster."

"And tell him he damn well better stay until he finishes," the voice in the background growled. "We need that building tomorrow to start shooting *Horror in the Prop Warehouse*."

"Tell him I'll do what needs to be done," Walter said, then clicked off the walkie-talkie, though he would gladly have chatted with Desiree for hours. He didn't have anything better to do that evening than work, anyway. He was very conscientious and would finish the job.

Chris Carmichael—producer of low-budget knock-off movies. The Jungo ape-man series, a bad Tarzan knock-off, had skated just a little too close to Tarzan's copyright line. The threatened legal action had caused the films to flop, even though they went direct to video. Walter had seen one of them and thought that the movies were bad enough to have flopped all on their own, without any legal difficulties to help them along. If anything, the publicity had boosted the sales.

He pulled out the other plastic elephant tusk, then some ugly looking tribal masks, three rubber cobras, and a giant plastic insect as big as his palm that was labeled DEADLY TSETSE FLY. Walter shook his head. He had to agree about the worthlessness of these props. There wouldn't be any collector interested in even giving them shelf space. If there had been enough fans to generate a few collectors, the Jungo franchise might never have disappeared.

Near the bottom of the crate he found a rattle, a shrunken head, and another tribal mask, but these props were far superior to the others. They looked handmade, with real wood and bone. The shrunken head had an odd leathery feel that made him wonder if it was real. He shuddered as he took it out of the crate.

It seemed unlikely that Chris Carmichael, a tight-wad with utter contempt for his audiences as well as his employees, would spend money on the genuine articles to use as props. Maybe a prop master had purchased them online or found them in a junk bin somewhere. Beneath the last of the witch doctor items, at the very bottom of the crate, he found a scrap of cloth that made him smile as he pulled it out and brushed off the bits of straw that clung to it.

A leopard-skin loincloth, the only garment Jungo the Ape Man had ever worn in the films—all the better to show off his well-developed physique, of course. Walter tried to remember. According to the story, Jungo had killed a leopard with his bare hands when he was only five years old and had made the loincloth out of its pelt. Apparently, the loincloth had grown along with the boy. Maybe the leopard had been part Spandex. . . . Jungo was probably the type of man Shirley would have fallen for—wild, tanned, brawny, and barely capable of stringing together three-word sentences. Walter groaned at the thought.

Now Desiree was another story entirely. Even on the big studio lot, they often crossed paths. He saw her in the commissary at lunch almost daily—because he timed his lunch hour to match hers. She was strikingly beautiful with her reddish-gold hair, her large blue eyes, her delicate chin, and when she smiled directly at him, as she had done three times now, it made him feel as if someone in the special effects shop had created the most spectacular sunrise ever.

But Walter still hadn't gotten up the nerve to ask if he could sit and eat with her. He was a nobody who did odd jobs around the lot for the various producers. Some of them were nice, and some of them were . . . like Chris Carmichael. The man was Dabney Coleman in *9 to 5,* or Bill Murray before his transformation in *Scrooged.* Carmichael had put in a requisition, and Walter had pulled the card: One man needed to clear prop warehouse. It was really a job for four men and four days, but Carmichael always slashed his budgets to leave more money in his own expense account. Carmichael didn't even know who Walter Groves was.

But Desiree did. That was all that mattered.

He gazed at the leopard-skin loincloth, hearing Shirley's words ring in his head. "You aren't a man's man. You don't let yourself go wild." He sniffed, trying to picture himself in the role she seemed to want him to play. What if Desiree felt the same way? What if all women thought they wanted a nice man but were only attracted to bad boys?

He picked up the witch doctor's rattle and gave it a playful shake, then put it down by the mask and the shrunken head. Even though she had hurt him, he wasn't the type either to put a curse on Shirley, or to transform himself for her into a muscular hunk of beefcake like Jungo. He would have needed an awfully large special effects budget to pull that off. Walter held up the leopard-skin loincloth to his waist and considered the fashion statement it would make. It looked ridiculous—even more so in contrast with his work pants and his conservative window-pane plaid shirt.

"If I wore this, what would Desiree think?" Would it convince her that he was a wild man, or would she just think him pale-skinned and scrawny? All alone in the prop warehouse, he had no particular need to hurry up. Carmichael, who never noticed anyone's hard work, had already said that the props were junk.

Before he could change his mind and think sensibly,

Walter unbuttoned his shirt and peeled it off. Taking a deep breath, he slipped off his shoes and trousers and tied on the loincloth. He surveyed the effect, looking critically at his skinny chest, thin arms, white skin, and the leopard-skin loincloth. He cast a skeptical glance at the witch doctor mask. "Exactly how did I expect this to bring out the wild man in me?"

Then something happened.

His heart began to pound like drumbeats in his ears. His skin grew hot and his blood hotter. He felt dizzy and then very, *very* sure of himself. The worries and confusion of his life seemed to float away like soap bubbles on the wind. His attention focused down to a single pinprick. Everything was so clear, so simple. He had worried too much, *thought* too much, suppressed all of his natural desires. He drew a deep breath, kept inhaling until his chest swelled. Then on impulse, he pounded on his proudly expanded chest. It felt good and right.

He didn't have to worry about the prop inventory or about Shirley. She had made a bad choice, and she was gone. He no longer needed to think of her. Outside the sun was bright. He was a man, and Desiree was a woman. Everything else was extraneous, a distraction. He was a hunter, and he knew his quarry. A real man relied on his instincts to tell him what to do.

He let out a warbling call, broadcasting a defiant challenge to anyone who might get in his way. Barefoot, he sprinted like a cheetah out of the prop warehouse and onto the lot. He had seen where Desiree worked. He knew where to find Chris Carmichael's trailer. His vision tunneled down to that one focus.

He streaked past the people working on various films. Someone made a cat-call, but most of the crews ignored him. Employees at Duro Studios were accustomed to seeing axe-murderers, Martians, barbarians, and monsters of all kinds.

Chris Carmichael's headquarters were in a dingy,

gray-walled trailer on the far end of the east lot. The success of a producer's films earned him clout in the studios, and Carmichael's track record had earned him this unobtrusive trailer and one secretary.

Desiree.

Walter yanked open the door and leaped in. He hadn't decided what to say or do next, but an ape-man took matters one step at a time. He reacted to situations, without planning in excruciating detail beforehand. Instead of startling Desiree at her keyboard and the producer on the phone, he blundered into a shocking scene that would have made his hackles rise if he'd had any. Carmichael stood with both hands planted on his desk, crouched like a predator ready to spring. Desiree shielded herself on the other side of the desk, trying to keep it, with its empty coffee mugs, framed pictures, and jumbled stacks of scripts, between herself and Carmichael.

He leered at her, moved to the left, and she shifted in the other direction. She was flushed and nervous. "Please, Mr. Carmichael. I'm not that kind of girl."

"Of course you are," he said. "If you didn't want to break into pictures, why would you work in a place like this? I can make you an extra in my next feature, *Horror in the Prop Warehouse*. Ten-second screen time minimum, but there's a price. You have to give me something." Now he circled to the right and she moved in the opposite direction.

"Please, don't do this. I don't want to file a complaint, but I'll call Security if I have to."

"You do that, and you'll never work in this town again."

Before she could reply, Walter let out a bestial roar. He wasn't sure exactly what happened. Seeing red, he acted on instinct and charged forward. He grabbed the producer by the back of his clean white collar, yanked him away from the desk, and spun him around. As he spluttered, Walter the ape-man landed a powerful roundhouse punch on his chin and knocked him backward into the chair he reserved for visiting actors.

Startled, Desiree gasped, but Walter was already on the move. He bounded over the desk, slipped an arm around her waist, and crashed through the screen of the trailer's open window, carrying his woman with him. The rest was a blur.

When he could think straight again—after the witch doctor's spell, or whatever it was wore off—he found himself on the rooftop of one of the back lot sets, sitting next to Desiree, his lips pressed against hers. With a start, he drew back. Her hair was rumpled, her cheeks flushed, and she wore an expression of surprise and amusement. "That was a bit unorthodox, Walter," she said, "but you were amazing. You saved me when I needed it most."

"What have I done?" Walter glanced down at the loincloth, flexed his sore knuckles, and knew with absolute certainty that he would soon die from embarrassment. He was sitting half-naked on a roof at work and had just made a complete fool of himself in front of a woman he had a genuine crush on. "I'm sorry. I'm sorry!" He scuttled backward, stood to look for a ladder or stairs, and quickly found an exit. "I didn't mean to hurt you. Mr. Carmichael's going to get me fired, for sure."

"Who, Chris? He has no clue who you are," she said. "Anyway, I'm going to hand in my own resignation. I've had enough of that man."

"I . . . I need to put something decent on. I can't understand what got into me." He felt his cheeks burning. His legs wobbled, and his knees threatened to knock together. Some ape-man!

Before Desiree could say anything more, he bolted, cringing at the thought that someone else might see him this way—that Desiree *had* seen him. He was sure Jungo never had days like this.

*   *   *

By the time he got home, Walter was consumed with guilt. He felt flustered, exposed, and too embarrassed for words. He couldn't believe what he had done, prancing around the lot in nothing more than a loincloth, crashing into the producer's trailer offices. He had punched out Chris Carmichael! Then, after jumping through a window with Desiree, he had somehow whisked her off to a rooftop and *kissed her*! He was the very definition of the word "mortified." To make matters worse, Walter had gotten dressed again, called in a friend to finish clearing out the warehouse, then slunk off the lot, taking Jungo's loincloth with him. He could justify this, since Carmichael had made it clear that the props could be thrown into a dumpster.

He sat miserably in his empty apartment—without Shirley—and wondered how he could possibly make it up to Desiree. He didn't much care about Chris Carmichael. The man was a cad, but Walter himself had stolen a kiss from Desiree, practically ravished her! Considering the power the loincloth had worked on him, he could easily have gotten carried away. In the process of saving Desiree, he had proved that he was no better than that jerk of a producer.

And Walter had just left her stranded there, on the roof of the movie set. No, no, that wasn't Walter Groves. That wasn't who he really was. Though he wanted nothing more than to crawl under a rock, he knew what he had to do for the sake of honor. He had to go find Desiree and beg her forgiveness.

For a long time he stood in the shower under a pounding stream of hot water, rehearsing what to say until he knew he couldn't put it off any longer. Every moment he avoided her was another moment she could think terrible things about him. He dried his hair, dabbed on some aftershave, and put on his best dress slacks, a clean shirt, and a striped blue necktie. This was going to be a formal apology, and he wanted to look his best. Pulling on his nicest, though rarely

worn, sport jacket, he rolled up Jungo's loincloth and
stuffed it into the pocket. Though it didn't make any
sense, he would try to tell Desiree what had happened,
explain how the magic had changed him somehow into
a wild man, someone he wouldn't normally be.

After dialing information, then searching on the Internet, he tracked down a local street address for D.
Drea. He knew it had to be her. Gathering his resolve,
he marched out to go face her. He didn't need the
crutch of a loincloth or some imaginary witch doctor's
spells to give him courage to do the right thing. He
would do this himself.

On the way to her apartment, he didn't let himself
think, forcing himself onward before the shame could
make him turn back. He had to be like Michael Doug-
las in *Romancing the Stone*, not Rick Moranis in *Little
Shop of Horrors*. Nothing should disrupt the apology.
Leaving his cell phone in the car, he walked to the
door of her apartment, raised his hand to knock, then
hesitated. He wasn't thinking clearly. He really should
have brought flowers and a card. Why not go to a
store now, buy them, and then come back?

He heard shouts coming from the other side of the
door, followed by a scream—Desiree's scream!

He froze in terror. What should he do? Desiree was
in trouble. Maybe he should run back outside, get his
cell phone and call 911. He could bring the police
here, or, better yet, pound on her neighbors' doors
and find someone who was big and strong. She
screamed again, and Walter knew there could be only
one solution. He tried the knob, found the door un-
locked, and barged in. He found Chris Carmichael already there, reeking of cheap cologne and bourbon.

"Leave me alone," Desiree said. She held a lamp
in one hand, brandishing it like a club.

Carmichael let out an evil chuckle. "Now that you
no longer work for me, we can have any sort of rela-
tionship I want. There are no ethical problems."

She raised the lamp higher. Walter stepped forward,

outraged but quailing at the idea of a fight. When Desiree saw him, her eyes lit up.

Carmichael turned.

Walter blurted, "Hey, what—what's going on here?" He wished he could hide or, at the very least, run back out of the apartment and return to do a second take of the scene. He needed to be a tough guy, like Dirty Harry in *Sudden Impact*—"Go ahead, make my day"—and the best he could come up with was a Don Knotts-worthy "Hey, what's going on here?" He groaned.

Carmichael recognized him, and his eyes grew stormy. Ignoring Desiree for the moment, the larger man lurched toward Walter, grabbed him by the shirt, yanked his tie, and drew Walter closer to him. "You're that little freak that sucker-punched me in my office, aren't you? Where's the spotted underwear?"

"I—I—I don't need it."

"You'll need an ambulance is what you'll need."

Indiana Jones would have done something different. He would have punched the villain, starting an all-out brawl, but as Carmichael lifted him and twisted his tie, he could only make a small "meep" sound.

"You put him down," Desiree cried, and Walter's heart lurched. She was actually defending him!

Carmichael laughed again. "You can't even save yourself. How do you expect to help this mouse?" He pushed Walter up against the wall, clenched his fist, and drew back his arm, as if cocking a shotgun.

Walter was sure his head would go straight through the drywall. "Wait. Wait, please." He swallowed and drew a deep breath. "If you're going to do this, let me face it like a man. I . . . I'd like to use the rest-room, please."

Carmichael blinked, then gave him a knowing smile. "Oh, afraid you're going to wet yourself, eh?" He let Walter slump to the floor. "Sure. Why not? Desiree and I were just enjoying an intimate conversation. We can wait."

He glared at her, and she sat down on the sofa, not sure what to do. Walter scurried into the bathroom and closed the door, his mind spinning. Maybe Desiree kept a gun in the bathroom, perhaps taped behind the toilet tank, like in *Godfather*. But he found nothing there, and a quick search of the drawers and the medicine cabinet revealed no other weapons he could use to save the day.

He stuck his hands in his jacket pockets and his fingers brushed a patch of sleek fur. The loincloth. It was his only chance.

Walter burst out of the bathroom wearing nothing but the scrap of leopard-skin. Barefoot and bare-chested. His mind filled with the thoughts of a hunter. Testosterone and adrenaline pumped through his veins, and he let out a wild yell, pounding on his chest. His hair was a mess, his eyes on fire. Seeing his enemy, the producer, he lunged toward him like a hungry lion attacking a springbok. Walter felt total confidence and did not hesitate.

Chris Carmichael, who used his position of perceived power to intimidate people, faltered. When he saw Walter leap toward him, he suddenly reconsidered what he'd been about to do.

Walter let out another roar. His lungs seemed to have twice their normal capacity. "*My* woman!"

Carmichael had probably never been challenged before. A producer, even a bad producer of second-rate movies, could boss people around in Hollywood. But Walter the ape-man, wearing nothing but his loincloth in Desiree's apartment, had no doubt that he himself was king of the jungle. Carmichael turned, took several steps in retreat, then paused. Through his hunter-focused gaze, Walter watched his prey, preparing to throw himself on the man if he made a move in the wrong direction.

Desiree decided for both men, though. As Carmichael started to turn back, she lifted her lamp, and smashed it on his head. He crumpled to the carpet

like King Kong falling off the Empire State Building.
The rush in Walter's mind drained away, and he found
himself standing naked in Desiree's apartment, except
for the ape-man's loincloth. He shivered, and goose
bumps appeared on his arms. "What did I do this
time?" he said, looking down at the producer with
dismay.

But Desiree was close to him. Very close and very
beautiful. "You protected me, Walter. You saved
me." She slid her arms around his waist and gave him
a hug. "You're my hero."

It was not the magic of the loincloth that made his
heart start pounding again. "You—you don't mind?"
he asked in surprise.

"I'll show you how much I mind in just a minute."
She stepped away and looked down at the unconscious
Carmichael. "But first, help me take out the garbage.
We'll put him in the hall and call the police." Walter
and Desiree rolled the man like a skid row drunk into
the apartment hallway.

Desiree closed the door, locked it, and turned to
face him. Suddenly he felt as if he were the prey and
she the hungry lioness.

He gulped. "I'm really a nice guy most of the time.
But I can be bad, if I need to be."

"Walter, I *like* that you're a nice guy. It's the first
thing I noticed about you, even from a distance. You
may not have known I was watching, but I've seen
you hold doors for other people, help them carry
things when their arms were full, lend them lunch
money, listen to what they say. Most of the time, that's
exactly what women want. It's what *I* want. But
women are . . . complex creatures. So once in a while
we also like a bit of a wild man. You seem like the
best of both worlds to me."

"You may never be safe," he pointed out. "What
if Mr. Carmichael comes back? I don't think he'll
leave you alone."

With a lovely smile, she led him to the couch and

sat him down. "In that case, maybe you'll just have to stay here to protect me."

There was a stirring in the loincloth, and he felt very self-conscious. "Maybe I should get dressed in real clothes."

"No, Walter. You stay just the way you are." Desiree leaned over to kiss him.

SEAMLESS

Michael Stackpole

"**O**h, Connor! This is nothing like the way I left it."

The genuine surprise on Daniella Granger's face matched the tone of her voice. Slender, but not short enough to be considered petite, Dani wore her dark hair to her shoulders and had light gray eyes that probably should have been called dove gray—soft and a bit timid.

"When you moved out from your boyfriend's place, you weren't so neat."

She slowly shook her head. "No. The break-up came just after my grandfather's death. I was a mess, and that's what I left the locker in."

I took another quick glance into the storage unit, looking for anything truly weird. Nothing except, maybe the way things were organized. All the stuff, from boxes crammed with papers to an old TV and some ragged suitcases, had been very neatly stacked against three walls, leaving a bare concrete slab directly below the single, unshaded light bulb.

Right there, in the spotlight, sat a small wooden box, roughly a foot and a half long, a foot in the other two dimensions. It looked old, had a rusty latch on it, and most of the black and gold paint had been worn away. The gold once had been decoration, but I couldn't make out what the designs were meant to be.

I entered the locker and dropped to a knee beside the box. "You ever see this before?"

"No." Dani rested her hands on my shoulders and peeked around me. "No, wait, yes. I think so."

"Which is it?"

"I saw it once in my grandfather's attic. He told me never to touch it and never to tell anyone I'd seen it. He moved it somewhere, so I'd not seen it since."

"You're sure this is the same box?"

She squeezed my shoulders. "I think so, but how could it get here? I mean, his estate was tiny, and my aunt said there was nothing for me. I never got anything, and I'd not have put it in storage if I did. I loved my grandfather."

I stood and took her hands in mine, squeezing them gently. "It's okay. It's no big deal. It's weird, like the rest of the stuff, but not a crisis."

She glanced down, but squeezed my hands back. "I know I'm acting silly, but ever since he died I've been rudderless. I thought I was holding it to together, but . . ."

"Not a problem. We'll figure this out." I picked up the box. "I'm sure there's a logical explanation for all of this."

"And if there isn't?"

I smiled. "Then my boss will find something else that will work."

Daniella didn't say much as we headed back to Casa Chaos, where my employer lives and, nominally speaking, works. Merlin Bloodstone bills himself as an *occultist*, but the IRS doesn't have a code for that, so I'm not sure it's a real occupation. Practically speaking, he provides spiritual advice for a bunch of very rich clients who could save themselves a lot of money if they'd just buy a gross of fortune cookies and read one every day.

That's unfair, but I didn't feel like being fair. I'd tried to brief him on Dani's situation, but he wanted none of it. Nor did he come down to meet her when she'd come to the house earlier. He remained hidden in his sanctum and sent me a note instructing me to do whatever I thought best.

That was inhospitable and rude—par for the course when he was in a mood. In his defense he'd note that we were under no obligation to help her. I disagreed, but then I'd heard her voice on the phone and had checked her out on Myspace. On a scale of one to Salma Hayek, Dani hit 7.5, and got a bonus point for being a damsel in distress.

We got back to Paradise Valley easily, parked and went straight to the office. Dani trailed in my wake, and the office won a big gasp from her. I rate guests on their reaction, and she scored solidly.

The office *is* impressive and extends up through the second floor. The west wall is made up of tall windows that provide a stunning view of Camelback Mountain's north face. Opposite it and all along the north wall are built-in bookshelves, with a catwalk about ten feet up to allow access to the top half of the shelves. A spiral, wrought-iron staircase in the southeast corner is the quick way to get up there, and there's a door for access from the second floor as well. The south wall is where Bloodstone hangs all the photographs of himself taken with lots of different clients, as well as plaques and awards, some of which are inscribed in languages I don't think even exist anymore. The doorway through which we entered splits that wall in half.

I carried the box in and plunked it down on Bloodstone's desk. The desk is this massive thing—only slightly smaller than the new US Embassy in Iraq. Save for a lamp, a blotter, a phone, a penholder and sometimes a book, he keeps it completely empty. I centered the box neatly and considered turning the lock away from where he would stand, but that would just be petty.

The middle of the room has a tan leather couch facing the desk but canted at some angle that has to do with the dictates of *feng shui*. Three rust-colored leather chairs—those big wing-back things that ought to be in a Victorian Gentlemans' club—face the couch. They have side tables between them, and a coffee table fronts the couch. I waved Dani to the couch, then retreated to my desk back by the wet bar.

I was going to ask her what kind of tea she wanted, but my boss decided to make his entrance, cutting me off. Bloodstone—more properly Doctor Merlin Bloodstone—*is* small enough to be considered petite—save for his head, his ego and this intensity he radiates. He wears his black hair slicked back, emphasizing his widow's peak. Compared to his body, his head is huge, and his violet eyes are large as well. Some folks built that way appear innocent, but Bloodstone looks on the verge of changing into some kind of monster.

He paused in the doorway and nodded to me. "*Ti Kwan Yin* for the both of us, Connor. You may have what you want."

Without giving me another glance, he turned and crossed to where Daniella was rising from the couch. Bloodstone had chosen to wear a gray suit with a blue shirt and a blue-green tie, the like of which I'd never seen him wear before. This worried me. His moods determine how he chooses to dress. We were off into the land of the lost, and I didn't like that.

"I'm so sorry I could not join you this morning, but I see you and Connor had some success. Please, sit." He waited for her to sit, then took the centermost chair. "Connor briefed me earlier, but I should like to hear it in your own words."

I shot Bloodstone a glare he ignored. The rat. He'd not wanted to listen to one word of anything I wanted to report, and now he made it sound as if he'd been engrossed in every little detail.

Dani didn't notice any duplicity. "It is about as simple as it is strange. I work as a server at Chelsea's Kitchen, over on Fortieth Street, north of Camelback."

Bloodstone nodded. "I know it. A very pleasant place."

"Thanks." Dani smiled up at me as I brought her the tea. "Two days ago I had a couple of four-tops, an eight, and a single. The single was a saint, just sitting quietly, not hurried at all. He knew what he wanted, liked what he got, lingered over coffee for a bit, but never hit on me or anything, the way some guys do."

I brought Bloodstone his tea, then joined Dani on the couch. She sipped for a moment, her smile widened, then she continued her tale. "The guy paid promptly in cash and left me twenty on a fifty-dollar tab. He also left me this."

She dug into her jeans and produced a small padlock key. "I thought he'd just forgotten it. I tried to find him in the parking lot, but he was long since gone. I pocketed it, assuming he'd call. Then, the next day, I get a package at work. It's got a cell phone in it. One number is programmed in. Yours."

Bloodstone glanced at me. "Possible?"

"Easy." I could have explained, but it would have been a waste of breath. Bloodstone makes the average Luddite look like Stephen Hawking.

"Please, Miss Granger, continue."

"The phone has a scheduler. An alert came up about my storage locker. Today, the lock I'd used was gone, and this key fit the new one. Everything had been moved, and that box—my grandfather's box—was in there."

Bloodstone set his tea down and walked around to the far side of his desk. "You said it was your grandfather's. When did you last see it?"

"Nineteen years ago. He raised me after my parents were killed in a car accident. He died four months ago, but no one ever sent this to me."

"Interesting trick, leaving it there after burgling your storage locker." Bloodstone bent down and peered at the lock. "Tell me about your grandfather."

She shrugged. "His name was Jack Granger. He was loving but low key. He used to say he'd gotten enough excitement in World War II, so he was content with a quiet life."

Bloodstone glanced at the return address. "What did he do in the war?"

"He was with the OSS. He was in Italy before our troops were."

My boss slid open a drawer and brought out a cigar-box that rattled as he set it down. He opened it, displaying a tangle of old-fashioned keys. "Do you have any objection to my opening the box?"

"I guess not." She hesitated for a moment. "I guess it's okay."

I glanced at him. "Her grandfather made her promise never to touch it."

"I see." Bloodstone nodded. "Miss Granger, you would agree that this prohibition may have expired. The box's presence in your locker and the delivery of the phone are indicative of someone's desire for you to bring this here."

"Yes, true, but I don't want to disappoint him."

"I suspect, if you ever had, the box never would have been entrusted to you." Bloodstone brushed his long fingers over the wooden lid. "This would have been beautiful when new."

Dani crossed her arms. "How old do you think it is?"

"At least a thousand years."

He said it so matter-of-factly that it took me a couple seconds to figure out what he was really saying. "You mean 'Before Columbus discovered America' old?"

"Without question." He rapped a knuckle against it, and it thumped solidly. "Cedar, probably from Lebanon. I believe it comes from Outremer."

Bloodstone pronounced it the right way, as French for "Beyond the Ocean."

I raised an eyebrow. "As in the Crusader Kingdoms?"

"The same." He fished through the keys. He inserted one into the lock. He twisted and the latch clicked up.

"Boxes like this are not unusual. In its day it would have been painted with images and symbols appropriate to the contents. Many such boxes arrived in Europe from Outremer. Sometimes the contents were genuine, sometimes fakery, but they were always treasured by those who possessed them."

Dani shook her head. "I kind of figured he got it during the war and brought it home. Looting, I guess, though I can't imagine him doing that."

"He would not have been unique in bringing back a treasure." Bloodstone's eyes narrowed. "I doubt this was a war relic, however."

Relic? Something clicked in my head. "Is that a reliquary? Are we going to find bones in there?"

"Unlikely. It didn't rattle." Bloodstone opened the box slowly, even reverently. He clearly had a clue as to what he would find, but the contents of the box blew past his preconceptions. Bloodstone's eyes widened almost as Dani's had, and there was no hiding his surprise.

We both came forward, and I was bracing myself for some skull-thing crawling with bugs or snakes or something. The look on Dani's face suggested she was dreading the same. We both took our first gander at it, then exchanged glances.

She put it into words. "I don't get it. It's a rag."

Bloodstone's voice shrank to a whisper. "Not a rag. It is a fine piece of weaving, definitely homespun. It is probably twice as old as the box."

I frowned at him. "You're telling me this came from the time of Jesus?"

He nodded solemnly. "I have little doubt it came from that time."

Dani reached out to touch the yellowed cloth, yet never quite did. "But if it's that old, why isn't in a museum?"

"That, young lady, is a very good question." Bloodstone slowly closed the box again. "With your permission, I shall do my best to find an answer."

That having been said, anyone else in the world would have hopped on his computer and done a Google search. Not Bloodstone. He doesn't have a computer. He only uses a phone because it was invented in the Nineteenth Century. And cell phones? Not a chance. For him, the very idea of mobile communications died with the last passenger pigeon.

He headed out of the office with the box tucked under his arm, then stopped and looked back at the two of us. "Miss Granger, because your place of employment seems to be the primary contact point, I will have Connor watch over you there. Under no circumstances should you return to your locker. If anything suspicious happens at your home, call the police, and do *not* use that cellular phone to do so."

She nodded. "Thank you, Dr. Bloodstone."

"And, Connor, see what you can learn about the source of the phone. I shall call the owner of the restaurant, and we will arrange a cover for you."

"Got it. How often do you want reports?"

He considered for a moment, balancing his desire to be left alone with his concern for what was going on. "Every two hours unless something peculiar is going on. Use the ring code."

"Done."

Dani looked at me as the man headed up the stairs to his sanctum. "He's a bit of an odd duck."

"He's a whole damned flock." I got up. "Let me see your phone."

Despite having a computer, a T1 line, a bunch of

friends to call, and favors to burn, I didn't learn much about the phone. It and the service had been bought for cash two days before she got it. It might have been possible to get the security tapes from the store where the purchase was made, but even seeing an image of the purchaser wouldn't mean much. If he wanted to remain hidden, he'd just pick someone off the street to make the buy for him. And even having his image wouldn't give us his name.

No sense in reporting a dead-end to Bloodstone, so we proceeded with the next part of his plan—my making sure Dani was not harmed. I'm not that big a guy, so it's not often I get to play bodyguard. I *am* licensed to carry a concealed weapon, but so far nothing warranted my packing a gun.

By the time Dani showed up for her shift that evening, Bloodstone had indeed called the owner of Chelsea's Kitchen, and they'd found something for me to do. I'd been thinking maybe I'd get to hang at the bar, which would give me an easy view of the interior and the patio, but they found something that would allow me to circulate and check everyone out.

This was how I learned that the term "busboy" is short for "bust-your-ass-boy." I don't know how folks in food service do it. My night was full of "More water," and "Less ice," or Goldilocks' complaints of things being too hot or too cold. Nothing was ever "just right." Folks were cadging for free this or to have something taken off the bill; and then servers like Dani, who did everything but bear a man's child or donate a kidney, would get stiffed on the tip.

The worst offenders were a party of four who'd just come from Wednesday night church services. After slamming some shots and wolfing down food as if it was *their* last supper, they put the bill on a credit card. Their tip was a small brochure. It invited Dani to join their church. They'd added a handwritten note— "Don't worry, dear, the Lord Jesus will provide."

Me, personally, I figure that Jesus would have

tipped better than 25%, and I made a comment to that effect.

Dani's eyes sharpened. "Servers are required to tip-out the bussing, bar and kitchen staff based on the charges rung up, not the amount of tip collected. When these folks stiff us for a tip, *we* end up paying for the privilege of having served them."

I fingered the brochure. "You mean the bartenders won't take their cut out of this?"

"Nope, and my landlord won't accept it for rent, either. Since the Federal Minimum Wage for servers is $2.13 an hour, I'll be screwed if I get much more Christian kindness. Once I figure out what the heck I'm doing with my life, it's adios food service and people like that."

Despite her remarks, she accepted the indignities with a smile and really did a great job making people happy. She might complain on break, but even when she was having a bad day, she turned on the charm. Between the great food and service, she didn't get stiffed all that often. Chelsea's Kitchen draws better-than-average customers who seemed to appreciate Dani's efforts. Still, after watching for only three days, I could begin to pick out the folks who would be high maintenance.

It wasn't until the following Saturday that I spotted anyone out of the ordinary. For a moment I thought it might be Dani's mysterious stranger returned to the scene of the crime, but this man was younger and so cadaverously slender that he'd bulge like a well-fed python if he tried to eat the rib-eye he'd ordered. I noticed him because he was seated in Dani's section, didn't order a drink, and watched her very carefully.

I didn't like it, so I eclipsed his vision of her. "I can get you a box so you can take that home with you."

Skullface looked up at me, and his smile shrank, which set my hair on edge. Piercing blue eyes raked me up and down, then he nodded to the seat opposite to him. "Please, join me."

"The help isn't allowed, sir."

"But you're not help, are you, Mr. Moran?"

I still didn't sit. "What's on your mind?"

"Your little friend over there has something which does not belong to her. I require it. I am willing to pay her for it."

"I don't know what . . ."

"Spare me, Moran." He slowly opened his jacket and pulled out a card case. The card he gave me had been printed in black over ivory, with a circle and cross device worked in red in the upper right corner. "Reverend Joseph Bernhard? I don't think I've ever heard of the Church of Jesus Christ Martyr before."

"Your employer will have. My cell number is on the back. You will have him call me." He regarded me as a vulture might regard road kill. "Not to be melodramatic, but this can work one of two ways. Either the girl can be enriched by this experience, or it will become a character-building exercise. I know that decision will be made above your pay grade. Pass on the message like a good boy."

I was tempted to hit him, and I probably would have, but he was expecting it. So, I just returned his smile. "As you wish, sir. Now, do you want a box for this?"

"Not necessary." He draped his napkin over the bloody steak, then dropped a pair of one hundred dollar bills on top of the growing red stain. "I look forward to the call."

I let him go, then retreated to the back and called Bloodstone. I let the phone ring twice, then hung up and called back. It rang four more times, then went to voice mail. I almost didn't leave a message because I knew Bloodstone would never find it—but maybe the CSI guys would. I read the information from the card, including the cell phone number, then repeated my cell number and asked for a quick callback.

I returned to the floor and looked for Dani, but she was gone. I asked another busboy, Luis, where she was and he pointed toward the parking lot. "Table five forgot their dinner. She took it out to them."

Table five. I closed my eyes for a moment. A pair of young men, well dressed, college or early career. Nothing unusual about them, really.

The squeal of tires from the parking lot snapped my eyes open. I ran for the door just in time to see a white Escalade bouncing onto 40th, heading south. They caught the light at the corner and headed west on Camelback.

Tony, the guy working valet, was sitting on the ground rubbing a hand over his jaw. "They kidnapped Dani. They just shoved her into the Escalade and took off. I tried to stop them but . . ."

"I know, they were big." I helped him up. "Did you see the other guy, tall, slender, young, blond hair trimmed short."

"Mercedes 500SL. Tipped me ten bucks."

"Which way did he go?"

Tony shrugged. "Out on 40th, same as everyone else. Do I call the cops?"

"Yeah. You have the plate numbers logged?"

"I'll give them to them. The Mercedes, too?"

"Give me an hour. If I don't call you, report it." I headed for the Cougar. "Some decisions need to be made above my pay grade, then I'm going to find Dani and get her back safely."

Bloodstone wasn't in the office when I arrived. That was good. It gave me a chance hit the net and Google Reverend Bernhard. I learned quite a bit about him and the weird crap he was into.

When I heard Bloodstone trotting down the stairs I turned my monitor to face the doorway and pointed to it. "This clown is Joseph Bernhard. He kidnapped Dani. He's seriously looney-tunes. He's the leader of a Christian Identity sect. His hobbies are loading his own ammunition, reading *Mein Kampf* in the original German, rescuing Nazi memorabilia from Soviet archives, and denying the Holocaust ever happened. And *that's* just what he says about himself on the Sean Hannity-fan dating-site."

Bloodstone nodded. "Christian Identity is a vile perversion of Christianity. They believe Aryans are the true chosen people, the Jews murdered Jesus and so forth. Racism cum religion."

"He wants the box. You're to call him."

His nostrils flared. "Dial him."

I did. The line rang twice, then Bernhard answered. "I'll hold for Bloodstone."

Bloodstone punched the speaker button on my desk phone. "The girl is safe?"

"You have something of mine, and I want it."

"Don't be coy. It was never yours."

"It was meant to be mine. I have searched long enough. You will bring it to me. An innocent life hangs in the balance." Bernhard hissed coldly. "Twenty-fourth and Camelback, near the bookstore. You have twenty-five minutes." He cut the connection.

I hit the speaker button again. "No cops?"

"Contra-indicated." He shook his head slowly. "Don't bother to bring your pistol."

"Bernhard is a kidnapper, and he likes to play with guns."

Bloodstone shook his head. "This time he is playing with something far more powerful, and it will consume him. No gun, no violence."

Our stares met, but it would be easier to win a stare-down with the Lincoln Memorial than with Bloodstone. I raised my hands in surrender. "No gun. No violence."

"Good." His eyes became violet slits. "I will get the box. We will take the Jaguar."

We loaded the box in the trunk, Bloodstone piled into the rear seat, and I slid behind the wheel. We made it to the parking lot with five minutes to spare.

Once I found a space, a van pulled up blocking us in. A man emerged from the back, opened our passenger door and dropped into the seat beside me.

I looked at him. "Box is in the trunk. Where's the girl?"

"Shut up and drive."

"If you think . . ."

Bloodstone squeezed my shoulder. "Bernhard suspects trickery. And he wants witnesses." Bloodstone settled back into the shadows. "Where are we going?"

My guide, who looked a bit rougher than the guys who took Dani, jerked a thumb toward the van. "Follow it."

I did as ordered, but I didn't like any of it. A quick swap would have worked well, but Bernhard wanting us there while he inspected the cloth was not a good sign. We were being kidnapped. We could identify our kidnappers. The easiest way to escape prosecution was to put a bullet in each one of us. After reading about Bernhard, I had no doubt he'd do that and likely declare he was giving us a sacrament.

Blessed is he who is anointed with 119 grains of lead.

We didn't have to travel far, just southwest to Thomas and 16th, to a mortuary. We drove around back to the receiving area. I pulled the Jaguar into an empty hearse bay, and the van blocked us in again. I popped the trunk, and Bloodstone retrieved the box.

Four men led us into the mortuary and to the first viewing room. The rectangular room had a dozen rows of seats, and I found them disturbingly full. It looked like a costume party and the theme was Nuremburg, 1936. Most of the men wore snappy Nazi uniforms, complete with the ceremonial daggers and an Iron Cross or two. The women wore stockings with seams running up the back.

Bernhard, however, took the cake. I was raised Catholic, so I'm used to priests being swathed in layers of cloth. Over a black cassock that had been belted with a Sam Browne belt, Bernhard wore a chasuble of red, with a big white circle in the middle of his chest. That featured a swastika in black, and what looked to be a holstered Luger sat at his right hip. He even wore a red miter fixed with the swastika, so he was all decked out for a High Unholy Mass.

We were directed to the front, toward the dais that had a massive Nazi flag as the backdrop. Three chairs had been placed over to my left, and Dani sat in one closest to the wall. I sat next to her and took her hands in mine.

"You okay?"

"Just scared." Dani gave me a hopeful smile. "Is this really happening?"

"It'll be okay." I tried to force confidence through my voice, but I was feeling as if I were trapped in some B-grade rip-off of an Indiana Jones movie. *And me without a whip or anything.*

Bloodstone delivered the box to Bernhard. The High Priest handled it reverently—as if the reliquary contained Hitler's bones—and placed it on a table opposite us. He centered it between two censers, scattering the thick ropes of sweet white smoke rising from them. Bernard brushed his fingers over the lid as if caressing a lover and then turned around and motioned for the congregation to be seated.

Between him and the audience lay a low bier, which wasn't too hard to imagine in a funeral home. On it lay something shrouded with a red cloth. It had that unique outline that suggested it was a body, but there were clearly parts missing. At least one foot was gone, and probably an arm. The chest wasn't that round and there definitely was a hunk of the skull missing.

Bernhard waited for Bloodstone to sit in the third chair, then raised his hand. "It is time, my friends, long past time. Bow your heads."

I didn't. I studied the crowd. A bunch of them looked the way I'd expect white supremists to look, with prison tattoos or shaved heads, but the others really sent a chill through me. They looked normal, even those of an age to have been fighting against the Germans in World War II. Out of the uniforms, they'd have been unremarkable, and they looked affluent, too. Hatred isn't cheap, and they could finance a lot of it.

Bernhard solemnly intoned a prayer. "Lord Jesus, by Your words, in Your name, great miracles have been wrought. Men have been raised from the dead. We ask You to look upon our brother, Adolf, and through Your love, restore him to the life so cruelly cut short, so he may continue the work of avenging Your murder."

As the others murmured "Amen," Bernhard whipped the red cloth off the thing in front of him. Desiccated, dried up, burned in places, with plenty of pieces missing and ivory bone visible through torn flesh, there was no mistaking it for a body. Somewhere in college I remembered reading that Hitler had shot himself, and loyal minions tried to burn his body. The Russians had interrupted them and had dragged the remains back for Stalin, never to be seen again. And, yet, I recalled hearing rumors that the body was still preserved in some KGB archive somewhere.

That can't be Hitler's body, can it?

Bernhard turned and opened the reliquary. From it he drew the homespun cloth and unfolded it. It looked like a man's cloak, all woven of one piece, which he draped over the corpse from toes to crown. He smoothed out the wrinkles, and Dani grabbed my left arm, burying her face against my shoulder. I gave her a squeeze, then dragged her to her feet as Bernhard gestured and the congregation rose.

"Lord Jesus, in Your name we ask that life again flow into our brother Adolf. The mere touch of the hem of Your cloak was enough to cure the blind, the leper, the ill and the dead. This perfect raiment, which could not be sundered and, therefore, was diced-for in fulfillment of prophecy, graced You as You raised

Lazarus. Bring us back our brother, for Your glory, and the glory of Your chosen people."

Bernhard modulated his voice, starting low and building higher. The intensity increased with each sentence. Enthusiasm filled the final words. It brought them to a peak. Everyone listening got caught in the cadence, leaning forward as his voice rose, settling back as it subsided.

As each sentence built the anticipation, Bernhard's hands clawed down through the air. They grazed bare millimeters above the cloak. His hooked fingers plucked at invisible strings. I could almost hear them thrum, and feel them vibrate through my chest.

And into the corpse.

Dani squeezed my arm hard. "Oh my God, Connor, it's moving!"

It couldn't be, but the cloak rippled. A corner slipped back from the blackened left foot. I searched the corpse for a sign of breath. I looked for any movement at all, to see a hand rising or the head turning.

Bernhard reacted with a triumphant hiss. "Behold the miracle!"

His words came faster now, and more power filled them. Members of the congregation gasped. They whispered. Some pointed, others hugged, and it was not out of fear. They were as exultant as Bernhard as the monster that had been Hitler began to regain life.

Dani's grip on my arm tightened. My fingers began to tingle. I stared, wanting to completely disbelieve. Then I thought I saw something. The flesh on the forehead, the edges around the hole turned pink. They were beginning to close.

Bloodstone's disdain shattered the trance woven by Bernhard's words and the swirling incense. "Nothing is moving, Bernhard. You were swindled."

The contempt in Bloodstone's words pierced the collective hallucination. Gasps became moans. Those who had hugged, broke apart. One ancient gentleman fainted. Others cursed. The incense became nothing more than cloying smoke. It swirled lazily, poisonously sweet, as if it rising from the burned corpse.

The wild fire in Bernhard's eyes dulled. His expression slackened, as if he could see himself as the rest of us did. He looked ridiculous standing over a carbonized mummy, wishing it to rise from the dead. Any credibility he'd had with his audience evaporated, and their ire was rising.

"No! This *will* work!" His eyes sharpened again. "We just need blood. A sacrifice."

Without missing a beat, Bernhard drew the Luger. I pulled Dani to me, twisting so my body shielded her. Bloodstone took a step forward, his right hand rising, palm forward. Bernhard, with hatred sparking anew in his eyes, thrust the pistol at Bloodstone's hand and stroked the trigger.

The gun went off. A single cartridge ejected. The brass spun up, glittering in the light. Gunsmoke from the chamber mixed with the incense. The pistol's extractor arm snapped back down, jamming a new bullet into the chamber.

"Don't." Bloodstone's voice sounded small compared to the mechanical click of the gun's mechanism. From others that single word would have been a plea for mercy. Bloodstone offered a warning.

And even before I wondered why the first bullet had not blown through Bloodstone's hand, Bernhard stroked the trigger again.

The pistol exploded. Fire and metal jetted back from the chamber, shredding Bernhard's face. He screamed horribly as the mangled pistol and two fingers fell toward the ground. Bernhard whirled away and slammed into the wall. The Nazi fell, dragging the flag down, draping himself and muting his screams.

Bloodstone turned to face the congregation, his unblemished hand toward them. He closed it into a fist, then pointed toward the door. His voice dropped into a rime-edged whisper that drilled into skulls.

"Leave now, lest your folly become your doom."

It really didn't surprise me as the crowd bolted. They'd all been locked into a trance. He'd broken it. He was shot twice at pointblank range and was unhurt. The gun exploded, maiming their champion. Though the audience may have been dumb enough to believe they'd been invited to Adolf Hitler's resurrection, they weren't completely stupid. With two strokes of the finger twitching on the floor, Bernhard transformed the Church of Jesus Christ Martyr from a "fringe Christian group" into a "murderous cult." There wasn't a single person rushing out that door who saw an upside to being associated with it.

"Connor!" Dani drew tight against me and pointed.

Bernhard had crawled from the cocoon of the Nazi flag and had extended his ruined hand. He caught at corner of the cloak, dragging it from the body. His head came up, his face expectant, his sightless eyes filled with blood. He began to tremble, then his head lolled, and his body went slack.

Bloodstone untangled the cloak's hem from the man's grip, then folded it and returned it to the reliquary.

Before sirens began to rise, we sped away in the Jaguar. Dani was shaking to pieces, and I couldn't blame her. I was trembling, too, but I held it together long enough to get us home. Only Bloodstone didn't seem to be reacting, and he did offer to drive, but the chances of our making it home in one piece with him behind the wheel were slightly worse than his surviving two pointblank pistol shots.

I ensconced Dani in a guest room and told her everything would be okay. I told her to get some sleep, then went to visit Bloodstone in the office. He stood by my desk listening to the 10 o'clock news. The radio squawked about a murderous Nazi cult whose leader had been found with a burned corpse. They said he'd survive his wounds but would lose his sight. He'd been arrested and was under guard at St. Joseph's Hospital.

I turned the radio off before the local sheriff could offer his thoughts on the matter. "What's more nuts? You telling me not to bring a gun, or you thinking bullets bounce off?"

He shrugged. "You know that the Righteous and Harmonious Fists, during the Boxer Rebellion, practiced spiritual exercises that made them impervious to Imperialist bullets."

I raised an eyebrow. "I don't remember that working out too well for them."

"Perhaps the ones who were shot lacked faith."

"Sure, and your faith saved you?"

"Do you believe otherwise?"

"Can't answer. Don't know what you believe in. What I do know is what happened."

Bloodstone smiled. "And what would that be?"

"Bernhard did his own bullet reloading. He primed a cartridge, but never added gunpowder. The primer kicked the first bullet into the barrel and it got stuck. The next bullet slammed into the plug. The hot gasses blasted back into Bernhard's face. The gun exploded."

"If you know what happened, why question my action?"

"My hindsight doesn't equal your foresight. No one could have predicted what happened."

He smiled in that annoying, all-knowing way he has. "Why do you think I told you not to bring your pistol?" Before I could reply, he continued. "Bernhard was right. The cloth in the reliquary *was* the cloak Jesus had worn. Can you imagine the Prince of Peace allowing violence in His presence?"

A chill ran through me. "But you said he was swindled, so that couldn't have been the true cloak."

"He was swindled by the Russians." Bloodstone shrugged easily. "Do you honestly think—no matter the profit—that any Russian would sell Hitler's corpse to a Nazi?"

"Good point. Putin probably has the corpse in a

box he can check just to make sure he's still dead." I shivered. "I just can't believe . . ."

Bloodstone laughed. "As a skeptic, you can't believe the cloak had any power, despite the statistical improbability of the gun's explosion. I, however, have no doubt about the cloak's authenticity."

I smiled quickly. "But if it truly *is* Jesus' cloak, why wasn't Bernhard healed when he touched it?"

"Luke, chapter eight, verses forty-three through forty-eight. The only person healed by touching the cloak was a woman who had been hemorrhaging for a dozen years." Bloodstone opened his hands. "All other healings were a matter of faith. Bernhard believed in the magic, not in the Christ."

"Is what you've said, true?" Dani stood in the office doorway. "Sorry, I couldn't sleep."

Bloodstone nodded toward the box on his desk. "I believe it to be true."

"Then how did my grandfather get it? Did he steal it from Italy during the war?"

"No. It has been with your family for far longer than that." Bloodstone smiled slowly. "In his history of the Knights Templar, Stephen Howarth suggests the mysterious 'Templar Treasure' was the Shroud of Turin. We know, from radiocarbon dating, this cannot be true. Your grandfather's cloak, however, may well have been that treasure. The Templars were wiped out without ever surrendering their treasure. Jacques DeMolay, the last Grandmaster, had an aide named Jules de Grange, who was never caught."

Dani hugged her arms around herself. "De Grange became Granger at Ellis Island."

I tried to lighten things up. "Sounds like you have the sequel to *The Da Vinci Code* all ready to go."

He waved that notion away. "Bernhard sought to profit from the cloak, and you saw what happened to him. The teachings of Christ are not friendly to capitalism."

"Tell that to televangelists." I glanced Dani. "What will you do with the cloak?"

"I don't know." Her face took on a determined expression. "Doctor Bloodstone, do you think my grandfather knew what it was and entrusted it to me after his death?"

"I see no evidence to the contrary."

Dani crossed to the desk and opened the box. She rubbed her hand over the cloak and smiled. Her head came up and her spine straightened. "What am I supposed to do with it?"

Bloodstone shook his head. "I am quite certain that is not for me to know. I am equally certain, however, that if you did not have the answer within you, the cloak would never have found you."

"You really believe that?"

"I have great faith in it, Miss Granger."

She touched the cloak again, then closed the box and snapped the latch shut. "So do I. I don't know what I will do, but I'll do something."

"Of course." Bloodstone bowed his head to her. "And you will make your grandfather proud."

ANCESTRAL ARMOR

John Helfers

Wreathed in the golden rays of the rising sun, the samurai stood motionless, one hand at his side, the other resting on the hilt of his *katana.* He was dressed in a magnificent suit of armor, with a *do maru,* or breastplate; *kuzakuri,* armored skirt; *haidate,* thigh guards, and *sode,* large square arm guards, all made of gleaming dark green lamellar: thousands of overlapping tiny scales lacquered into small plates and bound together with leather cords. All of the pieces had been decorated with hundreds of small, stylized pine trees, each one centered in a mountain peak so that they formed a pattern of larger scales on the armor. His arms were encased in dark blue *kote,* padded sleeves with metal plates attached at the end to protect his hands. His *suneate,* or shin guards, were made of dark blue lamellar, as was his *nodowa,* or throat protector. His *kabuto,* or helmet, was also colored in the same motif, with a dark green *shikoro,* or flared neck guard attached under the deep blue helm. Unlike other samurai, this warrior did not have a large crest on his *kabuto* but instead had a simple round medallion featuring the black pine tree affixed to the front brim. His unblinking, dark brown eyes were visible above a dark green *menpo,* a carved mask that covered the lower half of his face.

Four armed and ready men surrounded him, two holding swords and two wielding spears. They were clad in various pieces of mismatched armor, with plain helmets and iron breastplates. Each of the quartet was completely focused on the samurai in their midst.

A few steps away, Kitsune did his best to remain absolutely still, not wanting to disturb the scene that was ready to burst into furious motion at any second. Beside him, Ashiga Asano, his mentor in the arts of sorcery and court physician to the Emperor of Japan, regarded the men with his usual calm gaze, his arms folded inside his simple silk kimono, leaving the empty sleeves to flutter in the spring breeze. Next to him stood a broad, imposing man with his hair drawn back in the traditional topknot. He was dressed in a neat kimono with a large pine tree and mountain sigil embroidered on the back, and he carried the *katana* and *wakizashi* of the samurai sheathed on his *uwa-obi,* or belt.

Asano looked sidelong at Kitsune, a whisper leaking out of the corner of his mouth. "Would you care to predict what is about to happen?"

Kitsune stared at the five poised men, sensing their *ki,* or inner energy, rolling off in waves, battling across the field in a kind of psychic duel, each one waiting for their opponent's concentration to flag for even an instant—for that would be the time to strike. "I suspect that the next several moments will not go to according to the four men's wishes."

Asano nodded. "They have already lost—"

As the words left his lips, the five men exploded into furious action. The pair in front of the samurai attacked as one, the spear-wielder thrusting his weapon at his opponent's head while the swordsman raised his blade and lunged, ready to cleave the man from shoulder to waist. The two men in the rear were also on the move, charging the samurai's unprotected back.

The armored warrior stepped forward to meet the charge of his enemy, ducking underneath the spear's point while executing a flawless *iaijutsu* draw and slicing across the swordsman's abdomen. Before the man fell to the ground, the samurai whirled in a half-turn and brought his blade around in a deadly arc, opening the spearman's side even while he tried to bring the butt of his weapon up in defense. The spear fell harmlessly aside as the second enemy went down, his chest slashed open.

The samurai completed his turn to face the remaining two men as they closed. The swordsman came in first, with the spearman following. The armored warrior continued his circular attack, bringing the sword up in a diagonal slice across the man's chest as his opponent tried to swing his weapon down at the same time. The samurai struck first, and the warrior fell, the third victim of the single sword stroke.

The final soldier charged with his spear, but the samurai, his *katana* still raised, used the blade to parry the point and shove it to one side. As the spearman ran past, the armored warrior grabbed the wooden shaft with his free hand and jerked the fighter even farther forward. The man staggered, trying to keep his balance as the samurai executed another half-turn and slashed him across the back, sending him sprawling to the ground.

"—they just had not realized it yet." Asano finished.

The entire fight had taken less than three seconds.

The samurai sheathed his *katana* in one fluid motion as the four men rose, all bowing to each other. The victorious warrior untied his *mempo* and helmet and removed both, revealing the unlined face of a young man barely out of his teens under black hair shaved at the sides and back and bound in a topknot. Tucking the helmet under his arm, he strode toward the small group that had been watching and bowed to each of them in turn, including Kitsune. As he came up, he rocked back on his heels, his right hand never straying far from the hilt of his sword. Despite the casualness of the group, his eyes flicked from each of them, his body tense, as if expecting another attack at any moment.

"Your skill is impressive indeed, Nishina-san. Your province is certainly in the hands of a capable warrior." Asano studied the young warrior's helmet. "I see that your family's crest signifies longevity."

"Not only my family's crest, this was my grandfather's and my father's suit of battle armor, may their spirits rest in peace." The man noticed Kitsune's eyes on his katana. "My grandfather's and father's—and now my—blade, of course."

Kitsune knew what was expected. "A magnificent weapon, and superbly wielded this fine spring morning."

Nishina bowed. "Perhaps later I could arrange a closer examination of the entire *daisho,* if you wish."

Asano nodded. "It would be an honor for us to have a closer look at the famed Nishina blades."

The young man's eyes lit up at Asano's words, but his reply was interrupted.

"Morning practice is over, Nishina-san. Perhaps you should change before we break our fast." This came from the stocky man that had also observed the fight, the Nishina clan's sensei.

For a moment, the young man looked as if he was about to protest, but he nodded instead. "*Hai,* Inoue-san. I should review the terrain and mountain passes to the south again anyway." The young man bowed to the group again, then turned on his heel and stalked across the practice field toward the white multistory pagoda castle that loomed over everyone.

The sensei exhaled, and Kitsune noticed the older man's lips tighten and his shoulders slump ever so slightly as he watched the other man leave. Silence reigned among the three of them for a moment, and he breathed in the blossoming spring morning, en-

joying the scent of the immaculate lines of cherry trees
on the grounds.

"It is good to see you again, Ashiga-san." The
sensei did not look at Asano, but kept his eyes fixed
on the distant samurai as he climbed the steps to
the castle.

"It has been a while, hasn't it, Inoue-san?" Asano's
mouth quirked in a brief smile. "The last time we
spoke was at court."

"Your memory serves you well indeed. Afterward
I traveled north, until I found my current employment.
Nagai was very good to me, and his son, Satomi . . .
has been most kind as well." Inoue's pause was so
small it would have gone unnoticed in casual conversation. "I see that there have been changes in your life
as well." He nodded toward Kitsune.

"Of late I have felt the need to pass on some of
my wisdom to the next generation. However, given
my pupil's rapt admiration of your student, perhaps
he now feels that he has chosen a profession that does
not suit him." Asano turned his slitted gaze on his
protégé. "What are your thoughts on the matter, Kitsune? I'm sure Inoue-san could provide excellent in-
struction in the martial arts, even for one as old as
you, and then you would no longer have to traipse
behind an old man across the length and breadth of
our revered Emperor's majestic kingdom, never knowing what might await us around the next bend in the
road."

Kitsune kept his face impassive as Asano spoke,
quite familiar with his own *sensei*'s often-brusque
style. "There are those whom are fated to learn the
ways of bushido, as Inoue-san and Nashida-san have
expertly demonstrated this morning. However, my
path lies along a different route, and I must regretfully
decline my sensei's offer, in order that I may continue
traipsing behind him wherever he may lead." As he
finished speaking, Kitsune bowed deeply, eliciting
grunts and nods of approval from both. *Besides, the*

*study of the infinite world of magic and the realms
beyond this one holds more fascination to me than ten
thousand warriors,* he thought.

"Well put, young one, well put indeed." Inoue
chuckled. "Some things about you still haven't
changed, Asano-san. Come, let us stroll through the
gardens on our way back. After all, they are the highlight of the estate, and most relaxing, particularly in
the first bloom of spring."

The Nishina *sensei* led the way, with Asano falling
in beside him, and Kitsune following a few steps behind. He felt a presence several yards away and knew
that Asano's ever-present bodyguard—a tall, taciturn
bushi known only as Maseda—was nearby. The fact
that they had not seen him during the combat demonstration didn't mean that he hadn't been present, for
the man—at least, Kitsune assumed he was a man—
had uncommon powers of stealth and concealment.
More than once Kitsune had suspected him of being
a ninja, or thought that Asano had perhaps struck a
bargain with some kind of demon and bound it into
human form to serve and protect him. Whatever his
background, Maseda was loyal, efficient, and utterly
ruthless when dispatched against anyone that might
cause harm to Asano—or Kitsune. *He could probably
defeat the young Nishina leader without breaking a
sweat.* Kitsune had seen the tall man's katana in action, and the silent warrior's speed made the young
man seem positively glacial by comparison.

Asano's voice brought him back to the present. "It
would appear that Nishina-san is taking his duties as
leader quite seriously."

"Yes, perhaps a bit too seriously." The humor
slipped from Inoue's face. "That is why I had invited
you here as soon as the mountain trails were clear."

Still careful to keep a respectful distance from the
two men, Kitsune kept an ear on the conversation,
intrigued by Inoue's dispensing with the common
small talk so quickly. Asano said nothing, but merely

nodded thoughtfully while waiting for his old friend to continue. The three strolled though the large, gorgeous garden, with more white-studded cherry tree branches waving gently in the breeze all around them. Paths lined with crushed white stone led in several directions, around and to wooden bridges over calm ponds containing large koi fish gliding through the clear water. The land around them was a pleasant riot of fragrances, from graceful snow willow trees studding the garden here and there to the clusters of pink azaleas, violet hydrangea, white daphne, purple wisteria, and red and white lotus flowers planted in artful configurations. It was the exact opposite of the mountains in winter, and Kitsune felt a flash of dizziness for a moment, overcome as he was by the beauty of it all.

"Kitsune!" Asano's voice snapped him back to reality. "You are to be attending to your duties, not wandering along dumbfounded with your mouth hanging open at the wonders of this beautiful garden we are most fortunate to be touring."

With a quick bow, Kitsune quickened his pace and fell in behind the two men again.

Inoue continued as if nothing had happened. "Please understand that I have nothing but the utmost respect for Satomi. Indeed, over these past few years he has been my finest student. However, recently I have noticed a subtle yet definite change come over him."

"Indeed? From what I could see, he seemed a sober, serious young man."

"You speak the truth, but although he has always excelled in his martial skills, he also made sure to devote the time to hone a samurai's other talents. Over the past few months, his thoughts have turned darker, and he often speaks of battle, even proposing to start a war with the Yamazaki family to the south, which we have been at peace with for many years. He has neglected the spiritual side—poetry, the tea ceremony, origami—all these have been abandoned in favor of preparing for combat. The most unusual thing is that he has taken to wearing his armor more often, even during the day when there is no need for it. He has even hung it in his room so that he can don it quickly if necessary, as if he expects a surprise assault in the night."

"That would explain his comment about reviewing the land to the south of your border."

"Correct."

"And with the Shogun on his way to tour the northern lands, the last thing you desire would be to have him discover one of his loyal subjects tryign to provoke a provincial war." Asano brought his hands out from inside his pale blue kimono and folded them together.

Inoue frowned. "No one wants a war breaking out. The Shogun would order forces from all the surrounding provinces to march against Nishina's family. They would be utterly destroyed."

"Is there any reason that you know of why Nishina-san would wish to attack his southern neighbor?"

I believe that Satomi feels that there has been some kind of slight to his honor that he is using as a pretext. He has never said anything about it, but what other reason could there be?"

"And yet he does not make his grievance public, either by letter or in person at court, or demand restitution or compensation instead?" Asano asked. At the other man's shake of his head, he continued. "I am not sure what anyone save our honored Shogun, or perhaps our most noble Emperor himself, could do in a case such as this. A man who wishes to wage war will often seize on any reason, real or imagined, to do so."

"That may be true, but Satomi is not normally like this. I can only guess that something is affecting his mind, making him see enemies where there are none."

Inoue turned to look directly at Asano. "I hope that there is something that can be done in regard to this matter before it is too late."

"We shall see, Inoue-san." Asano had stopped on a wooden walkway that zigged and zagged at right angles over a large, koi-filled pond. "I would like to think about what you have told me in this place of tranquility. Kitsune and I will soon join you at the morning meal."

Inoue bowed deep. "*Hai,* as you wish, Asano-san. I look forward to it. Please let any servant on the grounds know if there is anything you desire."

"Your hospitality is most kind." Asano bowed back, and turned to look at the pond as Inoue left.

Kitsune approached his mentor's side, studying the pond and the ripples of water that the *koi* caused when they rose to the surface. He said nothing, but simply waited for Asano.

"What do you make of Inoue-san's statements?"

"He shows great concern for his daimyo."

"Do you feel that his words are sincere?"

Kitsune frowned. "He certainly looked and sounded genuinely worried about Nashima-san."

"Yes, he did. Even though I have known Inoue-san for many years, in speaking with him, as with anyone else, I always examine the conversation at hand for anything that may have changed, for things that should be there but are not, or new things that should not exist in the first place. Even an old friend's loyalties can change over time."

"But Asano, he asked you to come here. Surely inviting his trusted friend to help his daimyo proves his good intentions?"

"It might, or possibly he plans on enlisting my support in removing Nishina-san from his position, perhaps to install himself in the youth's place." Asano chuckled when he saw Kitsune's expression. "Do not be alarmed, my pupil, I do not believe that is what is happening here. However, that doesn't mean that people do not often hide their true intentions behind false faces."

"What do you intend to do?"

"Our challenge is to find out whether Nishina is behind these designs of war, or if someone else is manipulating events. For now, you and I will simply observe young Nishina-san for the rest of the day. Simply mark anything he might say or do that could prove of interest, and we will compare our findings this evening. Now come—the first thing we will need is full bellies if we are to get to the heart of this matter."

Although Kitsune thought Asano's plan seemed sound, he found that executing it was another matter. Although the staff of the Nishimas' hilltop fortress were polite and accommodating, the master of the province was maddeningly elusive, sequestering himself in meetings with senior members of his staff and, more ominously, officers in his standing army.

By late afternoon, Kitsune had grown frustrated with his lack of progress. Usually his perceived lesser stature as a child, combined with his unusual position as Asano's right-hand man, enabled him to glean information from the household staff wherever Asano and he found themselves. However, this time he had been met with blank looks and humble bows, accompanied by no useful information.

Where the hawk soars, it is difficult for the fox to follow, Kitsune mused as he walked among the flowered garden paths again, trying to figure out a new course of action. He considered meeting with Asano, but he dismissed the idea as there was nothing new to share. His thoughts were interrupted by an approaching shadow, and Kitsune looked up to see a servant girl bow low in front of him, her gaze respectfully on the ground.

"My pardon, Kitsune-san, but our daimyo requests

your presence in the main hall. The Nishina blades have been prepared for viewing."

At last, Kitsune thought as he bowed to her. "I am looking forward to it." He followed her out of the garden, up the broad sloped pathways, and through several heavily fortified gates and baileys that were designed to slow and entrap an invading force. More than once Kitsune passed small groups of guards hurrying somewhere or preparing horses and what looked like weapons and provisions. *Is Nishina-san planning on attacking sooner than Asano thought?* Kitsune wondered.

They reached the entrance to the main hall, where Kitsune slipped off his wooden sandals and put on soft slippers.

The large main hall was cool and shadowed, with the rice paper partitions drawn to enclose the room, even though it was still a beautiful day outside. As Kitsune stepped inside, his eyes took a moment to adjust to the dimness of the open space, and he thought he was alone for a moment. Then he spotted a sitting figure on a low dais at the other end of the hall, with an ornate, lacquered wooden rack holding three sheathed blades of varying lengths next to him.

"Welcome, Kitsune-san. Please, come, sit."

"You honor me, Nishina-san." Keeping his steps formal and precise, as his father had taught him years ago, Kitsune walked across the great hall until he was only a few feet away from the lord of Nishina Castle. He knelt and bowed low, touching his forehead to the floor, then raised himself up to sit cross-legged. Nishina bowed as well, lower than he was obligated to, an action that Kitsune found made the young daimyo seem more human. Unfortunately, that action was offset by the same dark green *do maru* and *kozakuri* armor he still wore over his kimono. He had removed his arm and leg guards, but Kitsune noticed that his *kabuto* was at his side, within easy reach. Even though

the samurai appeared relaxed, Kitsune felt the tense-
ness coiled inside the young man, ready to be un-
leashed at the slightest opportunity.

Steadying his breathing, Kitsune relaxed enough to
slip into a semi-meditative state, so that he could see
the psychic aura that surrounded every living thing—
including Nishina-san. The young lord's aura reflected
his turmoil, with tendrils of crimson and black swirling
around him and occasionally drifting off to dissipate
into the surrounding air. *He also shows an inner core
of light blue and white—purity and strength of purpose.
Whatever he's planning, he believes that he's doing the
right thing,* Kitsune realized. *Yet—something's not
right here.* The aura wasn't as crisp and defined as
usual; instead, it was as if the apprentice viewed the
man through a curtain of flowing water that blurred
the individual shades together into a smeared palette
of dark and light colors.

*There is a spirit at work here! But I will need
Asano's help to discern any more.* With a start, Kitsune
realized that Nishina-san was talking.

"—enjoyed the castle grounds?"

Kitsune wrenched himself out of the slight trance
with more force than necessary, turning the movement
into a graceful bow. "After seeing the cold, stark
beauty of winter for so long, the delicate flowering of
your magnificent gardens warms my heart."

Nishina-san bowed again. "We are privileged to
have Ashiga-san and yourself as our honored guests.
Your master has sent word that he would be along
shortly, and that we are to await his arrival."

"No doubt it will only be a small delay." Kitsune
knew otherwise; if Asano was delayed, there was a
good reason for it. *Of course!* Asano was delaying so
that Kitsune could find out something—anything—in
the time he was alone with Nishima-san. *Very well.
Now, how to begin?* "Your martial display this morning was most impressive. I don't believe that I've ever
seen a *katana* as exquisite as yours."

Nishina peered past Kitsune at the closed doors behind him, then leaned forward. "Thank you. To have Ashiga-san and yourself as an audience inspired me to make sure my performance was flawless." He waved Kitsune closer to him. "I know we should wait for your master, but I do not suppose it will hurt anything if I give you a preview of the Nishina *daisho* now."

"You are most kind." Kitsune bent his head to the floor again, then scooted gracefully over to the edge of the dais, right next to Nishina.

Draping a piece of silk over his hands, Nishina removed the middle blade, the shorter *wakizashi*, from the rack and offered it to Kitsune, who accepted the weapon, being sure to hold it only by the silk cloth.

"This is something you might find interesting." Nishima drew the blade out a few inches, revealing the gleaming steel, even in the dim light. "See the *hamon?*"

Kitsune examined the temper line of the blade, created by coating the back half of the single-edged weapon in heat-resistant clay and heating the edge until it became even harder, leaving a line that marked the border between the softer, more resilient steel, and the sharper cutting edge. This *hamon* was dark gray near the blade edge and faded into an almost black near the *mune,* or back of the *katana.*

"It is rumored, although it has never been proved, that this matched set is the only surviving *daisho* forged by Senzo Muramasa, student to the great Masamune himself."

As Nishina talked, a chill stole over Kitsune. While they traveled, Asano had often regaled his eager apprentice with tales of great leaders, warriors, monks, and others that lived in Nippon during centuries past, and he immediately recognized the name Nishima had uttered. A swordsmith of great renown during the fourteenth century, he had also possessed an unstable mind, and it was rumored that the blades he had created often took on the darker aspects of his personality, driving their wielders to unnecessary violence and even murder.

If the spirit in the sword is urging Nishima-san to begin this war, surely that would allow the blades to revel in as much blood as they could possibly want, he thought. Outwardly, he betrayed no physical reaction to Nishina's words as he replied, "Fascinating. I was under the impression that all of Senzo-san's blades had been struck from the official court records."

A guarded look of cunning appeared on Nishima's face. "True, but stricken from the records does not mean the swords were destroyed. But do not fear—as I said, it is only a rumor. The written provenance of these blades states that they were forged by a minor smith, one Rokugo Kagenori." The satisfied expression on Nishima's face, however, told Kitsume which version of the swords' history the young *daimyo* believed.

Which fits everything that has happened recently, Kitsune thought. Before he could attempt to elicit more information from his host, the main doors slid open, and Asano hobbled into the room, leaning on his carved wooden staff as he approached. As soon as the doors had moved, Nishima replaced the short sword on the rack and moved to the center of the dais, winking at Kitsune as he settled into the formal cross-legged position.

Asano bowed, straightening up with what appeared to be a visible effort. "Please excuse my tardiness, I came as quickly as I could once I had received your summons, but these old bones do not move as they once did, and I must admit that the beauty of your gardens was a distraction to my senses that delayed me even more."

"Your words honor my gardeners, all of whom labor mightily to bring forth nature's beauty around our castle."

"I hope I have not caused too much impatience. My apprentice is no doubt eager to see the famed Nishina blades, one of the last remaining complete *daisho* crafted during the end of the Masamune era."

Yes, there is much you need to learn about the Nishina blades, Kitsune thought as Asano took entirely too long to fold himself into the lotus position, his joints creaking and popping as he lowered himself to the ground. Kitsune tried to direct his attention to the swords, but Asano kept muttering and settling himself until both Kitsune and Nishina were hard-pressed to contain their annoyance.

"If Ashiga-san is ready at last?"

Asano paused for a bare second, and Kitsune realized that his mentor was delaying getting comfortable for a reason; apparently, he wanted to unnerve the samurai. His next words proved the boy's suspicions correct.

"I had a most interesting conversation with Inoue-san this morning, regarding the Yamazaki province to the south."

Nishina's features darkened, and his right hand reached over toward the sword rack before he brought it back to his side hard enough to slap the cloth of his *hakima*. "Inoue-san should keep to his training and not talk of things that he does not have full knowledge of."

Asano continued as if the younger man hadn't spoken. "Inoue-san seemed to think that you are about to move against Yamazaki family, which has been at peace with the Nishinas for the past century, and which would be in direct violation of our honored Shogun's edicts against aggression—"

"Enough!" Nishima's voice was loud enough to echo even in the paper-walled room. "How dare you, who come to my home as honored guests, presume to comment on the plans of my family, of which you know nothing!" He reached for the gleaming scabbard of his katana and pulled the weapon to his chest. "I, Nishima Satomi, demand that you leave this place immediately!"

Asano lifted his head, and his black eyes seemed alight with controlled fury in the dark room. "I would be most pleased to acquiesce to that order, if in fact it was given by the heir of Nishima. But—" His penetrating gaze seemed to burn straight through the furiously quivering samurai on the dais. "—that is not the case here, is it, Nishima Takahashi?"

Kitsune, his eyes riveted on Nishima even as he was about to call for Maseda, turned to stare at Asano with an expression of surprise that mirrored the young samurai's, who froze in the act of grabbing the hilt of his *katana*.

"Nishima Takahashi? Asano, the swords are—"

"—of no consequence here." Using his walking stick, Asano rose to stand in front of the Nishima *daimyo*. "I have spent the better part of today meditating on a possible cause of Nishima Satomi's sudden change of heart, and once I investigated your family's history, the truth became apparent."

The young lord angrily shook his head. "What 'truth' are you babbling about? The Yamazaki family has—"

"Been at peace with you since shortly after the time of the Sekigahara massacre. In fact, it was that very mention of the Yamazaki family that set me on the path to unraveling this mystery and Takahashi's role in it."

"My grandfather has been dead for more than a decade! He would not stand for your casual slandering of his name, and neither will I!" Lightning-fast, Satomi drew his *katana* and lunged at the unmoving Asano, sword raised to cleave him in two.

Kitsune had just opened his mouth to yell for help when a black blur leaped out of the shadows, a *katana* raised to parry Satomi's attack. The two swords clashed as their wielders slammed together in a tangle of arms, legs, and steel. Satomi and the other warrior sprang apart, each facing the other with their respective weapons poised to strike.

"Maseda-san, punctual as always." Asano inclined his head at the tall *bushi*, just as the main doors burst open and Inoue, armed with a *yori*, or long spear, and flanked by a half-dozen armed guards, rushed into the room.

"What is going on here? We heard shouting, and then the clash of swords. My lord, have these men attacked you?"

"They have insulted my family's honor with baseless claims!" Nishima pointed at Asano, Kitsune, and Maseda. "They have come into my home under the guise of friendship only to spread lies about my ancestors! They are to be placed under guard until I decide what shall be done with them!"

The guards spread out in a loose semicircle around the three, with Inoue still in the middle of his men. Maseda glanced at Asano, who made a small motion with his hand that caused the warrior to drop his guard and sheathe his sword.

Asano bowed low to Nishima. "Honored host, if I have said anything that is not true, then I humbly submit the three of us to any punishment that you see fit to mete out. However, as the royal physician to the court of our most noble Emperor, I also request the chance to prove that I have only spoken truth here."

Upon seeing Maseda relax, Satomi straightened as well, lowering his *katana* but not sheathing it. "It is only due to the knowledge of your renown throughout the kingdom that I will consent in this instance. Fail to prove the truth of your words, however, and the punishment for all of you will be swift, merciless, and final."

Kitsune gulped, but Asano ignored his unease as he walked over to the boy. "Did you use the spirit-sight on him?"

Kitsune nodded.

"As did I, when I saw him this morning. I did not wish to alarm Inoue or anyone else until I knew exactly what was transpiring here." As he spoke, Asano

brought forth a small paper box from inside his robes.
"This should enable us to bring forth the spirit that is
influencing Nishina-san." He handed Kitsune a small,
heavy egg with a tiny stopper at one end. "When I
tell you, throw this on the ground in front of the spirit
as hard as you can."

Kitsune nodded and stepped back, the strange missile heavy in his hand.

Asano turned to Nishina, who stood tensed in front
of him. "Honored Nishina-san, if I may ask for your
assistance as I reveal what has been happening here."
He held up the paper box." I know that your training
by Inoue-san is excellent, of course. If you would indulge me by slicing open this box when I toss it up in
the air?"

A frown on his face, Satomi nodded, his fingers tight
on the hilt of his *katana*.

"And . . . now!" Asano launched the box into the
air, the small container arcing over Nishina's head.
The samurai's blade flashed, and the box separated
into not two but four pieces that fluttered to the
ground, along with a fine spray of twinkling crimson
powder that enveloped the agile warrior.

"What—sorcery—is—this?" Nishima stared at the
cloud around him, his sword ready, but with no true
target to strike at. The dust did not affect him in the
least, but seemed to be drawn to his breastplate, coating it in a layer of sparkling red particles.

Asano mumbled something under his breath, then
raised his voice as he lifted his hand in a "come forward" motion at Nishima. "See now what has been
behind your quest to wage war on your allies to the
south."

As everyone in the room watched, the red powder
on the armor shifted and bulged, forming into a large
face with blazing green eyes, a proud, hooked nose,
and hair bound in a topknot on the breastplate,
snarling in silent rage. As the dumbfounded Nishima
watched, the face emerged from the armor, followed

by a neck, shoulders, long, spindly arms, and a torso that trailed off into a stream of vapor. The spirit flew from the armor to the ceiling, circling the room once, then streaked for a far wall.

"Now, Kitsune!"

Kitsune hurled the egg at the floor in front of the wall, the grenade bursting apart in a shower of hard rice grains. The spirit immediately stopped its flight and sank to the floor, peering intently at the grains of rice while pointing to each one with a spectral finger, its lips moving silently.

Asano bowed to Kitsune. "My apprentice was on the right path, but he was focused on the wrong instrument of Takahashi's—or should I say, his spirit's—plan for revenge from the afterlife." He turned to bow to Nishima. "Your grandfather was very active in the civil war leading up to the true joining of our great land that began in 1600. However, he harbored a deep hatred of the Yamazaki, even after the peace accord was drawn up. Apparently, much like Senzo-san's famed swords, his emotions against the Yamazaki were so great that a portion of his soul was imbued in the armor itself. Your father, Nagai, had no use for the suit and, therefore, never wore it; but when you began to use it in your training, the spirit was wakened from its rest and sought to finish through you what it had not been able to do in life."

Nishima's *katana* dropped from a shaking hand, and he fell to the floor, crawling toward Asano. "I have committed the gravest insult to you, Asano-san . . . I must absolve myself—" He grabbed at the hem of the sorcerer's kimono and wept.

Asano bent over and helped the young man to his feet. "Stand, Nishina-san, and be at peace. Not only have you not insulted me, but on this night you are responsible for assisting your honored ancestor's spirit to his final rest. That spirit is Takahashi's base emotions—hatred, lust, fear, jealousy—given form, albeit a simple one. That is why the rice grains stopped it—these types of spirits crave order in all things. Without that aspect of his personality restored to Takahashi, he cannot ascend to the great wheel and take his rightful place in the heavens."

"Can you—can you help restore my grandfather's soul?" Nishina asked.

"It is a simple matter." Asano produced another small paper box, walked over to the frantically counting spirit, and poured it out. A fine brown powder wafted over the apparition, and as it settled, the ghost became more and more insubstantial, until it faded into nothingness. "I have sent this *konpaku* to the spirit realm, where it will be drawn to your grandfather's soul to join with him, and restore that which was sundered between the world of the living and the world of the dead."

Nishina bowed deeply, holding the position for several seconds. "*Domo arigato,* Ashiga-san. My family is forever in your debt, myself most of all. You have saved my clan from eternal shame and dishonor."

Asano bowed low as well, a small smile on his lips. "You honor me with your words, Nishina-san. All that I would ask is that you take the strength of your grandfather and your father and turn them toward keeping the peace in your lands and the lands of your neighbors."

Nishina fell to the floor again. "On the souls of all my ancestors, I swear it will be done."

"Then rise, Nishina-san, and assume the true role of the leader of your family." Asano looked at Kitsune. "As for us, I think a good meal is in order, and then we will speak about the preparations for the Shogun's impending visit."

Still slightly dazed from what he had just witnessed, Nishina stumbled from the room, surrounded by Inoue and the other guards. Kitsune and Asano watched him go, flanked by Maseda, who stood impassively next to them.

Kitsune bowed to Asano. "You were correct about

the false faces, even if it was a ghost of the past that had caused all this trouble."

"Indeed, my apprentice, it is not always those of flesh and blood that seek to influence the living, but the spirits often have their own designs on our humble world as well." Asano leaned on his staff and headed for the door. "I expect that the rest of our stay will be a relaxing one, and I am looking forward to some peace and quiet—at least, until the Shogun arrives."

"My master is correct, as always." Kitsune bowed and followed as they left the main room—and the ghost laid to its final rest there—behind.

THE OPPOSITE OF SOLID

Linda P. Baker

"The more you live, the less you die."
Janis Joplin

Solid. That's the word that sums up my life.
Rock-solid, my momma called me. Rock-solid and steady. "You're gonna make some woman a good, steady, dependable husband," she would say, all proud and approving, as we sat in the kitchen, peeling potatoes for Sunday dinner. "Rock solid."

She thought it was a compliment. Wouldn't my momma have been shocked to hear her compliment turn into "stolid and plodding"? That's what my last girlfriend called me, as she slammed the door on her way out.

I think that's why I noticed the woman wearing a faded red hippie jacket, sitting on a park bench in the afternoon sun. It was her transparency that drew me. She was ethereal. Ethereal and luminous, with coppery, Irish-red hair and light like sun sparkling on snow around her head. It almost seemed I could see the wood slats of the bench through her shoulders. That's why she drew me . . . she looked so much the opposite of solid.

I wouldn't have normally had the nerve to ask a strange, beautiful woman if I could sit with her, but today, enjoying the early spring sunshine of Golden Gate Park, watching the flitting of butterflies and hearing the buzzing of bees, I felt particularly daring. I mumbled my request and remained standing, just on the off chance that she would refuse.

She looked up at me with eyes that for a moment seemed clear as water, then darkened to a good, solid blue. "You see me!" Her voice was like orchids, throaty and fragile, as if she didn't talk much.

"Yeah, sure I do." I answered immediately before I could think what an odd question it was. I sat down beside her as close as I dared and put my newspaper and my lunch salad and my bottle of fancy spring water between us.

Up close, she was less fragile, more visible, and the fairy light that danced around her head settled down and proved to be the noon sun reflecting off the bay. She smelled like gardenias with a touch of carnation, almost a taste rather than a scent. Almost funereal, but . . . pleasant.

Flower power. This woman had it, from her long red hair to her deliberately scuffed bell-bottom jeans to the tips of her sandaled feet.

"Don't people normally see you?"

"Not normally," she confessed. "They just sort of . . . look past."

I thought of how her shoulders had seemed to disappear into the back of the bench. But she was plainly solid up close. Thin as a model and pale, but substantial. She was wearing a jacket a bit too big for her that must have once been a deep, ruby red but was now faded to a streaked pink. It had gold embroidery around the cuffs and running up the front, a kind of flowery fleur de lis design that had frayed and cracked with age. It looked weirdly familiar, as if it were something I'd seen before.

I picked up my salad and fought with the supposed easy-open corner. "I don't see how anyone could look past you. Not with that hair."

She fingered a long copper curl as if she'd forgotten she was wearing a halo of fire around her head.

"It's beautiful," I offered, "especially with the sun shining on it."

She looked at me as if she was as startled at being paid a compliment as I was at giving one. She blushed, a pale pink that touched only her high cheekbones and just above her eyebrows. "Thank you. No one's said something like that to me in a long time."

I was smitten. In addition to a funky retro jacket and hair like new pennies, she had the smile of a siren, bright as sunflowers.

"I'm Charles." I held out my hand.

She touched her small hand to mine. Her skin felt strange, cool and there, yet . . . so not there. Like the brush of dandelion fluff. "Arizona."

I could help but laugh. "Arizona? That's your name?"

The smile faltered. Her hand slipped away, leaving a ghostly impression of coolness where her fingertips brushed.

I rushed to patch my faux pas. "With hair like that, I thought you'd be Caitlin or Maureen or . . . " I searched my mind for another obviously Irish name and couldn't think of a single one.

She relaxed, her smile returning. "It's from a song."

And immediately, the lyrics popped into my head. "Arizona, rainbow shades and hobo shoes. Paul Revere and the Raiders."

She smiled even wider, surprised and delighted that I got the reference. "My mom and dad were sort of hippies."

"I wanted to be a hippie. More than I ever wanted anything in my life. I even bought a map of San Francisco and a moth-eaten old duffel bag and kept it packed and hidden in the back of my closet." I

couldn't believe I'd just told her that. I'd never told
anyone about the stuff I'd dreamed when I was a teen-
ager. It all just seemed so silly and flighty. The exact
opposite of the rock-solid person my parents expected
me to become. And I guess there was a bit of disappointment in there, too, that I'd never shinnied down
the pear tree that grew right outside my window and
lit out for California.

I'd missed the summer of love and Woodstock and
Monterey Pops. The closest we'd come to anything
hippie in East Texas was Jimmy Johnston, who wore
his kinky blonde hair in a 'fro and went around saying
"Groovy, dude," to everyone, until he slipped and said
it to our English teacher in class one day and got sent
to the Principal's office. The Haight-Ashbury district
that had seemed so exotic and exciting was now just
The Haight, home to Gap and Starbucks. I hadn't
moved to San Francisco until I was forty-something,
and only then because I was promoted into it.

Arizona and her shining hair and the strangely familiar, flowery, faded embroidery on her sleeves
brought back the bittersweet smells and sounds of
those summer nights. Lying in my bed, listening to
Hendrix and Janis Joplin and Joe Cocker and Jeffer-
son Airplane, with the radio turned low so my parents
wouldn't hear. Smelling the warm, growing earth and
the green pears. Dreaming of hopping a freighter
headed west.

"What was in your duffel bag?"

I still remembered that, too. "A pair of bell-
bottomed jeans that I bought off a guy named Jimmy
Johnston. And a poster for a Janis Joplin concert. And
clean socks."

She laughed, a rougher sound than I'd have expected from such a delicate woman.

I looked down at my sensible leather dress shoes
and smiled. I would have been the only flower child
in Haight-Ashbury wearing clean, white cotton socks.
I guess solid and rebellious are strange bedfellows.

"Why did you want to be a hippie?"

I opened my mouth to be glib but, again, wound up telling the truth. "I didn't want to be sensible and steady. I thought being a hippie sounded like a magical way to live. Free and alive, the way Janis Joplin was. Unfettered, spontaneous. Music, drugs, free love."

She frowned, as if I'd said something goofy again.

"I know it probably wasn't like that. I mean, living moment to moment may sound glamorous, but not knowing where your next meal is coming from isn't all that . . . groovy."

We both grinned at my use of the word.

"I guess the fact that I thought I'd need clean socks tells you I wasn't cut out for it."

"I think you can be glamorous and free and still have clean socks," she said, and for a moment, I saw that sparkling light again and caught a glimpse of a Monterey Pine, needles shifting gently in the breeze through her forehead, as if her brain was clear.

I rubbed my eyes. Seeing things like that sounded like all the stories I'd read about LSD trips. When I looked up, her forehead was just a forehead again, solid and wrinkled by fine concentration lines.

"Why didn't you do it?" she asked. "Why didn't you run away and become a hippie?"

"I don't—I'm not sure exactly." I didn't like the sound of the words coming out. "I guess . . . I guess the right time just never came. And then it was too late."

"I was there once," she said. "For a while. It was cool, just like the books say."

"There where?" A bean sprout fell off my fork onto my thigh. I brushed it away. Why did I feel like our conversation lulled her into saying something she didn't mean to? Why did I, for just second, think she meant she'd been to Haight-Ashbury, in the Summer of Love?

Then she looked at me, straight into me. As though

she could see through me. "San Francisco, back then. I was there for a while."

"Huh?"

"I don't know about taking you there, but . . . I think I can take you somewhere you've never been before. If you want to go with me on my next trip."

Because I was still in that whole Woodstock, summer of love frame of mind, I immediately thought she meant a *trip*. A drug trip. But . . . would I do it? I sat there, staring at her. Kind of stupidly, I imagine. Like a big, dumb rock with a heart beating triple time. Would I do it? Wasn't that the kind of recklessness I'd always wanted? Hadn't I always intended to try tripping, just once? But I wasn't that fourteen-year-old dreamer anymore.

What if she was a cop? What if this was a set-up? My appetite shriveled, and I put the salad down on the ground. "Is this a joke?" I looked around, trying to do it casually. I couldn't see anybody who appeared to be watching us, but that was the point of surveillance, wasn't it?

"No, it's not a joke." She held out her hand.

I glanced over my shoulder, then at a guy who was sitting nearby on the ground, leaning back against a tree.

I looked back at her. She hadn't moved. She was just sitting there, her small hand extended, palm up. But she was doing that shimmering thing. One minute so transparent that she almost wasn't visible, the next as solid as . . . well, not as solid as me. Few people were as *solid* as me.

It must be something about the area, about the way the bench was positioned against the sun and the water. There was something about her. Something about the way she was barely there, but so much more there than anyone else I'd ever met, that drew me like a magnet. I took her hand. And the world shifted.

It felt like—it felt like sparkling. Like sparkling should feel, if you could feel it. It felt as though I'd

become one of those sparklers that all the kids played
with on holidays. As if I were giving off sparks, show-
ers of them, but they didn't burn. I didn't burn. I gave
off sparks of multicolored light, but I didn't diminish.
I was still solid and stable.

Then slowly the fiery pricks of light began to die
down, and I could see. The world around me was hazy
and thin, but I could see. The world was becoming
more and more solid, more and more color leaching
into the walls and the floor beneath my feet.

Floor? I was sitting in Golden Gate Park, watching
the noon sun sparkle on the bay, holding hands with
a girl named Arizona. There shouldn't be floor beneath my feet. Especially not floor with shag carpet.
Or walls with flocked gold and green wallpaper becoming more solid around me. There shouldn't be—I
looked around in a panic. Where was Arizona? But
there she was, right beside me, her thin fingers still
gripping my thick ones.

"Arizona? What's going on?"

"I don't know yet," she said, her voice calm and
even. There was none of the panic in her tone that I'd
heard in my own. "It'll come clear. It always does."

"What does?" I turned slowly, not going so far that
I had to let go of her hand. At the moment, she was
my only connection to solidity.

We were in a hotel room. It looked and smelled as
though there'd been a raucous party there. The air
was thick, almost unbreathable with the sour scent of
aged cigarette smoke and the sweet scent of whiskey.
There was an unopened bottle of booze on the
nightstand and one overturned on the floor just under
the foot of the bed. Cigarette butts and potato chips
overflowed from several ashtrays and from what
looked like a large, shell shaped soapdish on one bedside table. On the floor, beside the almost empty bottle of whiskey, was a newspaper. I leaned over and
picked it up. A Los Angeles newspaper, dated October 4, 1970.

"I don't understand. Where are we? Is this some kind of joke? Did you have this made up at that shop over on Page?" But of course, a fake newspaper wouldn't account for how I'd gotten here.

Arizona's lack of confusion and fear only made me more frantic. Up until that point, she'd seemed fluttery and ethereal, like a butterfly or a wispy cloud or some fey creature. Here, in this place that I couldn't account for, she seemed solid as stone and as dangerous as rattlesnake backed into a corner.

"How did we get here?"

"I don't know exactly. It just happens." Arizona said. "It has something to do with this." She caught the edges of her jacket and held it out from her hips.

The red jacket with its gold embroidery had seemed strangely familiar and strange from the moment I saw it. But that was some jacket if it could take me on a LSD trip without the LSD. "I don't understand."

"It'll come clear."

"Stop saying that! This doesn't make sense. Did you drug me? Have I passed out? Is this a dream?" Would I wake up in a few minutes, annoyed that the alarm clock had gone off and that yet another boring, plodding day was beginning?

"We've traveled in time."

"What?" That made even less sense, and now I was starting to get angry. I kept trying to remember if she'd touched my food. Or if I'd put my water down on the bench between us.

"I don't know how it works. I just know it happens. And we'll know what needs to be done. Once it comes clear."

For some reason, I wanted the panic of my first few minutes back. It seemed like a solid, logical response. At the same time, it didn't seem right, that a guy as big and broad as me should turn into a gibbering mess while a tiny woman stood by so coolly.

Arizona seemed to understand. She took my hands in hers, and it was only because her hands seemed so hot that I realized how cold my own were. "It'll be all right," she said. "I promise. It scared me, too, the first few times, but I got used to it."

"How many times has this happened to you?"

"I don't know. I quit counting after a while."

"How long is 'a while'?"

"I don't know. Ever since I bought this jacket at a junk auction. A long time, I think."

I circled the room. I stopped in front of the door and put my hand on the knob. The dull, tarnished gold of it was cold and solid in my palm. It gave me an idea.

I rushed over to the window and shoved the heavy curtains aside. The sliding glass door opened onto a dinky balcony that overlooked the street below. In the hotel parking lot right below was a mint Volkswagon van that I would have killed for in my youth. It had the finest psychedelic paint job I'd ever seen, even down to the giant peace sign on the front. And down the street, a yellow Corvair and a red Ford Mustang mixed in with a dozen huge, heavy period cars. So much for the theory that it was all just an elaborate joke. A newspaper could be faked, but an entire street of 1960s vehicles?

As I stepped back into the room, there was rattling and coughing behind a door that I assumed was a bathroom. A woman cursed softly under her breath. There was the sound of water running. More cursing, then the bathroom door opened.

I gasped, so loudly that the woman who strolled into the room should have heard me.

She looked exactly like Janis Joplin. The Janis Joplin I'd listened to long after my parents thought I was asleep. The Janis Joplin who epitomized everything I'd wanted in the depths of my unsolid soul when I was thirteen.

The woman walked past as though I weren't even there. I put out my hand to touch her, and it was like touching a cloud. It was like on the television when someone touched a ghost. My hand went right through her shoulder.

The Janis lookalike didn't even flinch. She just walked past and threw herself down on her stomach on the bed. The springs squeaked under her weight, then settled.

"What the hell!" There's only so much even a rock-steady guy like me can take. I crossed the room in what seemed like only two giant strides and grabbed Arizona. Her shoulder was thin, but solid. "What the hell's going on here? What kind of game is this?"

"No game."

But my mind wouldn't stop gibbering. It carried my tongue right along with it. "What's going on? I want to know right now. What is this, some kind of set-up? And where did you find that woman? She looks just like Janis Joplin." I knew about look-alikes, those people who do impersonations of celebrities. I'd seen a couple that could make you stop in your tracks, but this one . . . This one could have been Janis Joplin's twin.

"She *is* Janis Joplin," Arizona said, as matter of fact as if she'd been discussing next week's menu. "I told you. We've moved through time. You're connected to her somehow. That's why we came here, to this time. This place."

"I'm not connected to her. She died thirty years ago! Today." I picked up the paper from the floor and shook it at Arizona. "She died on this day. When I was just a kid."

Arizona nodded, but she wasn't paying me any attention. She was watching the woman on the bed.

She had rolled over on her back and pulled a large cloth purse up off the floor. Propping the bag on her stomach, she dug into it, scratching around as if whatever she was looking for was eluding her. Things began to fall out of the bag, an ink pen, a wad of papers, keys.

The next thing she found was a cigarette pack. She

ran her finger down in it, then shook it, as if there
had to be just one more cigarette in it. When it stayed
empty, she gave a sound of disgust and threw it into
the overflowing ashtray on the nightstand. Then she
sat up and pulled open the nightstand drawer and
stuck her hand in. She found another empty cigarette
pack. She cursed, eloquently and musically.

That's when I knew, really knew, that this really
was Janis Joplin. Because a lookalike might fake her
pockmarked face, or her eyes, or the frizzy hair. But
no one, *no one,* could sound like Janis. No one could
sound like that, rough and sweet, gravel on satin.

Then she pulled something else out of the
nightstand. A paper bag, brown and so new it sounded
crisp. She slowly opened the bag and upended it. What
toppled out made my breath freeze in my throat.

Janis stared at what had spilled out of the bag . . .
a syringe, a small folded packet that looked like wax
paper, a spoon, a short piece of rubber hose. Even a
stolid and plodding guy like me recognized a drug kit
when he saw one.

Janis picked up each item one by one and turned
them over in her hands. She picked up the wax paper
packet last, opened it slowly. It had fine white powder
in it. I knew what it was. So did she.

She looked like she might cry. Or laugh. Or scream.

I looked back at Arizona. She was watching us, her
gaze flitting back and forth between my back and the
packet in Janis' hands.

"Has it 'come clear' yet?" she asked. "Why we
came here?"

In a flash, I remembered why I'd never taken my
duffel bag with its carefully folded clean socks and my
guitar and hopped a train for Haight-Ashbury. It was
because of Janis Joplin.

Janis Joplin was a Texas girl whose hometown was
just like mine, uptight and boring and predictable. But
unlike me, she'd escaped. She'd lived her dream. I'd
dreamed of hopping a freighter for California and

standing right in front of the stage for one of her concerts. I'd dreamed of being carefree and unpredictable, of living for the moment.

Then Janis Joplin had died.

First Hendrix, then Janis just a couple of weeks later, of a heroin overdose.

And suddenly, I'd seen the dark underside of the carefree, hippie lifestyle. Several months later, Jim Morrison also died. But Janis' death had been the end of my dreams of Haight-Ashbury and life as a barefoot, dancing flower child.

I wheeled to Arizona. "I just remembered. This is why I didn't run away from home. Janis died, and all the light seemed to leak out of my dreams." I wasn't sure the light had ever come back.

Arizona nodded and smiled.

"Does that mean . . . ?" I stopped and squeezed my temples between my palms. It was all so weird, so very far out, that I couldn't quite wrap my mind around it. But I'd read science fiction, like every other kid with dreams of something different, something better. Some of the stories about time travel had stayed with me. "Does that mean that if I save her . . . my life will change? Does that mean that I'll be the person I always wanted to be?"

Arizona sort of shrugged and smiled and nodded, all at the same time.

I started to question that weird, ambiguous response, but I was too taken with the idea that I might not have to be stolid and plodding. That the woman behind me on the bed didn't have to die. But how would that work if I couldn't even touch her?

As I thought it, Janis jumped backward, sending the drug paraphernalia scattering across the bed. "God damn, man! Where'd you come from? How the hell did you get in here?"

She could see me! She was talking to me! For a minute, I just stood there, a big, dumb rock. Janis Joplin could see me. *Janis Joplin* was talking to me!

"I asked you what you're doing in here?" She was regaining her equilibrium, coming up on her knees on the bed, reaching for her purse.

My voice came back in a rush. My muscles decided they wanted to work. "I'm sorry, Miss Joplin, for scaring you. I just came for . . . I just came for this." I leaned over the bed and gathered up the drug stuff, dropping the syringe, dropping the hose, but making sure I tucked the little wax packet of white powder into my pocket. Then I gathered up the rest of it a second time and stuffed it back into the sack.

At any moment, I expected Janis to whack me over the head with her bag, or reach into it and pull out a gun, or start screaming her head off. But she just gaped at me, opening and closing her mouth like a guppie. When I got back to normal, if I got back to normal, maybe I would have a good laugh over making Janis Joplin tongue-tied.

"What—? How—? Who the hell are you, man? How the fuck did you get in here?"

"It's kinda hard to explain." I grinned with what I hoped was a reassuring expression. "I'm just a fan. A fan from Texas. I've been listening to your music . . . Well, all of my life, and I just—well, it's really great." I knew I was starting to babble, but, hell, who wouldn't babble, standing near enough a childhood hero to smell her toothpaste?

Arizona touched my elbow. Actually, she sort of pinched my elbow. Her fingers dug into the soft flesh right above it. I could see the sparkles starting around her head. She was losing her solid edge. Did that mean that we'd done what we were supposed to do?

But there was still one more thing I needed to say, even if it didn't help in the long run. "You've been clean for months now. You need to stay clean, to make more music for all your Texas fans."

Janis nodded, staring at my face. She was slowly losing her solidity, just as I suspected I was losing mine. The sparkles grew larger, stronger, and the burning arcs clouded my vision. The room around me faded, the flowered comforter and the wadded pillows at the head of the bed, and the petite, rumpled woman in front of them, losing their sharp edges. Janis had become even more transparent than Arizona had ever been.

Weirdly, as the room faded, it seemed to double. As though I were seeing two cloudy, see-through Janises, two fuzzy hotel rooms, slowly splitting apart, slowly, slowly becoming separate, y-ing out in two different directions. But there was only one Arizona, only one me, in only one of the rooms. The last thing I knew of the time and space we'd been in was Janis Joplin's husky, trademark voice, saying softly, "Godd-d-d damn!"

Going back, or traveling through time, or coming down from the trip, whatever it was, wasn't as easy as going out had been. Going had been like expanding, like turning into a sparkling cloud. Coming back was like being stuffed into a container that was much too small. Like being split in two, then twisted back together. The sparkly, transparent Charles was twisted and shoved and collapsed back down into solid Charles, and it hurt.

I hit the ground hard. Like falling out of the sky without a parachute. The scent of crushed and bruised grass slammed into my lungs. My eyes filled with tears. The weight and pressure of now was almost more than I could stand. The brown paper bag fell out of my numb fingers.

It was a rude way to ride back into San Francisco. I lay on the ground, gasping for breath, and watched Arizona rematerialize above me. Obviously, she had a better handle on time travel tripping than I did. It looked almost as if she floated into being, slowly becoming solid enough that I couldn't see the clouds above me.

Arizona leaned down and held out a hand, as if a flyweight like her could pull someone as solid as me up. "Are you okay?"

I was. But I wasn't, too. I felt weird and different. But . . . the problem was, I didn't feel different enough. I didn't feel like jumping up and running around Hippie Hill in my bare feet. I didn't take her offer of help. I just lay there, staring up at her and her faded red jacket, outlined in blue sky.

"I don't feel any different," I said. "If we just changed my past, why don't I feel different? Shouldn't I have different memories? Shouldn't I remember running away? Shouldn't I be—" I stopped myself before I could say it. "A better person." A *better* person. It was a revelation to realize that deep down, I'd always seen myself as a coward and a cop-out because I hadn't had the courage to make my dreams come true.

I sat up and picked at the knees of my wool-blend trousers, wiped a piece of grass off the toe of my shiny dress shoes. What if I'd changed my whole life, and it didn't make any difference? What if I was destined to be stolid and plodding and solid, no matter what? "Shouldn't I be a different person with a different job and, maybe, different clothes?"

"You are," Arizona said gently. "In that other universe."

"Other universe?"

"Didn't you see it, as we were returning? Didn't you see it branch off?"

"What the hell are you talking about?"

Arizona pulled her red jacket tight and sat down beside me on the grass. "I don't really know how it works. I just know that each time I go back, each time I change something, I see the result splinter off into another future. I've done a lot of research on it, and I think it's got to do with parallel universes. Did you know there's a theory that there are infinite universes, all running parallel to ours?"

"I don't give a crap about parallel universes! I care about this one. I thought I'd be different."

"Aren't you?" Arizona asked. "Aren't you different, just a little bit? Doesn't it make a difference that somewhere, sometime, the boy that you were took that step off the edge? Don't you feel . . . thinner?"

I stared at her. A cloud skittered across the sky, across one cheek, up and over her nose, out the side of her forehead. Thinner. Not transparent. She was thinner, so thin I could see through her!

"Oh, my god." I looked down at myself, felt my arms, my chest. I felt solid. I couldn't see the grass through my thighs. I couldn't see anything through anything. It was the first time in my life I've ever been glad to apply the word "solid" to myself.

"Every time it happens," she said softly, "a little bit of me splinters off, too. A part of me lives on in those other universes, goes on, in another life. I've been doing it so long, there's not much of me left in this one." She slipped the faded jacket off one arm. "I knew when you saw me that it was a sign. Then when you told me about what you wanted to be when you were a kid, and about Janis Joplin, I knew you were meant to take the jacket."

I could see individual blades of grass, swaying in the breeze, through her thin shoulder. I could smell the salt scent of the bay, blowing through her. I dug my fingers into the grass, into the ground. The earth was solid beneath me. The sky above had never seemed so hard and blue. It was my mind, my thoughts, that seemed wispy and skittering, like clouds. How crazy was she, to think a faded, old jacket could take her back in time? To think that she could pass her craziness on to me? To think that because I liked Janis Joplin's music, it was a sign.

She was shifting, trying to slide the jacket off the other shoulder.

I stood up before she could get any farther. "I—look—I've got to get back to work." I looked at my watch, as if just the act of reminding myself of the time of day could tame the skittering thoughts. As if doing something as normal and monotonous as checking the time could settle the panic that was battering around in my stomach.

She stopped tugging at the jacket and looked up at me with eyes that seemed to swim and waft and shift, clear, then solid blue, then clear again, like a fish's eyes. "I thought you wanted to be different."

For a moment, I smelled her again, a quick waft of funereal gardenias. I smelled ripe, ready-to-pick pears. Felt the lure of night stars and Janis Joplin's singular voice. "I'm sorry. I—" I looked at my watch again, but I couldn't see the hands. "I have to go. It was nice to meet you."

Before I could smell that scent again, that scent of Texas night, I rushed away. I hurried across the park, taking shortcuts over the grass. I didn't stop until I'd joined a clump of people who were waiting at the edge of the park for the light to change. After several seconds, I forced myself to look back.

Arizona had followed me and was standing several yards away on the grass. She was looking at me, but her expression was remote and sad and disappointed, as if she could no longer see me. She had put the faded red jacket back on. As I watched, she reached inside it and pulled out a pair of sunglasses. They were huge and round, pure Sixties sunglasses, nothing like the tiny, expensive aviator-shaped glasses that were so costly and popular today. She put them on. They dwarfed her small, luminous face.

Recognition hit me like a blow. I *knew* the red jacket. That's why it was so familiar. It was Janis'. There was a picture of her wearing it, on one of her albums. Janis sitting on a motorcycle, wearing a red jacket trimmed with gold embroidery and enormous sunglasses, her frizzy hair lit by the sun. Her expression was luminous and faraway, as if she could see something the rest of us couldn't.

The light changed. All around me, people started across the street. A couple of people shoved past me. Another one growled at me to get out of the way if I wasn't going to cross.

I stared at Arizona. Smelled pears mixed with salt air. I stepped off the curb and plodded after the surge of people heading back to work, Janis Joplin singing in my head.

THE TRAVAILS OF PRINCESS STEPHEN

Jane Lindskold

The dress had been in the family for longer than anyone remembered, for so long that no one quite recalled for whom the dress originally had been made.

It was commonly referred to as "great-grandmother's wedding dress." But as the generations passed, and the dress was handed on with more or less formality, the question of just how many "greats" should be inserted before "grandmother" was a point subject to occasional lazy discussion.

The problem was that no matter how many faded wedding photos were dug out of dusty boxes, no matter how many dingy paintings showing the dress being worn for this wedding or that a hundred years ago, or even two or three hundred years ago, the dress itself argued against the possibility of its age.

Taken from its storage chest, shaken out, arrayed on a stand, the dress was as good as new. Better, even, for new fabrics don't preserve in their folds the faint scents of roses and lilies, fragrant echoes of dozens of bridal bouquets. New dresses are not adorned with crisp, but not in the least scratchy tulle, embroidered with intricate hand-made lace set with minute beads that give back the light with the fire of genuine diamonds. New dresses may evoke the classic, but this dress—full-skirted with a daring but not vulgar bodice—

was the wedding dress dreamed of by every bride since days when brides began wearing white and transforming themselves into princesses, if only for a single, special day.

For those sentimental brides who decided to wear mother's or grandmother's gown, the choice was often accompanied by bitter disappointment. When the treasured heirloom wedding dress was removed from storage, many a bride-to-be discovered that pure white had faded to ivory, or worse, turned sour yellow. Stitches had worked their way loose. Hems were too short or too long. Beading had unraveled. Waistlines must be loosened or tightened up. Buttons needed replacement. Bows needed pressing. Trains showed evidence of trampling. Veils and the tiaras that held them in place had gone missing.

None of this ever happened to the bride who decided to be wed in great-grandmother's wedding dress. The dress was not worn for every family wedding, or even in every generation, since fashion is as fickle as love. However, when a bride-to-be was inspired to wear great-grandmother's wedding dress, and she opened the old cedar-lined trunk in which it was stored, she would find that the dress had held up remarkably well. She would also discover that it fit her beautifully. This oddity was excused as being proof that physical form and personal taste runs in families.

Nothing else. Surely nothing else.

Stephanie had begun life as Stephen.

He hadn't meant to become Stephanie, not full-time at least, but one thing had led to another. There had been the job-shortage after the dot-com bust. Stephen had heard that there was a really good post available with a very solid company but that the company was in trouble with the equal opportunity people and planned to hire a woman. They couldn't say so, of course, not without starting all sorts of reverse discrimination nastiness, but the fix was on.

So Stephanie, still Stephen at that point, had decided that one good fix deserved another. He'd apply for the job representing himself as a woman. Then, if he got an interview or, even better, if he got offered the job, he'd follow through right until the inevitable discovery that he was a man. Then he'd have his new employers in a bind. They could either offer him the job or face an interesting discrimination suit. He bet they'd offer him the job.

Up to this point, Stephen had been indulging in a bit of self-deception, concentrating on how much he needed the job, ignoring why he thought he'd have even a slight chance of being mistaken for a woman. Now, as he opened various closets and dresser drawers and pulled out a wide variety of attire, he allowed himself to face the headiness of his deception. The honest truth was that Stephen had indulged himself by dressing in women's clothing for the greater part of his life.

Stephen's first appearance as a girl had been the Halloween when he was eight. There had been a contest for the best disguise, and Stephen had set his heart on winning. He immediately ruled out rubber masks and the like. Too cheesy, too easy. After weighing and discarding numerous options, he fastened on the idea of going as a girl about his own age, a girl dressed up as a princess. That way his costume would have two levels. Everyone would look at him and try to figure out who was the girl dressed as Cinderella. They'd never guess it was a boy dressed as a girl dressed as Cinderella. At the culmination of the evening, he'd reveal himself and win.

Stephen's dad had died in a car crash when Stephen was two. His mother, who doted on him, thought the idea incredibly clever—so clever that she didn't think about how strange it was that just at the age when boys are starting to use "girl" as the greatest imaginable insult, her son would want to dress as one. On the night of the party, she helped him into his Cinderella costume and did his make-up.

No one guessed, and Stephen won the grand prize— an enormous jack-o-lantern filled with candy. He also won the nickname "Princess Stephanie." Stephen supposed the name should have bothered him more, but the truth was, it didn't.

Right before Christmas that year, he bloodied the nose of a boy who teased him a bit too much. The budding bully, horrified at what "the princess" had done, didn't tell his parents exactly how he'd gotten blood all over his shirt. He just said "another boy" had punched his nose in a fair fight. His parents, proud of their son's manliness in refusing to rat out a chum, didn't push.

After that, no one doubted that Princess Stephanie could stand up for himself. By spring of that school year, the joke was fading, and by the time the class merged with several others in junior high, no one remembered about Stephen's turn as Princess Stephanie. No one but Stephen. He remembered. More importantly, he remembered how right that Cinderella dress had felt. He remembered how he had enjoyed feeling beautiful and confident. He remembered his pleasure when he had overheard a few of the fathers say, "That little girl is going to be a looker," and things like that.

His pleasure was so intense that he never confessed it to anyone. Behind the closed doors of his bedroom he would dress up in the costume until he started splitting out the seams. He borrowed some of his mother's dresses when she was out at work, but no matter how carefully he hung them up, she noticed. Luckily, for Stephen, she thought he'd been after something else stored in that closet and only cautioned him to be more careful.

In junior high, Stephen joined the theater club, but the male parts he played only convinced him that he wasn't simply interested in dressing up. He skulked in the back of the theater when the director was coaching the girls—most of whom wore a dress about twice a year—how to move in skirts and high heels. If anyone noticed, they either praised him for his devotion to theater arts, or, more usually, figured he had a crush on one of the girls in the cast.

Stephen continued acting through high school, but he dropped it in college, when he would have had to be a theater major to get more than a walk-on role. By then it didn't matter. He had learned what he needed. He knew the secret tricks of make-up and hairstyling. He'd garnered some tips for dealing with excess hair. He could walk in three inch heels or a long skirt without tripping.

He'd learned something else that would have bothered him more except that just about everyone he knew had some confusion regarding either sex or gender identity—if not both. He'd learned that although he was not attracted to women, he was not attracted to gay men either. He preferred men who liked women, not men who liked men. That made having a love life rather difficult for Stephen, because the only people to whom he was seriously attracted were solidly heterosexual males.

Stephen's mother died from breast cancer a few months after proudly attending Stephen's graduation from college, so there was no one to pressure him to date or settle down. He took a job in a city where he knew no one and began to experiment. At work he was Stephen, but a few nights a week he would transform himself into Stephanie, and go out on the town.

He refined his techniques to perfection. Stephen did not attire himself as some flamboyant drag queen but instead transformed himself into the young woman he felt that, but for an accident of nature, he would have been. Stephanie dressed well, but not extravagantly or outrageously. She was demure, maybe even a little old-fashioned, preferring skirts and dresses to more casual clothing. This aura of respectability, combined with the cubicles in most lady's rooms, meant that Stephen had a lot less trouble with maintaining his masquerade than a woman would have had in a similar situation.

His natural physique made the transition even easier. Where Stephen was skinny and androgynous, with the addition of a little padding, Stephanie was willowy, slim, and wholly feminine. Naturally fair-haired, Stephen's beard-growth was so light that he could go three days without shaving, though he never did, of course. His chest was flat, but naked of hair, saving him the horrors of waxing such a large area. Happily, pony-tails were not uncommon among men in his profession, so he could wear his hair long enough to give Stephanie plenty to work with.

There were a few close calls, especially during the first year or so, but nothing Stephanie couldn't handle, especially since he had taken care to study aikido and other of the more defensive martial arts. The occasional man who got aggressive found his prey gracefully slipping away and was usually so embarrassed by his failure to hold on to such a slip of a girl that he would be the last to draw attention to it.

Stephen reviewed these events as he began to pack Stephanie's suitcase. The interview was in another city. Because of airport security regulations, he'd need to travel as Stephen, but once he got to his destination he could change. It was a blessing that no one could meet him at the gate.

Another new trend would work in his favor. Most large airports now had several restrooms meant for the use of handicapped travelers. They were private, unisex, and large enough to accommodate at least two people. Stephen could slip into one of these, change, and walk out as Stephanie.

His plan worked beautifully. Stephanie was met by Elaine, a personnel manager for her prospective employer. After Stephanie checked into her hotel and freshened up, she met Elaine for drinks. Conversation stayed general and pleasant, even when they met several other members of the company for dinner. The next morning, Stephanie toured the facility, and there were more meals with possible coworkers. By the time she was due to fly out a few days later, she had an offer, had countered, and a middle ground had been met that left them all quite pleased.

"We'll do a lot of the preliminary paperwork through email," said the personnel liaison on the way back to the airport. "I'm so pleased you've agreed to work here. Are you sure you won't mind relocating?

Stephanie smiled. "Not in the least. I actually like colder weather."

It's so much easier, she thought, *to masquerade as a woman when no one expects you to wear sleeveless dresses, or show up at a company picnic in shorts and a tank top.*

But for all Stephanie's smug contentment with the new arrangement, Stephen expected things to fall apart any moment. He already had false ID, correct in every detail but that his first name was Stephanie, rather than Stephen. He used these blithely and waited for IRS paperwork or a reference check to trip him up.

Apparently, though, no one checked his references. He had one tense moment when Elaine in Personnel told him that some tax form had come addressed to "Stephen." Then she laughed.

"I let it go. We know better than most how confused computers can get. What's important is that your social security number matched, so there'll be no problems with the IRS."

Most of Stephen's work friends had vanished when their mutual employer had gone under. Stephanie's social contacts were, by necessity, permitted only a certain amount of intimacy. She told them she was moving to take a new job, received congratulations, and knew she was forgotten almost before she was out the door.

Her new life began. Stephen was so completely forgotten that Stephanie occasionally was startled when hygienic necessity reminded her that she was not a young woman. She researched the various surgeries for transgendering, but she shied away from the procedures, squeamish about the physical truncation and large amounts of hormone therapy involved in such an extreme step.

Stephanie came to feel about Stephen's parts in the same way other people did about freckles or moles or other physical anomalies. They were something she had to deal with, but not really her. What mattered was that she was now a woman socially, and, at least superficially, physically. She was past the age when sex was the first thing on her mind, and she had gone so long without it that she missed intimacy more.

Everything was grand. Everything was wonderful. That is, until she met Donald Baxter and fell in love.

Don loved Stephanie, too, that was the tough part. He was as much interested in a pretty girl as any man. A swift glance at his trousers when they'd been cuddling in front of the television gave that away, but he respected her restraint.

"I think it's sweet you want to wait," he said repeatedly.

Stephanie thought that, if anything, the tantalizing novelty of her "nothing below the neck" rule kept bringing Don back, rather than driving him away.

They dated for eighteen months before the moment Stephanie had been anticipating, and yet dreading, came. Donald proposed.

He did it right, too, privately, over a romantic dinner in one of their favorite restaurants, the expensive one they saved for special occasions. The ring was marvelous, too. He'd remembered that she thought the more usual diamonds cold. Somewhere he had found an old-fashioned pink diamond. Stephanie reached toward its cobwebby beauty almost on reflex, and heard Don saying, "You'll have me then? How about a June wedding?"

What could she say? She wanted Don almost more than she could bear, but if she told him about Stephen, she'd lose Don. Still, didn't love deserve truth? She drew in a deep breath.

"Don, I want you to know how happy and honored I am, but there's something I need to tell you, something about who I was before I came here."

He reached across the table and cradled her hand in his.

"Darling, I don't care who you were before. You're the one I love now. Nothing will change that, I promise. I've often wondered if your restraint in . . . well, certain matters, meant that you'd had some painful experiences in the past. I don't want you to dredge them up, not now, not ever."

Stephanie tried again, "But, Don, you don't really know me."

"I know enough. You're kind and sweet, but you're also intelligent and witty. You're my best friend and my darling. Nothing would make me happier than to have you as my lover and my wife."

He slid the pink diamond in its platinum setting on her finger. It fit perfectly, and looked splendid.

"Don, I . . ."

Stephanie was going to tell him, but then a beaming waiter, obviously cued to wait for the ring to go on her finger, came hurrying up with a bottle of very expensive champagne and a silver tray holding her favorite dark chocolate truffles. She couldn't embarrass Don when he'd done so much to make everything perfect, not in front of all these people.

She'd tell him later. She'd must tell him, sooner rather than later. Otherwise the embarrassment would be all the more acute.

But somehow the right time never came. First his parents threw them a big engagement party. Then wedding plans seemed to take on a life of their own. It wasn't as if they didn't have time to themselves, but somehow telling Don that Stephanie was "really" a

"Stephen" while they were driving to listen to a band that might play at the reception or to taste samples of wedding cake or to interview a caterer didn't seem exactly proper.

And when she was alone, Stephanie had to admit she was enjoying all the fuss and excitement. Don was one of three brothers, and his mother was thrilled to lavish on Stephanie all the enthusiasm she would have given to a daughter. Since Stephanie's own parents were both dead, and Stephanie had no family of her own, Don's mother didn't even need to worry about taking some other mother's place. She could feel good about her generosity, and Stephanie couldn't bring herself to put out the light excitement had lit in that fine lady's eyes.

The wedding dress was a problem. After all, fittings and measurings were semipublic events. Stephanie couldn't have deceived a dressmaker for a moment. She hesitated.

"I could probably do quite fine with something off the rack," she said. "I'm a pretty standard size."

Don's mom smiled. "If expense is what you're thinking about, Stephanie, don't let it worry you for a moment. I know you and Don have insisted on paying for most of the wedding expenses yourself, but you're as close to a daughter as I'm likely to get. I'd love to buy you your dress. Don's dad agrees, too. I've even talked to a dressmaker I know, and she's free the day after tomorrow."

Stephanie's heart thudded in panic. She had to tell Don. He'd never forgive her—if he ever would anyhow—if he learned the truth from his shocked mother and a scandalized dressmaker. But Don was out of town on business and wouldn't be back for a week.

She couldn't tell him something like this over the phone—even if he'd listen. He was so committed to his position as the courtly gentleman who cared nothing for his beloved's past that he'd skillfully blocked her every attempt to broach the subject. She suspected that even if she said, "I'm a man, dammit!" He wouldn't understand.

Forget about dropping her pants. Ever since their engagement, Don had been careful, even overly so, about respecting her "above the neck" rule, so much so that they rarely spent more than a few minutes where they weren't chaperoned by at least a waiter or a semipublic situation. Stephanie knew why Don was doing this. He was showing her that getting engaged hadn't been an excuse for pushing her into premarital sex, but as much as she loved him all the more for his courtesy and kindness, there were times she could have punched him.

Don's mom was prattling away about her friend the dressmaker, showing Stephanie some photos of other gowns the woman had done, when Stephanie suddenly remembered great-grandmother's wedding dress.

"Those pictures reminded me of something I'd nearly forgotten. I have an heirloom dress that I think would fit me. I'd like to wear it, if there's any chance. It would be like . . . well, having a little of my side of the family in the wedding."

Don's mom looked momentarily crushed, but she was a good woman and livened immediately.

"I think that's wonderful. 'Something old,' the rhyme says. Maybe I can contribute the 'something new.' "

Stephanie beamed at her. "That would be wonderful! Why don't you come over the day after tomorrow and see the dress? That would give me a chance to make sure it hasn't perished in storage or anything like that."

Don's mom smiled, her happiness fully restored.

"Don't show Don," she teased, waggling her finger. "It's unlucky if the groom sees the bride's dress before the wedding day."

June came, and with it, the day of the wedding. Somehow, Stephanie had not found the right moment to tell Don about Stephen. She'd tried once, even getting so far as mentioning Stephen. Don had seemed ready to listen. Then a dog had darted out of a side street. Don had swerved to keep them from hitting it, and the moment had been lost.

All the hurdles Stephanie had expected hadn't happened. Blood tests were no longer done. Physical exams were no longer required. The bored clerk hardly glanced at their birth certificates, shoved across forms for them to sign, and barely glanced at any signature but the one Don scrawled on the check. That she checked against his driver's license.

Stephanie's bridesmaids were to be Pam and Elaine, her best friends from work. Stephanie had initially cultivated Elaine for purely practical reasons, figuring that the personnel officer would be the first to hear any hints that someone suspected Stephanie was not quite what she seemed. Somewhere the pretense of friendship had become real. Pam worked as a programmer in the same division Stephanie did. She was uninquisitive about anything but numbers and codes, but with those she was brilliant, even funny.

The three women had arranged to meet at Stephanie's house to get dressed in their finery and do each other's hair. Then they would take the limousine over to the church together. If Stephanie met them at the door already in her gown, neither of her friends thought this odd. Her physical modesty was well-known, and many a bride could hardly wait to put on the lovely dress that she would, after all, wear only once.

Besides, the dress itself provided ample distraction.

"It's amazing!" said Pam, a woman whose praise was usually reserved for the intricacies of some computer program.

"You showed it to us in the box," Elaine added, "but this is a dress that needs to be seen on to be appreciated. Spin a bit, Stephanie. Look how those beads catch the light. If it wasn't impossible you could believe they were diamonds. I love the netting over the neckline, modest without being in the least prudish."

Stephanie loved the netting, too, as it concealed her falsies from close inspection. The only things was, she didn't remember seeing the netting in any of the old photos. She supposed it had been too delicate to show.

"Even without your hair done or your make-up finished," Pam said, "you look like a princess."

"All hail Princess Stephanie!" Elaine said, making a deep curtsey, despite her jeans.

Stephanie flushed, remembering the boy of eight who had found his true self in a Cinderella costume.

"She's blushing!" Pam said. "Now, you're already half-way ready to go. Let's get to our hair and then we'll finish our make-up. Are you going to be all right in that gown? Wouldn't you be more comfortable in a bathrobe?"

Stephanie spun, letting the diamond beads catch fire in the sunlight streaming through the windows.

"I don't ever want to take it off," she said. "I wish I could be Princess Stephanie forever and ever."

Pam laughed. "Enjoy it while you can, though I'm sure Don is going to be an absolute Prince Charming, even after the wedding. You can tell he's not just madly in love, he's sincerely in love. Now, let's start with Elaine's hair. It's thicker than mine, and as I recall . . ."

The conversation drifted off into the intricacies of hairdressing. As Stephanie's hands worked on taming Elaine's thick chestnut locks, her mind insisted on returning to that morning. She'd sat there on the edge of the bed, naked, looking back and forth between the magnificent wedding dress on its stand and the undeniably male sex organs dangling limp at her crotch.

"I'm a man, Don! A man! The woman you love doesn't exist."

She practiced the words, but she couldn't imagine

saying them over the phone, and Don was taking his mother's superstitions very seriously. He'd even left the rehearsal dinner early, so he wouldn't take a chance of seeing Stephanie after midnight.

"I guess he knows that Cinderella changes back into her real self after midnight," Stephen said to the dress, "and he doesn't want to take any chances. How can I do this to him? But how can I stand him up at the altar? Better to go through with it, then let him find out the truth. Then we can figure out the best way to save face for him afterwards. It would be easy for him to have the marriage declared invalid. Then I could disappear. He could tell everyone whatever he wanted. Or I could pretend to die . . ."

Stephen started crying, hard tears that wrenched from the heart.

"But I love him so much! That's real, even if Stephanie isn't. I love him, and I'm going to lose him because even if a scullery maid can be changed into a princess, there's no way I can ever be."

"Ouch!" Elaine's exclamation brought Stephanie from her memories. "Not so hard! I don't mind wearing it up, but I do protest having it pulled out at the roots."

"Sorry," Stephanie said. "I think I've got the pins in now, and doesn't your hair look wonderful?"

It did, and Elaine was immediately mollified, turning her head side to side to inspect the effect. Pam's hair was easier to do, but Stephanie made herself concentrate on the task, not letting her mind wander. She took charge of the cosmetics, and each of her friends were overwhelmed at the transformation.

"You won't be the only princess at this ball!" Pam said, turning her head side to side to admire the results of Stephanie's skillful shadowing. "Mike won't know me."

"Mike will be awed," Elaine said, "but he's going to be embarrassed unless you get your dress on. We'd better get moving. The limo's going to be here before we know it."

And it was. Stephanie had hardly settled the heirloom tiara that went with the dress into her fair hair when the driver came to the door. He seemed pleasantly impressed with the entourage, escorting them to the long car with visible pride.

"Usually," Pam said when they were settled, "I consider stretch limousines an indulgence, but at a time like this, they make sense. We would never have fit your dress into a more usual car, Stephanie. Even ours would be a trial."

Stephanie could only nod. Her heart was in her throat, and she was suddenly overwhelmed with what she was glad to know everyone would take for bridal jitters. Then they were at the church. She could hear the organ notes floating out toward them as the church's big double doors swept open.

She stood straight. Great-grandmother's wedding dress glittered in the sunlight. Her veil fell into place as if arranged by invisible angels. Pam and Elaine looked radiant, but Stephanie glowed.

The bouquets were waiting at the back. Don's mom fussed about, making sure each woman got the right one.

"Stephanie, you look wonderful!" she whispered happily, pecking the bride on one cheek.

"Thanks, Mom," Stephanie said. "Now go ahead. The usher is waiting for you."

The parents of the groom were escorted to their seats, then the music shifted.

"That's your cue," Stephanie said, holding her bouquet just as she had practiced. "Take the lead, ladies. I'm right behind you."

No one was giving the bride away, although Don's dad had offered. Stephanie wouldn't accept that kindness, would not let that good man be part of her deception. Unseen Stephen would give Stephanie away, just as he would accept the responsibility at the end.

The service went by in a blur. Stephanie knew she said all the right things because no one looked at her strangely. The priest said "Husband and wife," and Don kissed her without a trace of shyness, never mind all the avid gazes fixed on them both.

Then they swept down the aisle to the thrilling notes of the organ recessional, and off to the reception. Stephanie had insisted that she could not bear a tyrannical photographer, so they settled for a few posed shots taken by a good friend, then joined the party.

Their first dance was to a song neither of them had selected, but which was so painfully appropriate that Stephanie smiled up at Don and pulled him onto the floor.

To the lovely notes of Cinderella's waltz with the prince from Disney's version of the fairy tale, Stephanie sang softly, "So this is love . . ." Don looked down at her, his eyes shining as brightly as had those of any prince in any fairy tale.

They left the reception early, and the limousine spirited them off to a room at a high-end hotel. Don had made the arrangements for this and for the honeymoon, and Stephanie only hoped he could get his deposits back when he explained that the wedding was off.

They were both a little nervous when they arrived at their room, so they took a moment to examine the elaborate setting. Don had reserved a suite, rather than a room. Champagne and truffles had been set out on a low coffee table before a cozy love seat.

Nervous of the bedroom and its enormous waiting promise, they gravitated toward the love seat.

I bet we're not nervous for the same reason, Stephanie thought. She glanced at the clock and saw it was a few moments before midnight. *How appropriate. Time for Cinderella to transform back into a scullery . . . boy.*

She got up from the love seat, stepped out of her high-heeled shoes, and peeled off her stockings with her toes. Then she moved across the room a few paces. Don half-rose as if to follow her, but Stephanie motioned him back, putting the coffee table between them.

"Don, whatever else happens," she said, "I want you to know that I love you with all my heart and all my soul. If I have done anything selfish, anything thoughtless, well, that's because there never seemed to be a right time."

She could see that he thought he meant her refusal to indulge in premarital sex. Before he could reassure her, Stephanie raised one hand for silence.

"The time has come," she said, and from somewhere she imagined she could hear a clock striking the first stroke of midnight.

The dress was remarkably cooperative in matters of fastenings. The little pearl buttons along the back had been easy to reach, and simple to fasten. They were even easier to unfasten.

Don had settled back in the love seat, his glass of champagne in his hand, his expression saying that he thought her surprise was far better than his. After all, who would have guessed his shy girl would undress before him?

Stephanie—for just this moment more, still Stephanie—smiled softly at him.

"I love you, Don," she said, undid the final button, and started peeling down the close-fitting bodice.

The soft fabric folded down easily, and Stephanie waited for Don's gasp of surprise when he saw that her curving bosom was an artfully stuffed bra and falsies.

He said nothing, and so she peeled the dress down to her waist. Still nothing, although Stephen's trim waist could never be mistaken for that of a woman.

Don's drunk! Stephen thought in desperation. *He's nearsighted and I never knew. He's a virgin, maybe, and has no idea what a naked woman looks like.*

Stephen dismissed that last. He knew perfectly well that Don was a normal, healthy heterosexual male.

He'd have seen naked women, in pictures, if not in person, and quite likely in person as well.

Stephen continued his agonizing striptease, opening the skirt and stepping free of those wonderful, all-encompassing, all-concealing hoops and tiers. He kept his gaze locked on Don, but the young man's face held only wonder and delight.

Stephen set the dress to one side and stood revealed but for his undergarments.

Come on! These panties don't exactly hide what I've got. Say something!

Without realizing it, he had spoken the last two words aloud.

Don shook himself from his entranced wonder and grinned, a merry, feckless expression.

"You are absolutely gorgeous, my darling. Are you going to stop there? I mean, some men might prefer sexy lingerie, but I'd like to see my real, live girl in all her glory."

Stephen blinked. He liked good undergarments, but the reality of keeping bound what needed to be bound and building up what needed to be seen had some restrictions. He had figured the game would be over by this point, so he hadn't gone out and bought anything particularly elegant in the way of lingerie.

But maybe Don was more innocent than was possible. Maybe he wouldn't understand until he saw the dangly bits.

Resolutely, Stephen reached to unhook his bra. The fabric felt silky to his touch, smoother than he remembered, and when it sprang loose the weight was all wrong. It should have hung, heavy with padding, but it swung as light as if it was made of nothing more serious than a bit of satin and lace.

"Oh, my god . . ." Don groaned.

Stephen braced himself, but the rebuke he expected did not follow. Don groaned again.

"Stephanie, get on with it, or this is going to be the most embarrassingly short wedding night in history."

Stephen dropped the bra without looking at it, but he did look as he slid his hand into his panties to strip them off.

They were not, most definitely, *not,* the French-cut briefs he had put on that morning. They did not have an inappropriate bulge in the front. These were the panties of his dreams, bikini-cut and trimmed with just enough lace to be sexy. They did not hide the awkward bulge of a penis for the simple fact that the bulge was not there.

Stephen/Stephanie stared, and felt a flood of delight. She inspected her chest and found she had two round and perky breasts, just like the ones she had always imagined. She had a waist, too, and very nice legs.

Don was laughing affectionately.

"Stephanie, it's as if you never realized that you were a girl! Come over here, right now. I'm going to carry you over the threshold in proper fashion while I still have the self-restraint to do so."

And so he did, gathering her close, and whispering wonderful things as he carried her to their nuptial bed.

Glancing over Don's shoulder, Stephanie saw the dress lying in a glittering heap on the floor and sent it a silent glowing whisper of thanks.

Then she gave Don her full attention and made him her man as he made her his woman.

LADY IN RED

A.M. Strout

When I packed in August for freshman year at NYU, my friends in Ohio warned me to get my degree and get out as quick as possible before New York City hardened my soul. "Lara," they said, "You're much too sweet, much too naïve, to make it in the Big Poisoned Apple."

To them I simply sang the old Sinatra line my Nana had used to convince me to move out east in the first place. "If I can make it there," I'd sing, smiling sweetly and giving a few Rockette-style high-kicks, "I can make it anywhere."

I had laughed at their warnings at the time, but two months into my first semester I was standing in a thrift store on West 8th Street engaging in a tug of war with an old crone over a red hoodie that I adored. I was beginning to see what they meant. Nothing comes cheap in the city, and with the chill of October setting in, I was on the hunt for a little warmth with my limited student budget. I had spotted the most perfect little red hoodie half hidden by the press of clothes hanging on either side of it. It practically called out to me, and when I saw the three dollar price tag, I was over the rainbow for it. I took it down, carefully folded it over my arm, and was on my way to the

counter when I caught movement out of the corner of
my eye and felt a tugging on my arm.

A gaudy looking woman in her early fifties had
latched onto my red hoodie. The Cinderella blonde
dye job on her wild hair was fading, and large clumps
of gray were seeping through, giving her a manic appearance that perfectly matched her actions. She
tugged again, harder this time.

"Excuse me," I said, clamping my arm against my
body to maintain my hold. I almost laughed at the
absurdity of her, but my amusement was quickly shut
out by my animalistic desire to keep the hoodie. I
viciously tore it away from her. "Mine!" she said,
lunging for it, but missing it completely. Instead, her
nails raked dryly against my skin, causing something
primal and protective to snap inside of me.

"No," I said politely but firmly, "it's not."

I held it at arm's length away from her. The crone
moved even closer, and the earthy old-person stink of
her choked me. Her eyes twitched back and forth,
following the hood that now dangled from my out-
stretched arm. She practically foamed at the mouth.

I realized everything seemed a little scary and off
kilter. This type of surreal behavior didn't happen in
the middle of a store. I felt my heart racing like a
scared little girl, and I wondered if my friends had
been right about me coming to city after all.

"I want that for my daughter," she screamed, spit-
tle flying.

I was startled as she raised her voice, but just then
the balding man behind the counter spoke up.

"Hey," he shouted, breaking the strange spell that
wove between us. "Mrs. Punzelli, knock it off. You
play nice or I'm gonna have to call the cops on you.
You got that?"

The old woman's body relaxed, but her eyes were
still intent on the hoodie. I backed toward the register,
calming a little with each step. I was thankful she
made no effort to follow. She glowered at me several

moments longer and finally made an unpleasant (and not to mention unsanitary) gesture flicking her thumb against her teeth. With that, she wandered off to the back of the store and muttered into a filthy gothic mirror hanging from the wall.

"What a pushy bitch," I said as I put my purchase on the counter.

"Sorry about that," he said. "She's usually not that bad."

"Why do you even let her in?" I took a crumpled wad of bills from my backpack and pulled out three singles.

The old shopkeeper shrugged. "I feel bad for her. She's got a daughter up in Bellevue. They've got her locked away up on one of them top floors, where they keep all the cuckoos. The old lady's just about gone crazy herself over that. I hear her daughter got in regular trouble too, helping other crazies escape out the window by letting them climb down her long, golden hair. I've seen pictures, girl's got the longest hair you ever seen!"

I suddenly felt a little bad about they way I'd duked it out with the old woman, but hey, what the hell was I supposed to do? Besides, she'd already lost interest, and despite the sad little tale I had just heard, the hoodie was mine now and I needed it. College students couldn't afford guilt in NYC. I paid the owner and thanked him.

"You need a bag?"

"No. I'll just wear it."

I waved as I headed out the door, and he smiled, instantly restoring my faith in the kindness of most people I had met during my short time in the city. Sure, I had noticed pockets of rude and indifferent folks living in The Big Apple, but I still held onto my optimism.

The sun was beginning its early descent, and I put down my backpack and slipped on the hoodie as the chill began to set in. It felt cozy, warm and familiar, and as I zippered it up, my cell phone went off in my backpack. I fished it out and checked the display. My mother's picture came up—my favorite picture of her in the whole world. It was from the governor's ball where my mother, a lowly impoverished intern at the time, had caught the eye of the young governor. Within a few months they were married, just like a storybook romance. It had angered her wicked and more privileged stepsisters to no end.

I flipped the cell phone open and put it to my ear.

"Little Red Riding Hood," I answered.

"What?" my mother said. "Excuse me?"

"Nothing," I said. "I just bought myself the cutest little hoodie for three bucks, that's all."

"Oh," she said stiffly. "I see. You have time to shop, but not enough time to study."

I had done little in the way of attending classes so far this semester, and, still wowed by being in Manhattan, I had already gotten chewed out about my impending miserable grades.

"Enough about me," I said cheerily, hoping to change the subject, "Is everything okay?"

She sighed into the phone. "Just another charity fund-raising luncheon for the victims of the latest Blunderbore Corporation's chemical dumping. You know your father."

Jack the Giant Killer they called him, always taking on the corporate big guns.

"But that's not why I called," she continued. "It's about your grandmother."

"Which?" I asked.

"The one in Queens," she said. "Nana."

Nana was by far my favorite, although I didn't get to see her as often as I would like. She was the one who had convinced me I'd be fine in New York. She was the hip grandma, active, the cool one I could actually talk to. She had never moved from the Russian neighborhood she had settled in when she arrived in

the States from her tiny European village. Her old
garden brownstone had been modernized since then,
and the Jackson Heights neighborhood had changed
over the years, but she was still the same old lovable
Nana. When my mother mentioned her, I was
concerned.

"Is anything wrong with her?" I asked.

"Nothing," she said. "Well, that's not entirely true.
She's a little under the weather and, well, I was hoping
you would be a dear and pick up some things and run
them out to her."

I utilized my mental planner book and ran my mental finger down the mental page to find today. I was
pleasantly surprised that today was blank.

"Not a problem," I said. I fished a pen out of my
backpack and a piece of paper, the trusty weapons of
any English major. "What does she need?"

My mother rattled off a list of items. Bread, milk,
something for her stomach, a couple of cabbages, fresh
beets, flour, eggs, and, last, red wine. I was going to
ask if Nana was hosting a cocktail party, but I held my
tongue. Would she be needing pigs-in-a-blanket too?

"And remember," my mother said in the infamous
lecturing tone I had grown up around, "I just want
you to go straight there, okay? Your father and I
worry about you. Make sure you give yourself enough
time to get out there and stay for a visit this time.
And be careful. Make sure you don't poke around her
place. *Make sure you spend some time with her.*"

My mother had always been borderline neurotic
when it came to protecting me, but this seemed beyond and above the call. I said a quick goodbye before
she could cycle conversationally back to my grades.
Then I immediately set out north to the organic market at Union Square.

Half an hour later, as I stepped to the curb with
four plastic bags full of Nana's groceries, a Manhattan
miracle happened—a cab pulled up before I had to

figure out how the hell I was going to flag one down with my hands fully loaded. I threw my stuff in the back seat, slid in, and slammed the door.

The driver was coughing, and I waited for him to stop. He looked Eastern European, probably in his forties. He wore a short black goatee that on a younger man would have been trendy five years ago, but on him, it was befitting.

"Where to?" he said when he stopped coughing up his lungs long enough to speak.

"Jackson Heights," I said, then checked the exact address I had scrawled on the back of the shopping list. "3352 85th Street. Between Northern Boulevard and 34th Avenue." I hadn't been there in a while.

"You want me to take the Willamsburg or 59th Street bridge?" he asked, pulling away from the curb.

"Uh, 59th is fine," I said. I sat back and closed my eyes. I relished the momentary silence of the cab ride, but sadly, it didn't last long. The driver was chatty behind his goatee.

"You live out there?" he asked, through the halfway-drawn partition between us.

I wanted to enjoy a nice, quiet, uninterrupted ride to the outer boroughs, so I decided to ignore the question. My body, however, had different thoughts on the matter, and before I even realized what I was doing, I began speaking.

"No, it's my grandmother's place," I blurted out. "She's not feeling well and I've got a bunch of food and wine I'm bringing to cheer her up. I love her, but she's a billion years old, and I honestly wish she'd hire someone to take care of her. It's not like she doesn't have the loot. Her place is huge."

As soon as the words were out, I clamped my hand down over my mouth to stop myself from going further. What the hell was I doing? Being a young woman in the city—not to mention how tiny I was— I rarely ran at the mouth around strangers. Here I was divulging all kinds of personal-ad info and family dish. I looked in the rear view mirror and saw that the driver was leering at me. His goatee looked devilish as I noticed a shift in his attitude.

"Its so sad when old people live alone, isn't it?" I could hear the clumsy craftiness in his voice as he spoke. "She *does* live alone, doesn't she?"

My hands were still over my mouth, but I still answered a muffled but discernible "yes" through them. I was confused and beginning to panic as we sped up Park Avenue toward Grand Central Station. I felt as though I had swallowed some truth serum with my morning Fruit Loops. We were just making every light as they turned green, and I began to wonder how the hell I might get out of the cab if it never slowed down. It felt as though I were being kidnapped. I looked at the license on display.

LUNA CANIDAE the name read. I committed it to memory. The driver began another coughing fit, this one longer than the first, and as I listened, the harsh staccato began to sound more and more like the bark of a dog. I pressed myself forward against the glass for a better look.

"Mister," I started, "are you all right?"

The driver was hunched over from hacking, and his once well-groomed goatee had gone wild and had grown into a full beard that was rapidly taking over the rest of his face. He was changing before my eyes, and as incredible as it was, I think the hours of blowing off class to watch old movies somewhat prepared me for coping with this. Everything about the driver was becoming more and more wolf-like. His coughing had indeed become a bark, and his hands elongated into the shape of sharp-clawed paws, making it nearly impossible for him to grip the wheel.

The traffic lights were still turning green for us, but his inability to control the vehicle sent us careening off the road and head-on into a lamppost. I was lucky enough to slam into the cushiony back of the seat in front of me, but the man-wolf yelped as his head hit

the steering wheel and he fell silent. I grabbed for my
bags, threw open the door, and tumbled out of the
cab onto the sidewalk. A small group of passersby
gathered, asking if I was okay. But I ignored them
and pushed through the crowd and ran the two blocks
to Grand Central Station. As I neared one of the main
entrances, I was blocked by a family apparently on an
after-dinner stroll—a hulking papa, a medium sized
mama, and a tiny toddler.

". . . was too hot, dear," I heard the father say as
I bumped into him.

"Hey," he growled, bearlike. "Watch it!"

"Sorry," I said quickly, and dashed into Grand Central Station. As I rushed down to the main concourse,
enormous trees the size of redwoods came shooting
up through the station's floor, bits of marble flying
everywhere. All around me the room was transforming into a forest. People ran back and forth to
avoid the debris and branches that shot past.

What the hell was going on?

Was I losing my mind?

Had living in New York City driven me insane?

I fervently wished I had listened to my friends back
home. They were right. I was having a mental break
from reality, and after only two months here. I
snapped my eyes shut, counted to ten, and opened
them again, hoping for some clarity.

Everything was still going crazy around me.

I made my peace with the fact that, crazy or not, I
was going to have to deal with it. I ran for the bookstore along the west side of the main concourse.
Things inside the store seemed normal compared to
what was happening out on the concourse, but I didn't
know how long that might last. The smocked clerk
only got out the "Can . . ." of "Can I help you?"
before I interrupted.

"Children's books," I said, somewhat breathless
from my run. "Fairy tales."

"Third aisle, last bay on the left," he said, pointing.

I hurried down the aisle and found the section. I dropped my grocery bags. An ugly little girl sitting a few feet away jumped at the sound, and her mother— far prettier than her—moved protectively close. I knew I must have looked crazy to them, but I turned away and began searching through the books until I found what I was looking for—a collection of *Fairy Tales by the Brothers Grimm.*

I flipped open to the tale of Little Red Riding Hood. The tale itself wasn't long, and by the time I was done, I more or less had confirmed my suspicions. I glanced over at the ugly little girl. She now was an anthropomorphic duck, and she quacked at me.

I didn't much care for the way the story ended. Sure, the grandmother and Red ended up alive, but only after a huntsman had cut them free from the wolf's belly. Of course, the tale didn't discuss the years of therapy Nana and I would have had to endure after such a traumatic experience. My brain was slowly accepting the insanity, but my heart was panicked. I had to stop this.

I grabbed the zipper on the hoodie, but it was stuck. I frantically tried tugging the whole top up and over my head, but the cloth seemed fused to my body and it wouldn't come free. I gave it a few more panicked yanks, feeling trapped, and broke several of my nails as I freaked out. The hood slipped onto my head as I tossed and turned, and the world slipped into cartoon colors.

My surroundings swirled, the trees outside the store looking more gnarled, the duck girl at my feet more threatening. I felt so tiny just then, so absolutely helpless, so afraid I was going mad.

I somehow knew I had to get to Nana's, and quick, but I wasn't sure if I wanted to chance another cab. I had never taken the train out there before, but I gathered up my grocery bags and followed the signs to the subway. After consulting the map, I decided that the train seemed the closest, and I dashed down to the platform, catching the last car as the doors closed behind me with perfect timing.

Two stops later, my empty car began to fill . . . and began to be affected by whatever cruel magic was in my hoodie. Any man who sat within ten feet of me began acting creepier than the usual guys I ran into on the train. One of them started by itching his hand, then his chin, and then started scratching at his whole face. Another snuffled and sniffed in my general direction. When a third's facial hair started growing out into a full beard in less than a minute, I stood up and hurried to the next car, dragging my bags with me and almost losing them between cars.

When the men on *that* car began behaving strangely, I moved to the next, this time tripping over a kid with the biggest nose I had ever seen arguing with an older man I presumed was his grandfather.

"Don't lie to me!" I heard the old man shout as the boy turned into a wooden doll with loose strings hanging from his legs and wrists.

The door between cars thankfully closed behind me.

The cars themselves were growing thick with vines that snaked after me. The forest path of the story was following my lead, and I shuddered at the audible cracks and slithers of it taking over the train. Underneath those sounds, I could hear the normal passengers shouting in surprise as the parade of man-wolves continued following me, several men jumping up from their seats to join in. They seemed to be intent only on me and hadn't made any attempt to harm any of the other passengers. Right now, the big, bad wolves had achieved only the level of "moderately annoying" as they slathered, drooled, and growled along behind me.

We pulled into the 82nd Street station in the proverbial nick of time. The stench of approaching wolves filled the car. It was the last car. I had nowhere else to go. I was trapped again.

I had never heard a sweeter sound when the doors dinged, and I was thrilled when they rolled open, but I stayed where I was, fighting my urge to flee. I waited until the last possible second—the wolves were mere feet away, and I could feel their hot breath on me— before I slid out through the closing doors. The now-trapped wolf-men could only stare through the glass and howl as their train pulled out of the station. Although scared, I waved goodbye to them in defiance.

Queens was like a foreign kingdom to me, so different from the inner city that I was used to and even more foreign in the strange cartoon Technicolor I was seeing in now. I asked the hunchback manning the booth for directions to Nana's house and then set off at a run, the muscles in my arms straining under the weight of my load. The plastic grocery bags had woven themselves into four wicker baskets.

I headed down the station stairs and tore off along the first block. A flurry of movement caught my attention, and I couldn't help but turn to see a large gray-brown tabby cat, standing on its hind legs, wearing hip-high boots, an Elizabethan neck ruffle, and a purple plumed Musketeer's hat. He was fighting off a pack of dogs like a champion fencer. The claws on one hand were extended like vicious looking knives, and although the cat was outnumbered, I had a distinct feeling the advantage was his. I pressed on.

One block left.

I passed two little roly-poly kids speaking what sounded to me like German. They were following a path of lollipops and candy bars up a walkway toward a brownstone that appeared to be made entirely out of candy, from its gingerbread paneling to its ribbon candy shutters.

"Hey, kids," I shouted as I stopped. They seemed to shake out of their fugue state and turned to look at me, their chubby little hands stuffed with candy already. "I wouldn't go in there if I were you."

They stood there, confused still.

"Unless you want the lady who owns that place going all Hannibal Lechter on you."

At this their eyes widened, and the boy turned to the girl, and said, "C'mon. Let's get out of here, Gretel." The little girl hesitated, grabbed a sticky bun that was part of the house's gate, and followed her brother. For a moment I actually felt good for helping them out. I felt the tiniest hint of optimism.

The feeling died quickly, however, when I turned back toward my Nana's and found the crunched in nose of the cab I rode back in Manhattan. It was sitting empty underneath the shade of a tree and was pointed at Nana's house half a block away. The panic of incredibility set in once again, and I broke into a heart-pounding sprint.

While most of the other brownstones in the neighborhood had been turned into three-family homes over the years, Nana's remained all her own. I walked timidly up the front steps, the fear pulsing thick in me. The door stood slightly ajar, and I eased it open farther and set the baskets down as quietly as possible.

The old house was silent. Even when it was busy with activity, I found the place creepy, but now it was like walking through a mausoleum filled with Russian antiques. Many of them were knocked over.

The trail of destruction led upstairs, and I followed it. Her bedroom was at the back of the house, and I knew from the Brothers Grimm that the wolf had headed there. I tiptoed the last few steps, hoping the pounding in my chest wasn't as loud as it sounded.

The door was cracked open, and I hesitantly pushed it wide. Sure enough, there in the bed was a shadowy figure. As I stepped closer, I could see the pronounced goatee of the cab driver beneath the furry snarl of the wolf's snout. The shirt he had been wearing was in tatters now. I checked the room for blood and was relieved to see none. Was Nana somewhere hidden in here or had she escaped? I stopped in the center of the room and looked around. She could have been under the bed or even in the closet, but I couldn't tell.

The wolf snarled.

"Finish this!" he barked, remaining tucked beneath the sheet on the bed. He seemed to be struggling, fighting the urge to leap up and devour me, but was bound by some power from doing so.

The power of the tale was binding him somehow.

I tried the zipper again, but it still wouldn't budge. I grabbed bunches of the fabric and tore at it, but it wouldn't give. I slipped my backpack off my shoulders and began searching through it for something, *anything* that might help.

"Why Nana," I said slowly, fighting against my compulsion to speak the words, "what big ears you have."

"Better to hear youuuuu," the wolf howled.

I shuddered as the sound ripped through me. I had to think. What were my advantages? I was much smaller than him, and I seemed to possess a greater knowledge of the situation.

"And what big eyes you have," I continued, as I kept rummaging through the bag. I was coming across nothing of use. I doubted my iPod would help, unless I could wedge my earphones into his ears and hope the old maxim that music hath charms to soothe the savage beast held true.

"Better to see you with, my dear," he barked. His body tensed in anticipation of the final lines of our roles being fulfilled.

"And," I said finally, fighting, dreading the words as they came spilling out, "what a terrible big mouth you have."

A clatter came from down the hall, and I craned my neck to see Nana. How the hell had she eluded the wolf? I had never really thought about it before, but Nana was in remarkably good shape for a woman in her seventies. She was moving at a brisk pace.

"The better . . ." the wolf began with finality.

I tensed with fear.

He threw off the covers and readied himself to pounce, "to eat you with!"

I dove for the door at the same time he lunged. My hand had wrapped around something small and cylindrical in my bag. The rest of the bag tore away from me as the wolf's claws caught the strap, the contents of my little life leaking out onto the floor. I screamed as I tumbled through the doorway, and slammed the door behind me. I held it shut as I felt the full weight of the wolf charge into the door on the other side.

"Run!" I screamed at Nana.

Nana did just that, making it to the bottom of the stairs at record speed and heading for the front door. I felt the doorknob twitching in my hand as the wolf clawed at it clumsily. It was only a matter of time before he smashed his way through.

A claw punched through the bottom of the door and snagged my leg. I yelped in pain. I felt blood trickle down my leg. I heard a large snuffle from the other side of the door and I imagined the wolf fully taking in the scent of my O Positive.

I decided it was better not to wait around for him to break all the way through. I bolted for the stairs, hurling myself down them without a thought for my safety. Behind me, the door flung open and the wolf leaped out, landing right where I had been standing a heartbeat ago. I swallowed hard and spun to face the beast, almost losing my footing on the stairs. My mind was racing, and I suddenly remembered one last component—one last *character*—to the story.

"No reason I can't be the huntsman too," I said and ducked low as he charged at me. In my hand, I gripped the lone weapon I had managed to retrieve from my bag. I thrust it up, and only after I drove it into the beast's chest, did I disappointingly realize was it was. A pen. What the hell good was a pen going to do?

The wolf cleared me and practically flew down the rest of the stairs, hitting the wall, spinning, landing on its back at the bottom. It writhed frantically, howling, clawing at its own chest, and smoke began to rise from the small wound I'd inflicted. The smell of acrid burning hair filled the room, and after what seemed like an eternity of screaming, the wolf stopped moving.

I stood slack-jawed, both horrified and pleased by what I had done.

Nana was crying, and my own breath was heaving in and out in great bursts. Outside, sirens went screaming by, and the two of us simply stood over the beast. Tears of relief started running down my face.

Nana stared. "How did you do that? How did you stop that monster?"

I shrugged, stepped over the wolf, and hugged her. I could feel her heart going a mile a minute.

"I have no idea," I said. "All I did was stab it with a pen."

I released her and leaned over the lifeless body. Holding back my own personal squick factor, I pulled the pen free, and lifted it up for examination. I began to laugh.

"What is it, dear?" Nana asked. I was sure I must have looked unhinged. And maybe I was. My mind was still reeling from the events of the past few hours.

"Well," I said when I could finally speak, wiping the tears from my face, "What else does every college freshman have from their Nana but a nice graduation writing set? A *silver* writing set, to be exact."

"And you said you'd get no use out of such a thing," she tsk-tsked.

I hugged her even harder than before.

"You're sure you're okay?" I asked.

Nana nodded. "That was a pretty fancy move you did on the stairs."

"I guess watching reruns of *Buffy* must have paid off."

"From what I hear," Nana said disapprovingly, "that's all that's paying off. About those grades of yours . . ."

"Nana, please," I said, "I just saved your life. Maybe you could call my mom and put in a good word for me?"

She thought for a minute, then smiled. "I *suppose* I could put in a good word or two for my favorite little Red Riding Hood."

With the mention of that name, I tugged at the zipper on the hoodie once again. This time it came free. The brightness of the Technicolor world faded and things around me turned to normal. The wolf melted into the floor.

I held the hoodie at arm's length.

It was a bittersweet parting; I had loved the way it looked on me, but what I had been through was definitely too high a price for fashion's sake.

The following day I returned to the thrift store, and asked for my money back. Hey, three dollars was three dollars. That was like three meals off the dollar menu or three midnight movies! Besides, I secretly held the wicked desire that that old crone who frequented the place, Mrs. Punzelli, might come back for it.

As I left, I caught the latest breaking news on the thrift store's one working television. The story concerned a pack of wolves that had reportedly leaped from the subway car at the end of the 7 line the previous night. No one had been hurt, luckily, and after dispersing they were all later found surrounding a brick high-rise, barely able to move, and exhausted— from prolonged huffing and puffing, I had no doubt.

ANOTHER EXCITING ADVENTURE OF LIGHTNING MERRIEMOUSE-JONES: A TOUCHING GHOST STORY

Belle and Nancy Holder[1]

Gentle Reader,
You may recall that in our previous story, "The Further Adventures of Lightning Merriemouse-Jones," Miss Merriemouse-Jones had fallen into the clutches of the evil Count Dracurat and his horrid Countess, who blamed dear Lightning for her husband's extramarital misadventures. The lovely young rodentina was rescued by the dashing private detective Quincy Dormouse, a strapping Texan of large fortune. Once Lightning had been restored to her doting parents, Mr. Dormouse began to woo her with all the ardor of a young mammal who has stared death in its beady red eyes and known, down to the depths of his furry soul, that the bell tolls sooner than one can ever imagine and that one must seize the day—or in this case, clasp hands gently—for the impetuous American believed his singular chance of earthly happiness lay in persuading Miss Lightning to be his bride.

As you may also recall, Lightning was quite dashing herself, and no stranger to passion—for she had left her family home in the wall of the Summerfield estate when pressed by her well-meaning parents to select a husband and "be settled." Our young heroine felt that the words "settled" and "Lightning" had nothing to do with each other. Therefore, to avoid such a fate mundane, she slipped into the pocket of Maria Luisa Summerfield, who was herself launching *into* matrimony via an elopement with her second cousin, Juan Eldorado Adelante-Paz.

It would be quite difficult to convey, in these more modern and, may one say, permissive times, what a serious breach of decorum an elopement was. But the two young misses were much of the same mind: Lightning herself was being sorely pressed to select a husband from the rats, mice, hamsters, and gerbils who came calling at her Papa's door, and she truly fancied none of them, not even Gerhardt von Ratschloss, who traveled all the way from Prussia to dance attendance upon our young lady. In a similar state of vexation, Maria Luisa would have none other than *Señor* Adelante-Paz, declaring that she would rather die than be separated from him.

Thus, Lightning and Maria Luisa decamped, and after the wreck of the frigate *El Queso,* Lightning found herself thrust into the nightmarish world we described at length (four thousand, one hundred words including eeks) in our previous (and may we say, with all modesty, well-received) tale. And when all was resolved—with the death of Count Dracurat, and the restoration of Lightning to her parents—her mama made it quite clear that she thought Mr. Dormouse would make as spectacular a catch for her daughter as a fragrant chunk of Blue Castello perched upon the most devious of mousetraps.[2]

One may recall the thrilling conclusion of our previous story,[3] promising more adventures of Miss Lightning Merriemouse-Jones, and so, we are happy to provide such a story here. We have the means at our disposal to entertain our readers for some time to come, for when Belle was approximately eight years old (she is nearly ten as we write this), we discovered an object of great fascination on the porch of our home. It was so tiny and brown that at first I, Nancy, sans my spectacles, thought it was some sort of bug.

But Belle, being keener-eyed and quite knowledgeable in the study of insects, declared it was no bug at all.[4]

She was quite correct: it was a tiny catgut notebook, labeled THE PRIVATE JOURNAL OF LIGHTNING MERRIEMOUSE-JONES. Imagine our delight! It is from this volume that we drew the material for our first story, and now do so again for our second. We happen to believe that it was deliberately left for us to read, and we have now accepted the commission to play scribe to this exceptional mammalian adventuress. The JOURNAL is filled with diary entries detailing her many deeds of derring-do, which pose some questions that we have yet to answer. Specifically, it appears that Our Heroine possessed (and perhaps possesses still!) some method of time-travel bequeathed upon her by her raternal uncle, Cheddrick Merriemouse-Jones. He was in his day either an innovative genius of the first water or a crackpot, depending upon whom one asks. He lived in the small English village of Stilton-Upon-Rye . . . and seems never to have died.

We mention this before commencing our actual story because you will see that our narrative opens in 1940, when Lightning should have been sixty years old, as she was born in 1880. And yet, in this tale, she is still a young, unmarried maiden as fresh as Devonshire cream. Indeed, as we began working, we were quite puzzled, and at first we thought the hero of the story was actually Cyclone Merriemouse-Jones, supposed to be a descendant of Lightning's, who is buried in the quaint and lovely churchyard in the village of Neufchâtel.

Bewildered, we determined to read the entire journal before we commenced this story, and approximately halfway in we read a trio of entries concerning an invention of her uncle Cheddrick's: a purplish-green taxi cab, which periodically arrived for Lightning at the exact instant that she presented herself at the heavenly Gates, in hopes of that final reward for

which all good Christians yearn. It seems to have been
the very conveyance by which Cheddrick himself
evaded the Scythe of Time that cuts us all down—
king or knave, queen or scullery maid—with the possible except of Lightning and her uncle. In other words,
we believe that Lightning and Cheddrick both may be
actual time-travelers![5]

When we have fully digested the complexities of
Lightning's discourse on the subject, we will happily
share them with you, our Devoted Reader. For the
nonce, suffice to say that despite the seeming contra-
diction in time periods, the heroine of this story is
indeed Lightning, as a young lady.

Thus assured, please read on, and enjoy "Another
Exciting Adventure of Lightning Merriemouse-Jones"
(including, as was the case in our previous work, anno-
tations from Miss Belle Holder.)

With great respect, and deep affection,
　　Belle and Nancy Holder, fille et mère

THE TALE ITSELF　•

25 September, 1940, London Town
　*They call it the Blitz! In the language of our Ene-
mies, that translates as "Lightning," just like my name!
And it is very like lightning, this nightly barrage of
explosives loosed upon poor, dear London. Herr "Fur-
rer" Adolph Ratler, who is surely the most evil creature
ever to run the wheel of Life, has dropped bombs for
over a fortnight on the beautiful warrens and mazes of
the very seat of Civilization. His hellspawn minions,
the bloodthirsty Katzies, fly in a parade behind a sinister black aeroplane unmarked save for what we assume
is a registration number: 070617. No one knows who
the pilot is, but he is merciless, shedding bomb after
bomb upon the helpless populace as if it is his life's
work. And so it is; many lie dying, or dead, and no
one is spared, be he King Rat or common field mouse.
Some say that the war will end when the pilot of the*

*black aeroplane is killed. But others say that this un-
holy war will never end.*

*As for me, I count myself as the recipient of great
personal tragedy. I am bereft. I have hastened to find
my family's London mousehole a ruin. Nothing can be
saved—not the beautiful pianoforte in the drawing
room, nor the exquisite tea service Mr. Dormouse presented my dear Mama in the halcyon days following
my deliverance from the evil Count and Countess Dracurat. All appears to be gone, lost to enmity and flame.
I shall dig through the debris with a heavy yet hopeful
heart, on the off chance that something remains of my
family's precious mementoes.*

*Hark! On the radio, we are warned to remain in-
doors! The brown-pelted Katzenjammers have landed
at the White Cliffs of Dover! I hear their jackboots on
the pavement outside! We are undone!*

26 September, 1940
*As I cower in my family's destroyed mousehole, I
have found something! It is an olive-green metallic
trunk, which was stowed beneath the attic eaves next to
the chimney. It appears that when the bombs hit, the
bricks tumbled in such a way as to create a protective
wall over the trunk, not unlike a Sumerian corbelled
arch, and so it was untouched. I have cleared a space
such that I may drag it out and am now endeavoring to
open it. Fingers crossed that something of value lies
within—nay, not of financial value, but which may bring
some measure of happiness to poor, wretched Lightning!*

And so it did, Dear Reader. Let us describe for you
in these next few pages what she indeed found, rather
than put you to the task of deciphering more of her
journal entries. For alas, there was another stupefying
Blitz attack, and a battle in the streets between the
Katzenjammers and various English ratriots—those
deemed too old to go to war, but nevertheless eager
to protect their kith and kin. Amidst the chaos, it took

our brilliant but pressured young lady some time to discern what exactly she had found inside the trunk, and by what means she should employ it. We hesitate to publicize that her immediate entries after the above couplet became a bit rambling; and those further on might stir pangs of utter disbelief and incomprehension. There too, as we are cognizant of the many demands placed upon our readers' time and attention, we ourselves shall attempt to summarize precisely what next occurred.

You may recall from your studies in school that the Great War, known also as World War One (1914-1918), was believed at the time to be the war that would end all wars. It was also a time of quite colorful personages, including the World War I Flying Ace, Count Orloff von Limburger, known far and wide as the Bloody Rat Baron. He won at least eighty air combats and was so beloved by his people that he was asked to retire rather than continue to fight, but he refused.

Von Limburger sustained a serious head wound on July 6, 1917, and was ever after much changed. He became distant, unemotional, and utterly devoid of humor. It was whispered that he was himself no longer, but a phantom. This caused joy among his own forces, but dismay among the Allies—for who could kill a ghost?

Yet he was killed . . . or so it was asserted . . . on April 21, 1918, from a lone .303 bullet (that is to say, from a Vickers-Maxim machine gun.) It has never been conclusively proven who exactly killed the Bloody Rat Baron, although credit was given to a Canadian named Brown. However, in Miss Lightning's family, the author of von Limburger's demise was firmly believed to be Edam ("Eddie") Merriemouse-Jones, whose plane went down in the wilds of Gouda shortly thereafter and who was never seen again.

After the war, however, some of Eddie's personal effects were sent home in the selfsame olive-green

trunk that Lightning retrieved during the London
Blitz. In this trunk lay his most beloved object, a WWI
brown leather bomber jacket painted with the initials,
BRB in scarlet, through which a black slash had been
painted. However, in the interior pocket of the jacket,
Lightning found the fragments of a sealed envelope,
which appeared never to have been opened. She hesitated not at all, but ripped it asunder at once.

Inside lay portions of a moldering letter, which read:

*. . . I did not kill von Limburger. I thought I had
him in my sights, but the plane I shot down contained
a mouse who very closely resembled the Bloody Rat
Baron. But it was not he! However, his death was proclaimed, and it was attributed variously to Brown, to
me, and others.*

*My superiors knew that I knew I had not rid the
earth of von Limburger. Therefore, I was pledged to
silence, as the populace of London had suffered griev-
ously at the hands of von Limburger, and morale
would plummet if the truth were known. I have been
ordered to say nothing, and I will not; and I swear
upon my loyalty to Crown and Country that I will secretly devote my life and those of my descendants, to
hunting down von Limburger, and ending him once
and for all!*

Imagine Lightning's shock! But her opportunity to
consider the import of her find was abruptly termi-
nated by the sounding of the air-raid sirens for yet
another furious attack!

Bombs rained down around the young lady, smash-
ing the chimney and extant walls to bits! *Boom!* they
sounded, all but shattering the place, and the nerves
of Lightning, trapped inside!

Despite the possibility that Katzenjammers awaited
her outside, Lightning determined that her best course
was to scurry to the nearest air-raid shelter, and so
she held Eddie's bomber jacket over her head to

shield herself from falling debris. However, there were skirmishes in the street, and as the falling bombs hit, the windows of the shops exploded; Lightning quickly put on the jacket, the better to protect herself as she ran for cover.

A moment here, as we caution you, Gentle Reader: This is indeed a ghost story, and there may those among you for whom this tale is too oversetting. If so, please move on to lighter fare, as we are determined not to shirk our duty in the presentation of this story.

For in the very moment Lightning put on the jacket, she found herself seated in a Sopwith Camel, directly behind her forebear, Edam Merriemouse-Jones himself! Like him, she wore the attire of a bomber pilot, complete with goggles and a silken scarf wound 'round her neck. The synchronized twin-mounted Vickers were rat-a-tatting at an enemy plane, and Lightning ducked down to avoid a return volley.

Forthwith, the Sopwith shot up into the clouds. The enemy plane did not follow. And there, Eddie turned round, saw Lightning, and looked quite pale and astonished.

He said, "How came you here, and who on earth are you?"

"No one on earth," Lightning replied, a bit sassily, despite her own astonishment (for she was, indeed, an intrepid adventuress and given to quick-wittedness even in the most perilous of circumstances). "If you are Edam Merriemouse-Jones, then I am Lightning Merriemouse-Jones, your relative." And she proceeded to describe how it was in London, and how she had come across his jacket.

As they flew through the gray mist, he shook his head and said, "Then it is true, and I have known it for some time, though I could scarce accept it: *I* am a ghost, and I have cursed myself for all time. Alas! For I swore I would kill Orloff von Limburger, but he is dead already!"

"I beg your pardon?" Lightning asked.

Gnashing his teeth, Eddie explained, "On July 6, 1917, von Limburger was shot through the head, and I and many others believed he had died. But he came back to the skies—much changed—and rumors spread that his evil masters had taken his body and performed blasphemous rites over it, creating the ghostly apparition that continued to mow down the valiant and the true! When I felled that mouse who resembled him, I wondered at the time if it was some ruse to throw us off his scent, but I did not dream that he had become a monstrous, undead killing machine."

He regarded young Lightning. "That you are here, in my jacket, tells me that my vow to kill him is impossible to keep, and thus I am doomed to fly throughout eternity, fighting a war that will never end."

Lightning was very sorry, both for himself and for her own sake, and she wondered aloud if she, too, had perished—in her case, during the most recent wave of the Blitz.

"What do you speak of?" he asked her, and as she proceeded to explain that England was again at war, he gnashed his teeth once more and raised his paws to heaven.

"Why do you misuse us so unfairly?" he cried. "How is it that British mousedom is so cruelly tormented throughout the decades of this century? Why were our trials not brought to an end on July 6, 1917?"

As Lightning bore witness to his anguish, his words caught her attention: for she remembered in that instant that 070617 were the numbers on the mysterious black aeroplane that led the bombing runs on England!

She cried out, "Mr Edam, I have had a startling revelation!" And she described to him the strange registration number on the black aeroplane.

"It is the date when von Limburger was killed!" she concluded. "And you swore to defeat him upon the lives of yourself and your descendants—and I am here!'' Her beady eyes shone.

"I believe I have been sent to help you defeat the Bloody Rat Baron, once and for all!"

As soon as Lightning uttered those words, a tremendous mist rose around the Sopwith Camel, followed by a ferocious thunderclap. She covered her ears with her paws and shut tight her eyes . . . and when she opened them again, she found herself in the front seat of the Sopwith Camel, quite alone . . . approximately ten thousand feet above the ghastly catillion of Katzie bombers unleashing yet another barrage of bombs over London. And there, at the head of the flotilla, flew the black plane numbered 070617—the plane of the ghastly von Limburger!

"Edam Merriemouse-Jones!" she cried, looking about. "Where are you? What shall I do?"

Then she tingled from head to toe as if she had been struck by, well, lightning—as if volt upon volt ripped through her slender, dainty frame. The brown leather bomber jacket crackled, energizing her and guiding her in her ensuing actions: she pushed the Sopwith down into a death spiral, aiming it directly for the black aeroplane!

"For Crown and Country!" cried the voice of Edam Merriemouse-Jones, deep within Lightning's being. "It will take a ghost to kill a ghost. Though it may mean your own life, are you with me, young lass?"

"Yes! Indeed!" Lightning cried. "I am!"

Her entire being filled with fursome terror and ecstatic joy as she allowed her relation full use of her limbs and faculties, preparing to dive-bomb into the black-cloaked plane of Orloff von Limburger.

The Sopwith Camel shuddered and whined as it hurtled through the English night. The other planes flying with von Limburger fired at her, but she and Eddie together dodged them all handily. A bullet zinged less than half an inch from Lightning's silky cheek.

Faster she fell, faster and faster, the Sopwith Camel screaming toward its target—a bomb itself now, racing to smash into the enemy!

Lightning prayed, and she thought of her dear Mama and Papa, and the Summerfield family, and of dear Quincy, who had never understood why she could not be settled. She kept her eyes wide open so that she could witness history—and the liberation of her relative from his ghostly torment!

"Eek! Eeek! Eeeeeeeeeeeeeeeeeeeeeeeeeeeeeeee!!!...." she squeaked, while flames blazed on the wings of her plane as she dive-bombed toward von Limburger's deathly craft.

IMPACT!

And before she could add the "k" to her final eek, Lightning Merriemouse-Jones stood before the graceful white gates billowing with mist and listened to the exquisite soprano chorus . . .

. . . when suddenly, the purplish-green taxi pulled up beside her, and the passenger door opened.[6]

THE ANNOTATIONS, PROVIDED BY MISS BELLE HOLDER

1. "Mom, my name should come first. B comes before N. I am a published author now, so let's play by the rules."
2. "Mom, that's great. I'm tired. I'm going to bed. Here are some interesting facts about lizards: some lizards live for as long as twenty years. Did you know that? Probably not."
3. To wit: "But do remember this, Gentle Reader: Lightning Merriemouse-Jones was destined for greatness."
4. When Belle was five years old, an approaching woman came to a dead stop approximately two feet in front of her. The lady's eyes widened with admiration, and she bent down to address Belle in that singsong voice which

some adults use when addressing children:

"Oh!" she said. "You are such a beautiful little girl! Look at those big blue eyes! Have you ever thought of becoming a fashion model when you grow up?"

Whereupon Belle replied, "Actually, I would like to be an entomologist."

5. N.B. from Holder the Elder: This may not be too surprising, as Cheddrick M-J was an admirer of the writings of H.G. Wells, and spent many an evening chewing upon the tomes of the esteemed author.

6. "No, it's a purple, blue, and green taxi cab arriving out of a royal purple mist, tinted with gold (unless it's hinted with gold. What does hinted with gold mean?) Okay, it's tinted."

REVOLUTION: NUMBER 9

Judi Rohrig

Not far from where Rose crouched in the dark, the leafy limbs of the thick bushes and low trees of the woods surrendered to harried chopping and hacking. The *Bachyrita* posse was in a fevered frenzy now, closing in fast.

Rose tried not to breathe, but her chest swelled and sank in ways she couldn't control after all the running. And even if she were able to stop her desperate gasping, surely the rataplanning of her heart would betray her. Not that her pursuers would "hear" the palpitations. The Bachyritas' BrainPods® would "see" her, though. That's why their posses were known as "pit vipers," because they could pick up her body heat through their sensors. Neither the dark nor the thick growth of the woods would offer Rose much in the way of cover from these *snakes*.

Here in the darkness, they would hold the advantage even if they hadn't dragged a Franklin along.

Rose lifted her head, squinting, begging the dim light to make meaning of the shadows. She'd been through this area before, and if she could just get to the river, she could connect with those still fighting for something that mattered.

But the knots in her deltoids and calves were screaming their exhaustion. She'd be lucky if she could

173

even make it to the river. Forget getting across the damned thing.

How much time did she have left? A few minutes? Then she'd have to face them, face the death she'd been running from since just before dawn.

A single fiery torch glowed brighter between the trees. Yes, they had a Franklin with them. That could be good. Those "real eyes" might actually slow them down. The flame from the torch in all this jumble of trees and thick bushes might confuse the Franklin.

Rose scrambled under the brush. Perhaps a few rabbits and squirrels could be startled from their havens, providing a muddled set of prickles for the vipers' super-functioning BrainPorts®.

Sharp thorns and ragged branches ripped at what was left of her already tattered jacket. She clasped her hands over her chest, not to still her ka-thumping heart but to secure the small case she'd tucked under her shirt. Inside the case was the real object of the Bachyritas' pursuit, and it was more than just a part of Exhibit Number 9.

"This way!" The words bellowed through the shadows of the trees.

Huddling as close as she could to the scabrous trunk of the large oak where a shaft of moonlight slithered down over her hands, Rose made out the stains of dried blood in the cracks and lines of her fingers: Roddy's blood.

A twinge of guilt wedged itself in there somewhere. And grief. But she had to make it to the outlaw camp of the Ungatosonrisas on the other side of the river. Her feelings could wait.

Another voice howled from the far end of the woods: "Over here!"

The snapping of twigs and limbs ceased for a second. If Rose remembered correctly, protocol for the vipers dictated confirmation of verbal instructions before they shifted directions. The Ungatosonrisas were said to employ annoying tricks to draw a posse from its prey.

Rose waited a moment, trembling against the craggy wood, wondering if the distant voice could indeed have been help. Was she close?

Not that the Bachyritas would ever give up. "Stop" wasn't an option for them, except to stop the masses from supposedly *harming* themselves. "For the protection of all" were the first words flashed through the pleasure goggles. That was their mantra, and it was the biggest lie ever. Bondage was not freedom.

Rose bit her bottom lip, cradled the case closer, and tried to see through the bushes ahead. She didn't know how to stop either. Moving as quickly and as quietly as she could, Rose shoved her way through the stands of prickly brambles and bristly scrub while legions of dark trees, limbs swaying low, clawed at her clothes and skin. She hadn't gone far when she reached a sharp drop. Below, in the moonlight, the waters of the river roiled on innocently enough. And for a moment, Rose wasn't a thief on the run. She was little Rosie MacGregor, big sister to Ellie Bug, and the river below was their secret fishing spot. There would be a "huge-mongus" tree whose long branch would stretch out over the water. And dangling from that branch would be the coarse rope she and Ellie Bug latched on to swing themselves out over the calm, plunging into the cool, deep murk amid unrestrained laughter.

Rose swatted a mosquito away from her ear. But those times were long gone, and the children of the Bachyritas might never know such innocent, carefree delights.

Swimming, like nearly every other endeavor, had to employ some element of pleasure. "All we are saying is give *piece* a chance!" was off-used expression. Nothing quite official, but certainly accepted. There was no reason to be embarrassed or ashamed about something so natural as sexual satisfaction. To "Make Love Not War"—which *was* one of the official slogans—was a beautiful thing.

The windows of the downtown department stores, which once had featured elaborate displays of animated skaters and Santas at Christmas time, had been redesigned to mimic the peaceful love-ins of still-revered writers and peace advocates John Lennon and Yoko Ono. Most people didn't really know a lot about the couple. The yellowed and peeling posters of what they did over a hundred years ago that lay plastered on abandoned storefronts or in alleyways all around the city did offer their images, but that was about all. What they had begun was far more important.

But people engaging in public pleasure was simply old hat, boring even, except for the few who engaged in the *bagism* ritual where the couple would enter either a black bag or a white one (if one of the parties was a true virgin). One by one, articles of clothing would be shed through the closing, dangled aloft almost theatrically before being dropped as the hand disappeared back inside. Unlike the couples who made love in the store windows, those employing bagism did offer the added feature of sound.

Self-reflection, self-actualization, self-satisfaction: Those were more watchwords of the renaissance. *Watchwords*. It always came down to the words. And choices.

Rose threw her hands to her face and felt her tears mixing with the scratches and grime. Maybe she had made the wrong choices and for the worst of reasons: selfishness. But she had told herself she wouldn't indulge her feelings just now. There would be time later. Later. There had to be a later.

Then Rose spotted the yellow glow of the torch.

"She's at the river!" someone shouted, unexpectedly and surprisingly close.

If her body heat had betrayed her before, the burning sensation she felt from the glasses case under her shirt was no doubt delivering her presence to the pit vipers this time. Their sounds could have all been a ruse to flush her out.

But as she glanced out at the waters below, Rose gripped more strongly the warm booty to her chest. A few hours ago, she'd determined this treasure was worth saving. And more. It was worth her life and Roddy's to get this to the Ungatosonrisas. They would know how best to use the treasure.

"She's ahead on the right. Less than a thousand feet."

"Get her!"

"I see her!" the Franklin shouted. "There!"

"We've got her now."

Taking only a few steps backward, Rose turned and broke into a run. Pulling the case close to her body, she sailed off the cliff, diving toward the dark water below.

"Think different!" she screamed into the night.

As the moonlit ink swallowed her whole, Rose thought of the color blue. Not black for death or white for baptism or even red for a fiery hell, but blue: the scrubbed denim of her father's workshirts, the crisp cold paleness of a winter morning's sky.

Roddy Bach-y-Rita's blue eyes.

On good days, Roddy called the pit vipers "Pop Rocks," after the candy that gave a fizzy, tingling sensation to the tongue. That was the same sensation the BrainPort® emitted when its helmet-held computer eye fixed on warm objects—its prey.

Roddy's chief beef with the entire movement was how it had besmirched his family's good name and his great-great-grandfather's honorable intentions by branding themselves "Bachyritas."

"They were the goddamned military. Soldiers!" He'd spit the last word. Roddy spit a lot in his screeds.

Yet like some ancient sage, he'd retell the same tale all over again, varying little except in the expletives he used.

Rose couldn't decide whether he played storyteller for her benefit, like a peacock with his feathers flaunted, or whether Roddy simply wanted to unleash his ire at the injustice done to him personally. He'd never asked to be born to such respected linage.

It didn't matter, because the telling was part of the fabric of who Rodman Bach-y-Rita was. Plus, anger made his blue eyes bluer. Like the searing cobalt in a flame.

They'd shared pleasure the first time following one of his tirades. For Rose, they used a white bag.

"They weren't even the *real* army," Roddy said. "Our *real* army was gone, mostly killed over all the oil crap during the Fifty-Year War."

"Bastards."

Roddy riveted his passionate blues on her.

"I didn't mean *our* guys were bastards, Roddy."

"You're tired of hearing this, aren't you?"

"No!"

"Yes, you are. You've become *complacent*."

"You're wrong. I'm as angry about what's happened as you are."

"You have no idea how friggin angry I am about anything. Was it your family that mucked it all up while selling everybody salvation? Hell in a handbasket . . . let's give peace a chance . . . fill in the blank . . ."

"Roddy, I—"

"Do you even have a family, Rose? Are you anybody's great-great-anything? You can't know what life is like for me. You can't have any friggin idea the generational burdens I carry. Sins of the great-great-grandfather . . ."

Every time Roddy turned on his heels, facing Rose, she flinched.

"Then who are the bastards, Rose? The stupid shits who perverted my great-great-grandfather's discovery and turned his good to evil? Why don't they call themselves the Lennon/Onos? No, they curse my family, curse me!"

Rose's head replayed known history: The Bachyritas had successfully put down an insurgency of foreign-born revolutionaries through primary employment of the guerilla device that allowed the army the shrewdness of "pit vipers." The signals of these "Brain-Ports®" were routed to soldiers' helmet-mounted cameras, allowing them to zero in on the enemy. Heat-sensitive signals were sent to a device on the soldiers' tongues as fizzy tingles, but their brains read the information as though they were "seeing." The one thing the rebelling Ungatosonrisas couldn't hide was the heat their bodies generated.

But Roddy told the story with more panache than the chronicles. That and his blue, blue eyes flashing angrily made the words worth hearing over and over again.

"Ole great-great-grandpa Paul was a neuroscientist at the University of Wisconsin. He explored brain plasticity as it relates to sensory substitution and brain-machine interfacing, in his search for a way to help the blind 'see.' Not a bad thing, huh? Anyway, his team—a *team,* Rose—routed camera images to different parts of volunteers' bodies. Trial and error, Rose. Basic shit. But what he found was that the tongue was more useful than tasting stuff like lemons, peppers, chocolate . . ."

Rose remained quiet as she rummaged through the papers stacked on her desk, scouring the photographs of paintings where the artists had added reading glasses of the famous to lend an air of scholarship and intelligence.

"Damned military." Roddy was making those grumbling sounds of his. "What could he have been thinking to have surrendered anything to them? He should have taken the BrainPort® and fallen down a hole somewhere. Gotten lost. Or given copies to the Ungatosonrisas. Leveled the playing field. Imagine that."

Rose perched two papers directly in front of her eyes and squinted at the images. One was a copy of Tommaso da Modena's painting of Cardinal Hugh of Provence seated at his desk, scribing away with rivet spectacles. At another desk on the other page by another artist sat a bespectacled St. Jerome. The latter was the patron saint of scholars and, in some quarters, the patron of glasses. Hadn't Roddy had her convinced that lying to the masses had been invented by the Bachyritas? Yet both the church men had lived and died before spectacles had come into use, and both works of art had been created a long time before Dr. Paul Bach-y-Rita had lived.

Rose tossed the papers back on her own desk and laughed. It was just a small chuckle, really, but enough to shake Roddy from his familial conundrum.

"You think this is all a joke, don't you?" Roddy's puffing face told Rose that no matter what she said right now, it would be the wrong thing. Roddy threw up his hands and lowered them in fists on her desk. "Dammit, Rose, you have no idea what it's like being a Bach-y-Rita."

"I'm one of the faithful, Roddy."

"Faithful? Faithful? What the hell does that mean?"

Rose backed against the nearest wall. When Roddy flew into one of his rants, it was useless to attempt reason; all she could do was try to avoid "accidentally" getting in the way of his flying hands.

He must have seen her fear, because Roddy chuffed and ha-rumped and then fed his explosion into his private office. It seemed the entire wall shook as he slammed the heavy wooden door. On the other side a few loud noises arose—books being thrown about, no doubt, or a chair in the way of his foot—and then there was quiet again.

Rose compressed herself against the wall a little harder until the familiar click of his lock broke the silence. It was only when she heard herself exhale that she realized she hadn't been breathing at all.

A month ago, when a bundle of historic spectacles had arrived, Roddy had gone ballistic over the haphazard way the specimens had been bundled. His airborne fist struck a bullseye on Rose's face.

She tried to contain the bleeding, but he'd broken her nose. Blood shot everywhere, drenching the papers on her desk and splattering several of the newly arrived spectacles she was to catalog and archive. The incident also caused her own brass frames to snap in the middle. Nobody fixed glasses. Few even wore them. If people had sight problems, they were either fitted with pleasure goggles for occasional use, left to squint, or offered a miracle surgery that gave them instant 20/20 vision. Only the perfect vision eventually dwindled to a horrible, painful blindness.

She'd managed to put off the required medical follow-up visits for her nose, returning to work just two days ago without a clearance. She was afraid the doctor might have strayed from her nose injury and decided to toss in a vision exam. That she couldn't risk. If anyone else found out her eyes were beginning to show their age, she'd be reassigned.

When Roddy had first caught her struggling to read a report, he seemed angry. He'd grabbed the box-cutting knife and aimed it at her only to slam it down at the last second, hacking into a newly arrived box, plucking out a pair of wire-rimmed glasses and placing them gently on her nose.

"Scared you at first, huh?" Roddy said.

"I hadn't cataloged those yet," Rose said.

"I know. I'm a bad boy, huh?" Roddy' s playful grins were nearly as magical as those eyes of his.

"But . . ."

"It doesn't matter, Rose. No one will ever know but us."

"But they're numbered. And they belonged to somebody famous."

"Ha! Famous? Who cares?" Then Roddy took the remainder of the box of glasses and tossed them all into the trash. "For some reason we catalog these spectacles. For some reason our jobs matter just now. But once we do all the research, checking the facts, comparing notes, examining the specimens, and entering it all down in our journals, then what?" Roddy's glower along with his fists set firmly on his hips told Rose he was truly expecting an answer from her.

"We . . . rebox the specimens, attaching the catalog number, and send them to the archives."

"Which are where?"

Rose gave that some thought. Was she supposed to know that? She'd never thought to ask.

Roddy removed her glasses, gusted a breath of fog on the lenses, then wiped them clean with the tail of his shirt. "My dear Rose . . ." He replaced the glasses on her face, adjusting them carefully. "There are no archives. Everything is destroyed once we finish with them. They think I don't know, but I do." His sarcastic laugh followed him all the way into his office.

Despite Roddy's unchecked brutality, he loved her. She knew he did. That's why he'd given her the glasses and hadn't told anyone about her failing eyesight. That's why she hadn't lost her job when the accident happened.

Roddy loved her. He was just afraid to let anyone into his miserable life. He was ashamed of what his family had done to society. If only he'd drop his own fear of truly sharing himself with her. Not inside some bag, but in one of the windows. Then people would know Roddy Bach-y-Rita and Rose MacGregor were making love and not war.

To the side of the stack of copies of artists' renderings of people wearing spectacles lay an official-looking paper. "From the Office of Rodman J. Bach-y-Rita," it said across the top. The page was a blanket woven with words, tiny words. The type he'd used for the single-page directive—whatever it was—had to have been no larger than nine points.

Straining to see, Rose made out: "Assistant Researcher Nancy Fleishman."

There had never been any other assistant as far as Rose knew.

Rose held the paper closer to the window, hoping to better discern the other words, only they were too small to make out. Holding the message directly under the lamp on her desk proved no better.

"Fleishman." Rose whispered the name as she sat down hard in the chair behind her desk. She knew that name well, but not a Nancy. Dr. *David* Fleishman was the most recognizable name in the study of spectacles. An esteemed former ophthalmologist, Fleishman had done the most exhaustive and extensive research and cataloging of eyewear ever. The stacks of papers on Rose's desk were copies of his work. Roddy nearly bowed every time the man's name was mentioned.

Rose's scrutiny of the paper blurred as her eyes refocused on the box of exhibits that had arrived the day of her accident. It sat wedged between several other boxes beneath one of the windows. Rose recognized it because of the dark stains left from her splattered blood.

Nancy, if she was some new assistant, obviously had not cataloged its contents.

Without moving her head, Rose flashed a look at Roddy's closed door and listened intently. Once he went inside his little sanctuary, he rarely popped out without her first being able to hear the click from his unlocking the door.

She kept her back to the door as she opened the box. Inside were the pitifully wrapped specimens. Several cases were marked with numbers only or had documents wrapped around them and secured with rubber bands. Just one had an aged and curling label attached to it, though a large #9 had been painted in red on the end of the case.

Rose shoved aside the rest and opened #9. They weren't metal-rimmed as she had expected. So many glasses that had survived from the era marked on the outside of the box—the 1970s and 80s—were like that. Styles had always varied through the ages, but some were more readily recognizable than others. The ancient Trig Lane and Swan Stairs with frames of bone, wood, metal and leather.

Roddy taught her all about the historical significance along with the minute details. He'd told her how spectacles evolved with class needs. The invention of the printing press begat books and newspapers and nudged the entrepreneurial elements as more people jumped on the bus, and the use of spectacles grew so common that baskets of them would be available at merchants, and people would simply rummage through them until they found what suited them best.

In the latter part of the Twentieth Century, glasses shifted from signaling the brainy people to recognizing the trendy. Though the well-known image of John Lennon from the peeling posters did depict him wearing glasses, it was Roddy who had made Rose truly understand that Lennon's "granny" style of wire frames had began its own revolution. Simply put, Lennon made it *cool* to wear glasses.

Though he didn't rant while talking about spectacles, he could go on and on. It was his first love, his passion.

Standing with the case in her hand and wearing the round-lens glasses that had been inside, Rose was able to make out the name on the faded label on exhibit #9: John Lennon.

She wasn't sure whether the tingles she felt all over her body were more fear or awe, but tingle she did. Unlike the pleasure goggles, which flashed "For the protection of all," what zipped through Rose's mind were the words from the ragged Lennon-Ono posters: "Think Different."

Think different. Think different.

Think . . . Nancy Fleishman.

John Lennon's old glasses were hardly perfect for Rose. His vision was obviously much worse than hers, but when she adjusted them a bit, the words on Roddy's official paper became very clear: Nancy Fleishman would be replacing Rose. Not because of Rose's failing eyesight or the accident or anything else.

"Due to the horrible accidental death of Rose Gregory, I am in need of another assistant. It was quite a moment of good fortune when I discovered Dr. David Fleishman's great-great-granddaughter had also been working in this field. I have arranged for her to begin as soon as she can make arrangements.

"The committee should also be advised that the archived spectacles are now ready to be auctioned to highest bidders."

Rose collapsed in a heap in the soft chair near the window in shock, the paper's words so hot in her hand that she dropped it to the floor.

She was dead, and Roddy hadn't even gotten her last name right. But she wasn't dead . . .

During her down time, she'd tried to wrestle with what her life meant. She'd walked the boulevards, noting the neatly trimmed lawns and thoughtfully planted trees. Yes, there was a pattern to the streets. And an eerie emptiness she hadn't had time or opportunity to notice before. Where were the children playing unabashedly in the yards? And bicycling gaggles of boys, fishing poles perched under scabbed arms with faithful tongue-dangling mutts running beside? And where were the young women with painted faces, strolling the boulevard as they shopped, sharing their banter about burgeoning careers and hopeful suitors? And the babbling and dowdy old men scraping their canes against the dry concrete sidewalks . . . where had they all disappeared to?

There were people on the streets and in the parks, mostly men and women in various uniforms, each keeping to himself or herself, making notes on hand-held units or engaged in some bagism ritual, which didn't always involve a second party in the bag.

The small light from her desk was the sole illumination when the lock finally clicked. Roddy's entrance into the room was his usual bold advance until he saw Rose wasn't at her desk. The hand behind his back clutched a box-cutter.

"It's *MacGregor*, Roddy. Rose MacGregor."

When Roddy turned to face her, his amazing blue eyes opened almost as wide as his mouth. "What the . . ."

Rose didn't know how many times she stabbed Roddy with the knife they also used to slit open the boxes, but she did note his blood splattered just like hers over the boxes, papers, and desk. "Give piece a chance, Roddy. Think different."

After a few gurgling gasps, Roddy's deep blue eyes froze in a stare at something far away, past Rose, past Roddy's terrible burdens.

A heady whiff of meat roasting and the crackling of a campfire confused Rose when she opened her eyes. "Ellie Bug?"

"Buenos días, Señorita." The man's face seemed to be more large white teeth than anything else, though his dark eyes actually glowed, reflecting the nearby fire. "Tu hables Español?"

Behind the man stood more people, all with darker skin than Rose's and all with straight black hair. Their garb was rough and simple, but of sturdy, coarse fabric.

"If you do not speak our language, we do speak yours." Strange how he could continue smiling even when he spoke.

"Are you the Ungatosonrisas?"

"You are Bachyrita, no? But one the *serpientes* seek."

Rose nodded.

"What have you done that the serpientes would chase you with *antorchas*? We could see them coming for a long time."

When Rose sat up quickly, her head boomed its disagreement with being upright.

"You jumped, Señorita. Did you mean to do that? The water here is not that deep. This is not Acapulco." This time when the man laughed, several others joined him.

As Rose rubbed her head, she fought to remember everything that had happened and why she had wanted to find the Ungatosonrisas. Roddy's last look flitted through her mind just before she remembered her precious cargo. She reached inside her shirt for the case with John Lennon's glasses. It wasn't there.

"This is what you now search for?" The man held out the case, which, though wet, looked no worse for its moonlight bath in the river.

Though the man's smile remained, his eyes were less friendly. Gently he handed her the case. No tricks, no resistance.

"Why are you still fighting the Bachyritas?" Rose asked.

"Who said we were?"

"Everybody knows you are."

"Everybody?" The man sat down hard on the ground neat to Rose. He sighed deeply as though he were exhaling a breath for thousands of decades.

"Why would the pit vipers, the serpientes, need to continue to exist if there weren't still resistance to the Bachyrita way? You're the resistance."

"They were not hunting any of us with BrainPorts® and antorchas."

Boldly, Rose foisted the glasses case out to the man. "This. They want this."

The man opened the case, unfolded the glasses as he examined them closely. "A pair of glasses? It has come to this where *espectáculos* are forbidden?"

"No, but not everyone can afford them. These aren't ordinary glasses, though. They're special."

"Mágico?" The man's Cheshire Cat grin had faded into a puzzled look.

"No, not magical. Real. Before I looked through them, I believed the lies of the Bachyritas. I believed my life was happy and full. I believed peace was the absence of war. But after I put these on, I saw the truth."

"Verdad?"

"Yes."

All of the others handled John Lennon's glasses, holding them every which way, getting a better look near the fire. Rose, still a bit disconcerted from all that had happened, retrieved the glasses, blew a puff of steam on the lenses, and then set them on the man's nose. "See for yourself, Señor. See the truth. Think different."

After all of the Ungatosonrisas tried wearing John Lennon's spectacles, the man returned them to the case. He handed it back to Rose. "We did not see this mágico, Señorita. Maybe it works for you only." His smile had faded fully away.

"Then you were trying to see through them. Lennon never did that. He imagined peace despite what he saw through his eyes, through his glasses." Rose handed the man the glasses again. "Look again. Imagine peace. Real peace. The Bachyritas can see with their eyes and their tongues, and yet they see nothing."

Once more the man sat down, facing the open space just beyond the camp where the sky had begun turning a hopeful blue. Soon the sun would rise again. Soon it would be another day with all its possibilities.

"Imagine . . ." Rose whispered in his ear. "Imagine."

CURSORY REVIEW

Donald J. Bingle

Kim Wasserman's eyes scanned the neatly hung and folded clothes in the master bedroom closet. Two months of Jenny Craig® meals, and she was about to show off the sizzling results at the DeMarco's annual Fourth of July barbecue.

"C'mon, Kimbo, we're going to be late," called her husband, Ken, who, as usual, was twitching to leave when she had barely even started getting ready.

She rolled her eyes and smiled. "You know, you're going to call me Kimbo in public some day, and then I will have to kill you." She headed toward the back of the closet, where she had hidden all of her favorite outfits that had no longer fit back when her weight had started creeping up. "Just because you don't care about your appearance doesn't mean I don't have to take a few minutes to get ready."

Ahh, there were those cute jeans she had gotten at that adorable little shop in San Juan on their honeymoon. They'd been a bit snug, but she had bought them anyway. She'd never worn them. She had gotten them when she was at her wedding weight, fifteen pounds below her high-weight mark. Now she was twenty-two and a half pounds lighter than her high, thanks to Jenny. Seven and a half pounds below her wedding weight. The jeans, with their colorful, intricately embroidered pockets and cuffs, would be perfect for the barbecue.

She grabbed the jeans and headed out into the bedroom. Ken was waiting with arms crossed, his head tilted to the right, chin down, eyebrows raised. He unfolded his arms and tapped his watch. "No, still working," he mumbled.

Kim tried to give him a stern look, but a mischievous grin crept through. "I'll be ready before you are," she declared, continuing before he could protest, "because there is no way in Hell you are wearing that Hawaiian shirt."

Ken dropped his arms and sighed. "Yes, ma'am."

Kim quickly slipped on a white, peasant-style blouse and stepped into her jeans. They didn't slip on as easily as she had expected. She tugged at the waistband and sucked in her now smaller tummy, not that it really made a difference for the hip-huggers. Finally, she got the pants pulled up and the zipper closed. Tight jeans were fashionable, but she felt like a boa constrictor was swallowing her.

Ken stepped out of the closet with a clean rugby shirt on. "Do these jeans look too tight to you?" Kim asked, her mouth in a frown.

Ken froze, his eyes darting down and up her figure and then up and to the right, searching the heavens for the right answer, if there possibly could be a right answer to such spousal inquiries.

"Uh . . . er . . . m-m-my wife is right," he stammered.

She pursed her lips and gave him an icy glare. "Nice try, bucko. Now, what's the real answer?" She folded her arms and thrust her hip to one side to await his answer, when the button holding the jeans closed popped, bouncing along the floor and under the bed.

Damn it. She was down twenty-two and a half pounds. How could the jeans not fit? Ken better not have been monkeying with the bathroom scale . . .

*   *   *

Grznarb snarled, his yellowed fangs dripping sulphuric saliva onto the institutional, metal desktop.

"I transfer you in from another department to head up the *Cursed Clothing and Frivolous Fashion Accessories Division* and this is what I get? Something that could be accomplished with a 3-for-1 sale on Häagen Dazs or accidentally washing the jeans in hot water?"

Threkma was sweating profusely, and it wasn't just from the typically infernal heat. His horn-nubs glowed red from embarrassment and stress. "No, no, your Unholy Toadliness. It's not just that the pants have shrunk or the woman has not lost weight. The jeans are cursed. No matter who tries them on or when or where, they will always be just one size too small. It's actually a variation of the cursed camera gambit, the one which automatically adds a double-chin and twenty pounds to everyone in the picture, back from when I worked in the *Cursed Electronics and Other Incomprehensible Technology Division.*"

"Fah!" yelled Grznarb, a bit of Hellfire bursting forth from his mouth and singeing off Threkma's eyelashes. Grznarb had always found singed eyelashes to be a particularly effective management technique. He couldn't imagine how humans had never stumbled upon it. "And what does this cursed clothing get us? Mild aggravation on the part of the would-be wearer?" He knew his saliva was still steaming from the burst of Hellfire, distracting the underling, but he liked his minions terrified and confused, especially during their performance reviews.

"M-m-much more than that, sir. Diet failure, or at least perceived diet failure, can lead to bingeing. I think gluttony is the classic word, your Pus-Filled Putrescence."

"Gluttony!" roared Grznarb, a glob of still steaming saliva spewing forth onto the desktop and starting to eat away at the tally sheets and memoranda, then the metal beneath. "What kind of penny-ante curse-works are you running here? Your latest curse produces occasional gluttony? Who in Hell cares? As if gluttony wasn't endemic in human population anyway!"

Threkma swallowed hard. "More than that, your Unclean Maggotness. The cursed jeans can lead to domestic quarrels, displaced anger, depression, and, in a small number of cases, suicide. That's a mortal sin, there, your Vomitous Abomination. A mortal sin."

Grznarb snarled. "Even the little black dress thing was better than this."

Threkma straightened his thrice-broken spine at Grznarb's words. "The little black dress of infidelity did have some good results."

"Fah. You have been spending too much time around humans. Your speech offends me and not in a good way. Call the thing by its true name."

Threkma's spine began to curl, the previously broken vertebrae grinding against each other with excruciating pain. "The micro-mini of sluttishness, you mean, your Diseased Ferretbreathness?"

"Yes," grumbled Grznarb, "but even it had limited effectiveness. The problem with cursed clothing is that the curse begins to fade too quickly when you take it off. Extended foreplay can lead to second thoughts. That's a real structural dilemma in dealing with fornication fabrics."

"Still," squeaked Threkma, "we did have that high profile political success with the little blue dress variant made out of fellatio fabric . . ."

"Fah! You can't rest on old successes for eternity." Grznarb nested his pointed chin in his scabby hand, letting a talon hover just a millimeter from his own eyeball, just to unnerve his unworthy subordinate. "What we need is something people wear every day, like the old eyeglasses of impure thoughts. Why aren't we making them anymore?"

Threkma trembled. "People switched to contacts, so we had to miniaturize and increase the potency of the cursed material. Then the humans switched to disposable contacts, creating a black hole in our supply and production budgets. Lately, they've started flocking to laser eye surgery. We rigged a few of the lasers to malfunction and boil the insides of the eyes 'til they exploded, you know, just to try to buck the trend, but the whole subgroup has completely fallen apart, your Metastasizing Worminess."

"So, just what are you doing?" demanded Grznarb. "You keep requesting more and more of Hell's powers of damnation for your department, but I'm just not convinced it's being used well. The Dark One's power to curse is finite, you know. Not like the infinite blessings of our . . . competitor."

"Yes, your Festering Warthogness, but curses do last forever, so the total damnation in the world increases at all times. That should please you and The Horned Slayer."

Grznarb tapped his talon on his eyeball lightly, causing a yellow trail of bubbling ichor to ooze out and eat through the scabs on his cheek. "The total damnation increases, but so does the population. Besides, these fabric curses are especially problematic. The power of the curse dissipates as the item wears, fiber by fiber, leaving the item ultimately ineffective and a level of damnation in most lint filters that swallows errant socks whole."

The sock-less Threkma did not respond to the revelation of the answer to one of life's great mysteries, so Grznarb continued. "That's why hard items work the best—the curse can last for centuries, undissipated, especially with gems and gold. Why aren't we using our limited power of damnation for the old classics, like the cursed sword that damages whoever the wielder loves most in all the world equal to the damage inflicted by the sword in battle? Death to kings and comrades, wives and wenches. Now, there was a good time."

Threkma shuffled his feet, the claws clacking audibly on the rough stone floor. "Although occasionally used as fashion accessories, swords are really in the

Cursed Weapons and Things That Blow Up Real Good Division, your Oozing Snotfaceness. In that vein, we did produce some wedding rings (in contemporary styles in both gold and platinum) of infidelity . . . er . . . sluttishness. Cursed diamonds really are forever, your Drooling Hideousness. But the humans took the damned rings off whenever the urge to be promiscuous took hold, generally well in advance of removing their clothes to rut. The rings were, accordingly, no more effective than the fornication fabrics and matching fetish footwear."

Grznarb snarled.

Threkma blathered on. "Wedding rings of shrewishness and wife-beating have been much more successful in eliciting the behavior sought to be induced."

Grznarb's snarl turned into a full-throated roar, sending a glob of glowing phlegm onto Threkma's foot. The minion endured the pain as it melted through to the floor. "Then why aren't we producing more of those?"

"Unfortunately, the effectiveness is high, but the overall duration tends to be short, failing to justify the expenditure of curse power needed to infuse the precious metal. Women's shelters, high divorce rates, and increasingly effective law enforcement in the area of domestic violence have all been an issue. And, once the ring is removed, whether because of divorce or incarceration, it is essentially a wasted curse. No one passes down family heirlooms anymore. High precious metal prices have resulted in the rings being melted down and the power of the curse diluted and spread across newly manufactured jewelry and electrical components, leading to hardware freeze-ups in most major computer brands and a general low-level of irritation across the population, but no more."

Grznarb picked his nose with his tongue. "So, jewelry no longer is effective?"

Threkma brightened a bit, whether from the question or because the glob that had been on his foot had finally eaten its way deep into the stone floor. "We have had some success with bling."

"Bling?" Grznarb hated human slang.

"Heavy, gaudy necklaces and rings worn by youthful enthusiasts of hip-hop music."

Grznarb tapped his foot on the stone floor. "Get on with it. What sin is this 'bling' cursed with?"

Threkma smiled weakly. "It was meant to increase the popularity of the . . . er . . . singers."

Grznarb's brow furrowed. Threkma rushed on. "The so-called music is truly horrendous to hear, your Decomposing Vileness. It was hoped that insanity and mass suicide would result."

"And did it?"

"No. We did achieve some midlevel chaos and sin, however." Threkma didn't look at Grznarb as he continued sheepishly. "Moderate hearing loss and theft of digital music."

Grznarb thrust two razor-sharp talons into the nostrils of the minion and hefted him off his feet, blood flowing down Grznarb's scarred and scaly arm as the talons bit deep. "There is something you are not telling me. You are not the Prince of Lies! You, underling, cannot fool me."

"There was a production error," gasped Threkma with a nasal gurgle from Grznarb's talons and the blood flowing down the back of his throat.

Grznarb twisted his hand. "Yes?"

"Instead of cursing the bling, the bling causes the wearer to curse. It's . . . it's proven quite effective at that. Hip-hop music is full of emphatic and descriptive cursing of all types, including all known and several unidentified forms of damnation and graphic representations of all bodily functions. And a sin is a sin, your Cancerous Moldiness."

Grznarb flung Threkma down into the minion's desk chair. "Have you nothing else?"

"Just the usual. Post Office uniforms with the curse of rage, Mont Blanc® pens cursed with arrogance, pretension, and condescension, adult diapers cursed with incontinence, and candy striper uniforms cursed with kleptomania and/or nymphomania. We did some cigarette lighters of pyromania, but everyone uses disposables now, so fireballs have declined noticeably." Threkma seemed to tense for a more localized fireball and the resulting incineration that he, no doubt, thought was coming.

Instead, Grznarb shook his head. Lice and sloughed skin spattered to either side. "When I brought you from the *Cursed Furniture and Decorative Lawn Ornament Division*, I thought you would shake things up here, Threkma. The cursed couch of false confession you placed in psychotherapists' offices really caught my good eye. And using the skin of Chinese dissidents to upholster it was an especially loathsome touch. Lots of guilt, a steady stream of suicides, some sprees of murderous mayhem, and trafficking in human parts sewn together in sweat shops by slave labor. All evil work."

Threkma managed a half-smirk of pride and self-satisfaction as Grznarb continued. "Of course, the straight-back institutional chair of false confession placed into police interrogation rooms was the big highlight of your stay. Anger, guilt, depression, false witness, suicide . . . the list of sin is infinite."

Grznarb approached the minion, looming over him. "Your stay here in The Lower Realms is infinite, but your job-security is not. One four-letter word from me and you could be chewed for all eternity by an Arch-Demon with breath that makes mine smell like peppermint schnapps."

Threkma quaked in fear, or maybe it was just another of the aftershocks of Beelzebub's Fall from Grace.

Grznarb jabbed the damned bureaucrat in the chest with a bloody talon. "Tell me what you were going to use this latest allocation of eternal damnation to curse now, right now. And it had better be good. I want a cursed wearable that has enormous impact but does not wear out and get tossed in a box for Goodwill. Something that passes from generation to generation. Something insidious. Something delicious. And by delicious, I mean truly evil."

Threkma made no attempt to stem the bleeding that now flowed from both his snout and his chest, as he replied. "I did find an old recipe, almost a half-century since its last use. It has a tremendous impact not only on the wearer but also on his victims, the victims' extended families for generations to come, and on the misguidedly faithful."

"Why haven't you produced these to date?"

"They take an incredible amount of evil, your Rancid Hatefulness. They have to ward off constant blessings and that is not easy."

Father Breen returned to his room once most of the parishioners had left. He took off the stole that lay across his shoulders, kissed it, and placed it reverently on his desk. He sat down at the same desk with a weary slump and put his face in his hands. When he had first been called, he had been counseled by the monks who had trained him that celibacy was no easy task but that he must put his mind and his energies to holy work instead. So many years had passed since that day, and his normal sexual urgings had lessened with each passing year. He had performed well in his duties and had moved up the church hierarchy. Celibacy was no longer a struggle. His sexual feelings were a faint and distant memory.

But lately, since his promotion and transfer, he had felt new, disturbing, urgings. Urgings that excited him one moment and horrified him just a few hours later. Urgings he could not understand and could not tell anyone about, lest all his good work be destroyed. As he stroked the brocaded symbols of his stole, passed to him by his predecessor at St. Basil's and his predecessor before that, he thought of what he should do.

He got up, kissed the stole, muttering a quick blessing, and draped it once again across his shoulders. It was time to meet with the new altar boy.

As he left his room, he no longer thought about what he should do, but he knew what he would do.

He smiled.

Somewhere in the firepits of Hell, Grznarb smiled, too. "A pleasing result, but expensive and, of course, not your recipe," rumbled the demon to Threkma.

Threkma quavered and lowered his eyes, but he spoke in a rush of words. "No, it's not. I mean, yes, it's not, your Coagulating Rottenness. But, it gave me an idea. Perverted symbols of allegiance. Not really jewelry, but tokens of membership or belief that are worn every day. Little gold crosses of cruelty, for example."

"Fah," snorted Grznarb, "you focus only on the faithful. Blessing resistance will need to be built-in at extra cost. Besides, The Dark Angel requires a broad spectrum of sinners. Each and every soul should have an equal opportunity to damn itself for all eternity."

Threkma's eyes darted from side to side. "Not crosses," he murmured, no doubt stalling for time. "Been done before, anyway," he blathered on, punctuating his words with a cracking, maniacal giggle. "Although both the Crusades and the Spanish Inquisition did have their moments. No, your Regurgitated Sliminess, but perhaps nonreligious icons. We can pervert all of their symbols against them."

An excellent suggestion. But Grznarb was an excellent manager. He knew that he had to make his underling sweat just a bit more. "Symbols of allegiance? This is not the Middle Ages, my misguided minion. Heraldry is no longer in style." He curled his lips in a faux grimace.

"Modern symbols," insisted Threkma, "Frat pins of homophobia, perhaps."

"Too narrow a base," growled Grznarb, making a mental note of the suggestion.

"Union pins of racism," proffered Threkma, obviously desperate to please his taskmaster.

"Declining union membership," replied Grznarb, secretly pleased at his servant's creativity.

"Corporate logos of greed . . ."

"Nobody publicly identifies with their employer these days."

"American flag lapel pins of intolerance and warmongering . . ." shouted Threkma, in revelation.

Grznarb roared in laughter, unintentional Hellfire incinerating the office desk, the straight-backed chair, and his erstwhile employee.

"How do you think *I* got this job?" he mumbled to himself as he strode off to the pits to find a damned replacement.

JACK'S MANTLE

Joe Masdon

Bob was miserable. The kids were away for the day with Brenda's mother, and her idea of quality time with her husband involved book fairs and consignment stores. She had been smiling all day, and he irritably began to wonder if part of her smile came from the knowledge that she was driving him violently insane. The novelty of morning romance had been good, but that had been the only ten minutes that he had enjoyed of the past three hours. Enjoyed? Tolerated. Ten minutes of routine, passionless sex with his wife was way too little payment for a day filled with flea markets and pottery shops.

She despises me.

As they entered crap-for-sale shop no. 5, she smiled blissfully at him as if they were part of some happy cruise ship commercial. His weary half-smile as he held the door didn't slow her down. She hurried into the shop purposefully, cooing about some sugar bowl she'd noticed as they entered. Clearly the sex was better for her than it was for him to keep her in this gooey-eyed mood all morning.

God, I hate her.

Fifteen minutes later, Bob wasn't sure where Brenda was in the store, and he didn't much care as long as it was away from him. He was ambling care-

lessly down a few aisles, looking spitefully at the junk
that stuffed the store claustrophobically. It was a big
store, and shelves and clothing racks went from floor
to ceiling. He had been stomping around angrily, but
misery took a lot of effort to maintain, particularly
when it was really just exaggerated boredom.

After a while he found himself looking lazily
through the men's coats. For some reason, there
seemed to be more men's coats here than just about
anything else. They were too tightly packed to actually
move the hangers, but he fingered the fabric and
pushed a few coats a half-inch or so, pretending that
it gave him a better view of the merchandise. Amid
the tightly bunched rows of shoulders and sleeves he
would occasionally pull out a coat that he would
vaguely reject and be unable to squeeze back into the
rack. He left a trail of protruding half-coats and limp
sleeves dangling into the narrow aisle.

Almost buried under the faded shoulder of a baby
blue Members Only jacket and a stained London Fog
trench coat was a garment that caught Bob's eye. He
jammed his hand in and felt something rough and
woolen. He pulled on the hanger once, twice, and
slowly pried the long black overcoat into view. Bob
noted that the black overcoat had one of those
peculiar-looking capes attached to it. It was worn
thin in a lot of places, and even though it was bulky,
it seemed a little narrow for him. More for amusement than for any serious intent, Bob looked for a
size tag in the collar. There was no tag or label of
any kind. It occurred to him that the overcoat was
probably so old that all of the tags had frayed away.
It looked like one of those things that got donated
to community theaters and showed up in everything
from Victorian England costumes to WWII Ameri-
cana musicals.

Feeling theatrical, Bob pulled the ratty old overcoat
off its hanger. Smiling at his silly impulse, he twirled
it over his head and wedged his arms into the sleeves.

He expected the shoulders to be narrow as he pulled his arms to his sides, but the coat slipped down very comfortably. The smell wasn't that bad, but it could use a dry cleaning, he thought. The waist was in fact a bit tight, but the sleeves were close enough, and the shoulders felt good. He had planned to lose some weight anyway, so he sucked in his gut and buttoned it halfway. At the end of his sleeve, he felt the tickle of the cardboard price tag against his thumb. Catching the dangling tag, he glanced at the faded yellow sticker and nodded at the odd price of $18.88.

He decided that the cape part was stylish and gave him an international look He slid his hands down the sides of the coat looking for pockets, missed, tried again, missed again, then feeling around finally realized that there were no pockets on the outside. Bob was a bit deflated. No pockets . . . a deal breaker. He smiled disappointedly and prepared to return the overcoat to menswear limbo.

"What on earth are you wearing?" the voice was a mixture of amusement and reproach.

God, NOW she appears.

Holding out his arms, he turned toward his wife without looking, "You like it? I think it's kind of neat."

Sighing gently and shaking her head, Brenda raised her chin as she spoke, "I'm sure it is. I'm done. Sorry I took so long. Come on, put that back on the rack and we're out of here, I promise."

A command wrapped in an apology. Nice.

His breath shortened, and his lips tightened slightly. Bob did not look at his wife. "Winter's coming. I could use a new coat."

Her mind already jumping to the next location, Brenda offered, "Okay, let's go to the coat outlet and find you something. I'm glad you mentioned it; I can look for a raincoat for David while we're there. He's outgrown the one from last year."

* * *

Bob pulled a hatchet out of his pocket and slammed it into his wife's skull. This time it only took one chop to shut her up.

Without a word, Bob picked up his old coat and the hanger and walked sideways down the aisle toward his wife.

"Honey, what are you . . . ?" Brenda sighed in minor annoyance as her husband brushed past her and up to the checkout counter. He held out the price tag at the end of his sleeve for the clerk. He turned to his wife and noted the silver soup ladle and the commemorative RC Cola bottle in her hands with the yellow tags still on them. "You said you were done . . . ?"

Plus the 6% sales tax, his black wool overcoat cape came to $20.01. The clerk called it $20 even.

Despite her misgivings about the ratty-looking old overcoat, Brenda had dutifully taken it in to be dry cleaned that week. She didn't want the musty odor lingering in the closet, so she tossed it in with Bob's work shirts and her dress suits. She resolved to get it cleaned as often as possible under the guise of showing concern for this thing that obviously meant so much to Bob. Her real hope was that it would fall apart under the cleanings.

It was Sunday evening, and they had just gotten home from visiting relatives. It had been a good day, and when Brenda had indicated that she did not feel like cooking, Bob suggested Mexican. Bob sat in the booth across from his wife and eight-year-old son. His teenage daughter sat next to him pretending that her parents and brother were strangers who had the audacity to sit at her table without asking. Autumn weather had come early that year, with lots of chilly wind.

To Brenda's surprise, the old overcoat cape had not really drawn that much attention and it really didn't look any worse than the denim jacket with the phar-

maceutical company logo that her husband wore all
too often. Bob had long ago learned not to ask his
daughter to put his jackets on the inside of the booth
next to her or, for that matter, to make any effort on
his behalf. So he sat there wearing it, leaning over his
plate when crunching salsa and chips. Bob eschewed
his usual enchilada and beans and ordered the low-
carb fajitas. The good mood of the day was still in full
swing as Bob and Brenda laughed along with their
children.

A dozen girls walked in the restaurant, chattering.
Facing the door, Bob saw them as they came in, and
he tried very hard to look without being obvious.
From the distance, they all seemed to be varieties of
beautiful. His eyes lingered a few extra seconds at the
moving jumble of firm young body parts that strained
against T-shirts inside half-opened jackets and hips
that curved into tight buttocks. With the practiced restraint of the middle-aged voyeur, he managed to suppress the words, "Oh, good God . . ." even though
his lips still went through the motions.

Dear God, just tell me they aren't high-schoolers.

There was the brief thought that looking at such
young girls was revolting, or at least illegal, if they
were underage. But the firm, full bodies still waved
unabashedly at him from the edge of his vision. Besides, if they were in college, it was probably only
revolting, not illegal. Yes, had to be college. Bob decided that a group of high school girls would not be
out at a restaurant on a Sunday evening; they were
probably from the private college down the street.

Bob noticed a couple of waiters quickly pulling tables together, and the dozen or so little packets of
young female body parts were being led to them. The
tables were off to his right, and behind Brenda's field
of vision, so Bob took a moment to give the female
buffet a closer look. They were all attractive in that
young way, and one or two made a definite impression. None of the girls actually giggled, and Bob recog-

nized the casual, yet restrained, social dynamic of the college sorority in action.

He was disappointed to see that a few of the girls were wearing those blue jeans that squeeze a woman's hips too low so that her bottom looks more narrow and boyish. But those same jeans that were so annoying from the back rode low in the front, providing a sample glimpse of tender, tanned stomach flesh. Jackets were being stripped off and hung on the backs of chairs. Bob spent a few too many seconds watching that particular spectacle, unable to look away. Round breasts shifted and heaved as arms and shoulders wriggled out of jackets. A couple of the T-shirts were tight enough that letters and logos across the front were hidden underneath curves that were far too perfect to be real, Bob thought.

He stifled a small groan by vigorously crunching into a chip he had been absently holding. Back to reality for the briefest of moments, he stole a glance toward Brenda and was relieved to see that she was fully occupied with trying to get a civil response from their daughter to some question or comment.

Careless. Don't stare directly at it, moron.

Bob's dinner arrived in a steaming cloud of sizzling red meat, onions, and peppers. Young David was impressed with his father's loud meal, and for a few minutes Bob played with his food and his laughing son. When he finally glanced back toward the table of sorority girls, they had settled into their seats, and his view was mostly limited to the two girls on the end. One was wearing a blue blouse that hinted at money in her family. The blouse did not hug her body, so Bob had to settle for what entertainment he could derive from her face and hair. She was dark blond, with a sexy face that needed the help that her makeup gave it. Sure, she was pretty, but her eyes were a little too small for her face, and her nose was a little crooked. She tried to make her eyes look bigger by wearing too much eyeliner.

She spoke with confidence, and the others were quiet when she talked. The other girl on the end was tall and slim, with frosted blonde hair that framed a pixie-like face of doe eyes, a pert nose, and lips that stayed slightly open. She wore too-tight T-shirt and jeans. Bob noticed that she seemed to have very large breasts, but it was hard to be sure because she sat with her arms in front of her, and she leaned slightly toward the table. She was quiet, and her meal was very simple, and, Bob could tell, inexpensive.

He stole glances off and on during the meal, and he caught her a few times with her arms away from her body. Her breasts looked large and perfect, which Bob concluded was probably due more to bra than to nature. He mentally downgraded her beauty, chalking it up to technology in women's underwear. He shook his head at his own foolishness for ogling a padded bra inside a T-shirt. Then a hint of shame kicked in. She was a little girl who was insecure and self-conscious and was beautiful, but far from a sexual fantasy for a respectable, middle-aged family man.

This is a new low, even for you.

For a while, he made a conscious effort to avoid looking at the girls half his age. Then he stole another glance.

The frosted-haired beauty on the end sat quietly on the fringe, submissively listening to the other girls while half of the chicken quesadilla grew cold on her plate. She had leaned back in her chair and stretched her legs until her body was almost straight under the table. Her thumbs were in her pockets, pulling the waist of her jeans low against her stomach, and her T-shirt rode up a little more showing about an inch of tanned stomach.

Bob could see soft ripples of firm female muscles that no specially designed lingerie could fake. His breath quickened as his gaze lingered on her. She laughed slightly at something that one of the others said. Her stomach tightened as she leaned forward, and the softer parts of her body moved gently along with her laugh, dispelling any criticisms.

His breathing got shallow.

He imagined feeling her narrow shoulders in his hands.

He touched the warm, smooth flesh of her arms under his fingertips. She held her wrists above her head, making her body even leaner and firmer. Her head turned slightly to the left, eyes looking away. Her body quivered as he ran his hands back up her arms and across the hollow of her neck, down between her breasts and along the amazing line of her stomach. Stopping at her stomach, he could feel her flesh tingle in anticipation. Her body tensed as his finger again cut a teasing line from her neck down her rigid, muscular stomach. She groaned and started to protest.

The shy, needful little slut.

He raised his hand back between her breasts, and his finger swept slowly to the right, under the soft, yielding flesh, tracing the muscles of her rib. His finger returned to caress the rib.

She awaited his masterful touch, like the good little whore she is.

Growing bolder, he set his finger tracing along her left hipbone, starting at the center and moving away as a tease. Then he traced the right. She was ready for him, he knew. He could feel the heat of her body. He reached down her smooth, tanned legs. He was poised above her now as she gasped in pain. He reached down to her warm, wet body and gently pulled the intestines aside so they would not obstruct his view. His hands retraced her remarkable stomach muscles again; then he wrapped both hands around her stomach, cradling it as he lovingly pulled it from her.

There was something wrong, he realized. Looking at her firm, beautiful body, he saw that his finger had been too sharp and too insistent. He had stabbed her tender stomach into raw strips. As he stood there feeling the warm, dripping flesh in his hands, he saw strips of partially eaten meat spilling from her stomach. Blood covered his hands and clothes, dripping on his suit and overcoat, down to his shoes. Where the blood dripped on his jacket, it disappeared into the fabric.

His pulse quickened, and his head began to spin. He saw the frost-haired beauty beneath him, the smooth, tanned skin of her torso peeled back to reveal the warm, wet, bloody organs glistening under her mutilated flesh.

Bob's eyes were glassy and blinking, and his chest began to heave. His breath was coming in shallow bursts, and he began to twitch in the seat.

"Bob?" Brenda noticed his distress, and dread began to creep up on her.

Bob's breathing became more urgent. He felt a pain under his left armpit, and he could smell the awful taste of seared flesh and stomach acid. He started at the sound of his name, and he heard a small cry of fear. He shook his head hard, and the image that filled his vision was of a woman's face. In his hands was a stomach, still dripping blood, acid, and strips of seared flesh, red peppers, and brown onions, uneaten on his festive plate. He pushed back from the table and away from the plate of steak and peppers.

Then he felt a horrifying pressure against his pants. He felt his bile rising, even as other fluids worked for release. With the odor of acid, bloody flesh, peppers and onions screaming in his head, he jumped up from the table and stumbled toward the door. With just enough presence of mind, he pulled the caped overcoat closed in front as he bent over and staggered crookedly for escape.

Outside the restaurant, he fell to his knees in a patch of grass and vomited. Between heaves, he prayed to a god he did not believe in to take away the painful, intolerable erection.

What the hell is happening to me?

Brenda fell to the ground beside her vomiting husband and put her arm around him. She was shaking in fear. Slowly, Bob's stomach slowed, and the smells in his head faded.

Don't touch me!

The disgusting presence in his pants was still straining.

"Honey?" a timid, hopeful voice reached Bob.

"I'm okay." He said. Realizing how weak it sounded.

She was crying a bit, but she was still holding his kneeling, hunched-over form. "Bob, what happened? Should I take you to a doctor? I'm calling an ambulance!"

"No!" His voice bordered on panic. "No. I just got sick. Bad peppers maybe." He was running out of composure. "Go back inside, I'll be right there. I just need a minute." The smell of vomit was lingering in his mouth and from beneath him on the grass, but he could not stand up yet. Not yet.

"I don't think I should . . ."

"Brenda!"

Bitch! Do what I tell you!

"Brenda . . . go tell the kids that I'm okay. David looked scared."

Stupid cow!

She slowly rose, her hands still on him.

And stop touching me when I'm puking!

"I'll be right back, Bob, I'm just going to go tell the kids you'll be all right. I'll be right back!"

Go!

He heard her retreating steps, and she was saying something to some other people, one with a Hispanic accent. Bob vaguely noted that someone from the restaurant had made it all the way to the door and had been watching from the safe distance of the doorway. A small, concerned crowd was gaping through the windows. The embarrassing pressure in his pants was easing. To his surprise, he heard in a trembling voice, "Sir, are you all right? We know first aid. Can we help?"

Looking up, Bob saw a girl. He had to look up past her chest to see a concerned face, pure and unblemished, ringed by frosted blond hair.

NO!

A part of him stirred, and he said viciously, "Go away! Go very, very far away!"

Another Saturday without the kids. It was cold and raining outside, so rather than rush from the car to an annoying succession of junk stores, the wife had given him a dutiful dose of bland morning sex and dragged him to the mall. The mall was a little less fatiguing sometimes, because it had a Cookie Hut and the store with the expensive electronic toys. After forty-five minutes in Macy's, Brenda finally acknowledged the reeking boredom on Bob's face. He stood with bags from Yankee Candle and Bath and Body Works drooping in the one hand.

"Honey . . ." No response from Bob. "Honey?"

"Hmm? What?"

What now?

Brenda started to reach out to take the bags from him but then changed her mind and decided that he could roam free, but he had to carry the heavy candle and healing hands lotion. "Go," she announced with a wave of her hand. To her own surprise, her voice held little irritation.

"What?"

"Go. Shoo. Wander." Her fingers brushed at him. "Get out of here. You're driving me crazy," she lied. "I'll call you when I'm done shopping. Make sure your phone is on."

Now Bob was walking alone in the mall, looking at the people and thinking about stopping for a Guinness at the faux British pub near the food court. It was cold today, so most of the young women were wearing jackets or coats, and it made it blissfully easy to dismiss the haunting, firm young flesh that occupied his thoughts. Bob was glad that the weather had forced all these young sluts to cover up.

A tall red-haired woman wearing a tight minidress came breezing out of one of those lingerie stores. She was not wearing a coat, and her body and hair bounced as she sashayed, moving toward Bob. As she got closer, he saw deep gashes on her face, and a red line shimmering across her neck, releasing blood down her plunging neckline. The skin and muscles along her left cheek peeled down and plopped wetly to the floor.

Bob stopped and closed his eyes, breathing slowly and calmly. He smelled the rush of blood as the woman's high heels clicked louder and louder toward him, beside him, and then the noise trailed away, fading into the crowd.

He opened his eyes slowly, still facing the store the red-haired woman had come from. Bob saw a plump brunette woman whose breasts had been sliced off standing in the window. She was holding up a black and pink lace brassiere in one hand, and a skimpy orange one in the other hand, comparing the two. Her blood stained the front of her shirt, dripping between her feet as she considered the price tags.

Bob's throat tightened. He turned slowly away and resumed walking. He was careful not to step in the bloody footprints left by the red-haired harlot.

A few minutes later, Bob felt normal again. He was in control. Again.

Bob continued to window shop without any real destination. He dismissed the cigar shop, blew past the cell phone kiosk and the puppies, and he did not even notice the model train store. He slowed as he approached a shop with electric razors in the window display. Thinking about his old Remington electric, he went in to see if they sold blades for his old model.

The store was filled with red velvet display cases glimmering full of silvered blades. Razors, scissors, and electric shavers were prominent as well, but the vertical display cases with the hundreds of exquisite knives captured his imagination. Along with half a dozen other men, Bob walked along the displays, admiring the seemingly endless assortment of stainless steel. There were entire cases of straight-bladed hunting and fishing knives, military fighting knives, diver's knives, and replica daggers. As he ogled the fine craftsmanship, he came upon the folding knives. His pulse quickened slightly when he saw an assortment of small, razor-sharp knives with unusual blades. Some were partially serrated, and others were so straight that light sang across the edges as he moved by. The blades were small and extremely thin, even when folded up. Most of the men were window shopping the larger knives, but Bob was transfixed at this case of small, efficient blades that folded into your pocket.

Hello there!

It was nestled in red velvet beside a knife touted as a special police design. The blade was less than three inches long, and it was serrated almost all the way to the tip. It hooked at the end like a talon. The special description indicated that it was designed for use by sailors to cut rope at arm's length, and the beak-like tip provided leverage on moving targets. The blade had a small hole where you were meant to place your thumb knuckle so the blade could be opened one-handed. The knife was named the Harpy.

Well, well.

Suddenly sweating and short of breath, Bob gladly paid one hundred twenty dollars and quietly returned to the traffic of the mall.

He was entirely too old to be in this bar, and he knew it. The wife and kids were out of town visiting family, and he was stuck working the weekend.

Hope Sonya isn't driving Brenda crazy.

The majority of the clientele was from the college down the road. He knew the place well by now and knew that he could charm young college women with

JACK'S MANTLE 213

his quiet confidence and willingness to buy them
drinks without asking the waitress how much they
cost. Bob would sit and pretend to listen to them as
their blood dripped off their pretty, mutilated faces
onto the little umbrellas that sat in their fruity drinks.

It was crowded tonight, and Bob was at the bar,
holding his overcoat in his lap because there was no
safe place to drape a coat. It occurred to him that
there were no less than a dozen guys his age sitting
at tables by themselves, leering at the young girls.

Losers.

He fidgeted with the buttons on the overcoat and
noted that Brenda had tightened up the loose button.

Wow, that was nice of her.

After a while, a woman sat next to Bob. She was
almost his age, also too old for this place, with overdone blonde hair and a tight red dress that exposed a
lot of hanging cleavage. Her skin was weathered,
showing years spent in the sun. She ordered a drink
and did not immediately pay for it. As she raised the
glass, she cast a sidelong, dirty glance at Bob, then
she drained the gin and tonic.

Bob motioned the bartender to bring her another
one.

Roxanne was the name she gave, and she was not
as loud as the younger girls. Her voice was husky, and
she smoked. Bob hated cigarettes and women who
smoked them. In fact, he didn't like her at all. She sat
there in the tight red dress, with her rough tanned
skin, long legs, and her slightly overdone eye makeup
looking at him like she was interested. She smelled of
sickly sweet perfume and cigarette smoke. Bob did
not have to look away, or close his eyes, or suppress
any urges from under his folded overcoat as long as
he focused on her.

They talked for a time, and Bob gave her his attention without listening. He did not allow himself to be
distracted by the firm and blood-soaked bodies of the
sorority girls on the dance floor. After her third drink,

she leaned in close to make sure he heard her. "Honey, don't take this personally, but you should know that I have bills to pay. We can take this party somewhere private, but it will cost you. I hope that doesn't spoil the mood."

A distant feeling of familiarity threatened Bob's composure, but he remained calm. He ignored the blood that was now slowly dripping from the gash where Roxanne's nose should be, and gazing into her mutilated eye sockets said, "No, not at all. In fact, I think you just said the magic words, Love."

Standing in the bathroom, Bob washed the blood from his hands. The small apartment stank of stale smoke and fried foods. There was a litter box in the kitchen that stank, too. He dabbed at the sleeves of the overcoat, but there did not seem to be any blood on the wool. In fact, looking in the mirror, he was remarkably clean considering the past hour's activities. He was certain that some blood had sprayed across the sleeve, but looking at it now, it was dry and soft with no trace of blood. He finished washing off the knife, grateful for the ingenious design that prevented it from holding water in any crevices.

He walked through Desiree's bedroom one last time and saw her lying peacefully on the bed. Her hair was rumpled across the pillow. Her breasts and an ovary were arranged on her bedside table, beside most of the tissue from her face. Someone had already gotten to the other ovary years before Bob met her, it seemed. Her legs were splayed open, and the soles of her feet were pressed together, near her buttocks. He had taken his time, and treated the dirty whore with the care she deserved. He hated rushing.

He felt a vibration near his right hip. He reached down and noted with surprise that his cell phone was somewhere in his overcoat. Fumbling with a strange pocket he wasn't sure he'd noticed before, he pulled it out. He was on full alert, as if Brenda might somehow know where he was through the phone. His voice was artificially cheerful, "Hey Sweetie. No, you didn't disturb me; I'm on my way home right now. No, it's okay, I'm just wrapping up here at work. You aren't bothering me at all."

Bob walked outside, talking quietly. "Say, did you sew a pocket into my overcoat? You did? That's the sweetest thing, thank you. You're becoming a regular little seamstress. Be home in a flash. Love you. Bye-bye."

The kids rushed out the door to catch their various school buses. Bob was surprised to see Brenda come back in the house. She would usually hurry over to the school and sit there out of view, waiting to make sure David got inside safely before driving to work. She denied doing it, but Bob knew better. Bob did not discourage her paranoia. After all, there were a lot of sickos in the world.

But this morning, she was still there after the kids were gone. Bob noted that she was bringing a small armful of dry cleaning in from the minivan.

He drank coffee and read the local paper. There was a short article on the front page about another hooker who had been found murdered downtown. A redhead. She'd been dead a couple of days. No other details were released. Bob turned to the sports section.

"Honey?"

"Yes, Dear?" Bob set his paper aside and looked at his wife. Her brown hair was pulled back and she was wearing one of the dark blue and black dress suits that she wore when she was trying to hide her weight. She held her overcoat across her arm, stroking it absently as if she were on her way out the door. Her freckles were obvious this morning, despite the fact that she had actually used a little makeup today to cover them. Bob recalled her saying something about her boss having a presentation that she was helping with.

I'll have to call and offer encouragement later this morning.

"Are we . . . are we okay?" she asked.

"What do you mean? Of course we're okay." Bob was genuinely confused. "What do you mean?"

There was a long pause as Brenda looked around, "It's just that . . . I mean . . . I worry that we don't do things together anymore."

"What do you mean, Dear?"

Where is she getting this?

"Well, you've been staying out late a lot and coming home smelling like you've been in bars. And . . . well . . . I don't have to tell you how long it's been since we've made love." The last bit was almost mumbled, but Brenda had momentum going and didn't want to stop, "Bob—is there another woman?" she blurted out fearfully.

"No, of course not." Bob said almost laughingly but without a trace of mockery.

"Well, it's just that . . . well . . . sometimes I can smell the perfume, I think."

"Dear, there's no other woman," Bob said dismissively and convincingly.

She offered him a weak smile. "I hate to say anything. It's just that you've been so different these past few months. I mean, you're more thoughtful, more . . . and you don't even peek at other women when we're out anymore, which is actually kind of nice, but . . ."

Bob shifted a bit uncomfortably at that. He felt like a kid who finally realized that his mother always kept a count of how many cookies were in the jar.

"But at the same time, we haven't had . . . sex . . . for almost four months." She ran through the speech quickly, with rehearsed speed, and kept going. "*Cosmo* says that these are signs that a husband is cheating."

Smiling a bit, Bob repeated, "Dear, I haven't had any kind of sex with any woman but you since we started dating. I'm sorry if I ever looked at another woman. The sight of most other women makes me ill compared to you, Dear, and I am grateful that your face is the one I wake up to in the mornings." Bob's words rang with surprising sincerity.

Relieved, but a bit unprepared, Brenda pressed an issue. "Where have you been going at night?"

Chuckling, Bob said, "I've been hanging out in bars and patrolling street corners finding hookers and eviscerating them for my sick pleasure, Dear." Bob's heart almost stopped.

Where the hell did that come from?!

Brenda chastised him, "Bob! That's tasteless to laugh about those poor murdered women like that. Shame on you! I don't care that they were prostitutes, they were still people."

"I'm sorry, Dear, I didn't mean to upset you."

What in god's name did I say that for?

"I love you just how you are, Brenda, and I like us the way we are. I'm not cheating on you."

I told her . . . about the hookers. I can't just let her walk out of here now.

"Don't read too much into my behavior, Brenda. Midlife crisis, maybe."

Now I have to keep her quiet!

Bob felt the tremor of fear grow into a knot.

Brenda smiled sweetly and came close. He could smell the fresh, clean scent of the morning shower and fabric softener. She was incredibly plain, and Bob felt absolutely no desire to have sex with her. He inhaled the scents again and remembered all the anger and hatred he had felt for her all these years. He summoned up the apathy and rage, building to a sharp, razor's edge as he looked into her eyes.

He saw her freckles, her concerned brow. He had nothing. No blood, no stench, no rage, no visions . . . nothing compelling him to silence her. Just fear. If he had to kill her, he had to do it *alone*. He did not have the knife or his treasured coat.

He averted his eyes in wilted defeat.

"I'm glad we talked, Bob. And I'm glad you were honest with me. Couples should be honest with each other." The tone of her voice had changed, and when he looked back up to her, he noticed that the coat she was holding over her arm and stroking lovingly was *his*. She bent down and gently kissed his head, holding her hand on his shoulder. "Be sure that it stays that way."

She handed him the coat and then reached into her pocket and extracted something that flashed silver in the kitchen lights. She placed his knife on the table in front of him. Bob's heart jumped into his throat, and his breath froze.

"Bob—don't be out too late tonight."

IRRESISTIBLE

Yvonne Coats

Sandy slumped against the wheel of her old-but-it-still-runs Toyota Celica and tried to figure out how her day had gone to hell. A tap on the window startled her: It was Billy, one of the regulars, smiling at her in a way she'd gotten far too familiar with. Not a bad guy—none of them were bad guys, usually—but she surely did not like that smile.

She rolled the window down a crack, and Billy didn't say any of the things she'd anticipated, like how unfair it was that she'd been fired. He didn't ask if she'd be okay, or offer her a loan. What Billy did say was, "I wonder, I mean, could I call you sometime?"

"No. I gotta go now, Billy." *Shit shit shit,* she thought as Billy reached for the door handle. She turned the ignition key and had never been more grateful to hear the little Celica's sewing machine engine turn over.

She pulled away from Billy as fast as she could without knocking him down and zipped through the parking lot and out into the street. She'd made good money serving drinks at the Silver Dollar, but she hadn't put much away. She didn't think finding another job would be all that easy, especially since Shelly, the manager, said she'd fired her "cause she couldn't keep her hands off'n the customers."

Tears welled in Sandy's eyes. It hadn't been her mauling the customers, but the other way around. *I need a drink,* she thought when she saw the Handy Pantry sign.

She pulled right up to the door—*good, it's not busy*—and went inside for some cheap beer. She hoisted the six-pack onto the counter and rummaged in her purse for her wallet.

"Hi," the clerk said. He was a skinny redheaded guy who looked about seventeen years old but had to be older if he could sell beer. And he had *that smile*.

"Hi," Sandy said, extracting her wallet. "How much?"

"Drinkin' alone?"

She kept her eyes down but was sure he was still smiling.

"Preferably."

"Not very friendly, are ya?"

"Sorry. Just tired and not in a very good mood." She smiled slightly and forced herself to look up. *Yup, he was smiling, like a man about to take his first bite of a really good steak.* "How much is the beer, please?"

"Onna house."

Damn. "Come on, how much is it?"

"Onna house," he said again, louder.

"If you don't let me pay for it, I'm not taking it."

When he just kept smiling, Sandy thought, *I am not leaving without beer.* She pulled out a five, slapped it on the counter, and walked out.

"Hey, wait! This is too much." The redhead came out behind her, but he was too slow. She had the Celica in reverse and out of the parking lot before he stepped off the curb. In the review mirror, she could see him waving her five-dollar bill.

When she got home, to a former garage some thrifty soul had turned into a dollhouse of a rental, she was glad she lived alone. Right now, she was glad she wasn't dating anybody. *Do Lutherans have convents?*

she wondered, though she hadn't been to church since she left home.

She popped the top on one of the beers, took a long swig, and snorted at the brand name, Blitz. *How come cheap beers have all the best names? I guess names are cheaper than ingredients.*

She flopped down on the squashy red plaid couch, pulled off her spike heels, and rubbed her toes and arches. Groaning, she stood up and peeled off her stockings, tossing her fancy garters on the coffee table and aiming the stockings toward the bathroom.

She sat back down, took another slug of beer, and considered her situation. She had a couple of hundred in checking, nearly seven hundred in savings, maybe two months' worth of money if she really watched it.

Her gaze settled on the garters. Last week, they'd seemed perfect. Last week, her sister Cheryl asked her to be a bridesmaid, said she'd buy Sandy's dress—hallelujah—and asked Sandy to find her something "old and blue" that Cheryl could "borrow" and wear on her wedding day next month. Before Sandy could panic about finding something wedding-appropriate, she saw an ad in one of her magazines. There was a tiny photo of a pair of garters, and they sure looked blue. Underneath was printed, "Be irresistible," and a description of the garters as "antique."

Sandy had called the phone number, and a soft southern voice answered, "Blue Ridge Bazaar, Rennie McCoy speaking."

"Um, I'm calling about some garters."

"I got them when my grandmother died. I believe they'd been in the family for a long time. They're handmade, probably late Nineteenth Century and, since I assume you want to wear them, the elastic is in remarkably good shape."

"That's nice," Sandy said, in a hurry because it was long distance. "I can't tell from the picture . . . are they blue?"

"Yes, royal blue satin with lace trim, which has yellowed a bit, but the garters are quite lovely. My grandmother said they, how did she put it, 'contributed to a memorable wedding . . . and wedding night.' She wouldn't let my mother wear them at her wedding, though, I remember someone saying . . ."

"So they really are old. Great. Um, how much are you asking?"

"A hundred dollars."

"Shit. Sorry. That's a lot of money."

Rennie McCoy had listened to Sandy talk about her sister's wedding and her request, and they had haggled for a couple of minutes. Finally, he'd agreed to let them go for seventy dollars, shipping included. Maybe it had been a great deal, but now Sandy wished she had the money back.

She woke up with a hangover—it'd been a long time since she'd killed a six-pack by herself, and she vowed it would be an even longer time before she did it again. Looking at her dull skin and red eyes in the mirror over the sink, she decided to stay home and clean house before hitting the pavements to find a new job.

She got lucky and found work the next day, glad that Shelly from the Silver Dollar had not, apparently, said anything too awful about her to Kent, her new boss, who owned the Westerner. She still couldn't figure out what had gone wrong at the Silver Dollar, but none of the men at the Westerner paid her more than ordinary attention. Some harmless flirting, a couple of propositions from guys she expected to pour out the door at closing time—nothing unusual. Nothing weird.

Things went well until Friday. Kent had told Sandy that he wanted her to dress more provocatively on the weekends. "I can buy you gear if you need it, but go ahead and wear your own stuff tonight."

Sandy looked in the full-length mirror in her bedroom. She'd put her hair up and wore big silver hoop earrings, snug black tank top, bleached denim mini-skirt, sheer black nylons, and shiny black stilettos. *Maybe a little plain.* She pulled one of the blue garters halfway up her left thigh, where it would be highly visible. *Not bad,* she thought. She wondered if guys would put dollar bills in it, the way she'd seen them do with strippers.

At the Westerner, Kent came across the room to greet her. "Wow. You clean up nice, Sandy."

"I don't exactly think of this look as 'clean,' Kent." She liked Kent.

"Guess not." Then he smiled in a way that made Sandy's neck hairs quiver. "Well, we both got things to do, so I'll talk at you later."

Sandy nodded. Maybe it hadn't been *that smile* after all.

The evening went well, at first. Sandy's tips were incredibly generous, which she figured was due to it being a weekend and more crowded. Then she heard one of the other servers complaining about her to Kent, telling him that Sandy was "doing something" because her customers kept asking for Sandy to serve them. Sandy figured she was just a better server, that was all. It wasn't like at the Silver Dollar. Nobody had groped her. No fights had broken out.

But by ten o'clock, the Westerner was bursting at the seams. Nearly all the single women and couples had left, and the bar was starting to look like a men's club.

Feeling stupid, Sandy went into the ladies' room and took off the garter. She wrapped it in a paper towel and stuffed it behind the toilet tank in the back stall. Squaring her shoulders, she walked back out into the bar.

At first, it didn't seem to make a difference, but within twenty minutes Sandy saw fewer men staring at her. In an hour, enough men had left that couples could get in to dance to the live band that Kent brought in on weekends. Sandy's tips went down, but her spirits rose.

She thought about leaving the garter where it was, but in the end she shoved it in her skirt pocket before she left. Kent, who had ignored her all evening, looked up as she crossed the room. He seemed to be thinking about saying something, but she waved and made it out the door before he spoke.

It was nearly three a.m. by the time Sandy got home. She kicked off her shoes, drank a big glass of water, flopped down on the couch, turned on the TV, and fell asleep.

She dreamed about her sister, Cheryl, but in the dream she turned into somebody else and found herself in a heated argument.

"He was gonna marry me, Nancy, and you knows it!" Sandy shouted with another woman's mouth. She felt small and worn out, and she looked down to see her hands folded on an obviously pregnant stomach.

The other woman, if sixteen years can make a woman, smiled slyly at her.

"Where'd ya put 'em, Nancy? Where?" Sandy felt a stabbing pain in her back and reached around awkwardly to rub her spine. *Does pregnancy really feel this bad?*

"Whatever do you mean, cousin Roseanna?" The blonde girl simpered and smoothed her pale yellow frock.

"*I* made them garters, and you knows it. I 'broidered his name and mine, and I done all the carryin' on like grandmam taught me. They're mine, and no good can come from your thievin' of 'em." Roseanna/Sandy needed to pee. She felt hot and itchy. She needed to sit down.

In a very low voice, Nancy said, "I took your name off them garters, Roseanna, and stitched in mine. 'Nancy and Johnse' is what them garters sez now." Her face glowed with confidence, and Sandy/Roseanna saw what a child Nancy still was. *Big bosoms and a husband don't make you a woman.*

She looked around for the nearest chair and fell into it. Nancy's smooth brow creased. "You look awful red, cousin. Lemme go get your mama."

She was too tired even to protest. She whispered, "I thought I could make it right. I thought, 'cause I loved Johnse, that I could make everybody stop fighting. The magic worked on Johnse. He loved me." She sucked in air like there suddenly wasn't enough. "I thought I could work magic on his papa, Devil Anse. Maybe stop the feud." She felt herself sliding off the chair and came to rest on the hard mud floor, gloriously cool against her face. "I shoulda put the feud first, ahead of Johnse. It ain't never gonta stop now. That fool girl broke my magic, I don't know what'll happen."

Her ears rang, and she closed her eyes. The ringing continued, and Sandy woke to the answering machine taking a message from somebody selling something.

She sat up, blinking in daylight. Slowly she reached into her skirt and pulled out the wadded paper towel. She unwrapped the garter and set it on the coffee table. After a while, she went and got the other one. She examined them inch by inch, inside and out, but didn't find anything that looked like lettering, just a few tiny needle holes where, maybe, thread had fallen or been picked out. She grabbed the phone and called Blue Ridge Bazaar with a few questions for Rennie McCoy.

When she'd finished telling him about wearing the garters and about her dream, McCoy didn't say anything for a moment.

"Hello?" Sandy said.

"You're pulling my leg, aren't you?" His voice sounded uncertain.

"I'm not a liar, Mr. McCoy." Sandy thought she was calm, but her voice shook.

"I'm sorry, it's just . . . Does the name McCoy mean anything to you?"

"Doctor, classic Trek." She thought again. "And the real McCoy, whatever that means."

"Nothing else?"

She thought hard. "The Hatfields and the McCoys. Hillbillies. They didn't like each other much."

She heard a sigh, probably over the word 'hillbillies.' *Oh well, it's said now.*

"In 1880, Roseanna McCoy and Johnson Hatfield acted out the Blue Ridge version of *Romeo and Juliet*. They didn't marry, though she was pregnant and that would've been the normal thing to do. A year later, Johnson did marry a McCoy—not Roseanna but her cousin Nancy. There was never a good explanation for why Johnse had switched women, especially after Roseanna saved him from being killed by three of her brothers."

Sandy looked at the garters, blue satin gleaming in the morning sun. She picked them up, so light, so lovely to be so dangerous.

"Over the next ten years, thirteen people died in the feud, including Roseanna's sister, four of her brothers, and Roseanna herself."

"What about the baby, Johnse's baby?" Sandy remembered being pregnant in the dream.

"Roseanna got measles and miscarried."

"And I've got her garters," Sandy said. She stroked the smooth satin and thought about Roseanna McCoy.

"Yes, I guess you do." She heard regret in his voice. "What are you going to do with them? I mean, it's none of my business, but if you don't want them, I'd be hap—"

"Well, I'll have to find something else for my sister, but I plan to keep them."

She heard McCoy sigh. "Just be careful."

Sandy laughed. "Worried that I'll use my powers for evil instead of good, Mr. McCoy?"

He didn't laugh, but she thought he might be smiling when he said, "Excuse me, your 'powers'?"

"I really don't know what use these things are, other

than the obvious. I'll keep them safe, though." Sandy wondered, "Do you have any other family heirlooms in your store, Mr. McCoy?" *Wouldn't it be great if he did,* she thought. *I'd love to see what else the McCoy women might have conjured up.*

"Call me Rennie. I'm the last of my branch of the family, so I've inherited the lot. The stuff from my grandmother's house was what finally pushed me into opening this store. I wonder what other surprises there might be?"

Sandy thought fast. "I'm going to be traveling soon, and I might be coming your way. If there are other things Roseanna, or anyone else in your family made, things like the garters, it might take a woman to make them work." She crossed her fingers, hoping that he wasn't married. He seemed nice on the phone, but even if he looked like Quasimodo crossed with a muskrat, Sandy needed to see what might be in his store.

"Do you know when you'll be in Kentucky?" he said slowly. She definitely heard a smile in his voice this time.

"Not exactly. But you might want to keep an eye out for a woman in stockings."

SEEBOHM'S CAP

Peter Schweighofer

Major Prentice Vance of St. Louis, Missouri, peered across the table at the supposed German spy. Headquarters claimed the man could betray Operation Overlord, but Vance couldn't tell how an ordinary army rifleman might have useful strategic knowledge about the impending invasion of Europe or how he could have transmitted it to Germany without detection.

And why would the man be foolish enough to carry around any evidence betraying his allegiance to Nazi Germany like that cap?

Vance gazed at the cap in fascination. It sat limp on the vast table between him and the spy—nothing more than a crumpled piece of faded tan fabric with a bent visor and worn patches halfway down the top seams, and marks that seemed to indicate its former owner wore wireless headphones over it. A spattering of blood dried brown in the harsh desert sun dotted one side. Such a worn, mundane cap seemed out of place sitting on the highly polished massive table, centerpiece of the palatial dining room in the countryside mansion the Office of Strategic Services had requisitioned from its British cousins.

Private Benedict Kelly of Culbertson, Nebraska, army infantryman and alleged German spy, stared at the cap as if it were some kind of malevolent demon waiting to pounce on him and consume his very soul. He craned his head as far back as the tall dining room chair would allow, his white-knuckled hands gripping the armrests. Vance couldn't tell whether the sleepless, bloodshot eyes and the sallow skin came from several days of imprisonment and questioning or from sheer dread of that cap.

Vance's assistant, Lieutenant Laura Jackson from Peekskill, New York, didn't take any notice of the cap and didn't display any discernible emotion at all. She sat in a chair pushed well away from the table, one leg draped over another just enough to show off her nicely turned ankle. Someone had pushed back the heavy curtains to allow light from the tall French doors nearby to filter through the sheers, casting a diffused light throughout the dining room and giving Jackson a deceptively angelic aura. She might only serve in the Women's Army Corps, but Jackson possessed an uncanny knack for disappearing on errands and returning at the right moment with exactly what Vance required (a baffling trait Vance secretly intended to investigate someday.) Jackson maintained her focus on the steno pad balanced on her leg, occasionally glancing up from her notes to size up Private Kelly and his reactions to Vance's polite queries—questions phrased more as conversation starters than demands.

"It says here you bought the hat from Private Sewell. Where did he get it?" Vance removed his steady stare from fidgety Kelly and casually perused the file set before him. His lithe fingers nonchalantly turned the pages as he gazed down his nose at the reports. Vance spoke with even tones, measuring his speech more as if they were having a relaxed tea than a military interrogation.

Kelly blinked a few times, shrugged his skinny shoulders, and stuttered. "I . . . I dunno. Uh, Africa, I guess."

Vance's fingers touched the pencil-thin mustache over his lips, drawing attention to the faint but friendly smile. "Surely Private Sewell mentioned something about the hat's provenance." He noted Kelly's perplexed expression—he wasn't much more than a gawky farm boy who more than likely dropped out of school—and corrected himself. "Where the cap came from. Didn't Sewell weave some fanciful tale bragging how he acquired the cap?"

Kelly made that exasperating shrug of his shoulders again.

"We could always send for Sergeant Mullen to refresh your memory." Vance's grin took a slightly menacing curve. Sergeant John Mullen of Moose Lake, Minnesota, took care of the heavy work during Kelly's earlier interrogations with the Military Police. "But I don't think Lieutenant Jackson would like that." Vance's assistant looked up, batted her eye lashes with a doleful look, and pouted her ruby red lips in a possibly mock frown, right on cue. Vance expected she'd reprimand him later for involving her in his mind games.

"No, ma'am," Kelly drawled. He allowed himself a glance from the cap to Lieutenant Jackson with a bashful smile, then glared at Vance. "I told them before, more than once, dammit, that Sewell got the cap in a battle in North Africa."

Vance's lips maintained their sinister curve. He smoothed his mustache before reaching across and closing Kelly's file. "Fine. Perhaps, then, you'd like to give us a firsthand demonstration of what happens when you wear that cap."

All color drained from Kelly's face. His hands gripped the chair, and his army uniform visibly trembled on his lanky frame. Vance thought a bit of drool leaked from Kelly's quivering lips. He recalled the reports in the folder. Kelly's unit occupied one of the sealed training camps in the south of England where troops waited to embark on the imminent invasion. Kelly's friends found him twitching on the ground near his tent, eyes rolled into the back of his head, his mouth spitting foam and frenzied words that sounded like German . . . all while wearing the *Afrika Korps* cap.

"Sprechen Sie Deutsch?" Vance asked in fluent German. *"Sind Sie Deutscher?"*

Kelly controlled his tremors and shot Vance a befuddled look.

"Obviously not," Vance answered. "Do you have any knowledge of the imminent invasion of Europe?"

"Huh?" Kelly shrugged. "Sure, everyone's getting all ready for something big, but nobody knows exactly what or when. Come on, anyone looking around here knows something's about to happen. Why else would American troops swarm all over southern England, doing invasion exercises and practice drills?"

"Well, then, I think we're done for now. Sergeant!" Vance called. An army sergeant—not the bruiser from Kelly's earlier interrogations—entered the dining room through one of the tall, double doors and stood at attention. "Escort Private Kelly to the room we've prepared—not a cell, Kelly, but a real room—and make sure he gets something decent to eat. As I recall, the kitchens here are as well-stocked as a Chicago steakhouse."

Kelly didn't budge. "When can I go back to my unit?"

"Oh, I doubt you'll be returning to combat, though that should prove a relief," Vance said with an understanding grin. "Not after all you've gone through. I'm sure they'll put you on the next ship home. Oh, don't worry about your patriotic duty. You've done your part, soldier, that's for certain, and there's no disgrace in what's happened. If I'm right, you might have delivered to us a valuable weapon in the fight against fascism."

Kelly pulled himself out of the chair and stumbled over to meet the sergeant, never taking his terrified eyes off Vance and the cap.

Vance knew Kelly wouldn't really go home to Nebraska. He'd most likely enjoy a lengthy stay at St. Elizabeth's, the hospital in Washington where the OSS and other government agencies sent "mentally ill" psychiatric patients—devoid of any right to *habeas corpus*—to languish in guarded isolation for the duration.

With all he'd seen, and would see, Vance wondered if he'd end up there himself before war's end.

"Should I tell Colonel Donovan we have a spy on our hands?" Jackson asked, looking up from her notes.

"Of course not," Vance replied. The head of OSS wanted straight answers, not conjecture, before he made any report to General Eisenhower. "Kelly's just some country bumpkin from Nebraska. Doesn't know a damn thing. Looking over his file, there's no possible way the Germans could have recruited him either in America or during his service in Italy, and he seems to have no means of communicating any intelligence to them, certainly not from a sealed camp with rigorous security restrictions. Besides, Kelly wouldn't know good intelligence if it came up and kicked him in the pants."

"But he knows about that cap."

Vance stared a moment at the cap, brow furrowed with curiosity, his fingers caressing his mustache. The crumpled cloth sat there lifeless, the German eagle patch emblazoned on the front, a ghostly aura of dust settling around it on the veneered tabletop. The hat's former owner obviously belonged to the German *Afrika Korps,* which had ranged across the deserts of North Africa until General Montgomery had begun beating him back from Egypt at el Alamien and Patton drove him from Morocco and Algeria in Operation Torch. Defeating Rommel there led to a swift invasion of Sicily and then Italy, but the Allies needed another foothold in Europe from which to strike at the heart of Nazi Germany.

Who was the *Afrika Korps* officer who wore that hat? By the worn marks midway along the fabric, Vance figured the fellow wore headphones a lot, meaning he served some function in communications, possibly with a wireless company or as a radioman with a mobile reconnaissance unit. His glance followed the trail of dried blood tracking up one side.

Soldiers always picked up souvenirs of their experiences, badges of courage proving they had participated in particular battles and had come away alive once more. Why was this cap special? Vance leaned forward, enthralled by the potential power of this simple, crumpled hat.

"Where do we go from here, sir?" Jackson asked, a glint of suspicion in her eyes.

Vance leaned back in his chair, the opulent dining room suddenly coming back into focus and diminishing the cap's presence in his mind. He turned to Lieutenant Jackson with a charming smile. "Why don't you contact our British cousins and track down this Sewell fellow. Kelly was with the First Infantry Division stationed near Poole on the southern coast of England. Follow his deployment to determine when it came in contact with any British units. Probably some element of that British army division stationed around Southampton. I want to know exactly when and where Sewell found that cap."

"Should I forward any recommendations to Colonel Donovan?" she asked.

Vance peered back at the cap. "Not at this time," he replied. "This situation calls for a bit more investigation on our part before we make any concrete recommendations."

"General Eisenhower can't wait," Jackson noted. "They're deliberating even now whether to launch Overlord in the next few days."

Simple strategy for invading the continent dictated an amphibious landing with the shortest crossing from England to France at Calais, not a longer, riskier crossing to Normandy. All intelligence from agents behind the lines pointed to Hitler expecting an invasion at Calais given the deployment of his armies. German army wireless traffic intercepted and deciphered by the British code breakers at Station X confirmed the field reports. But even they could only provide a small view of the overall picture.

"They have more intelligence to corroborate than we can provide," Vance countered. "At this point, with British and American forces poised to strike after months of planning, Hitler's armies deployed somewhere along the Atlantic wall, and Eisenhower watching the weather reports, Eisenhower's taking as low a risk as he can get."

"I don't think SHAEF would quite see it that way," Jackson countered.

"Well, we have nothing conclusive to give them until we uncover more about that cap." Vance walked over to stare out the window over the carefully manicured English gardens outside.

Jackson closed her notebook and collected Kelly's file. "Do you want me to lock that up in the vault?" she asked, nodding at the cap.

Vance didn't interrupt his examination of the light rain falling on the gardens and a few visible portions of the great old manor house. "Just leave it there," Vance said. "I'll take a closer look at it in a few moments, thank you, Lieutenant."

Jackson sauntered out of the dining room, her heels clicking severely on the ornately patterned parquet floor. Vance stole a glance at her as she slipped out the tall double doors and closed them behind her.

Vance stood at the windows a few more minutes taking in the scenery outside. He found such peaceful contemplation of the natural world or mundane matters necessary in steeling himself for encountering the unnatural. He inhaled the lingering scent of candle wax and perfume that haunted the room, heard the patter of raindrops against the windowpane merge with clattering typists in a nearby room, felt the muggy air close about him in his woolen uniform.

Vance casually walked to the table and picked up the cap. It electrified the goose bumps on his arm and sent shivers up his spine. Though he slicked back his wavy hair, it seemed to stand up on end and tingle as if covered with excited bees. His ability to detect items or people with otherworldly qualities had brought him to the attention of the OSS, which appointed him head of its Bureau of Special Investigations (derisively named "BS Investigations" by those ignorant of its true purposes). By now Vance knew Kelly wasn't a German spy; he was more interested in the cap, what it did to those who wore it, and what it might do to help the Allies win the war.

Vance ran his fingers over the cap, ran his thumb over the Nazi eagle patch on the front. He felt granules of warm sand, leather-padded headband and earphones, sticky sweet blood. Vance inhaled its scents: dust, sweat, cordite, and fear. Then he put the cap on his head.

Information, sensations, and emotions flooded every corner of Vance's mind. He reached out to steady himself against the dining table. His vision narrowed into distant tunnels; he breathed more rapidly to delay the unconsciousness racing up to meet him. He fought to focus on the ancient family portraits and ornate candle sconces on the far wall to keep his eyes from rolling up into the back of his head.

The burst of paranormal energy dropped him to the floor. A maelstrom of dots and dashes, clicking, blinking, typing, spinning metal rotors, clumps of four-letter groups, and finally cohesive German words rushed through his mind, a tempest of sensations not simply of the man who had fought and died wearing that *Afrika Korps* cap, but of all those past and present involved in the wireless telegraphy, codes, and ciphers the Nazis used to coordinate their vast war machine. For a fleeting second Vance realized no ordinary soldier like Private Kelly could possibly comprehend, let alone maintain mental and emotional control over this overwhelming storm of information. But Vance fought, shaking his head and body in apoplectic convulsions in an effort to physically and mentally discern the sensations flooding his mind.

Once he managed to isolate and understand streams of seemingly dissonant information, Vance tried arranging them in a logical order, much like conducting an interrogation or sifting through a file, starting with the basic information and working deeper. The originating signals pounded through his head, overlapping drumbeats of dots and dashes of multiple transmitters broadcasting messages in Morse code. These rapidly passed through stages of clicking typewriter keys, smooth electrical current passing through advancing metal rotors, and finally blinking letter lights. The letters gathered into groups of four, then transformed into comprehensible abbreviations and even entire words.

Vance realized this cap somehow channeled and deciphered all German radio communication within Western Europe through its wearer.

He doubted anyone intentionally designed the cap that way—the Nazis would be fools to allow such a fantastic weapon to fall into Allied hands—but surmised the emotional heat of combat and anguish of death imbued it with the knowledge and expertise of its wearer, who must have served with a wireless communications company in North Africa.

Vance's body twitched as he focused on the nearest messages, those most clear that translated into lucid intelligence about Nazi units guarding northern France. Orders to march, divisions held in reserve, units reforming after combat elsewhere. He started forming a vast strategic picture of towns and units between Normandy and Calais. One static and one active attack infantry division sat directly along the coast where the Allied amphibious forces hoped to establish a beachhead. Three smaller infantry groups stood in reserve south of the operational theater. Rommel had deployed his much-feared German panzer divisions far from the invasion point, with the 21st Panzers moved ten miles southeast of Caen and the infamous 12th SS Panzer Division more than fifty miles away, just west of Dreux, and the messages coming through the cap indicated they were stationed in the rear for rest and recuperation. Vance knew Eisenhower would like to know exactly what kind of opposition he was facing once American, British, and Canadian troops took the beaches of Normandy.

But the way he deployed his divisions confirmed that Hitler fully expected an Allied assault at Calais. Although a handful of divisions stood ready to repel any invaders at Normandy, Hitler had ordered at least nine infantry and four panzer divisions into the vicinity of Calais. The Lehr Panzer Division sat in reserve just west of Chartres to counter any Allied attack on either target. Clearly the Nazis expected an attack at Calais.

Vance could not comprehend how long he'd been unconscious exploring the mysteries of the cap. He heard the dining room door swing open and Lieutenant Jackson's shoes clicking evenly on the parquet floor, then halt abruptly.

"Call a medic!" Jackson screamed.

Vance opened his eyes wide, shook the cap off his head, composed his expression, and smiled calmly at Jackson. "No, everything's all right," he said, trying to sound confident despite the enduring tremors coursing through his body. He pulled himself up to his elbows, used the table to help him rise unsteadily to his feet, and then found coordination enough to make a show of dusting off his uniform jacket sleeves. Vance addressed the cautious yet curious crowd of sentries and typists who had gathered at the gaping double doors. "No need for alarm," he said. "I'm fine." The others reluctantly dispersed.

Vance leaned down to retrieve the cap from the floor and faltered; Jackson reached for it, but Vance grasped her arm. "I'd advise against touching that, my dear," he said. He saw her eyes go wide in response to his menacing look. Jackson quickly regained her composure and stood up, stony faced. After taking a few deep breaths, Vance bent down to pick up the cap himself and casually tossed it onto the table near his seat. Jackson knew it was an act and pulled his chair out so he could sit down.

"Tell me, Lieutenant, what you discovered about our friends Kelly and Sewell and how they acquired this cap." Vance's lithe fingers crept along the table and began absently fingering the dusty fabric, hoping simple contact might endow him with some of the cap's supernatural insights.

Lieutenant Jackson drew up a chair, crossed her legs, and flipped open her notebook. "I tracked down Sewell encamped near Southampton as you thought," she began. "Sewell traded the hat to Kelly for an amazing amount of booze and cigarettes for his unit. It's a long and twisted trail of trades, but I tracked the cap's original owner to Rommel's *Afrika Korps* at Gazala. During a counterattack, General Montgomery's forces overran Rommel's communications detachment, 3rd Company, 56th Signals Battalion, what the Germans call a *Fernemeldeaufklärung Kompanie* or *Horchkompanie*."

"A long-range radio intercept unit," Vance interjected. "Probably handled all of Rommel's headquarters-level code and cipher work, with broadcasts heading into the field and back to Berlin. It probably also carried out interception work targeted against Montgomery's wireless traffic."

"Exactly, sir. I pored over the operational reports, both for the army and intelligence, and determined this *Horchkompanie* helped Rommel stay one step ahead of Montgomery's forces . . . at least until Gazala, when things started falling apart."

"Yes, because he was woefully disorganized at el Alamein and certainly while retreating afterwards." Vance's other hand began smoothing out his pencil-thin mustache as his brows furrowed in thought. "Lose your ability to intercept and decrypt enemy wireless messages and you lose your advantage."

"Sewell's buddies destroyed the unit and took souvenirs. He claimed the cap came from the *Horchkompanie* commander, Captain Alfred Seebohm. Apparently he was a genius regarding anything to do with codes, ciphers, and radio work."

"That would explain this," Vance said, patting the cap and withdrawing his hand. "Seebohm was undoubtedly wearing it when they killed him. The trauma of death might have imbued it with his expertise and, well, quite a bit more about the workings of the German cryptographic system. On par with Station X at Bletchley Park, only through a different medium." Vance flashed a playful smile.

The two remained silent for a moment, respectfully contemplating the cap. "Where do we go from here?" Jackson asked.

Vance's lips curled in a sinister smile. "We put Seebohm's expertise to our own use. Sergeant!" he called. The fellow posted just outside peered around the door. "Would you kindly fetch me an operational map of northern France and a handful of pencils?"

"What should I tell Colonel Donovan?"

"Assure him that Operation Overlord can go ahead on whatever schedule Eisenhower chooses," Vance stated confidently. "The impressions from this cap confirm that Hitler's fully expecting an assault at Calais and give us a good view of those forces waiting for us in Normandy."

The sergeant returned with a large, rolled-up map under his arm and a handful of pencils. "Thank you,

Sergeant," Vance said with a disarming smile. While the sergeant returned to his post outside the door, Vance unrolled the map and began marking German unit placements with a pencil.

"They won't believe it," Jackson said. "It's absurd. A German wireless operator's cap imbued with all his knowledge, all the workings of the codes and ciphers, even intercepting radio waves."

"It's as reliable as any intelligence Colonel Donovan is ever going to get out of our bureau," Vance countered. "Ike may not believe it—heck, if Donovan's his usual cagey self, he'll obscure the source of this seemingly dubious intelligence—but the Colonel himself wouldn't have authorized our bureau if he thought our investigations didn't have merit."

"Say what you want about the cap, there's no way you can know all that," Jackson said, pointing to the map on which Vance continued jotting notes.

"True," Vance conceded. "Though operatives in France might confirm it, probably too late or after the fact. I doubt anyone would believe the veracity of the unit deployment I'll sketch for reference. I guess in retrospect it will seem uncanny, if not downright suspicious."

The cap sat next to Vance and the map, no longer an object of horror or curiosity, but another weapon to use in defeating Hitler's Nazis.

"Trust me, Lieutenant, I don't think we've seen the last of such strange occurrences during this war."

CAKE AND CANDY

Kelly Swails

A sk most people what death smells like and they'll
  say earth mixed with decaying leaves, or formal-
dehyde and old makeup, or maybe unwashed skin
overlaid with disinfectant. For me, death will always
smell like licorice and wedding cake.

I'm standing beside a casket in a funeral parlor,
alone in a room full of people. Staring at the body, I
wonder what it is like to be dead. He knows the answer to the question in the back of everyone's mind.
My existential angst and morbid curiosity mix to a
form of jealousy, and I wonder what is wrong with me.

Almost everyone is dressed in black, their murmurs
audible over the soothing music coming from the
walls. One brave soul, a formidable-looking woman
wearing a steel-gray dress, approaches the casket and
slips a gift to the deceased. The ice broken, the other
mourners form a line behind her.

I know what's coming. I correct my posture and will
myself not to cry.

"Gladys, I'm so sorry. Tad was too young."

My mother-in-law accepts the woman's embrace
and says, "Thank you for coming, Judy." Tad's mother
is the picture of refined sorrow. Her hair is perfectly
coiffed, her eyes have the merest hint of red, and she

241

dabs her nose with a pressed hankie. I hate her perfection as much as Tad does. Did.

"And who is this, Gladys?" Judy turns her gaze to me, and I shrink. She is wearing expensive cologne, probably something French, and for some odd reason I wonder if this is what hell smells like.

"Tad's wife."

I force a smile. I will be polite if it kills me. "Nice to meet you. I'm Anne."

Judy does not blink, nor does she take her eyes from mine. "I didn't know Tad was married."

"About six months ago. Eloped." Gladys says. My jaw clenches.

At that, Judy's eyes slide to my stomach before moving over the rest of me. I can see her taking inventory and placing tick marks on a list in her mind. Flat tummy: check. Pantsuit: check. Blotchy face: check. I watch as she places me under the "Unacceptable" column.

"I see why you didn't tell anyone, Gladys," Judy says, her gaze returning to mine. Her gray eyes tell me it's my fault that Tad is dead before she moves down the line to offer condolences to Tad's brother.

I cannot hate her, because I agree.

I am curled up in bed. I have tacked blankets over the windows, unplugged the alarm clock, and turned off the phone. I do not know if the world exists outside, and I do not care.

A knock sounds on the door. "Anne, are you in there? Are you okay?"

I grimace. My grandmother. "Yes, I'm in here, and what do you think?" I call. Keys jangle in the lock and I groan. Tad never fixed the chain on the door, and so there is no way to keep her out. I curse him in my mind and instantly feel ashamed.

Grandmother sweeps into our—my—bedroom and stops short. "Holy Mary Mother of God," she says. "How long have you been holed up?"

"I dunno. What day is it?"

She gives me a considering look. "Tuesday."

"A week, then."

"It smells like it," she says as she pulls a blanket off a window, pushes open the curtains, and raises the sash. Blinding light fills the room as a warm breeze brings in the city sounds from below. I try to burrow deeper under the blankets, but Grandmother yanks them off me before I can resist. "Up you go. Get showered and dressed. I'm taking you out for lunch."

"I'm not hungry," I say.

"I don't remember asking if you were. Up."

I know it is pointless to argue. Sighing, I roll off the bed and walk to the bathroom. Before I start the water to brush my teeth, I hear her rummage through my closet. I stop myself from telling her I am capable of dressing myself. This way I don't have to see Tad's clothes hanging useless next to mine.

After Grandmother approves of my appearance, we walk two blocks to the Korner Kafe. We sit outside, and she orders daiquiris and salads for us both. I find that I don't mind being told what to eat and drink, and I wonder what is wrong with me. I never would have let Tad order my food.

"Tad hates this place," I say after the drinks are delivered.

Grandmother takes a sip from hers, nods in approval, and says, "Why is that?"

"Pretentious. He thinks it's someplace his mother would like." I cry when I realize what I've said. "He thought that, anyway. Tad hated this place."

"I know you'll find this hard to believe, Anne, but you will survive this." Her normally brisk voice is soft.

"I'm glad somebody thinks so."

She gives me one of her penetrating looks, the same one she used to give me as a child when she knew I was hiding something. Back then I could withstand about ten seconds before telling her everything I knew. Age has granted me the ability to last twenty.

"I never asked to be a widow at twenty-five. I didn't sign up for this."

"Actually, you did. It's called a marriage license."

"Whose side are you on?" I ask, angry.

"Yours, but there aren't any guarantees in life. You should consider yourself lucky because you've learned that lesson early." She takes a breath and leans back in her chair. "I didn't pull you out of bed to make you upset."

"Yeah? Could have fooled me." I say.

"I wanted to give you these." Grandmother fishes a red velvet box from her purse and places it on the table between us.

I uncross my arms and open the box. Inside is a pair of topaz-and-diamond chandelier earrings. The stones are flawless, their facets catching the sunlight and sending rainbows onto the tablecloth. "They're beautiful," I whisper. I brush my fingers over them lightly and find them warm to the touch.

"They were given to me by Fred's mother, after he died."

I look at her, startled. I had forgotten that she was a young widow, too. She is looking at the earrings, but the smile on her face and the far-away look in her eyes tells me she is seeing something else. I close the box with a snap and place it back on the table. "I can't accept these. They're special to you."

She comes back to the present and smiles at me. "They'll be yours one day anyway, you know."

"That's beside the point," I say. I cannot think of my grandmother dying, not yet. "I've nowhere to wear them."

"Nonsense. You could wear these to the grocery store, provided you have the right shoes."

"Grandmother—"

"Tell you what. We'll call them a loan. When you don't need them anymore, you can give them back."

I can see there's no use in arguing. "You'll have them back next week," I say as the food arrives.

"I'll think you'll be surprised," she says as she places her napkin on her lap and gives me a wink.

"I can't believe I let you talk me into this," I say as I pull on an embroidered velvet shirt and grab a pair of jeans from the cluttered closet.

"You need to get out of this apartment, Anne. It isn't healthy," my friend Pandora says.

"I get out." I try to keep the defensiveness from my voice without much success.

"Yeah? When's the last time you bought groceries? Or shoes? That's what I thought," she says when I don't answer. She begins to pick through my jewelry box, and I am reminded of the first time she did that. We were thirteen, and my collection had consisted of rings that turned my fingers green and a single gold cross necklace. She had been appalled at my lack of style. Not much has changed.

"Just because I haven't bought anything doesn't mean I haven't left this place."

"Whatever. At least you're getting out now. Today. With me. This movie we're going to is supposed to be pretty good. That's what Brad said, anyway."

"Since when have you listened to your brother?"

"Since he started having good taste. Ooohh, where did you get these?" Pandora holds up the earrings.

"They're on loan from Grandmother. She says I can keep them as long as I need to."

"You're definitely going to need these for at least the next five years. They're gorgeous! Put them on."

"Panda! I'm wearing jeans."

She rolls her eyes. "So wear a pair of heels. Jesus, this isn't rocket science. Put 'em on."

I give her a look and take the earrings from her. She rummages through my closet while I struggle with the old-fashioned screw-posts.

"You've got too much shit in here," Pandora says as she tosses a handful of Tad's shirts to the floor.

"Watch it," I say, my voice sharp.

"You'd have more room if you got rid of his things. It's not like he's gonna use them." Her soft tone dissolves my anger.

"I know. But seeing his things reminds me that he was here, once."

"I'd think seeing his things would remind you he's dead."

I sigh. "Yeah." I finish fastening the left earring and wipe my face. The amber stones against my skin makes my complexion less sallow, my dark circles less noticeable. They are surprisingly light, and they warm my earlobes. I shake my head to feel their pendulum-like weight.

"Life's a bitch, huh? Wowza," Pandora says as she takes in my appearance. "You look hot. Here, wear these." She hands me a pair of jeweled heels.

I suddenly feel too alive to object.

We are in the darkened theater when I hear it. I am enjoying the movie, laughing at an absurd scene, and I am thinking that Tad would enjoy this, too.

You're right, I am enjoying it.

I stop and look around, catching a faint scent of licorice. "Did you hear that?" I whisper to Pandora.

"Hear what?" she whispers back, wiping tears from her eyes. I am jealous, because the last time I laughed so hard that I cried I was laughing with Tad.

Cut the shit. You were laughing at *me that time.*

"That! Did you hear it?"

"No," she says, watching the screen. Laughter erupts through the crowd again, and Pandora joins the cackles.

I sit back and pretend to watch to rest of the movie.

Afterward, I resist Pandora's insistence that we get a martini. Being social has exhausted me, and once I get to my apartment, I shed my clothes and fall into bed. I roll onto my side and an earring pokes behind my ear, reminding me I am not completely undressed. Grimacing, I sit up and begin to unscrew the post.

Don't.

I freeze, hold my breath, and listen hard. I only hear my pulse in my ears. Licking my lips, I whisper, "Tad?"

Yeah. I just want you to hear me for a little longer. Please. Don't take the earrings off.

Gooseflesh covers my body, and I smell licorice again. "Am I going insane?" I am afraid to speak above a whisper.

Tad snorts. *You've always been insane. Why should you be any different now?*

"Not possible. It can't be you. You can't prove . . ."

As to proving it's me . . . I have been dead two months. The last food I ate was leftover cake from Susan's wedding, and the last drink I had was a shot of Jaeger. The last time we—

"Stop," I say as I begin to cry. "But that's not proof. Tell me something else."

Silence stretches out so long, and I am about to pull the covers over me when the voice comes again.

On my side of the closet there's a shoebox on the top shelf, way back in the corner. Inside is a bracelet I bought you for your birthday.

I push the covers off, whip open the closet door and pull down stacks of neatly folded sweaters. Finding the shoebox, I rip the lid off and pull out a square velvet box. Inside is a delicate gold band with a single ruby set in the center. Slipping it over my wrist, I say, "It's beautiful."

Tad buying a gift four months in advance of my birthday is—was—so typical of him.

"It's the earrings, isn't it?"

Isn't what?

"The earrings. That's why I can hear you."

He doesn't answer, but I know then that I will never give these earrings back.

"What's it like to be dead?" I ask.

Can't tell you.

"What do you mean, you can't tell me? Is it that hard to describe?

Oh, no, it's not that. I mean it's a rule. I had to sign papers and everything.

"They made you sign a contract?" I laugh. Having a conversation about the afterlife with my dead husband is just absurd enough so that believing the dead have contractual obligations is easy. "Did they notarize it, too?"

I've already said too much. Listen, do me a favor.

"Anything."

It's time you donated my things. I'm dead, remember? Don't think I'm gonna need that Cubs hat anymore.

The irony strikes me and I laugh. Tad is pragmatic even when he's dead.

"Tomorrow," I promise.

What's wrong with tonight?

"What's right with tonight?" I say too quickly.

Anne. You will never get over my death when you have reminders of my life slapping you in the face everywhere in the apartment.

" 'Get over' you? One doesn't 'get over' a spouse's death in sixty days," I say.

You'll end up like that batty old woman down the block.

"What have you got against Mrs. Neadlebeck? For all we know, the CIA *did* murder her husband."

When I was alive you thought she was creepy, too.

"When you were alive . . . I . . . oh, fuck you," I say. All of a sudden I'm so angry I can't breath. "Sometimes you're just so impossible, Tad! Did you come back from the afterlife just to piss me off? Well, you succeeded." I regret the words as soon as I say them, but I am too stubborn to apologize.

First off, Tad says, and I can hear the smile in his words, *I didn't "come back." I've been here all along. And second, I'll piss you off if that's what it takes.*

"Takes to do what?" My curiosity takes the edge from my anger.

Remember when my boss at work died? The bald guy everyone hated?

"Ye-e-e-ah." I know where he is going with this, and I don't want to hear it.

Everyone I worked with thought he was an incompetent, selfish, small man. But if you were at the funeral and didn't know better, you'd have thought he was the most beloved man at the company. His eulogies made him out to be this big philanthropist.

I smile at Tad's vocabulary. "Human, even."

Right. And remember how I made you promise not to do that? That, if I died, I wanted you to be honest about who I was?

"Yeah."

I still want that. Don't make me a martyr, Anne. Don't be a martyr yourself. There's plenty you didn't like about me.

"Like what?"

Like how I used to eat rare beef. Or how I used to ignore the dirty dishes in the sink when it was my turn. Or how I used to fart in my sleep.

"That was actually kind of funny," I say. "I didn't mind it as much as I let on."

I'm so glad you finally told me.

His sarcasm makes me chuckle.

Sobering, I say, "But what if I forget the good things? What if I throw out your hats and I forget how insane you got during baseball season? What if I throw out your ties and I forget you liked stripes? What if I throw out your cologne and I forget how you smelled?"

You won't. My dad died when I was five, and I still remember him helping me break in my first ball glove. The baby oil smell, the rubber band around the ball and the glove, him showing me where to crease it—all of it is right there. If I close my eyes, I can still hear him laughing when I caught my first ball with it. I can

*remember how the ball just fell into the spot I'd made
for it, like he said it would. You can't forget me. I've
marked up your heart too much.*

"But how can I be sure?" I don't realize I'm crying
until I hear my creaky voice.

You'll just have to trust me.

These are the exact same words he said to me after
he proposed. I had asked how he could be sure he
would love me in fifty years. He said I'd have to trust
him. And I did, completely. I am pleased to find that
I still do.

Should we start with the kitchen or the closet?

"The kitchen, I think," I say. While I would not say
I am happy, my smile doesn't feel forced. "I've always
hated those dishes you bought."

"You're in good spirits," Pandora says as she peers
into her reflection in the bathroom mirror.

"Am I?" I am on my knees, scrubbing the bathtub.
This was Tad's job, one of many I've taken over since
he's passed. Perhaps I am not resentful because I can
hear him snickering about Panda's outfit in my ear.

"Yeah. I would have thought cleaning out Tad's
stuff would have made you sad. What did you keep?"

"Nothing," I say, tackling a stubborn patch of
soap scum.

"Nothing?" she says, not believing it. "Not one single thing?"

"Give me some credit. I kept a few things, but most
of it's gone." Why do I need his things when I can
talk to him anytime I want to? "I don't need constant
reminders of what I lost to remember what I had."
My earlobes tingle, and I know that Tad agrees.

Pandora squints at me. "Have you seen a therapist
without telling me?"

"No." Unless you count talking with spirits as therapy. "Why do you ask?"

"You just seem so *healthy*. It's disturbing. Next
you'll tell me you've gone vegetarian."

"That's going a bit far."

"And you've finally been converted. Wearing that bracelet to clean the tub is so right it's almost wrong."

"Good thing I'm done," I say as I splash rinse water around the porcelain. "Wanna go grab a drink? My treat."

"That's my girl," Pandora says.

I do not realize until I change my clothes that Grandmother's earrings are on my bureau and not my ears.

"You're finished with them? Are you sure?" Grandmother says, her eyes trying to read my face.

"I've never been surer of anything. I don't need jewelry to feel Tad beside me." I place the box on the table between us and dig into my fruit salad.

"You'll be surprised how long they stick around," she says, casually. "Between Fred and George and Ray, I'm never alone. Sometimes I wonder if they take shifts or if they're all there at once, bumping into each other and cursing."

I laugh at the picture her words make in my mind. "You could wear the earrings and ask them."

"I could," she agrees, "but that would be intruding."

"Is that so different from what the dead do to us?"

"I'd like to think it is," she says, smiling. As she slips the earrings into her purse, I think I see one of her dead husbands beside her. I blink, and the moment and the image are gone.

A CLEAN GETAWAY

Keith R.A. DeCandido

"Watch where you step!"

Lieutenant Danthres Tresyllione was already in a bad mood when she arrived at the house in Unicorn Precinct, and finding herself being yelled at by one of the guards did not improve it. Looking down, she saw that the floor of the house was covered in some kind of dark muck.

Her superiors were generally amenable to paying for a Cleaning Spell to get blood stains out of her boots and earth-colored cloak. This whatever-it-was, on the other hand, would be a harder sell, and Danthres was in no mood to fight that particular battle with whatever functionary in the Lord and Lady's court oversaw the appropriations for such things.

"I'll stay out here, then," she said, stopping in the threshold.

"Not a problem," said a familiar voice from inside. It was her partner, Lieutenant Torin ban Wyvald. "I've already been soiled, so I'll provide the gory details."

Danthres peered inside to see a large sitting room that would have been considered fancy and high-class but for the fact that it was covered in a truly impressive amount of dirt and grime and muck. Tramping around in it were the guard who had cautioned her to step lightly—whom she recognized as Manfred, one of the few grunts in the Cliff's End Castle Guard who had anything approaching a brain—and Torin. Hovering about a hand's-length above the floor was the M.E., Boneen. Typically, the magical examiner refused to degrade himself, so he used his wizardly abilities to levitate; just as typically, the cranky old bastard didn't offer the same courtesy to the others.

"I'm surprised to see you here already, Boneen," Danthres said. "It usually requires a team of dragons to get you to a crime scene with any dispatch."

Glaring witheringly at Danthres from his position over the floor, Boneen said, "Does it disturb you, Tresyllione, to make so many attempts at wit and yet fall short of the mark?"

"Not in the least." Danthres turned to Torin. "So what happened?"

Torin cleared his throat before speaking. "This house is owned by the Jaros family. The actual owner is the family patriarch, Millar Jaros, and his son, daughter-in-law, and four grandchildren all live here as well. This morning the daughter-in-law, Abbi, came downstairs to prepare breakfast, and discovered this."

While Torin was talking, Danthres had been looking at the muck and noticing something. "All right, this is odd—there's a pattern to the gunk. Like it all exploded outward." She'd seen similar patterns in blood when someone was struck with a heavy object, especially in the head, but it wasn't something she ever expected to see with dirt.

"Yes, it did." Torin was now pointing at a closet door. "It seems to have come out from there."

Crankily, Boneen said, "No 'seems' about it. I did the peel-back, and it showed this garbage literally explode outward from the closet." On loan from the Brotherhood of Wizards, the magical examiner's primary purpose was to cast an Inanimate Residue Spell, commonly called a "peel-back," which allowed him to see what recently happened in a particular place. "And once I did that, I had this young man call you two in."

That, at least, explained why Boneen's arrival preceded theirs. She looked at Manfred. "You summoned the M.E., Manfred?"

"Yes, ma'am." The guard sounded pleased that she remembered his name. "And he had me bring you in, like he said, ma'am."

Danthres's mood grew darker by the second. "Pardon me, Boneen, but I was under the impression that the function of lieutenants in the Castle Guard like myself and Torin was to investigate crimes that occur within the Lord and Lady's demesne."

"What are you driving at, Tresyllione?"

Angrily, Danthres said, "What I'm driving at is that what I see here is an accident, not a crime—unless there's a dead body I'm missing under all this?"

Torin's long red hair and thick red beard obscured all of his face save for his humorous eyes and aquiline nose—except when he smiled broadly, as he did now. "No, but there is a bit of a wrinkle."

She sighed. "Of course there is."

Manfred said, "I talked to Abbi Jaros and then her husband, father-in-law, and children, and they all say the same thing: until this morning, there was no closet there, just a blank wall."

"So there's magic afoot." She fixed her irritated gaze upon Boneen. "Isn't magic the Brotherhood's concern?"

"Licensed magic is, yes. This is unlicensed magic." Sniffing, he added, "The Brotherhood does not consort in magicks that cast dirt about."

"What, your desire to keep from getting your hands dirty extends to the rest of the world, too?"

"Something like that, yes. In any case, I've already communicated with Lord Ythran, the local Brotherhood representative, and he and I agreed that this is an unlicensed commercial spell, and therefore not within the Brotherhood's purview. So have at it."

With that, Boneen gestured, muttered something, and disappeared in a flash of light.

After blinking the spots from her eyes—Danthres was half-elf, which made her more sensitive to the bright lights that accompanied Boneen's Teleport Spell—she said, "This doesn't answer my question."

"What question is that, Danthres?" Torin asked as he slogged through the muck toward the front door.

"What crime has been committed?"

Torin looked down, smiled, and then looked back at Danthres. "Well, vandalism at the very least."

"A crime easily solved even by the pea-brained idiots of the guard rank." Turning to Manfred, she said, "Nothing personal, Manfred."

Manfred grinned. "Honestly, ma'am, most guards' brains aren't that large."

Danthres found herself laughing against her better judgment, then quickly grew serious again. The last thing she wanted to do was get chummy with one of the guards. "So why are we handling this?"

Torin walked slowly to the closet door. "I said vandalism was the very least this could be. I've examined the closet door—it doesn't match the design of the rest of the house, and the space it takes up can't be accounted for by the shape of the house. It's definitely something magical. It might be some sort of attack on the Jaros family. Since we haven't actually spoken to them yet, now might be the time to do that, and see if this is part of something larger."

Rolling her eyes, Danthres said, "Somehow I doubt that very much." She sighed far louder than perhaps she should have and asked Manfred, "Where are they?"

"Next door, ma'am—they said they didn't want to stay in here until it was cleaned up."

Torin gingerly walked across the sitting-room floor

toward Danthres. "Perhaps you can recommend that cleaning service of yours?"

Her face darkening even more, Danthres said, "Not likely. I spent half the morning trying to find where they *put* everything." At the behest of a rather aggrieved landlady, Danthres had hired a cleaning service for her rooms. Said landlady had rented Danthres the two rooms on the upper floor of her house in Dragon Precinct on the condition that Danthres keep the place clean and neat. However, Danthres had not been keeping up that part of the bargain especially well, thanks to the long hours she put in as a detective for the Castle Guard as well as her own inherent laziness when it came to matters of housekeeping. Since the landlady was threatening to toss Danthres out on her ear if she didn't comply, she hired a cleaning service.

They'd done a thorough job of making the place neat and shiny and clean. It was far more thorough than Danthres would have believed possible—so much so, in fact, that Danthres couldn't find a single thing she was looking for this morning. It was what had set her on her bad mood in the first place.

As Torin did his best to wipe his feet on the welcome mat, he said to Manfred, "Seal off the house for the time being, and get Sergeant Arron to send someone to guard both the front and back doors."

Danthres rolled her eyes. "Waste of time."

"Perhaps, but I'd rather have guards there and not need them than the other way 'round."

"Fair enough. If you're done, let's go talk to the family."

The family, to Danthres's lack of surprise, was singularly unhelpful. That lack of surprise was due to the way her day had been going. First there was the scavenger hunt for her every personal item. Then she arrived at the east wing of the castle, where the sergeant informed her that the magistrate had returned

a not-guilty ruling on her and Torin's most recent
murder case, which did nothing to improve either her
mood or her opinion of the magistrate. She couldn't
complain to Torin about it because he was late as
usual—only he wasn't coming in at all, because he'd
been summoned to the crime scene in Unicorn.

To add to the annoyance, none of the Jaros family
seemed to be in any way insincere about their confusion over what had happened. Danthres had been a
detective in the Castle Guard for a decade now, and
she had gotten a good ear for when people were lying.
While Millar Jaros did lie about his monetary worth
and Abbi Jaros lied about how she was a good and
faithful wife, and the children lied about any number
of things, they all seemed quite sincere to her trained
ear when they discussed the suddenly appearing closet.

Just as Torin and Danthres were about to leave the
neighbor's house, Abbi asked, "Excuse me, Lieutenants, but, well, I mean—" She threw up her hands.
"What are we supposed to *do* about that?"

"Hire a cleaning service, I would expect," Danthres
said dismissively.

"I'm a good housewife," Abbi said stubbornly. "I
don't believe in cleaning services."

"Have at it, then," Danthres said with a wicked
grin. "But if you decide you'd rather not get on hands
and knees and muck out your own house, I can recommend a service to avoid. They're called Forak's Perfect Clean, and they've made a mess of my own
place."

Abbi frowned. "What kind of cleaning service
leaves a place a mess?"

"That's kind of my point." With that, Danthres left.

Danthres' mood was even worse when she came in
the next morning. After spending the morning wasting
their time interviewing the Jaros family, they spent
the afternoon wasting their time interviewing Alfrek
Jaros' coworkers. Alfrek, Abbi's husband and Millar's

son, worked in the Lord and Lady's castle as a deputy to the transport minister, Sir Lio. That, at least, made tracking them down easy, as they were in the same building where Danthres and Torin worked.

They were no more helpful in revealing why someone would mess up the Jaros sitting room from a hidden closet.

Sergeant Jonas came dashing in from the kitchen, shuffling parchments, his green cloak billowing behind him. He scowled at Danthres as she approached her desk. "You're late. And where's your—"

"Jonas, so help me, if you ask me where my cloak is, I will ram my sword so far up your ass the point will stick out your left ear. Just fetch me another one, will you?"

The sergeant twisted his lips, as if considering saying something, then thinking better of it, and then zipped off to fetch a fresh cloak. All members of the Castle Guard wore leather armor, a crest emblazoned on the chest to indicate posting: a gryphon for the castle, and a unicorn, dragon, goblin, or mermaid to indicate the precinct with the same name in the city-state proper. Those above the level of guard had a cloak to indicate rank; lieutenants wore brown.

Danthres saw, to her shock, that Torin was already at his desk, which abutted hers. True, she was later than usual, but for Torin, late *was* usual. He was also holding some parchments in his hands. "Paperwork," he said dismissively as he set them aside. "What happened to your cloak?"

"Forak's. I'm guessing one of their cleaning people made off with it when they cleaned the place. That's why I'm late, I had to go over there to complain. They promised to search and get back to me." She sat down at her desk. "What have you been doing?"

"I was thinking about what other avenues we could explore, and I thought we might try the architectural angle."

Danthres frowned. "Excuse me?"

"Millar, Abbi, and Alfrek all said that the closet wasn't part of the original design of the house, that it was a blank wall until yesterday morning."

"Right. Whatever magic cast the muck also created the closet."

"Perhaps. But this house dates back to when the city-state was first being built. Lord Galmar, Lord Albin's late father, insisted that all constructions have their blueprints filed in the castle. Lord Albin didn't continue that practice—the city-state grew too large for it to be practical to keep track of every single building—but back in the old days it was a requirement." One of Torin's smaller smiles peeked out through his beard. "So I've requested the blueprints."

Instinctively, Danthres wanted to object. In her experience, the best way to find out what happened was to figure out who was most likely to have committed the crime and interrogate them until they confessed.

But they'd tried that, and didn't turn anything up. Torin's notion was as good a one as any.

"What's wrong?" Torin asked.

"Hm?" Danthres looked up. "What do you mean what's wrong?"

Torin smirked. "I expected at least a grouse about what a pain it is to paw through records when we should be questioning people."

"What would be the point?" Danthres said with a dramatic sigh. "Besides, I used up most of my invective this morning with those shitbrains at Forak's." Waving off the platitude Torin was likely to espouse, she said, "It's fine, don't worry about it. Let's get to work."

"Well, we can't until—"

One of the castle page boys came in, laden with massive rolled-up parchments, and looking nervously from side to side. "Lieutenant bin Givald?"

Chuckling, Torin got up. "Close enough. Over here, lad."

The page boy dashed over to Torin's desk, dropped

the parchments unceremoniously on its surface, then dashed out of the squad room as fast as his spindly legs would carry him.

"No doubt concerned about overexposure to the thugs," Danthres said irritably, using the word far too many of the aristocrats in the castle used when speaking of the Castle Guard.

Torin grinned. "No doubt." He unrolled the dried old parchments, one for each floor of the house.

Danthres got up and walked around to Torin's desk. As she started to peer down at the blueprints, she noticed that Torin was wearing new boots. "What happened to your boots?"

Shrugging, Torin said, "I couldn't get that muck off, so I sent them to be cleaned, and they issued me a new pair."

"I should mark this day down," she said dryly. "In ten years, I think that's the first time you've changed boots without being threatened with bodily harm." She was also impressed that Torin had managed to convince the service to do the job in the first place.

"It takes forever to break them in," Torin said testily. "I have wide feet."

She shook her head. "They're *boots,* Torin, not pets." Not wanting to get into this argument *again,* she looked down at the ragged material. "I'm amazed these things haven't fallen to pieces. Aren't they over a hundred years old?"

"Magic, probably," Torin said, "cast when it was realized that they were, in fact, falling to pieces." He studied the first floor. "Interesting. There isn't a design for a closet—but there is a space there." He put his index finger on the spot where the closet was now. "That's odd."

"What is?"

"Feel that."

Looking at her partner as if he were crazy, she asked, "What?"

"The parchment, on the spot where the closet is, feel it."

Shrugging, Danthres did so—and was surprised to feel something etched into the parchment. "It feels like a character of some kind."

Torin looked up just as Jonas came zooming in, a cloak in his hand. "Sergeant, could you fetch Boneen, please?"

Jonas handed Danthres her cloak in the manner one would give a diseased rat to a waste disposer. After Danthres snatched it out of his hands, the sergeant said to Torin, "He's on a call right now—Dru and Hawk found that invisible robber's house, and he needs to do a peel-back on it."

Nodding, Torin said, "Fine, when he gets back, could you ask him to tell us what the sigil is on this section of the parchment?"

Jonas looked at where Torin was pointing and nodded. "Oh, by the way," he said as he turned to leave, "they couldn't do anything for your boots. The Cleaning Spell didn't work for some reason." With that, the sergeant left the squad room again.

"You know, it might not even *be* a sigil," Danthres said, "though I agree that's the most likely thing."

"Either way, best to sound sure with Boneen—otherwise he'll yell at us for wasting his time."

Danthres snorted. "Like he won't anyhow."

"Fair point. I wonder what the problem was with the boots."

Shrugging, Danthres said, "They probably got a cheap Cleaning Spell that doesn't actually work."

"Probably."

"Lieutenant?"

Since no name was given, both Torin and Danthres turned at the sound of the voice, which came from one of the guards assigned to the castle. Danthres couldn't remember his name, so she just thought of him the way she did most of the guards: he was the stupid one.

"Yes?" she said.

"There's someone here to see you both—she says it has to do with the Jaros case."

"Who is she?" Danthres asked.

The guard said, "Her name's Amaralla, and she says she—"

Suddenly, a very short, dark-haired woman barrelled past the guard and said, "Enough of this, I'm *busy,* dammit, don't have time for this. Are you two Trestle and bag Wyverin?"

"I'm Lieutenant ban Wyvald," Torin said slowly to make sure the woman realized just how badly she'd mangled their names, "and this is my partner—"

"Yes, yes, yes, you're the ones investigating what happened to the Jaros house, right?"

"We are," Torin said. "How may we—"

"You can do your damn *jobs,* that's what you can do. You're supposed to be able to stop this kinda thing, right?"

"Actually, no," Danthres said with as insincere a smile as she could manage—which was pretty insincere indeed. "Our job is to find who did it and stop them from doing it again."

"Well, then who's responsible for stopping it?"

"I'm sorry, who are you again?"

Sighing dramatically, the woman said, "As I told this mouth-breather with the mite-sized brain—" She indicated the guard, who took the insult with aplomb. "—my name is Thea Amaralla, and I represent the Amaralla Cleaning Service."

That's two cleaning services in Cliff's End I despise, Danthres somehow managed not to say out loud. "And what is your connection to the Jaros case?"

"If you'd just *listen,* I'd tell you. They hired us to clean up the mess in their place."

"In that case," Danthres said, "the answer to your question is you."

"I beg your pardon?"

"You wanted to know who's responsible for stopping it. It's a mess, you're a cleaning service—I would think the answer would be obvious?"

Turning to Torin, Amaralla asked, "Is she always like this?"

"No," Torin said cheerily, "usually she's belligerent. Madam, I'm afraid my partner is correct, cleaning up the mess is your job. We simply need to find out who did this and—"

"Not *did*."

"I'm sorry?" Torin frowned in confusion.

"Not *did*. *Is* doing. The mess is getting worse. And every attempt we've made to clean it up has met with failure. Nothing will make it go away—and now it's growing." She stomped her foot. "So will you *please* figure it out? The Jaroses are demanding their money back!"

Just as Danthres was about to speak, Torin cut her off. "I'm afraid that issues of payment must be worked out between you and the Jaros family, madam. However, you can rest assured that we will be looking into this new development." He looked over at the guard. "Will you please escort the lady out?"

Smiling nastily, the guard said, "Gladly, Lieutenant." He grabbed Amaralla by the arm and yanked her toward the door.

"I will not be *treated* this way! Let go of me! This is an outrage! This is—"

Whatever else it was became lost in her rapid, guard-aided retreat. Danthres made a mental note to be less nasty to that guard in the future.

Torin looked at her. "There would appear to be more to this than we thought. I suggest we go back."

Danthres desperately wanted to argue the point, but she found she couldn't. And that only made her mood worse.

Before they could even make it to the door of the Jaros house, Millar Jaros intercepted them, screaming a blue streak.

"What the hell's wrong with you people? You see the *mess* in there? Well? Didja? It's a *mess*! How're we supposed t'live in there if it's such a *mess*?"

Next to him was Abbi, who put a hand on his shoulder. "Father, take it easy, they can't—"

Whirling on his daughter-in-law, Millar said, "How'm I supposed t'take it easy when there's such a *mess* in there!"

"I know, Father, but—"

Torin finally said, "May we please take a look?"

Throwing up his hands, Millar said, "Sure, take a look, but all you're gonna see is a *mess*!"

Danthres shot Torin a look, as if to say, *What else were we supposed to see?* Torin shrugged back, and the two of them then walked past the Jaroses to the guard who'd been assigned by Dragon Precinct to stand at the front door.

"Open it," Torin said.

Nodding, the guard opened the front door.

The smell was the first thing to hit Danthres. On their previous visit, the place had smelled bad, but no worse than the thoroughfares of Goblin Precinct during midsummer, or the docks of Mermaid Precinct in the afternoon after the fish came in.

Now, though, the Jaros house made the docks seem like an orchard by comparison. Danthres's nose wrinkled up immediately and pretty much stayed that way as she surveyed the sitting room.

Not that there was much of the sitting room to survey—it was covered, wall to ceiling, in the same dark muck. She could make out small shapes under the muck that she assumed to be the furniture, and she also saw other bits and pieces jutting out from it.

"Lord and Lady," Torin muttered.

"Close the door," Danthres said to the guard. "We need to get Boneen in here."

It took the better part of an hour for the magical examiner to make his appearance. During that time, Danthres tried to ignore Millar Jaros's complaints, mostly by coming up with entertaining ways of flaying the old man alive.

When Boneen did arive via a Teleport Spell, he looked even more perturbed than usual. "I've already *been* here."

"Yes," Danthres said, "and all you told us was that it was unlicensed magic. What *kind* of magic was it?"

Boneen sneered. "The unlicensed kind. Why am I wasting my time with this?"

Torin asked, "Boneen, did you identify the sigil on the blueprints on my desk?"

"Yes, right before I was told to come here. It's the symbol for hiding something."

Looking at Danthres, Torin said, "Like a closet."

Millar stepped forward. "What do you mean?"

"The blueprints for your house have a mark on the spot where the closet is now," Torin said. "It would seem that the hidden closet was part of the building's original plans."

"Excuse me," Boneen said before Millar could go off on another rant about messes, thus marking the first time Danthres had ever been grateful for Boneen's crankiness, "but why am I here?"

Steeling herself, Danthres told the guard to reopen the door to the Jaros house.

Boneen seemed unperturbed by the stench. He simply looked inside and said, "Oh, dear."

"Well put," Danthres muttered.

Shaking his head, the magical examiner looked away from the muck-covered sitting room. "I had assumed this to be a one-time event—someone using the Duality Spell once for whatever arcane reason—but it looks like it's been used for some time, and still is being cast on a regular basis." He regarded Torin and pointed at the closet in the back of the sitting room. "That sigil I was translating—it was on the spot where that closet is?"

Torin nodded.

"Can we please close the door before I die?"

Danthres asked plaintively. The elven half of her heritage came with a sensitivity far greater than that of humans, and the smell that irritated them was going to kill her ere long.

Waving his hand dismissively, Boneen said, "It won't do any good, but go ahead." The guard did so, to Danthres's relief.

Millar drew himself up to full height. "What do you mean it won't do any good? And who's going to clean up that *mess*?"

"And what exactly," Danthres asked, "is a Duality Spell?" As a rule, Danthres preferred to avoid magic, but reality didn't allow for that, and ten years in the Castle Guard made her painfully aware of the most common spells—particularly the ones that were commercially available. This one, however, rang no bells.

"To answer your earlier question, Tresyllione," Boneen said, folding his spindly arms across his chest, "this magic is of a type devised by a wizard named Ivano the Misguided. He pioneered an entire system of magic that involved checks and balances—every time you cast a spell, there was a concomitant reaction elsewhere. This way there'd be no effort on the part of the spellcaster, and anyone could wield magic."

"Anyone *can* use magic," Danthres said impatiently. "All they have to do is buy a spell—"

"—that's already been cast." Boneen sounded just as impatient. "A wizard casts the spell into the scroll, which then goes on the market. The purchaser then uses it, but the energy of the spellcaster has already been spent. With Ivano's magic, one didn't need any kind of training to cast a spell, nor did one need to purchase a spell—you simply needed to incant it."

Torin nodded. "That explains why that Amaralla woman's people couldn't clean the place—and why my boots resisted the Cleaning Spell."

Seeing an out, Danthres said with a smile. "So that means this *would* be a case for the Brotherhood, wouldn't it?"

"If I bring this to the Brotherhood, the first thing they'll ask is why I didn't bring this to them sooner." Boneen for once sounded abashed. "If it's all the same to you, I'd rather not bring that to their attention."

"Oh, no," Danthres said angrily, pointing an accusatory finger at Boneen, "you're not getting out of it that easily. I've had far too many murders and assaults shitcanned because it's 'Brotherhood business,' and everything gets swept under the rug. Now, the one time when they'd actually be a *help,* which only happens once every third blue moon, and you're telling me you won't *inform* them?"

"I'll help you," Boneen said.

That brought Danthres up short. The M.E. had never used those three words in sequence before that Danthres was aware of. Boneen considered the work he did for the Castle Guard to be a waste of his precious time and energy, and he begrudged every second of it. For him to volunteer . . .

Boneen went on. "Give me a minute to gather myself up and let me examine the house more closely. I might be able to trace where the spell's being cast."

"Uhm, excuse me?" That was Abbi Jaros, whom Danthres had briefly forgotten, having focused most of her ire on either her father-in-law or the M.E. "What kind of spell *is* this exactly? What's happening to our house?"

Boneen started waving his arms about. "Ivano's magic always has a secondary effect. Someone is doing something pleasant, and that requires that somewhere else there be something awful. However, the awful can be directed, and in this case, it was to the closet that was hidden in your house when it was built." He cast a glance at the shut door. "But they've obviously been casting this spell for some time. The muck in your closet has become too big to fit therein, and it has spilled out into the house." Now he looked at Danthres and Torin. "We need to find out who's doing this. At this rate, it will expand to take over and destroy this house. In a week, it will have consumed the entire block.''

Danthres blinked. Perhaps she didn't want the Brotherhood involved, after all—not if she wanted this solved properly. "All right, then, what do we do?"

"First, I examine this house." Boneen slowly got down onto the floor and sat in a lotus position; Danthres could hear his bones creak and crack as he did so. The aged wizard muttered something, waved his right hand about, and then started to float upward.

About a minute later, he unfolded his legs, while still floating, and placed them on the ground. "This is worse than I thought. It's been going on for at least a decade, possibly longer. I can't tell for sure—there are magically enhanced items in there interfering." That last was said with an accusatory look at Abbi and Millar.

"That's impossible!" Abbi said. "We don't keep anything magical in the house."

"That's right," Millar said. "Got rid of it all. Filthy stuff, magic."

Noting that was the first thing Millar had said that hadn't made Danthres want to punch him, she asked Boneen, "Is there any way to extract those items? If they don't belong to the family, they might belong to whoever cast the spell."

"It's possible, but I'm already rather tired, and—"

"Fine, then." Danthres turned to Torin. "What's the name of the Brotherhood representative?"

"Ythran," Torin said. "I'm sure he'd be overjoyed to hear all about Boneen misreading the peel-back."

"I didn't misread it!" Boneen was almost pouting. "All right, all right, I'll cast the blessed spell."

This time, Boneen didn't bother with the lotus position, but the muttering took longer, and he gesticulated with both hands.

Danthres had to blink away the spots in front of her eyes that the resultant flash of light caused, but when they were gone, she looked down at the ground in front of Boneen to see seven objects, all encrusted with the muck that had taken over the Jaros house, all looking like articles of clothing.

Boneen pointed at one of two items that looked like cloaks. "That looks like a Protector Cloak—a low-level one, it'd just keep the shit off you walking around Goblin—but that explains the magical interference."

However, Danthres was more interested in the other cloak.

Breathing through her mouth to avoid the stench—which, while not as bad as the room had been, was still pretty awful—Danthres bent over to grab it. Grateful that her uniform included gloves, she picked it up by one end with her right hand, wiping the center of the cloak off with her left glove.

Then she smiled grimly. "I know who did this."

Forak's Perfect Clean had offices in Dragon Precinct, only a short walk from Danthres' rooms, which was why she had chosen them in the first place. That evening, she entered their waiting area, accompanied by Torin. As had been the case when she had gone there to make the appointment, and again when she filed the complaint about her missing cloak, the waiting area consisted solely of a bench, a desk behind which sat a prim young woman, and a door leading to the back.

The prim woman—whose name, Danthres recalled, was Emanuela—looked up at their entrance. "Ah, Lieutenant Trellis, isn't it?"

"Tresyllione, actually," Danthres corrected automatically.

"Of course. I'm afraid we haven't found your cloak yet, but I can assure you that it will turn up. We here at Forak's guarantee customer satisfaction—it is our watchword, after all." Emanuela said all that without once changing her inflection.

"Well, I'm afraid that isn't good enough," Danthres

said, trying to sound like an outraged customer—
which wasn't too difficult an act for her just at the
moment. "I want to speak to your supervisor
immediately."

"I'm afraid Mr. Forak isn't available right now,
Lieutenant, but if you wish to make an appointment—"

"*I'm* afraid that I must see Mr. Forak right now, or
I will shut this place down."

Emanuela opened her tiny mouth into an O, then
closed it. She didn't have a prepared response to that,
it seemed, and it took a few moments for her brain
to actually function. "Can you *do* that?"

Torin smiled his most pleasant smile. "We are lieutenants in the Castle Guard, madam. The Lord and
Lady have granted us considerable leeway in such
matters, and all we would have to do is pronounce
this place a menace to the well-being of Cliff's End
and its inhabitants, and it would be shut down. Mr.
Forak could, of course, appeal to the magistrate, but
that might take days."

"Weeks, even," Danthres added. "And you would
not be permitted to conduct business until that—"

"Mr. Forak!" Emanuela cried out in a tone very
much like a mouse's squeak, apparently unable to handle any more disruptions to her world. "Some people
here to see you!"

A short man with thin hair and a thick mustache
came out through the door to the rear. "What? What?
Dammit, Emanuela, I told you not to bother me, I'm
trying to— Oh!" That last word was spoken upon
sighting two people in leather armor and earth-colored
cloaks, symbolizing that they were detectives in the
Guard. "Dammit, Emanuela, why didn't you tell me
that the good people of the Cliff's End Castle Guard
were here?"

"But—" Emanuela tried to protest, but Forak didn't
give her the chance, bounding forward with a broad
smile peeking out from under his mustache.

"You're Mr. Forak?"

"Yes, Lieutenant, yes, I am most definitely him, yes, I am. Now then, who might you be, and what service can Forak's Perfect Clean do for you on this lovely day?"

"I'm Lieutenant Tresyllione, this is my partner, Lieutenant ban Wyvald. I'm one of your customers, actually."

"Ah, yes, well, of course," Forak said, sounding relieved. "Are you satisfied with our service, Lieutenant Tresilon?"

"Tresyllione, and I mostly am, yes, although an item has gone missing. A cloak—just like the one I'm wearing now. I told your girl about it there—"

"Right, of course, yes, we're getting right on that. My best people are searching for the cloak even as we speak."

"Your best people?"

"Of course."

Danthres nodded. "Fascinating."

"Mr. Forak, I apologize," Torin said, "but I'm a bit befuddled. You see, before coming here, we went to the castle and examined your tax records. They say that you only have one employee." He nodded his head at Emanuela. "I have to wonder—who does the actual cleaning?"

"And who's looking for my cloak?" Danthres added.

Forak started to shuffle from foot to foot, and twisted the end of his mustache with his right hand. "Yes, well, ahm, you see, I mean, that is to say, uh—"

"Let me save you the trouble of lying, Mr. Forak. You don't have any employees, do you? You charge one gold per room cleaned, which, when I first came here, you said was to cover cleaning supplies and labor costs. Other cleaning services usually charge two gold, but they also give the option of providing your own supplies—which you don't do."

"Erm, yes, you see, I—"

"This is because you don't actually have a staff, do you, Mr. Forak?" Danthres started moving slowly closer to Forak, who backed up until he bumped into Emanuela's desk. "Instead, you cast a spell to clean the room and send the dirt to a closet hidden in a house in Unicorn, where no one will ever find it. There are only two problems, Mr. Forak."

"Oh, ah, yes? What's, er, what's that, then?"

"First of all, the closet filled up and exploded. The dirt from all the homes you've cleaned has now taken over the house, and soon it will encompass an entire block. Do you know who owns that house, Mr. Forak?"

"Er, well, no, actually, I—"

"Alfrek Jaros. He works for Sir Lio, the transport minister. Do you know what Sir Lio will think about someone doing this to one of his deputies?"

"Uhm—"

"The second problem is that it isn't just dirt that goes to the Jaros closet. According to our magical examiner, the spell requires sending the items from one closet to another, and some items in the closets of your clients got mixed in with the dirt. They included two pairs of boots, a Protection Cloak, three tunics—and *my* cloak."

"Ah, yes, well, you see, I can, er, that is to say, I—"

Torin grabbed Forak's arms. "I would reserve comment until you've seen the magistrate."

Puffing himself up, Forak said, "Hang on, you can't arrest me! I've done nothing wrong!"

Danthres snarled. "You've done quite a bit wrong, Mr. Forak. Fraud, for one thing."

"I didn't defraud no one, I didn't! I said I'd clean your place, and I *did!*"

Torin glanced at Danthres. "He has a point."

"True. But there's also littering. And vandalism to the Jaros house." She smiled a most unpleasant smile, then. "And, of course, there's the Brotherhood."

Forak went white. "Th—the Brotherhood? You mean, that is to say—of Wizards?"

"Yes, that Brotherhood. They don't take kindly to people using unlicensed magic."

That deflated him, and he took Torin's advice and refrained from further comment. They led him out the door and handed him off to one of the four guards from Dragon they had left waiting outside. That guard would take him to the castle for imprisonment until the magistrate—and the Brotherhood—could deal with him. Torin instructed the other three to escort Emanuela to Dragon for questioning and to close up the offices of Forak's Perfect Clean.

Danthres looked up at the sky, seeing the sun starting to set into the horizon, and she realized that she was in a good mood. Justice had been done, she'd found her cloak, and she didn't even have to deal directly with the Brotherhood.

Then Torin said, "You realize that when this is all over, he's going to have to reverse the spell in order to salvage the Jaros house. That means all the dirt will probably have to go back."

"Actually, I hadn't realized it." Danthres snarled, her foul mood back full force.

"Yes," Torin said with a smile. "You've been left with quite a mess."

Somehow, Danthres managed not to kill him.

OFF THE RACK

Elizabeth A. Vaughan

Sarah yanked the offending strip of paper from the calculator, crumpled it, and threw it at the basket. It bounced off the rim, hit the wall, and fell to the floor.

With a curse, she jerked out of her chair to retrieve it. The chair obeyed the law of physics and thumped back against the wall. Sarah cursed again, this at the black mark it left on the wall.

Pam stuck her head into the tiny closet Sarah called her office. "Problem?"

"No." Sarah kept her face down as she picked up the crumpled wad and dropped it in the trash. She wasn't going to tell her only employee about the red ink on that slip of paper. "Just got up too fast."

Pam accepted that, as she accepted the meager paycheck each week, with a shrug. "Listen, can I leave early? There's no customers, and I gotta—"

"Sure." Sarah didn't really want to hear it. "Go. I'll lock up."

The door was swinging shut before the words were out of Sarah's mouth. She heard the door chimes marking Pam's exit even as she turned off the calculator. She paused long enough to watch the negative number fade as the display went dim.

Sarah sighed and stepped out into her store, to watch as the last few moments before closing ticked off. She stepped to the counter and started to clear away the clutter.

Outside, through the glass windows of the store front, soft white flakes of snow started to fill Pam's tire treads. Painted on the window, backward from this angle, was "Sarah's Closet," the gold and cream lettering still as bright and promising as it had been a year ago on opening day.

Sarah looked away from the bright promise and cleared the counter, straightening pens, dusting the unused credit card machine and the register.

Opening day of her consignment shop had been just as bright and promising as the window. She'd spent a year researching, planning, taking out the loan, making the business plan. She'd collected the clothes for a year, searching garage sales and auctions, talking to friends of friends to build her inventory.

But consignment needs more consignments to survive, and as the months wore on, there'd been few visitors who had brought in things. She'd found it hard to replace the stock and watch the store at the same time, forcing her to hire help. A cost she'd left out of her detailed and perfect business plan.

Sarah sighed again. There'd been traffic, sure, but somehow people didn't find what they were looking for, or it was not the right size, or it was the wrong color. Why go to her store, when they could go the big discounters?

She glanced at the clock. Another three minutes and she could go home and lose herself in a bubble bath, a favorite romance novel, and ramen noodles. Time enough tomorrow to think about negative numbers and looming bills.

Movement drew her gaze back to the window. Someone was trying to wrestle an old shopping cart up on the sidewalk in front of the shop. A shopping

cart piled high with bags and cans, and with more
plastic bags tied to the sides, all filled with question-
able items.

Sarah frowned. She'd picked this location because
of its higher-end clientele, and she'd never seen a
street person here before. Dressed in a thin, stained
sweat shirt, with old jeans almost falling off his hips.
His, it had to be, she caught a glimpse of a ratty beard
when his head turned. One of the legs of the jeans
was pulled up over his knee, displaying a naked leg
covered in scabs and sores. A thin ankle, covered in
an old cotton sock, pushed into even older tennis
shoes. No hat. No gloves. Sarah shivered at the
thought.

The man was pulling at the cart, trying to get the
wheels over the curb. She could hear it rattling and
squeaking as he tugged. He got the back wheels over
the curb and pulled until the front wheels clanged into
the obstacle. He kept pulling, as if it never occurred
to him to go to the front and lift it up.

Or maybe he couldn't.

The snow that had fallen in his hair was melting,
and water drops glistened in the scraggly depths.
There were damp patches on his shoulders where his
muscles moved underneath. Sarah looked at him with
an expert eye, sizing him up without really thinking
about it. A medium, easily.

There was a coat on the men's rack, a high-end
winter coat that would fit him. And a warm woolen
hat in the bin. Gloves too.

She hesitated, surprised by her impulse. Generosity
wouldn't put food on the table. But the loss wouldn't
make any real difference. And it was closing time.
And he was in front of the door.

Without another thought, she gathered up the coat,
stuffed the hat and gloves in the pockets and
stepped outside.

The snow was a swirl now, the wind making patterns
in the light of the parking lot lamps. Sarah took in a

breath of cold air, faintly scented by the Chinese restaurant next door. The man was still tugging on the
cart, and in frustration, Sarah stepped around him and
lifted up the end to clang on the sidewalk.

He looked at her, startled, with pale gray eyes.

Sarah didn't bother to say anything, just held out
the coat.

His eyes flicked to it, then back to her face. His
beard and mustache covered his face, leaving no hints
to his reaction.

Sarah shivered in the cold. "Take it." She held it
out again. "Put it on."

He reached for the coat with a filthy hand. Sarah
watched as he eased it over his shoulders, moving
carefully as if it would break. She swallowed hard,
afraid to look too close at his leg, or take too deep
a breath.

The man pulled out the knit hat from one pocket,
and pulled it over his matted hair. He looked at her
with those washed-out eyes and said nothing.

Sarah hadn't really expected much else. Her impulse
of generosity had left, leaving her only a desire to
close up and get home. But as she turned to go, the
man mumbled something and started digging in the
cart.

Uh-oh. Sarah winced at the idea that the man was
going to reciprocate, and prayed that whatever
emerged was—

He held out a hanger.

She reached out and accepted it. It was one of those
old wooden hangers, with the metal rod that rein-
forced the wood. It felt warm and smooth under her
fingertips, and she caught a faint hint of cedar.

She looked back at the man, intending to say
"Thank you." But he was already shoving the cart
past her shop, mumbling something, intent on his
own business.

So Sarah went back in, and put the hanger on one
of the empty racks, right by the counter. She gathered

her own coat and purse and shut off the lights. The
man and his cart was into the next block when she
stepped out into the snow and headed for her car.

Intent on bubble bath and book, she drove off into
the night.

Sarah overslept the next morning; thankfully, Pam
had opened the store on time. Pam was chewing gum
and bent over the counter, looking over one of those
gossip rags, when Sarah rushed in with coffee and the
paper. Sarah nodded and said "Morning" as she
headed toward the office door, trying not to look as
embarrassed as she felt for being late.

There was a ball gown hanging from the rack. On
the hanger. It was a lovely low cut blue silk, with a
full gathered skirt.

Sarah stopped dead in her tracks. "Where did that
come from?"

Pam opened her mouth, but the chime on the door
made them both turn and look. Two women, stylish
and made up to perfection entered. Sarah's brain was
processing the cost of their labels when the first one
spoke.

"Good morning! I'm looking for a vintage—"

The other woman squealed. "Look!"

Stunned, Sarah watched as they descended on the
dress.

"It's my size!"

"It's perfect for you!" One reached for the paper
price tag that hung from a small ribbon off the dress.
She nudged the other to look at the tag.

"I want it." The first woman announced.

Pam stood up right and reached for one of the
longer garment bags. The woman dug out a credit card
and placed it on the counter.

Sarah still stood there, coffee in one hand, paper
and purse in the other. One of the women gave her
a pat on the shoulder. "I'll be back, if you get in more
treasures like this!"

"That will be $1,590.00. With tax." Pam murmured. The credit card zipped through the machine.

Money worries temporarily forgotten, Sarah still stood there, stunned.

Pam denied all knowledge of the dress, claiming that it had been hanging there when she'd walked in. Sarah had her doubts, of course, but Pam wasn't the type to do something on her own initiative, that was for sure. Sarah decided that someone was trying to help her, except that no one had a key, or access to that kind of dress, that she knew of.

But then it happened again.

And again.

Each morning, Sarah would open the store, to find a garment hanging from *the* hanger. Each time someone would come in that day, looking for that particular garment, cheerfully paying the price on the tag.

A business suit.

A sun dress.

A leather jacket.

A wet suit.

The prices varied, the clothing varied, but without fail the hanger had something suspended from it every morning, a small paper price tag dangling in front.

Sarah couldn't figure it out. She had the locks changed, she set up a security camera. But the camera didn't work and the clothing kept appearing. As did customers, new ones who became repeat ones, who brought clothes to consign, who came back and bought other clothes.

Within a month Sarah was in the black.

Within six months, she had back inventory and Pam was full-time. She could be pickier now, setting aside the older and worn items to donate to the Salvation Army.

During this time Sarah became a bit superstitious. She forbade Pam to touch *the* hanger, and left it on the rack in all its glory. Pam, of course, just shrugged.

She didn't seem to notice or care about anything other than her paycheck.

And the clothes kept coming.

A christening gown of linen and lace.

A slinky little black dress.

A XXXL wedding dress, with veil and slippers. Sarah waited all day to see who would show up for that one.

And sure enough, close to the end of the day, in walked a large woman with her groom-to-be. She fit the dress perfectly. And never blinked at the price. Once the sale was made and Pam had left for the day, Sarah stood in front of the rack and stared at the hanger.

"I don't suppose you could find me a man? I'm not fussy, although I prefer brown eyes to blue."

The hanger just hung there in silence.

Sarah laughed, and shook her head. "That's okay. I'm grateful for the clothes and the help." She eyed the hanger seriously. "But it won't last forever, will it?"

The hanger remained silent.

And so it went.

Sarah's Closet became the in place to shop, with both the society crowd and the young people looking for bargains. Sarah had enough stock that she was starting to think about the Internet, getting a website, and putting pictures of the clothing on-line. But something deep within made her hesitate. "Nothing good lasts forever" echoed in the depths of her brain. "Wait and see" was another thought. After all, magic never lasted, now did it? In all those stories. She took the prudent and cautious route.

So she wasn't really surprised the morning she opened the shop, a year and a day later, to find that there was nothing on the hanger.

The cold air and snow blew in as she stood there in the doorway, staring at the rack. It was indeed empty, swaying slightly in the draft.

She stomped the snow off her boots, stepped in,
and let the door close behind her.

A year and a day.

It had been a year and a day since she'd seen that
odd man and given him a coat. He'd handed her the
hanger in exchange, a more than fair exchange for the
magic that it had brought with it.

Magic that had saved her dreams.

Sarah sighed, mild disappointment flowing through
her like a wave. She'd expected it, but it still hurt. It
had been a wonderful year, and she was in good shape
financially. The store would still need hard work, but
she knew that she could make it, after this year.

The magic was over and done.

But to see the hanger just . . . hanging there . . .

It hurt.

She sighed, and went about the day.

Business was brisk in the morning, but the snow
kept falling all day, large wet flakes. Customers slowed
to a trickle, and the radio spoke of businesses closing
early. Sarah let Pam go home and settled behind the
counter and watched the snow. She tried to ignore the
hanger, which was still on the rack.

Once or twice it occurred to Sarah to pack it in and
treat herself to a bubble bath, but she had the oddest
sense of waiting, as if something was going to happen.

There were no more customers, and the only call
she got was from the Salvation Army, asking if she
had anything to be picked up. She said she did, and
they'd be by shortly.

Sarah'd wait for the truck and then close the store
and go home. Yes, a bubble bath, that new hardbound
romance she'd just bought, some General Tso's from
the Chinese place next door. Good plan for a snowy
night.

The Salvation Army truck pulled up; it was the regular guy, so he went in back and carried out the box
crammed full of clothing. He set it down on the floor
and handed Sarah the clipboard with the paperwork.

She signed off, and he put it under his arm and reached back down.

When he lifted the box up, *the* hanger was tucked in among the clothes.

Sarah darted a look at the rack, and sure enough, her hanger wasn't there. She looked back as the man headed for the door.

She could just see the wooden corner of the hanger, as if it were waving goodbye over his shoulder. It seemed right somehow. Fitting, even.

At the same time, the door opened, and a customer walked in, dancing around the man with the box with a laugh and an apology. Sarah was still focused on the box, and she watched as it was loaded on the truck, the big metal door coming down with a muffled clang.

"Excuse me." The customer placed a coat on the counter.

Sarah looked down. It was a well-made coat, from a high-end designer. Warm and thick, with deep pockets. She reached out to touch it.

"You want to sell this?" She was still oddly distracted. There was something familiar about the coat.

"No," came a warm, deep voice that carried a hint of laughter. "Actually, I found it, and your business card was in the pocket, so I brought—"

It was the coat that she'd given away, a year and a day ago! It had to be.

"Where did you get this?" She looked up into a smiling face and the warmest pair of brown eyes she'd ever seen.

The man laughed again. "Well, that's kind of a strange story, truth be told." He smiled even wider, and Sarah caught her breath. "I'll tell you," he continued, then hesitated for a moment as he seemed to study her. "I'll tell you, but only over some dinner. Do you like Chinese?"

THE RED SHOES

Sarah Zettel

Once there was a clergyman who had a stout wife and a fine family of children. He was a kind man, though in the great dark church on solemn Sundays he preached sermons warning against all sins—great and small.

One day the clergyman came home accompanied by a young girl just in the first flush of her woman's beauty. He called his wife and children into the parlor and said to them: "This is Karen. She is in need, and God has sent her to us. She will help you watch the children, my wife, and do such other tasks as may make her useful. Make your greetings, my children."

One by one, the children all said hello, for they were all raised to be polite. But they were also children, and they could not help but stare. For though Karen was a pretty girl, she had no feet. At the ends of her legs were two crudely carved wooden slats, and she got about on two wooden crutches.

The children were naturally very curious as to how she came to lose her feet. Their mother, though, hushed and scolded them so that they eventually stopped trying to ask. But still they wondered, especially the youngest girl, whose name was Elsa.

Karen tended the fire and stirred the kettle. She sewed and she knitted. She rocked the cradle and sang a lullaby when the baby boy was lonesome, and she did any other thing that was asked of her. But she never spoke of her feet. Elsa sometimes stood in the shadows of the chimney corner and watched Karen move about. *Thump, thump* went her crutches. *Creak, creak* went the wooden slats, and tears of pain ran down Karen's pretty face.

One day, Elsa could contain herself no longer. "Oh, Karen!" she clasping her hands together. "Tell me how it is you have no feet! I'll give you Clarissa, my best doll, if you tell me. Please, Karen!"

Karen looked at little Elsa with the tears shining in her eyes. *Thump, thump, creak, creak,* Karen moved to the chair by the fire and pointed to the spot on the hearth next to the cradle. Elsa sat on the hearthstone at once, drawing her own feet under her skirts and hugging her knees to her chest.

When Karen spoke, she spoke to the fire and did not look at Elsa at all. "When I was a little girl, I was very poor and I had no shoes. A shoemaker's widow made me a pair of shoes from scraps of red leather. They did not fit well, but they were the only gift I had ever been given. When my mother died, a kind old lady saw me and took me in. She called my red shoes ugly and had them burned.

"I lived with the old lady, and she was very good to me, and when it came time for me to be confirmed, she took me to a shoemaker's to have new shoes made. This man had a pair of red shoes in his case that would fit my feet. They were so very beautiful. The old lady could not see their color, and she bought them for me when I begged her. I wore them to church, and everyone looked at me. That made me very proud. When she was told, my old lady said I was wicked to wear red shoes to church. She ordered me to always wear black.

"I did not listen. Next Sunday I wore my red shoes again. There was an old soldier outside the church door. He wiped people's shoes as they passed to get alms. He bent down to wipe my shoes, and he said, 'What pretty dancing shoes! They fit so tightly when you dance!'

"I did not think much on it. I was just proud someone had noticed my beautiful shoes. We went into the church. The whole world saw my red shoes, and pride swelled my heart. When we came out, the old soldier with his red beard was still there. He said again. 'What pretty dancing shoes! They fit so tightly when you dance!'

"And the shoes began to dance. They danced me up and down and would not stop. No matter how I cried and begged and tore at my stockings, they would not stop and I could not get them off. The shoes danced me out into the woods. They danced me through the graveyard and back to the church. There was an angel in a white robe, and he said to me I could not enter the church, but must dance and dance.

"At last, the shoes danced me to the house where the executioner lives. I begged him to strike off my feet, and he did, and my feet in the red shoes danced away through the woods."

Elsa sat hugging her knees so tightly with her mouth open and her eyes wide. "Then what?" she asked.

Karen just shook her head. "Then I came here, and I wait until God may grant me mercy."

Elsa jumped to her feet. "That's not a proper story!" she cried out. "There should be a prince, or a fairy. They should have made you feet of silver so you could walk through the king's orchard at night and eat pears until the prince sees you and falls in love."

Karen shook her head again. "That is not my story, Elsa. You must not be wicked and say so. I must try to be patient and good and wait for the mercy only God can give."

But Elsa burst into tears. "It's not a proper story!" she cried again and rushed from the kitchen.

All that week, Elsa brooded about the red shoes and about Karen's story. She would not play with her best doll, Clarissa. She would not eat her supper, and when her father read from the big Bible at night, all she saw were the tears of pain on Karen's face, and all she heard was the *thump, thump, creak, creak,* of her crutches and the wooden slats.

"It is *not* a proper story," she told herself over and over again.

At last, her father grew concerned. He came to sit at the foot of Elsa's little bed, where she lay in her white nightgown all tucked up under the colorful quilts her mother had made. He asked Elsa what troubled her. Elsa, who was by nature a truthful child, told her father the whole tale. When she ran out of other words, she whispered. "Papa, I wish I could go find the red shoes and bring Karen's feet back to her!"

Her father thought on this for a long moment. "You know that it was wrong to ask Karen what became of her feet," he said. "Your mother has told you so many times."

"I know but . . ."

"Karen is right. She must wait for God's mercy. Leave her to God, my child." He smoothed Elsa's hair back from her brow.

At these pious words, Elsa stuck out her little chin and said, "But God is in the church, and her feet cannot go there."

Her father scolded her then and told her she should have no dessert tomorrow for her impiety. He left, and Elsa lay in the darkness with the moonbeams shining through the curtains, until she made a decision.

"I will go find the red shoes," she said. "I will make them give Karen her feet back. It was not right that they stole them from her."

Carefully, so as not to wake the other children, Elsa crept from her bed. She wrapped some bread in a pretty handkerchief her mother had given her, and poured some milk into a silver cup her father had given her, and took her best doll, Clarissa, for company. Then she went out into the darkness to look for the red shoes.

The night was vast and cold. The houses looked quite unlike themselves, being only velvet shadows beneath the thousand stars. The Moon, however, took pity on the little girl walking alone and spared some of its best silver beams to light the street, making the cobblestones gleam so that she might see her way.

First, Elsa went to the church, as that was where Karen said she first began to dance and where she had seen the angel. As this was God's house and her father's, Elsa knew no fear of the church, even in darkness. The spires and arches rose up stern and hard against the silvered night.

Elsa climbed the broad, shallow steps and gazed at the closed doors with their knockers held in the mouths of lions. Above them waited the carving of the angel Michael with his wings spread open and his sword held up high.

"I am looking for the red shoes," said Elsa to the doors. "Have you seen them?"

But the lions only shook their heads until the knockers swung as if blown by the wind. The angel above them, though, cried out, "She shall dance! She shall dance from door to door; and where proud and haughty children dwell, she shall knock, that they may hear her and be afraid of her!"

"I am not afraid of Karen!" cried out Elsa, stamping her foot. "And she cannot dance anymore! All she can do is thump and creak on wooden feet, and it is not right!"

"Don't mind him," mumbled the right-hand lion around his knocker. "It is just his way."

"The executioner might know where the red shoes have gone," said the left-hand lion. "It was he who saw them last." The left-hand lion gave Elsa directions to the executioner's house. Elsa said *thank you* and made her curtsy, even to the angel.

It was a long way to the executioner's house. No one wished to have the man who might one day hurry them to the grave living beside them. Elsa walked on. The sun came up to warm her. She ate a little of her bread and drank a little of her milk. As she struggled across the plowed fields and into the tangled fields lying fallow for the year, she hugged Clarissa to her breast and went doggedly on.

The executioner's house was small and mean, cramped and crooked. A raven perched on the roof beam and sang a harsh song as she walked beneath the eaves. Holding Clarissa close, Elsa knocked on the door.

"Who is that!" cried a gruff and terrible voice from within.

"It is Elsa!" Elsa answered. "I am looking for the red shoes!"

The door flew open and the executioner came out. He seemed bigger than his house, and his bald head gleamed in the sun. His hands were hard and stained from his work. In one, he held the great, notched axe that had sent so many condemned from the world.

"Who are you that you ask after the red shoes?" he roared.

He is trying to scare me, thought Elsa, and she would not be scared. She told him of Karen and her story, and as she did, he seemed to grow smaller and sadder.

"I remember her," he said, hunching his shoulders up. "She came to my door. She was only skin and bones. Her legs were scratched and bloody. She could not stop dancing although she could barely breathe and could no longer hold her head up straight. She begged me to strike the shoes from her body, and I could see nothing else to do. I used my axe as best I could, and she bled terribly and fell against me. The red shoes danced away into the woods, carrying her feet with them." He looked off towards the north, to where the woods loomed dark and green, and the sunlight feared to go. "I have never been afraid of what I do until I did that thing. Nor yet have I ever been able to forget that sight of her feet set free to dance in the red shoes."

"The shoes stole her feet," said Elsa firmly. "And I am going to find them."

The executioner looked into her eyes for a long moment. Then he nodded. He took her into his cramped, crooked house. He fed her thin soup and black bread and replenished her milk. He found a comb so that she might straighten her hair and retie her doll's ribbons. Then he took her to the path that led into the woods.

"Further I dare not go," he said. "I have killed too many men. Though I only did as the laws required, they do not know that, and they wait for me in the woods. But you are a good child, and they cannot touch you."

Elsa thanked the executioner and walked down the rutted path into the woods. All the while, the executioner watched her go.

In the deep woods, it quickly became dark as night. The few sunbeams were paler than the moon's had ever been. The path was pitted with the tracks of deer and the wolves that followed them. The roots of trees crisscrossed the way and caught at Elsa's toes to trip her up. Overhead, invisible in the branches, the crows called to one another to come see this new thing. They laughed hard and harsh when she stumbled. The wind wormed its way between the tree trunks to make her shiver and tease her hair. The whole world smelled of moss and old graves.

Elsa walked on. She looked this way and that for some sign of the red shoes in the gloom, but she saw only the white ghosts of the dead men, their heads lolling on their shoulders, waiting for the executioner to come to them. But they did not come onto the path, and they did not touch her.

Elsa walked on. She ate her bread and drank her

milk, and she held her doll. The path grew narrower
until it was only a winding thread. Gnarled trees and
unkind bracken reached out their crooked twigs to
poke and prod her. They tore at Clarissa's dress and
tried to snatch away her ribbons.

At last, when Elsa was so tired she was afraid she
could go no further, she saw a woman sitting on a
great, arching tree root. She was as brown, knobby
and gnarled as that root, with a great hump over her
left shoulder. Indeed, Elsa might have thought she was
just another part of the tree if her eyes had not
gleamed so brightly in the darkness.

"Hello, my little maid," the old woman said in a
voice as soft and rich as loam. "Where are you going
all alone?"

"I am going to find the red shoes," replied Elsa.
"Have you seen them?"

"Well, now." The old woman tapped her chin.
"That is a large question. Let us have some of that
bread and milk and think about it."

So, Elsa sat beside the old woman and shared out
her bread and milk, which the old woman took with
great smackings of her lips and slurpings of her
tongue. She belched and rubbed at her wagging dew-
lap and scratched herself about the body and the head.
Elsa did her best to remember her manners and not
stare, but it was very difficult.

"Now then," said the old woman, when all the food
was gone. "You say you are looking for the red shoes?
They are here."

"I must make them give Karen her feet back."

"Ah!" she exclaimed archly. "Well, finding them is
one thing, and catching them, that's another
altogether."

Elsa stuck her chin out as she had with her father.
She did not have to say anything though. The old
woman nodded.

"Very good," she said. "So. You must follow the
path. It will go under a tree and over a stream. On

the other side of that stream, you will come to a clearing where a great oak has fallen. There you will find a soldier with a red beard playing on a fiddle. Do not let him see you. After a time, he will call the red shoes and make them dance for him. They will not look as you think they might, and you must not be afraid."

"I will not be afraid."

Again, the old woman nodded. "Good. The soldier will make the shoes dance until they cry out, "Give us rest! Give us rest!" And the soldier will answer, "You will have no rest until I grow weary, and I never grow weary while I watch you dance!" You must cry 'Soldier, soldier, give me the red shoes!' He will answer you, " 'Little Elsa, Little Elsa, give me a dance!' Then he will play his fiddle, and you will dance."

"Then what do I do?"

"Ah. Then, my child, you will dance until you give him something he wants as much as the dance."

"What is that?"

But the old woman shook her heavy head and shrugged her humped shoulder. "That is what you must find, Little Elsa." Then she sprang down from the root and scampered into the forest, and she was gone before Elsa could draw her next breath.

Elsa sat there for a long time, listening to her own heartbeat and to the laughter of the crows. Then she gathered her empty cup and handkerchief and climbed down off the root. Elsa walked on. The woods grew darker, and the path grew narrower still. There was a place where a tree root arched over it like a doorway, and Elsa walked through. A stream cut it neatly in two with silver water and muted laughter. She jumped over it, landing unsteadily on her tired feet.

Ahead she saw a place that was gray instead of black. Gradually, her aching eyes saw it was a clearing, and she saw the black corpse of a tree lying like a fallen giant in the middle. Her breath seized up in her throat, and she left the path that was her only guide, and, one hesitant step at a time, she moved toward

that gray place. The trees laid their branches on her
head and shoulders, cautioning, trying to hold her
back and turn her away. She had to push past them
as she pushed past her brothers and sisters to see the
parades in the streets. As she drew closer, something
tickled at her nose, a strange smell she did not expect
in such a place. Tobacco.

Elsa dropped down to her knees. Awkwardly, for
she kept hold of Clarissa in one arm, she wriggled
forward. The ragged hem of the tree trunk pointed
toward her, and past it she could just see a man's
black boots, and a brown hand, and a trickle of white
smoke rising toward the gray evening sky.

Elsa made her decision. She crept carefully into the
hollow of the great fallen tree. The worms and beetles
paused in their work to see who this new neighbor
was. The punk wood turned to powder as she touched
it and showered down into her hair and eyes. She
rubbed her eyelids, held in her sneezes and peered
out through a slit in the bark that allowed her to see
just a little slice of the clearing. But that slice held the
soldier with his red beard wild and uncombed and his
scarlet coat shining with gold braid.

The soldier sat on a stone, his legs stretched out
and his black boots crossed. He puffed contentedly on
a long-stemmed white pipe. Thick smoke poured from
the bowl and from his mouth as it opened and closed,
rising up as if it were what made the clouds that had
gathered so thickly overhead.

After a time, he seemed to weary of smoking. He
knocked out his white pipe against his black boot heel
and tucked it into his coat. Then, from somewhere
Elsa could not see, he took out a little fiddle and
curving bow. He drew the bow across the fiddle strings
and the music leaped up as merrily as the flames in
her home's hearth. He set to playing at once. The
swooping, soaring notes rang through the forest, making the air shiver. The tune he played was strange and
sad and merry and frightening all at once. Elsa's feet

itched at the sound of it. They were tired no more
and wanted to be up and moving. Her ears strained
to hear more. She clutched at Clarissa and bit down
on her tongue. She tried hard to remember the other
sound, the one that brought her here, the *thump,
thump, creak, creak* of Karen's crutches and wooden
slats on the kitchen floor. As she did, the tune did not
call quite so loudly.

The soldier finished his tune with a flourish of notes,
each higher and brighter than the last. He laughed, as
if delighted at his own cleverness, and lowered the
fiddle from under his chin.

"It is dull," he said, tapping the bow against his
boot. "To play all alone. It is much better to have
someone to dance to the music." Once more, he
touched the bow to the strings and began to play. It
was a schottiche he played, merry and sprightly, a song
about swinging around and leaping up high and holding hands while you both spun together about the
floor. It broke Elsa's heart to hear it in the wilderness
where there was no one to dance to such a pretty
thing, but she held herself still.

The red shoes came.

They crashed through the bracken, loud and clumsy.
Once, they might have been shining leather with embroidered toes and gilded heels, but now they were
black with blood. It spilled out of the horrible stumps
of Karen's lost feet, severed so cleanly above the
ankle. Elsa had thought Karen's feet would be worn
away to bones by now, but they were not. The blood
poured like a flood of tears, running down onto the
forest floor so that the shoes and Karen's feet must
dance in her own blood, without stopping and without
rest, while the soldier played his merry tune about
lovers spinning around the floor. The schottiche finished, and then came a polka, and a waltz tune, a reel
from England, and a jig from Ireland. All the dances
of the world were drawn down by the soldier and
poured out so that the shoes must dance.

Elsa thought and thought. It was hard, because the soldier's tune kept pushing into her mind and filling it up so that her thoughts had to crowd around the edges of the music and could not come together to make ideas. She held Clarissa tighter and tighter. She watched the soldier's fingers fly on his fiddle strings and the bow dart back and forth. She watched the red shoes dance. The soldier laughed louder than the crows even, and there was so much blood.

You must give him something he wants as much as the dance, the old woman had said. *Something he wants as much as the dance.*

Then, an idea came to Elsa. She bent her head and whispered to Clarissa, who listened in silence, as she always did.

"Give us rest!" cried the shoes, the voice muffled by blood and torn by exhaustion. "Give us rest!"

The soldier laughed, and Elsa saw that his eyes were as shiny and black as his tall boots. "You shall have no rest until I grow weary, and I never grow weary while I watch you dance!"

Elsa thrust her doll through the split in the fallen tree trunk and in the high voice she used to make Clarissa speak in all her games, she cried out. "Soldier! Soldier! Give me the red shoes!"

The soldier turned toward her, and she saw his black eyes shining with a merriment that cut through the air like lightning. He did not hesitate, not for an instant, in his playing. The tune changed seamlessly from one lively reel to the next.

"Little Clarissa! Little Clarissa!" The soldier called out. "Give me a dance!"

The doll twitched in Elsa's hand, and Elsa dropped her swiftly. Instead of falling to the ground in a heap as she was used to, Clarissa landed neatly on her own two white cloth feet. She lifted up the hem of her lace dress and skipped as merrily to the center of the clearing as if she were on her way to a birthday party. The doll danced up to the red shoes and back again, bowing politely and circling 'round them, her white feet treading in the fresh blood and soaking it up, becoming red themselves. Elsa wondered whether they ever be clean again.

But she had no time to mourn her doll. Now she had both hands free, and she could creep from the hollow tree and ease herself around the clearing's edge. The soldier played faster, and the little doll and the bloody red shoes danced together to his laughter and his music. His bow flashed and his fingers flew. He attended to nothing but the show in front of him as Elsa crept behind.

Then, quick as a cat, Elsa snatched the bow from the soldier's hand and ran back to the fallen tree. The soldier stared at his knobby hand for a moment, as if he could not believe what had just happened. In the middle of the meadow, the shoes hesitated, turning this way and that on their toes, and Clarissa stood, smiling, holding her hems in her hand, waiting patiently, as she always did.

"Soldier! Soldier!" cried Elsa holding the bow high. "Give me the red shoes or I will break this bow over my knee!"

To her surprise, the soldier threw back his head and laughed so hard it seemed he'd split stone and tree with the noise.

"You are too late, little Elsa," he cried when his laughter was done. "Karen has given herself to God, and God has taken her away." He snapped his bony fingers and pointed to the middle of the air. It seemed as if the world split open, and Elsa saw the streets of her city. She saw a wagon drawn by a single black horse wearing a black plume. All her brothers and sisters walked behind. In the wagon was a coffin. She knew without knowing how that this was a true thing she saw, and her heart broke in two. The hand that clutched the bow trembled a little

"It was all for nothing, you silly child," said the soldier while the tears began to run down Elsa's face.

"Give me my bow, and take your doll." He snapped his fingers again, and Clarissa fell to the ground, nothing more than a doll in a pink dress and ribbons, her feet horribly stained by her naughty mistress who let her go play where she should not. "Go home. Pray on your knees for things that you can understand, and leave the red shoes to me. If you are a good girl, you will never have to see them again."

Suddenly Elsa felt smaller than she ever had. The music had brought all the world and time into this clearing, and they watched her with the bow held high in a silly game. The red shoes still stood beneath their coating of gore with the hideous stumps of Karen's abandoned feet thrusting out of them. Karen had not lost her feet. She'd given them away with all her pride. Given them to God, and God had taken them. The old soldier was only doing his duty, like the executioner. She had not understood, because she was a little girl and nothing more. Her hand trembled again.

"No!" she said, stubbornly. "It is not right! It is not a proper story! Give me the red shoes or I will break this bow over my knee."

"Elsa, Elsa." The soldier folded his arms and shook his head, just as her father did when he thought she was being silly. "Do you think I need a bow to make music?" He snapped his fingers once more, and the fiddle's strings trembled, though the instrument lay on the ground. They trembled and they shivered and the music began again. It swirled and looped, catching at Elsa's mind and tugging at her heels. Beside her, the red shoes began to dance again, hopping and gliding, all the blood making a scarlet train behind them.

Elsa's arm fell to her side and the bow slipped from her fingers. The music snatched and pushed at her, and she did not know what to do. She looked down at Clarissa with her red stained feet, and felt tears prickle again at her eyes. She had come all this way, and done all these things, and she did not know what to do anymore.

You will put on the shoes, and you will dance, the old woman had said. Elsa swallowed. Her throat was dry as dust. It was the only thing she had not done yet. The only thing, the last thing.

She straightened her shoulders and stuck out her chin. "Soldier, soldier!" she cried out as loudly as she could. "Give me the red shoes!"

The soldier laughed again, a low chuckle that made the ground tremble. He raised his hand and the fiddle strings stilled and the world was so silent that her ears rang.

"Little Elsa, Little Elsa," the soldier said, and his voice was a wolf's growl. "Give me a dance."

Elsa crossed the clearing to the red shoes that waited still in the silent world. She lifted them from Karen's feet. The blood smeared all over her hands. The feet lay on the forest floor, white and forlorn, ridiculous things without their owner. But the thing begun could not be stopped, and Elsa stepped into the red shoes. It seemed the world swept 'round her, and for a moment she saw the shoes as they had been, the gleaming red satin and embroidery and shining gold heels. She saw what Karen had loved, the love of beauty, of something that was her very own, and for that she had been taken away to die.

"Such pretty shoes!" laughed the soldier in his low, dark chuckle. "They fit so tightly when you dance!"

He did not move his hand, he did not blink, but the fiddle strings shivered and the music began again. The red shoes, weeping out the remnants of Karen's blood, began to move, taking Elsa's feet, and the whole of Elsa, with them.

Elsa danced.

She turned and swayed, she kicked up high and spun. She held out her arms for the partner who was not there. She danced, and the blood—Karen's blood, the shoes' blood—ran down and darkened the forest floor. She saw herself, a skeleton in rags dancing through the dark forest and up the streets of the town

so that people shut their windows against her and
murmured prayers as they would against a ghost. She
saw her mother weeping by the fire for her daughter
whom she thought dead.

The soldier laughed, and the music drawn down
from the sky and up from the roots of the world
played on, and in her mind she heard the weeping of
the shoes.

Her legs were already tired, and tears threatened.
The soldier laughed, and his voice was the crows'
voices. The music played harder, twirling her around
and pulling all the breath from her lungs. But the
blood in the shoes, Karen's blood, slipped between
her stockings and the shoes—and the shoe did not
cleave yet. Not yet. She had a moment, a moment
only and she had to do something.

The shoes whirled her around again, and she saw
the bow where it lay beside Clarissa. She saw Clarissa's button eyes gleaming, up black as those of the
old woman in the woods. She thought she saw the
ghosts looking on, she thought she saw Karen, dancing
all alone, lost in the darkness, her only hope the axe
and death.

Dancing alone.

Dancing alone to music that she could not hear but
that would not ever stop.

Little Elsa, Little Elsa, give me a dance!

The shoes did not yet hold her, not all the way,
not quite.

She had two steps that were her own, two, three,
one more, enough to cross the clearing and grasp the
soldier's crabbed hand with her little bloody one.

"Soldier, soldier!" Elsa cried out. "Here is your
dance!"

The blood stuck his hand fast to hers, and the dance
that swirled around her pulled him to his feet, catching
him up in its current and drawing him in. Elsa
snatched at his other hand and held it up.

Father was a clergyman, but he did not fear the

dance as some did. Elsa knew the schottiche and the polka. Elsa knew jig and reel. Elsa also knew the dances that every child knows, the twirling and the jumping, the high laughter that comes from moving fast and free. All these dances Elsa danced, holding tight to the soldier's hard, calloused hands while he gaped at her, moving clumsily in his tall black boots. But he couldn't stop. The blood held them together. While she danced, he must dance.

"Let me go!" he screamed.

"How can I let you go?" Elsa asked as she skipped round the clearing, swinging their arms. "I am only a foolish little girl who does not understand. How can I be stronger than all the dances you know and the red shoes you've put on my feet?"

The soldier threw back his head and howled until the smoky clouds shook. Elsa twirled them around, the music and the roar of her blood singing in her ears. She did not try to stop. She danced him up the line and down again, and he howled once more, and she spun them around. Her breath was going. She was so tired. She must dance. She must not falter. For while she danced, he must dance, and he knew it. He had asked for this dance that they now danced together, little girl and red-bearded man.

His dance, her dance.

His choice, her choice, and all the music of the world to spin them 'round.

"Take the shoes!" he cried out. "Take them! I give them to you, only let me go!"

With that, all the strings on the fiddle broke at once, a terrible, twisting cacophony that knocked Elsa backwards. She fell onto the earth, skidding through the leaves until she rolled to a stop beside Clarissa and the bow. Her feet were still. She heard the crows calling to one another, but she heard no music and she heard no weeping, and the soldier scowled at her and snatched up his broken-stringed fiddle and was gone.

After a little time, Elsa picked up the bow and her

doll. Wearing the red shoes, she walked from the clearing to the path. The hump-shouldered woman waited there, her black eyes shining. Elsa had no more food, so she gave the old woman the fiddle bow. The old woman laughed loud to receive it and lifted Elsa onto her humped back and carried her from the woods to the executioner's house. The executioner met her at the door and embraced her with his strong arms. He gave her soup and black bread and water to wash herself with and walked her home.

Her mother and father scolded her and wept over her. Mother bleached Clarissa's feet white again, and Father bought her a new pair of black shoes and made her learn twelve whole psalms and stay inside for two weeks.

When she was allowed out again, Elsa wore the red shoes to church, and the lions smiled at her, and the angel fluttered his wings and lifted his nose in the air. But in the shadows Elsa saw Karen, clothed in white as the angel was. Karen stood on her own feet and smiled.

After that, Elsa did not wear the red shoes except for dancing, and when she danced she felt as if their freedom poured out over the world as a blessing, like music, like love.

When she could dance no more, Elsa gave the red shoes to her daughter, and she to hers.

And that, Elsa knew, was a proper story.

ABOUT THE AUTHORS

Kevin J. Anderson has more than twenty million books in print in thirty languages, including Dune novels written with Brian Herbert, Star Wars and X-Files novels, and a collaboration with Dean Koontz. He just finished the sixth book in his epic space opera, "The Saga of Seven Suns." He and his wife, Rebecca Moesta, have written numerous bestselling and award-winning young adult novels. An avid hiker, Anderson dictates his fiction into a microcassette recorder. Research has taken him to the deserts of Morocco, the cloud forests of Ecuador, Inca ruins in the Andes, Maya temples in the Yucatán, the NORAD complex, NASAs Vehicle Assembly Building, a Minuteman III missile silo, the aircraft carrier *Nimitz,* the Pacific Stock Exchange, a plutonium plant at Los Alamos, and FBI Headquarters in Washington, DC. He also, occasionally, stays home and works on his manuscripts. Visit his websites at: www.wordfire.com and www.dunenovels.com.

Science Fiction/Fantasy author **Linda P. Baker's** internationally published novels are *The Irda* and *Tears of the Night Sky,* with Nancy Varian Berberick. Her short fiction has been published in several anthologies, including *Dragons of Krynn*, *The New Amazons*, and *Time Twisters*. Linda credits her mother, Lena, and sister, Lisa, for the genesis of "The Opposite of Solid," because they reinfected Linda and her husband, Larry, with the auction bug, begetting the question: "What if I bought something at an auction that . . . ?"

Donald J. Bingle is a frequent contributor to short story anthologies in the science fiction, fantasy, horror, and comedy genres, including the DAW anthologies *Time Twisters, If I Were an Evil Overlord, Furry Fantastic, Fantasy Gone Wrong, Slipstreams, All Hell Breaking Loose, Renaissance Faire, Sol's Children, Historical Hauntings, Civil War Fantastic,* and *Earth, Wind, Fire, Water: Tales From the Eternal Archives #2.* He is also the author of *Forced Conversion,* a science fiction novel set in the near future, when everyone can have heaven, any heaven they want, but some people don't want to go. His latest novel, *Greensword,* is a darkly comedic eco-thriller about a group of misfit environmentalists who are about to save the world from global warming but don't want to get caught doing it. He is cursed with a long commute to his day job as a securities attorney, but he is blessed with a lovely wife, Linda, and two rambunctious pooches: Mauka and Makai. Don can be reached at www.orphyte.com/donaldjbingle.

Yvonne Coats is originally from Dubois, Wyoming, a town where the wintering bighorn sheep outnumber the humans about ten to one. She now lives in Albuquerque, New Mexico, a city with more people than the entire state of Wyoming—lots less snow, though. She shares space with her smart spouse, Mike Collins, and their rotten cat, Magpie. Her stories have appeared in small-press magazines and in anthologies *Treachery & Treason* and *Turn the Other Chick.* Yvonne was shortlisted for the first James White Award in 2000. When not writing, she enjoys gardening, knitting, lifting weights, and trying to learn Japanese.

Keith R.A. DeCandido (www.decandido.net) first introduced the characters of Torin ban Wyvald and Danthres Tresyllione and the world of Cliff's End in the 2004 novel *Dragon Precinct*. They've also appeared in the short stories "Getting the Chair" (*Murder by Magic*, 2004), "Crime of Passion" (*Hear Them Roar*, 2006), and "House Arrest" (*Badass Faeries*, 2007). Keith's other short fiction can be found in *Amazing Stories, Did You Say Chicks!?, Farscape: The Official Magazine, Furry Fantastic, 44 Clowns: 11 Stories of the 4 Clowns of the Apocalypse, The Town Drunk, Urban Nightmares,* and various Doctor Who, Marvel Comics, and Star Trek anthologies. He's also written a great deal of fiction in the media universes of Star Trek, World of Warcraft, Starcraft, Doctor Who, Buffy the Vampire Slayer, Marvel Comics, Serenity, Farscape, Andromeda, and tons more. He lives in New York City.

"Ancestral Armor" is Kitsune and Asano's fourth short fiction appearance (with other stories published in *Battle Magic, Historical Hauntings* (both available from DAW Books), and *100 Crafty Little Cat Crimes*). **John Helfers** has published more than three dozen short stories in anthologies such as *Millennium 3001, Liftport, Time Twisters,* and *Places to Be, People to Kill*. His media tie-in fiction has appeared in anthologies for the *Dragonlance®* and *Transformers®* universes, among others. He also writes nonfiction, including a comprehensive history of the United States Navy and a critical look at the impact of culture on military operations in the collection of essays *Beyond Shock and Awe,* edited by Eric Haney. Recent novels include the YA illustrated novel *Thunder Riders* and *Shadowrun: Aftershock,* co-authored with Jean Rabe.

Belle Holder is a beginning author, yet quite good for a beginner, and she loves animals. She has a pet mouse, Lighting, whom she writes about a lot; and she hopes to become a lawyer, an agent, or a farmer who uses scientific research to grow incredibly good crops. "Another Exciting Adventure of Lightning Merriemouse-Jones" is her second published short story. She and her mother are members of Persephone, a women horror writers organization.

Nancy Holder has sold approximately eighty novels and more than two hundred short stories, articles, and essays. She is currently working on *Athena Force: Disclosure*, due out in August 2008. *The Rose Bride*, a fairy tale retelling, is out now.

An unreformed tomboy, **Jane Lindskold** came late to her appreciation of the magic of clothing. However, she is now a complete convert and can occasionally be glimpsed wearing satin and embroidery. She has written most of her eighteen novels and over fifty short stories while wearing battered jeans and T-shirts. Her most popular character, Firekeeper (the protagonist of six novels, beginning with *Through Wolf's Eyes*), often wears very little and prefers not to wear shoes unless absolutely necessary. The characters in the stand-alone novels *The Buried Pyramid* and *Child of a Rainless Year* also have clothing issues. Lindskold is currently involved in a new series, one that has immersed her in an appreciation of Chinese lore . . . and clothing. You can get a look at her at her website, www.janelindskold.com.

Louise Marley is a recovering opera singer who now writes science fiction and fantasy full time and teaches a creative writing class at Bellevue Community College in Washington State. She is the winner of two Endeavour Awards, has been a Nebula, John W. Campbell, and Tiptree nominee, and was a Clarion '93 graduate. Her work has been published by Ace, Viking, Puffin, *Asimov's*, *SciFiction*, *Talebones*, and others.

Joe Masdon grew up in Macon, GA, and graduated from Oglethorpe University in Atlanta in 1988. He moved to North Carolina in 1995, pursuing a woman that he caught and married in 1996. He graduated from the University of North Carolina at Greensboro in 2004 with a Master's Degree in accounting. He has managed to get two short stories published and is always glad to hear from Jean Rabe when she is working on a tight deadline. He and his wife Sherrie live in Elon, NC, with their two children, Jonathan and Robert.

Rebecca Moesta is the author of twenty-eight books and numerous short stories, including the award-winning Star Wars: Young Jedi Knights series and two original Titan A.E. novels, which she co-authored with husband Kevin J. Anderson, and a Buffy the Vampire Slayer novel, *Little Things*. With Anderson, she has written an original young-adult fantasy series, *Crystal Doors,* for Little, Brown. In comics, she has worked with Anderson on the hardcover Star Trek: The Next Generation graphic novel, *The Gorn Crisis* from Wildstorm and *Grumpy Old Monsters* from IDW. Moesta is the daughter of an English teacher and a nurse, from whom she learned, respectively, her love of words and her love of books. Moesta, who holds an MBA from Boston University, has taught every grade level from kindergarten through junior college and worked for seven years as a publications specialist and technical editor at Lawrence Livermore National Laboratory.

Chris Pierson has been a writer since he was a kid up in Canada. He has written seven novels for the Dragonlance series: *Spirit of the Wind, Dezra's Quest,* The Kingpriest trilogy (*Chosen of the Gods, Divine Hammer,* and *Sacred Fire*), and the Taladas trilogy (*Blades of the Tiger, Trail of the Black Wyrm* and *Shadow of the Flame*). In addition, he has been published in *Dragon Magazine* and in the anthologies *The Dragons At War, Dragons of Chaos, Rebels & Tyrants,* and *Time Twisters.* During the day Chris works as a game designer for Turbine, and has been involved in the Asheron's Call series, Dungeons & Dragons Online: Stormreach, and Lord of the Rings Online: Shadows of Angmar; he also writes and edits game material for Wizards of the Coast and Sovereign Press. He lives in Boston with his wife and fellow movie addict, Rebekah.

Judi Rohrig is just an Indiana housewife with a computer in her kitchen. Her fiction has been published in *Masques V, Furry Fantastic, Dreaming of Angels, Extremes V,* and *Cemetery Dance Magazine,* and her essays have been published in *On Writing Horror, Personal Demons,* and *The Orbit #2.* The former editor and publisher of *Hellnotes* was honored with a Bram Stoker Award in 2005 and the Richard Laymon Award in 2001. Visit her online: www.judirohrig.com.

Michael A. Stackpole is an award-winning author, game and computer game designer, and poet whose first novel, *Warrior: En Garde,* was published in 1988. Since then, he has written thirty-six other novels, including eight *New York Times* bestselling novels in the Star Wars® line, of which *X-wing: Rogue Squadron* and *I, Jedi* are the best known. Mike lives in Arizona and in his spare time spends early mornings at Starbucks, collects toy soldiers and old radio shows, plays indoor soccer, rides his bike and listens to Irish music in the finer pubs in the Phoenix area. His website is www.stormwolf.com.

Peter Schweighofer lives in Virginia, and is primarily known for his writing in role-playing games, including work done on the *Star Wars® RPG, The World of Indiana Jones,* and the *Men in Black Roleplaying Game.* His fiction also appears in such anthologies as

Alien Abductions, Far Frontiers, and *Historical Hauntings.*

A. M. Strout was born in the Berkshire Hills, mere miles from writing heavyweights Nathaniel Hawthorne and Herman Melville, and currently lives in historic Jackson Heights, New York (where nothing paranormal ever really happens, he assures you). His first novel, *Dead to Me,* will be published by Ace in 2008. He is the cocreator of the faux folk musical *Sneezin' Jeff & Blue Raccoon: The Loose Gravel Tour* (winner of the Best Storytelling Award at the First Annual New York International Fringe Festival). In his scant spare time, he is an always writer, a sometimes actor, sometimes musician, occasional RPGer, and the worlds most casual and controller-smashing video gamer. He currently works in the exciting world of publishing—and yes, it is as glamorous as it sounds.

Kelly Swails is a Clinical Laboratory Scientist by day and a writer by night. She and her husband, Ken, live in Illinois with three cats named Kahlua, Morgan, and Moonshine. She never wears earrings.

Elizabeth A. Vaughan is the author of *Warprize, Warsworn,* and *Warlord,* the three books that make up Chronicle of the Warlands. She believes that the only good movies are the ones with gratuitous magic, swords, or lasers. Not to mention dragons. At the present, she is owned by three incredibly spoiled cats and lives in the Northwest Territory, on the outskirts of the Black Swamp, along Mad Anthony's Trail on the banks of the Maumee River.

Timothy Zahn has been writing science fiction for more than a quarter of a century. In that time he has published thirty novels, more than eighty short stories and novelettes, and four collections of short fiction. Best known for his eight Star Wars novels—the latest,

Star Wars: Allegiance, was recently published—he is also the author of *Night Train to Rigel* and the young-adult Dragonback series. The Zahn family lives on the Oregon coast.

Sarah Zettel was born in Sacramento, California. Since then she has lived in ten cities, four states, and two countries. She started writing while still in high school and has never stopped. To date she has published twelve novels, as well as a series of short stories and opinion essays in a variety of genres. She currently lives with her family in Michigan. When not writing she gardens, plays fiddle, practices tai chi, and reads lots and lots of picture books to her son Alexander.

Sherwood Smith

THE FOX

Book Two of Inda

"Smith's lush descriptions evoke a fantastic yet credible world, where magic spells and enchanted stones are everyday facts of life." —*Kirkus*

Attending the military academy had been Inda's greatest dream. But academy reality was far from what he imagined—for by defending the second son of the king, Inda became embroiled in a vicious political struggle he could have no hope of winning. Before growing to manhood, his fate will sever him from all he holds dear, from friends, family, and the life he thought he'd been meant to live, onto the decks of pirate ships and beyond...

0-7564-0421-5

To Order Call: 1-800-788-6262

www.dawbooks.com

Violette Malan

The Sleeping God

A Novel of Dhulyn and Parno

Masters of weapons and the martial arts, mercenaries
Dhulyn and Parno have just saved one of the Marked,
one of those with special powers, from a mob under
the influence of the Sleeping God. Dhulyn's own gift
may make her a similar target, so the pair takes ship for
safer shores. On a seemingly simple escorting mission,
not even Dhulyn's talent can warn them of the threat
lurking at the end of their journey.

0-7564-0446-8

Raves for Violette Malan:
"Believable characters and graceful storytelling."
—*Library Journal*

"Fantasy fans should brace themselves:
the world is about to discover Violette Malan."
—*The Barnes & Noble Review*

To Order Call: 1-800-788-6262

www.dawbooks.com

DAW 58

OTHERLAND

TAD WILLIAMS

"The Otherland books are a major accomplishment."–*Publishers Weekly*

"It will captivate you."
    –*Cinescape*

In many ways it is humankind's most stunning achievement. This most exclusive of places is also one of the world's best-kept secrets, but somehow, bit by bit, it is claiming Earth's most valuable resource: its children.

Tad Williams

THE **WAR** OF THE **FLOWERS**

"A masterpiece of fairytale worldbuilding."
—*Locus*

"Williams's imagination is boundless."
—*Publishers Weekly*
(Starred Review)

"A great introduction to an accomplished
and ambitious fantasist."
—*San Francisco Chronicle*

"An addictive world ... masterfully plays
with the tropes and traditions of
generations of fantasy writers."
—*Salon*

"A very elaborate and fully realized setting
for adventure, intrigue, and more
than an occasional chill."
—*Science Fiction Chronicle*

0-7564-0181-X

To Order Call: 1-800-788-6262
www.dawbooks.com

DAW 45